T0354544

Devil's Paintbrush

ONE'S PAST DOESN'T PREDETERMINE ONE'S FUTURE

K. L. Arthur

Editor: Dianna Susan Byrd

Order this book online at www.trafford.com
or email orders@trafford.com

Most Trafford titles are also available at major online book retailers.

Print information available on the last page.

ISBN: 978-1-4669-7767-9 (sc)
ISBN: 978-1-4669-7766-2 (hc)
ISBN: 978-1-4669-7768-6 (e)

Library of Congress Control Number: 2013901781

Trafford rev. 03/29/2016

 www.trafford.com

North America & international
toll-free: 1 888 232 4444 (USA & Canada)
fax: 812 355 4082

Contents

DEDICATION

To the following Vietnam War and Afghanistan War veterans—all brave and honorable men:

Timothy Lancaster, US Army

Dennis W. La Cerda, US Army

Ralph Lindsey, US Army

Everett Mattson, US Marines

David McCarthy, US Marines

James M. McGowan, US Army

James McParlin, US Navy (Seabees)

Gilbert L. Ouellette, US Army

Keith Watson, US Army (Afghanistan)

In memory of

Joseph F. Cook, US Marines

Mark W. Grigsby, US Army

ACKNOWLEDGEMENTS

I would like to extend my deepest appreciation and gratitude to all the professionals within the VA Healthcare System's PTSD program, Veterans of Foreign War's Legislative Representatives of Boston, Massachusetts, and the Veteran Services of North Attleboro, Massachusetts for their ongoing support of the men and women of our Armed Services.

And, to the founders and current staff members of the YMCA of America. Through their efforts and enormous generosity, a 12 year old boy growing up in poverty of 1960s Baltimore learned how to brush his teeth for the first time, swim for the first time, write a letter for the first time, and experience the joy of eating 3 meals a day for the first time.

K. L. Arthur

ACKNOWLEDGMENTS

STORY SYNOPSIS

Devil's Paintbrush

An epic fiction drenched in reality. *Devil's Paintbrush* tells the life story a young boy who grows up in a violent and abusive home within the Projects of Brooklyn, Baltimore during the 1960s. Then, as a young man, he once again finds himself thrust in another hostile environment—South Vietnam. Somehow he survives both worlds.

Decades after receiving "The Bronze Star" in combat, Ken Callahan's long suppressed memories and fractured emotions compel him to enter yet another threatening battlefield and engage a very different enemy—a foe deadlier than any Viet Cong or bird-eating tarantula he ever confronted as a younger man.

This new battlefield is the private office of the Veteran Administration's top PTSD clinician.

His new enemy is . . . himself.

Within the relative safety of this clinician's office, Ken is reluctantly dragged-back in time to unearth decades of buried memories of war. That's when the PTSD professional community becomes stunned as they discover Ken's combat experience was not as lethal as the domestic violence and sexual abuse he endured at the hands of a disturbed older brother and sinfully wicked mother long before he even went to war.

In short, Ken Callahan's PTSD was deeply entrenched well before he stepped foot on the battlefields of South Vietnam.

"Discovering" the truth about his own past proves to be challenging enough, but in order to "accept" such truth, Ken must cross a line from which there is no return. The man who ultimately emerges is not the same "Bronze Star" recipient who reluctantly enters PTSD treatment; nor are the people he touches along the way. Only the qualities of a *Devil's Paintbrush* can provide the caliber of personal resilience needed throughout every step of Ken Callahan's life-long journey.

Readers of this story will be either shocked and disgusted or enlightened and educated. There is no safe place between these two extremes.

Readers' Alert:

Even though this story is a fiction, it reflects historical and social events spanning a fifty year period. As such, some era-based racial language, domestic conflict, and war-time situations may be too intense for non-adult readers.

(Pilosella aurantiaca)

Wikipedia, 2012

Devil's Paintbrush . . . a flowering plant found throughout
the world. It is one of the most resilient and adaptive plants
on earth—survives in highly hostile climates as well as within
the safety of well-kept home gardens. It has a beautiful bloom,
thrives best in isolation and can be dug-up and replanted
often without causing much trauma or shock. This plant is
extremely difficult to damage permanently or destroy totally.

So goes . . . Kenneth A. Callahan

Photo Attribution:

(Wikipedia, 2012, Creative Commons; CreativeCommons.ogr)

CHAPTER 1

Routines
(Brooklyn, Maryland, 1961)

THE THREE O'CLOCK SCHOOL BELL screamed off the wall freeing the students of PS 239. Kids scampered onto yellow school buses that would soon take them to the safety and comfort of their loving homes scattered throughout Brooklyn, Maryland—one of Baltimore's southern communities. Eager mothers would be impatiently waiting to welcome their kids back to the warmth of their home on this bitter cold, overcast afternoon in February 1961. Hugs, hot cocoa, and endless questions about their school day would undoubtedly be unleashed from very caring mothers as they wait for their fathers to arrive home around 5:30 p.m. Traditional *Leave It to Beaver* dinners would then be politely shared among all 4.5 members of the average suburban, nuclear family—consisting of one working father, one stay-at-home mom, and 2.5 children (one boy, one girl, and a half of one or the other). Very appropriate conversations about school, family, and neighborhood events would then be discussed at dinner as they continued bathing in each other's love and security.

Later on, their black and white TV set would be watched by the entire family. The kids would then set off to complete homework, enjoy a late snack of milk and cookies, and brush their teeth before heading off to bed. Peaceful sleep would come quickly after being gently tucked in bed by both parents. A series of soft kisses to foreheads along with the standard "Sweet dreams . . . I love you" would accompany each tuck.

Such "routines" provided ample nurturance and stability for the kids to meet the demands of the next day's adventure growing up in South Baltimore. This caliber of interpersonal routines was repeated like clockwork every day for the majority of students attending PS 239—Ben Franklin Middle School. Healthy, normal children sprouted from the safety of these well-kept homes, and more importantly, personal values were subtly embedded into the self-identity of these trusting children. Entire generations of mature and caring adults would naturally evolve as a result of these routines yielding future senators, teachers and parents of America. They, in turn, would do the same with their own children.

After all, this was America in 1961—at least that was Little Ken Callahan's view of the world around him. Of course, he was dreaming and wishing. When the three o'clock school bell screamed for him, he did not scramble aboard a yellow school bus nor was he safely hustled home by any other means. Instead, his personal journey was on foot through the back alleys of Brooklyn. His destination was the Projects—his home, his neighborhood, his world, and his only reality.

Little Ken was about twelve years old.

The Projects

This community was a complex of government-built, one and two-story row houses constructed for the GIs returning from World War II. It was a low-cost thank-you given by a grateful nation to the men who bravely defended their country on the battlefields of Europe, North Africa, and the Pacific; a well-deserved reward for those who gave so much, for so many, for so long.

This highly segregated (100 percent white) community consisted of approximately sixty separate buildings spread across a square mile in one of Baltimore's most southern neighborhoods. Tenth Street ran through its center neatly dividing it into perfect halves. A management office, maintenance department, and recreation center were located in the heart of this social microcosm and served the needs of approximately four hundred low-income families. Each building consisted of eight side-by-side units, one family per unit. This meant eight families shared a single, flat-roofed redbrick building. Each unit had one rectangular window in the front and back on each floor, and identical white cement porches marked their front entrances in an attempt to replicate the look of Baltimore's more affluent, historic neighborhoods. It was a noble, but futile attempt.

The rear side of each unit consisted of a small clump of grass with a single narrow asphalt path leading to its back door. Running parallel to the buildings were winding strips of asphalt called alleyways. Columns of sagging clotheslines also spaghettied their way along these backyards and alleyways and were accented by an endless array of dented garbage cans and random chain-linked fences (some erect, others not so erect). And countless telephone poles and power lines were defying the law of physics by magically leaning at different angles, except straight up. This unique combination of neighborhood characteristics brought a bizarre yet artistic quality to the Projects. Any well-educated person driving through this neighborhood after taking a wrong turn off Patapsco Avenue could easily conclude they were entering a surreal painting by Salvador Dali. Others could easily pinch themselves into believing one of Picasso's postimpressionist designs was coming to life before their eyes. Of course, the residents of the Projects were just too close, too intimately involved, to truly appreciate the richness of their own backyard in such ways.

Because of astonishingly similar designs, the only way anyone could distinguish one building from another was by living there. To help locate people, the name of each building was solidly drilled on the front corner of the first and last units. Street numbers were never used to identify individual family residences; rather, one's official mailing address assumed the name of their building (not their street). Buildings sharing a similar proximity were grouped together into collectives called courts. And because it would have been politically incorrect, even in 1961, to name such a special community—the Government Projects, the city of Baltimore instead gave it a special name—Brooklyn Homes. This identity just felt more humane to city officials.

Little Ken lived at 4139 Martin Court, Brooklyn Homes, Baltimore, Maryland. Zone Improvement Plan (ZIP) 21225.

Nevertheless, everyone in Baltimore still referred to this unique neighborhood as the Projects of Brooklyn. While not much could be done to humanize the design of the Projects, two positive things could be said about them. They were well constructed and very well insulated. Most important to Little Ken on this cold afternoon in 1961, his unit was also extremely warm. The Callahans living room at 4139 Martin Court was sparsely furnished with one long sofa stretching across the entire right wall; it was the only place to sit. There were no hanging pictures on any walls, actually there were no pictures anywhere in the house except a very special portrait hanging upstairs in the bedroom of Little Ken's mother. A fourteen-inch Sylvania television sat on a small folding table two feet in front of the sofa, and a huge rectangular section of linoleum covered nearly two-thirds of the living room's cement floor. A two-foot high, S-shaped ashtray stand towered in front of the sofa next to the TV, and a single shadeless bulb hung from the center of the ceiling throwing a bright, harsh light down upon everything in its view. The kitchen, even smaller than the living room, was as sparsely furnished. There was a card table in the center of the kitchen that served as a kitchen table. It had four folding chairs—two were opened next to the table and the others were folded and leaning against the wall. There was also a General Electric stove and a Schilling refrigerator in the kitchen. Several cabinets hung over the kitchen sink, and a small cupboard was adjacent to a fully exposed floor-to-ceiling furnace, where Little Ken usually applied his most important personal routine of the day after returning from school—getting warm fast. That is, if he was allowed back in his house.

Kenneth Callahan—Youngest Son

He was about five or six years old when his family moved into the Projects of Brooklyn, and he would live around there with his mother, two older brothers, and younger sister for about ten years—1955-1965. On this specific overcast afternoon, Little Ken tried to run all the way home from PS 239; it was just too bitterly cold to walk. But the folded cardboard serving as the sole of his left shoe had prematurely worn through earlier that day, making his trip home even more difficult. Usually a single piece of cardboard lasted several days before it had to be replaced, but not this time; and he knew the longer it took for him to get home, the longer it would take to reduce the swelling and numbness in his left foot. Actually, Little Ken didn't mind the touch of his sockless flesh hitting the frozen ground on every down step; he could handle that. What really got to him though, more than anything else, was how winter's stabbing air seemed to always find a way underneath his open sole and consistently dart between his partially exposed toes during the up steps. That's what he dreaded the most—the up steps, not the down steps.

The gray sky was beginning to darken as winter's evening quickly approached. Little Ken nearly made it running all the way home, but his lungs gave out at the outskirts of the Projects. He decided to walk the remaining distance. *Little Ken* was the nickname the kids in the neighbor had given him. He had two older brothers, Butch and Walter; both were much bigger and taller than he; so the kids called him *Little Ken*. However, some adults around the Projects called him Little Ken too but for very different reasons.

He possessed his mother's British, northern-Euro complexion—light blonde hair, blue eyes, and strong cheekbones. Little Ken also had a blush of freckles running from cheek to cheek giving him that eternal youthful look even on this cold winter's day.

Both of his older brothers were just the opposite—taking after their respective fathers. They both had much darker features and were much bigger in size and weight.

He was a good-looking kid who, more than anything, wanted to fit in with his schoolmates and neighbors, but instead, he always ended up keeping them at a distance somehow. To teachers and even his own mother, he appeared to have an eternal look of sadness on his face despite his natural good looks. To his classmates, he just seemed more serious about his schoolwork than they were. He was a quiet, easy to get along with kid who never caused trouble and never drew undue attention to himself. Even though Little Ken was always present in class (seldom missing a whole day of school), the other kids and teachers had to look hard to find him. He was an inconspicuous young boy.

It really wasn't sadness that made him appear so forlorn; rather, Little Ken had just become unsure and suspicious of most people already in his short life. This concerned attitude seemed to etch an ever-present look of worry into his cute, boyish face. His mother, Hilda Callahan, always described him to her new boyfriends, strangers, and neighbors in the following way. "Yeah, he's a good-lookin' kid alright, takes after his mother . . . dat's for sure . . . but he always looks like he's carryin' the weight of the world on his shoulders . . . like he's got somethin' on his mind . . . always worryin' . . . I don't know, never figured it out 'bout him. He's a gud' kid, my quiet one . . . don't give me much trouble . . . not much."

Even though she'd always described him in such a way, Hilda knew the exact "weight" Little Ken was actually carrying on his shoulders (as she put it), but she could never openly share that with anyone. Even though his classmates liked him, they still made fun of him because of his serious nature. The older kids liked him too, but for different reasons. Little Ken made a great punching bag and a fine target for perfecting their gang maneuvers. At first, he disliked being a "target," but he gradually became used to it, even started enjoying the attention it brought. He was seldom invited to join pick-up teams in sports except for an occasional football scrimmage and only then just to provide some blocking for a smaller, speedier quarterback. Little Ken was never allowed the privilege of carrying the football. The routines associated with being a target came to suit him over time and even helped prepare him for many combative situations he was destined to face throughout the remainder of his life in the Projects, along the streets of South Baltimore, and later in Vietnam. And the kind of attention he got from his mother made him a target of a different kind—a very special target that June Cleaver certainly would never approve.

On this extremely cold afternoon, Little Ken finally arrived home from school. It was about 3:25 p.m. He tried opening the front door of 4139 Martin Court, but it was locked. He was just hoping for an unlocked door this time due to the extreme cold and because his exposed left foot already had numbed. So he backed off the front steps and looked up at the second-story window. His mother's bedroom light was on, which meant she was home; it also meant she had company. After several minutes of continual knocking, which also achieved routine status in his mind, the upstairs window flew open. His mother then yelled down at him. "Jesus Christ . . . cut da' shit, will ya'? What da' hell ya' want, anyway?" Her tone was demeaning and uncaring.

Hilda Callahan's light brown hair was being held up on one side of her head by several bobby pins. A cigarette was dangling from her mouth as she yelled down to her son, who now was turning a deeper shade of blue. The cutting edge of the northeast wind was whipping through the Projects faster than a speeding train down a mountainside. It was relentlessly punishing Little Ken's exposed left foot, gloveless hands, and hatless head. So he started another well-practiced routine—pleading. Little Ken knew he would get only one shot at convincing his mother to open the door, so he was direct. "Mom, please . . . it's real cold today. Let me come in, OK? I won't bother you guys, I promise. I promise," he said, looking up from the sidewalk as his hands, arms, and legs continued moving in vain to keep his blood circulating. But the window closed as fast as it opened. She gave no reply.

A half hour later, the front door finally opened. Little Ken's mother was wearing a thick red robe with a long flamingo design running from top to bottom on the right side. It was loosely tied around her waist, and one of her breast was nearly fully exposed.

This was not a new sight to him.

Hilda Callahan—Mother

Hilda Callahan was a tall, lean, muscular woman. In some circles, this thirty-eight year old mother of five would be considered quite attractive. However, in other circles, she would be viewed as cheap, a onetime fling, unworthy of even a second glance. Hilda also had a very hardened look about her. She was tough to catch, tougher to hold, and even tougher to escape especially if someone crossed her. People didn't mess with Hilda Callahan. She had "mileage."

Little Ken loved his mother very much; he feared her even more. When the front door finally opened wide enough, he tried to swiftly race by her to the warmth of the kitchen, but his stiffness slowed him down just long enough for her fist to land squarely on the back of his head. He was momentarily stunned but recovered quickly. Little Ken had this specific routine down pat too. He then made a beeline directly to the kitchen and began virtually hugging the steel furnace without really touching it. It was located in the far corner of the kitchen next to the back door. In a loving response, the furnace returned his embrace by starting to spread its magical warmth throughout his entire body. He dropped to the floor and ripped off his shoes. He then placed the bottoms of both feet less than an inch from the front of the blazing hot furnace. Simultaneously, he placed the palms of both hands as close to the furnace as possible without burning himself. This was always an awkward and "vulnerable" position for him—it was as if his feet and hands were seized by four huge furnace magnets holding him motionless in mid-air. The only part of his body actually touching anything was his butt on the floor. He usually stayed in this magnet position as long as it took to get warm, that is, as long as she would allow. He was just wishing his mother would give him a little extra thaw time on this especially cold afternoon.

His wish did not come true.

She entered the kitchen after a minute or two and walked directly toward him. Still magnetically connected in his mind to his loving furnace, he felt totally defenseless as she approached. Hilda Callahan knew it too. So Little Ken braced himself for the next inevitable blow; he was just too good of a "target" right now for her to willingly pass up such an opportunity. But to his surprised (and delight) a blow did not come this time. Instead, her words, not fists, landed hard. Towering high above her magnet boy, she said, "What da' hell ya' doin' home so early, anyway? I told ya' d'er wasn't gonna' be nutten' here ta' eat today. Why didn't ya' just head over to the Jacksons or Johnsons or Baumanns . . . bet d'ey feed ya' 'somethin.'"

Hilda's voice had become deep and raspy over the years. Thousands of Lucky Strike and Camel cigarettes had taken their rightful share of this woman's throat. To some men, she had a very deep, sexy voice. To others, she sounded like a worn-out contralto singing underwater. Hilda also spoke with contractions. That is, she always dropped the g's off words or ran words together resulting in the creation of her own language. She felt English should be changed to her style of talking, not the other way around. For example, she would say cookin' versus cooking, gonna' versus going to, and ya' versus you. Also, her "th" sounds were usually conveyed as "d'at" . . . for "that," "d'ose" . . . for "those," or "d'ere" . . . for "there."

"If ya' don't like da' way I speak, d'en just shove it where da' sun don't fuckin' shine," she would proclaim loudly and proudly to anyone who corrected her. If Hilda Callahan could have had her way, the entire English language would have been overhauled to suit her unique style. The entire world, for that matter, would also have to change and get in step with her way of thinking and behaving.

Looking up at her from his furnace seat on the floor, Little Ken tried to answer without being perceived as challenging; she hated to be contradicted, challenged or ignored. So he chose his words carefully. "Ah, Ma, I hate going over to the Johnsons anymore. It's as if I'm begging or something after so many times, you know. And besides, I think they're on to me . . . showing up exactly when dinner is about to start, leaving afterwards, and all. I know they really don't want me there . . . they're just being kind, that's all. Why, just the other day I overheard Bernadette talking about me and she said I was . . ." But, Little Ken wasn't allowed to finish his plea; her fist landed on the left side of his head this time, stopping him in mid-sentence. Her blow drove him to the other side of the kitchen, ten feet away from his loving friend, the furnace. "Listen ya' little terd . . . when I squat ya' out twelve years ago, I didn't make ya' no promises, did I? D'ere's da' door right over d'ere . . . swings both ways. Anytime ya' get tired of livin' here, just head west like d'at dam older brother, Walter, did. Guess ya' and yur' udder' brother, Butch, are next . . . right?" she said with as much condescension as possible.

Hilda Callahan was an angry, bitter woman. She hated anyone whose skin was darker than her own, anyone who didn't speak English and anyone who was smaller or weaker than she was. Most important, she needed a bottle, a cigarette, a dollar, and a man nearby at all times—in that precise order. She also needed to have control of everything and everyone—kids, husbands, relatives, and neighbors. She was a manipulative, selfish, mean woman who had no real close friends, only temporary male friends who never seemed to last long enough to become real friends—only brief enough to be physically friendly. Hilda Callahan either destroyed men swiftly, or she married them and then damaged them slowly over time. Either way seemed fine with her. It also seemed to depend more on her mood than on the quality of the man. However, all the smart men she met learned who she was very quickly and never returned after their first embrace. She certainly would be willing "at times" to relinquish a little control over the short term in order to maintain control over the longer term. Her manipulative talents were only surpassed by her selfishness and her well refined self-survival skills. As such, she was relentless getting what she wanted. Hilda was a very dangerous disturbed woman, especially regarding people and relationships. At this age, Little Ken didn't fully understand the inner workings of his mother's mind, but he clearly understood everything he saw her do, everything he heard her say, and most important, everything he experienced firsthand, up close and personal. That's all he really needed to understand and survive her many moods, seething temper, and relentless wrath from day to day.

Meanwhile, back in the kitchen . . .

Little Ken had been violently separated from his furnace friend as a result of his mother's accurate head blow, and was now scrambling back to his warm magnet position. Her blow had landed effectively, but it didn't really hurt him. He was strong and resilient enough to withstand most of her body blows if he was prepared; it was her surprise blows that took the greatest toll on him, lingering long after the actual impact.

However, her fists were one thing, but there was another weapon far more terrifying to him—her "extension cord." Getting hit by her fists or kicked by her was something he came to tolerate, but he couldn't handle the searing pain inflected by her extension cord—a ten-foot insulated wire with a hard-rubber, double-pronged plug at the end. It was originally manufactured to help connect appliances, like irons or radios, to wall sockets beyond the reach of the appliance's standard length.

But Hilda had found another application for this cord.

Little Ken feared the extension cord simply because it not only stung and slashed his skin immediately upon impact, leaving lasting welts and rips, but it also could reach him in tight-squeeze areas within the house; his emergency escape hatches in time of need. In such "safe places," blows from her fists, arms and feet just could not land squarely because of the confined space he was in, but her extension cord could. For example, sometimes Little Ken just wasn't fast enough to make it completely out of the house when being attacked by her (or by his brother Butch, who also enjoyed "playing" with his little brother in such ways). If he couldn't make it out of the house, his backup strategy was to always try for one of his "safe places" in the house, including the tight area between the back of the kitchen furnace and the wall. Or, he'd try to make his way upstairs and dart under the big bed in his mother's bedroom or between the bedroom's door and closet space. Either place would be out of the direct-impact range of her fists but not out of reach of the extension cord's cutting teeth. Her wrath would be reduced somewhat, but not completely eliminated. The extension cord proved to be a viable, lethal substitute for her fists in such tight places.

Hilda Callahan had been standing next to the kitchen window just looking at Little Ken who was once again in his magnet position near the furnace. She lit a cigarette and drew deeply, swallowing as much of its loving poison into her lungs as possible. He'd always watch her as she smoked and was curious why his mother seemed to enjoy watching the fire eat away the cigarette's paper with each deep inhale. He noticed how much she savored each puff, seemingly sucking the life out of cigarettes and transferring it into her body. Somehow she was able to hold each puff in her mouth for a very long time then swallow it effortlessly. The leftover smoke that didn't make it all the way into her lungs just seemed to leisurely crawl out of her nostrils, dance up the front of her face, and then magically disappear into nothingness. He never once saw her blow smoke out of her mouth after inhaling like her boyfriends did. However, each time she inhaled, Little Ken sensed she was savoring something much more than just the taste of smoke, but he didn't know what it was. Her mind seemed to go somewhere else during such private moments—a place that was comforting or concerning to her. He didn't know where, but he did know she really seemed to enjoy her smokes.

So it was only natural that Little Ken couldn't wait until he was old enough to smoke himself. If it made his mother feel so good, he wanted to do it, too. So one Saturday morning when his mother was sleeping off another hangover, he took a cigarette and a pack of matches out of her purse. He went outside and ran to the far end of Martin Court to try it himself. He looked around first to see if anyone was nearby. It was all clear. He then placed the cigarette between his nervous lips, just as he saw his mother do so many times before. He removed a single match from the match pack. Once he dragged the match across the striker area, the flame came alive much faster and was much bigger than he expected. His finger was immediately burned because he wasn't holding the match properly, and that's when he also felt for the first time (the last time), sulfuric fumes darting into his raw, virgin nostrils. He wasn't ready for all this happening so fast and so close. He panicked, dropped the match pack on the ground, spit out the cigarette, and tried to clear the fumes from his nose all at the same time. This happened in a split second and caused him to fall to the ground in the midst of a sensory overload and immediate disorientation.

Before getting up, Little Ken looked around to see if anyone saw what just happened. No one was nearby. He was glad but also embarrassed. So he stomped on the cigarette and the whole match pack. Once he was satisfied it would never rise up or try to burn or suffocate him again, he ran back to his house. Without having tasted true cigarette smoke, that which his mother obviously enjoyed so much, he decided never to try it again. Little Ken stayed "tobacco-free" that day, and he would remain a non-smoker for the rest of his life.

Fathers, Husbands, Brothers and Sister

There was a long silence as Hilda, once again, drew deeply from her cigarette while standing next to the window in the kitchen. She continued staring at Little Ken who was still sitting next to the furnace in his magnet position. That's when her mind usually went to an unknowable place. During such faraway moments, Little Ken sensed she was thinking about her first three husbands or her elder son, Walter, who ran away from home just two years before. To Ken, her husbands and Walter may have gotten away at different times, but at least each made it out "in one piece." But, at this moment anything Little Ken would have said in his brother's defense would have fallen on deaf ears anyway, even worse, it could have agitated her even more. So he didn't reply to her comment about Walter. Instead, he just continued embracing the furnace, keeping his eyes on her.

Little Ken was still trying to get warm for the first time since leaving school at 3:00 p.m. when she eventually walked out of the kitchen, and headed back upstairs. She was in one of her restless, unpredictable moods, and he didn't know which one was going to resurface next, but he knew he would find out soon. Hilda didn't make any ex-husband references to Little Ken this time either, not on this occasion. She always seemed to reserve her most elegant language, most colorful expressions, about her ex-husbands for very, very special times. Her most favorite adjectives used to describe them included "scum suckers," "chicken shits," "wimp bastards," "weak, good-for-nothin' cowards," and, of course her most favorite description— "hemorrhoid husbands." Hilda's creative vocabulary could rival even the most erudite psychology professor when it came to classifying various types of human personalities. No one could ever deny her that distinction. Hilda's tongue and mind were as quick and lethal as her fists and feet.

All in all, Hilda M. Callahan had been married five times from about 1942 to about 1969. During that time she gave birth to five children that Little Ken knew about. He could have been wrong.

Her first husband was Connors Lang and she had two sons by him— Randall Stanley (1941) and Walter Jake (1943). He divorced Hilda in the mid-1940s and took his son Randall with him; Hilda kept their younger son, Walter, for herself.

Her second husband was Jamieson Archer. He and Hilda also produced two more boys in the late 1940s—Butch Errol in 1947, and Kenneth Allan in 1949. Jamieson Archer, was also able to successfully escaped Hilda's grasp in time to save his life as well as his soul. In the wake of Archer's great escape, he also abandoned all three boys, leaving Walter, Butch and Ken behind, alone with Hilda.

Her third husband, Milton A. Callahan, managed to survive in Hilda's war zone for three full years (an Olympic record when measured in "Hilda time"). In the early stages of their marriage, Milton did an honorable thing. He legally adopted all three boys—giving each of them his last name. That's when Walter, Butch and Ken officially became a Callahan. This occurred around 1953. But eventually even Milton Callahan, like his predecessors, successfully fled leaving all three boys alone with Hilda once again.

Her fourth husband, Ryan O. Mytus, was the smartest of all Hilda's husbands. They were married around 1963 or 1964 and apparently he was a very fast learner, quickly discovering the essence of Hilda's true character. He safely bolted after only a few months of marriage. It's highly likely that Mr. Mytus never looked at another woman the rest of his life.

Hilda finally seemed to settle down a little around 1965 or so, but only after unleashing nearly thirty years of endless havoc on the male population of Brooklyn and South Baltimore. That's when she met a good man named Joseph Smith. She married him in the late 1960s and stayed married until his death in the mid-1990s. Little Ken would come to remember this man very fondly, but never really understood how he lasted so long in the same environment with his mother. But he did. He felt Joseph Smith should have been nominated for sainthood.

During her life, Hilda's name would change at least six times: Hilda Harrington (maiden name) changed to Hilda Lang (first husband); to Hilda Archer (second husband); to Hilda Callahan (third husband); to Hilda Mytus (fourth husband); to Hilda Smith (fifth and final husband).

Hilda Harrington, Lang, Archer, Callahan, Mytus, Smith certainly loved men, and she loved marriage, unfortunately she never mastered the art of keeping either for very long.

Walter Callahan—Oldest Brother

Little Ken didn't reply to his mother's comments about Walter running away from home either. Walter was a good big brother, someone Little Ken trusted; someone who never harmed him, not once. He wasn't at all like Butch, his other older brother, who loved to bring pain into Little Ken's life. At fifteen, Walter was a kind boy, very tall with thick black hair—a mix between a young Elvis Presley and a younger Frank Sinatra. He also was very protective of Little Ken as well as with other kids in the neighborhood and those at school. Whenever school bullies were picking on smaller, defenseless students, the kids would run to Walter for help and protection. He was also much bigger and taller than most kids at school, and the little kids came to trust him over the years, just as Little Ken trusted him at home. When Walter graduated from the ninth grade, he was awarded the Gladys Mitchel Humanitarian Award by his school principal. It was bestowed upon him at his graduation ceremony in 1958 or so. Little Ken, Butch and Hilda attended that graduation; and when his name was announced as the winner of that award, the entire assembly of kids and parents stood to cheer for him. Little Ken was never more proud of his brother, Walter.

This seemed to be the last good thing to happen to Walter Jake Callahan growing up in the Projects. Something happened to him later that year that would be forever unknown to Little Ken—something so impactful that compelled Walter to drop out of school, evacuate 4139 Martin Court, leave the Projects altogether, and strike out on his own. Consequently, he never had a chance to make it through the tenth grade or further his education. Little Ken ran into him by accident from time to time in different places throughout Brooklyn. Walter had gotten a job working on a traveling vegetable truck delivering fresh veggies to various neighborhoods across South Baltimore, including Brooklyn.

However, he never saw Walter Callahan set foot inside 4139 Martin Court ever again.

Meanwhile, back at the furnace . . .

Little Ken normally could keep track of his mother pretty well when she was in the house. But somehow his attention on thawing out and warming up at the furnace distracted him this day. That's when he turned his head from facing the furnace to see her standing right behind and above him—like a storm cloud just waiting to burst open. "Listen, I want ya' ta' go to Giles Food Market and get me some cigarettes . . . and get back with 'em right away. Someone is upstairs that I want ya' ta' meet," she directed. It wasn't a request. "Ah, Mom, I still haven't warmed up yet. I promise to go in a few minutes after I . . . ," But before he could finish his sentence, he saw the back of her fist coming up from below her waist once again, and it was coming directly toward his face this time. He swayed at the last moment and avoided the full impact of her blow. "Don't give me any crap, ya' hear. I'm goin' out later ta' night, and I don't need any of ya' bullshit . . . understand? Just do it."

With that, she threw a quarter on the table and departed as quickly as she appeared. She wasn't waiting for Little Ken to say "Okay." It was not an option; she knew he would comply. So Little Ken put on his shoes and coat then headed out the back door. But first, he checked to see if the other door was unlocked. Then he unlatched the kitchen window just to ensure at least one way was available for him to get back in, if needed. He didn't want to go through another after-school beg-to-get-in routine, not on this bitter day. About thirty minutes later, he returned with her cigarettes and yelled upstairs to her that he was home. Little Ken threw his coat on the sofa and began re-embracing the furnace. Once his thawing was well underway, he headed to the refrigerator to see if there was anything to eat. Only the usual suspects were there:

- one container of Carnation's canned milk
- several bottles of beer
- a small bowl of leftover pancake batter with a thin film on it

- half a jar of mayonnaise, and
- one "untouched" bag of M&Ms

Not a great selection but at least it was something. He knew the M&Ms were off-limits, way off-limits. To even touch them would unleash the full wrath of Hilda Callahan's fury. M&Ms were hers, only hers, and always hers. So he took out the pancake batter and canned milk, got the frying pan from the cabinet, and started making his dinner—an exact replication of the previous night's dinner and the night's before. It was the same frying pan his mother used on Walter's head numerous times. There never was any syrup or jelly in the house for the pancakes, but even "naked pancakes" (as he called them) were filling and hot. And that's all he needed right now, anyway.

After several minutes passed, he heard his mother calling again. However, her tone was much different now. She was using her most contrived, most loving voice—the one usually reserved for only special occasions. Little Ken knew every one of his mother's many moods and voice tones; this was her most maternal voice: "Ken, won't ya' please come up here for a moment, darlin'? I want ya' ta' meet someone. And please bring up da' cigarettes too, OK, sweetheart?" Whenever he heard that specific tone of voice coming from upstairs, filled with words such as *darlin'* or *sweetheart,* he knew the nature of the next routine and what was about to happen. So Little Ken replied to her immediately in his most submissive voice to ensure she would not misinterpret his reply as disobeying. "Mom, I can't right now . . . got pancakes going on the stove. I'll throw the cigarettes up the stairs to you, though. Here they come, OK?"

With that he threw the pack up the stairs. They landed in the second-floor hallway. There was no reply—not a good sign. So he went back into the kitchen to keep his pancakes cooking. There was a long period of silence. Then he heard the weight of her footsteps making their way across her bedroom, then along the short narrow hallway between the other two bedrooms and the bathroom, then down the stairs. Each step became louder and louder in his mind, vibrating the whole house. Subconsciously, his grip on the frying pan handle tightened with every step, every vibration. By the time she entered the kitchen, his senses were on heightened alert and he had to be ready for, not only the impact of her words, but also her fists. He sensed both would be arriving shortly.

He was wrong.

Rather, she very sweetly said the following to her son: "Ken . . . please turn-off da' burner now and come upstairs w'it me, darlin'. I'll give ya' some money later on so ya' can go and get somethin' ta' eat down at Central's Restaurant, Okay? So com'on now." Hilda Callahan didn't wait for a reply. She reached over and turned off the stove's burner herself and then took Little Ken by the hand and led him upstairs to her bedroom—to what he knew to be "high times." This was the name she gave to such special moments in her bedroom. It was nothing new to him, just another routine about to unfold in 4139 Martin Court in 1961.

They then walked down the short hallway to her bedroom. They entered together, hand-in-hand.

Sandy Callahan—Sister

After giving birth to her four boys, Hilda then had a little girl. Her name was Sandy. She was born in 1960 during a seemingly downtime between Hilda's many marriages. Before her birth, Hilda had been dating a man named Leonard Flint, who worked at Baltimore city's waste incinerators facilities. He would come to 4139 Martin Court on a regular basis around 1959 and early 1960 to see Hilda and always bring along boxes of expired cookies and candies. Instead of burning such expired, discarded foods as required by law, he brought some of it to Hilda and her boys. Butch and Little Ken called him the Tang Man because he would also bring a case of Tang on every visit.

Tang was a fruit-flavored, powdery mixture that exploded with a strong orange taste when water was added. The drink was not popular during the early years of production in the 1950s, therefore Flint would find lots of it showing up at the city's incinerators being dropped off by store owners who no longer wanted to carry the stuff on their shelves. However, Tang became quite popular and famous when it was used on John Glenn's

Mercury flight and subsequent Gemini spaceflights conducted by NASA in the early to mid-1960s.

To the Callahan boys, Leonard Flint was just another man at the house, coming and going; his only distinction was Tang, nothing more. Little Ken sensed, didn't know for sure, that Flint was Sandy's real father. It didn't seem to matter because when Sandy was about three or so, she was adopted to another family. And, Hilda Callahan was paid $200 in the "transaction." "Yea . . . it was a gud' deal, alright. I got $200, and Sandy now gets ta' eat regular . . . like . . . whatever and whenever she wants . . . and she even gets a bedroom of her own ta' grow up in . . . and has a real backyard ta' play in too . . . I dun' seen it myself." Hilda said this in a very proud and boisterous way as if she had just successfully negotiated the car sale of the century. At least that's how it came across to Butch and Little Ken after they both returned from Camp Canoe (a two-week, free summer camp for a few of Brooklyn's underprivileged kids). It happened in the summer of 1963 when Sandy was about three years old and was also the first time they learned their little sister had been adopted to another family—gone forever.

Yet, Little Ken knew his mother failed to mention another tangible benefit for his sister—Sandy would also be much safer physically, emotionally, and socially in another home. He didn't really know how many times his sister was abused by his mother in her first three years or so, but he sensed it occurred more than once. The one incident he recalled involved his little sister, his mother and two of her new boyfriends. The incident happened a couple months before Little Ken and Butch went off together at Camp Canoe.

The "Accidental" Ashtray

Sandy's "accident" occurred late one afternoon on a weekday when Little Ken was working with Mr. Williamson, the director of the Projects' recreation center (RC). Ken was helping Mr. Williamson prepare for the kickoff of a brand-new athletic program—the John F. Kennedy's Physical Fitness Program. This was a special, popular program sponsored by the US government. It was not just for the Projects people; it was also a nationwide initiative. This program was designed to help "Soft America" (as JFK put it) shape up, work out, and get healthy. After winning World War II, many Americans apparently were becoming fat, dumb, and happy—severely out of shape. This national program, implemented via state recreation departments across America, was designed to turn this trend around. All the residents of the Projects and surrounding communities were encouraged to participate—kids, parents, relatives, neighbors and even local business community members. Mr. Williamson was just about set to kick-off the program when an ambulance came screaming up Tenth Street and headed straight to the Projects. It made a sharp left turn into Martin Court, right across from the RC. That's when a kid from the neighborhood came running over and told Little Ken the ambulance went to his house—4139 Martin Court. So he told Mr. Williamson he had to leave to see what was happening, but he would return as soon as he could. Ken then ran across Tenth Street, went around the back of the first building in Martin Court, and darted toward his unit in the middle of the next building. There he saw his mother and two strange men standing near his back door. They were huddled, smoking cigarettes, and whispering. The ambulance was idling, the siren had been turned off, and several neighbors had come out of their units and were watching everything.

His sister, Sandy, was being placed into the ambulance when his mother saw Little Ken coming. She yelled at him to go back to the RC, and then she slid into the ambulance alongside her daughter who was covered with a white sheet pulled up to her neck. Little Ken disregarded his mother's direction and approached the ambulance anyway. He could see Sandy's scared face and bulging eyes. She called out to him, even though her mother was at her side. The sheet around her had several red stains around her abdomen and legs.

When the ambulance pulled away, Little Ken didn't go back to the RC as his mother directed either. Instead, he went through his back door following the two men who had been there with his mother. Beer bottles were spread across the kitchen table, and the kitchen smelled as usual—like a warehouse of old cigarette butts and older whiskey. That's when he asked the men what happened to his sister. Both of the men were three times the size of Little Ken and much older, but he confronted them anyway. They didn't answer right away; instead, they started exchanging glances. Then one of the men nervously stumbled through the following explanation of things. "Ahhh . . . ummm . . . your sister had accident . . . that's right . . . she sat down on that big ashtray stand in the living room . . . that's right . . . and she cut herself pretty good on the sharp pointy edge . . . that's right . . . we tried but couldn't stop the bleeding . . . so your mom went next door and called an ambulance . . . that's right. Hope your sister will be alright, kid . . . she's a good little girl." Little Ken never heard so many "that's right" in such a short talk. Something didn't make sense to him.

Something wasn't "right."

So he left the kitchen and walked into the living room. Little Ken knew all about his mother's big ashtray stand; it was her second most prized possession in the house (second only to the portrait of Elvis Presley in her bedroom). The ashtray stand was certainly big and unusual, but he couldn't understand why or how his little sister could "sit" on it. The ashtray stand was nearly two feet high (about Sandy's height.) It had a huge round base on the bottom and a circular dark brown glass cigarette butt holder on top. The base and holder were connected by a long S-shaped, thick metal bar in between. It was very solid and very heavy— virtually immobile unless it was dragged, titled, or rolled on its side somehow. He just didn't understand how Sandy could have sat on it or even accidently fallen against it, knocking it over. The ends of the curved S-shaped came to a point as the men said, but each end was rounded, not sharp or pointed at all, certainly nothing that could cut or rip skin.

What was it then that actually cut Sandy? He couldn't figure it out. And the men were not talking any longer either. That's when Little Ken realized loud country music had been blasting from his mother's bedroom upstairs. So he went up the steps and down the hall to turn it off. There, he noticed the blankets on her bed were in shambles, and the sheet also had red stains in a lower corner, just like the ones on the sheet in the ambulance that Sandy was wrapped in. Again, something didn't make sense.

Nearly three years old now, Sandy had been walking and running on her own for some time, but she still couldn't go fast enough to even budge that big ashtray stand no matter how fast she ran or even if she fell right on top of it. That's when he sensed his little sister had been upstairs with his mother and the two men when the "accident" happened. So, he ran back downstairs to talk more with the men.

They were gone. He never saw them again.

Sandy was kept at the hospital for a couple of nights. His mother came home that evening but didn't explain what happened to Little Ken or Butch. She only said Sandy was going to be fine. Three days later, Sandy was brought home. And a few months after that, when Butch and Little Ken returned from a two-week summer camp for low-income kids, Sandy was gone. She had been adopted by another family. "Yeah, it was a . . . GUD' DEAL" was the phrase his mother once used to describe Sandy's adoption—a phrase that Little Ken would never, never forget.

That's why he sincerely felt that Sandy would be better off growing up elsewhere. No matter where she went, she would be fine as long as it was away from 4139 Martin Court and far away from the Projects of Brooklyn. In a strange way, he was actually happy and relieved that his little sister had gone to a much better place. As such, Little Ken thought perhaps his mother really had done the right thing after all, especially for Sandy.

He and Sandy would not see each other again for nearly a decade.

The Recreation Center (RC) and Mr. Williamson

While growing up in 4139 Martin Court, Little Ken came to dread (really dread) many things other kids at school naturally enjoyed and looked-forward to throughout the year. He called such times "special events" and included:

- Hearing the school bell ring "ending" each day.
- Weekends.
- Holidays.
- Summer school breaks.

Such "special events" meant he had to spend more time at home, something he just didn't want to do. Ken's secret philosophy during those days was—"*Any place but home.*" He did sense it was kind of weird thinking this way especially knowing all the other kids at school just could not wait for the school bell to ring and weekends to come. Ken also felt doubly-weird after he first saw *The Wizard of Oz* (MGM's 1939 mega-special effects fantasy staring Judy Garland). Despite all its wonderful characters, locations and memorial scenes, this movie's major message was—"*There's no place like home.*"

He never trusted MGM afterwards.

So, during such "special event" times, Little Ken sought-out safe places to go. The main place he liked was the recreation center (RC). It was located in the middle of the Projects. Ken's home, 4139 Martin Court, was close by, less than a half block away. The RC was funded as a part of Baltimore City's recreation services. It was a fun place, a learning place, and a "safe" place for Little Ken. The RC had board games, Ping-Pong, pool, indoor and outdoor organized sports, and a water fountain splash pool in the summer months. Teen dances were also held there on Wednesday evenings, and teenagers from nearby communities including Brooklyn Park and Curtis Bay attended. Little Ken was too young to attend the dances; he was not quite a teenager yet. Still, he would volunteer to help out the director of the RC, not only get ready for the dances, but also with other recreation activities scheduled throughout the week.

The RC's director was Mr. Carl B. Williamson.

He was a smart, good man and a natural athlete. Little Ken idolized him just like he idolized John Wayne. Mr. Williamson was about thirty-five years old and a former lieutenant in the US Army who worked for Baltimore City's Bureau of Recreation. This was his first job as a director of an entire community center, and he appreciated the help Little Ken would so freely give to him, especially considering most of the other kids seemed to complain about everything and never offered to help him with anything. For his help, he'd taught Little Ken many things, including how to use athletic equipment, how to schedule events, how to keep records, how to coach, how to recruit other kids to participate in events, how to create posters and advertisements for new recreation programs, and even how to master the rules of baseball, basketball, and football. Equally important, Little Ken learned how to compete and win while also following the rules . . ."how to win (and lose) with "grace," as Mr. Williamson would say to him.

One set of ideals he helped instill within Little Ken early on in their relationship became a long-term, personal value that he carried with him throughout his life. "Listen, Kenneth . . . you can lose a game but still be a winner. It's all about *how* someone loses—and wins—that tells everyone else who the real victor was. A final score of a game is just a number—only one part of winning and losing anything. Go shake the hand of the person who just beat you and congratulate him in front of everyone, and I bet they will view you differently the next time—not just as a competitor but as a man too . . . and as a winner, even though you may have lost. So you see, it's possible to win even when you lose. Try to remember that. Okay?"

Little Ken did remember it and practiced it . . . forever.

After a while, he became sort of a "sidekick kid" to Mr. Williamson. They tackled problems together, traveled to other RC's events, opened and closed the RC in tandem, and even refereed competitions together. In the process, Little Ken started to feel proud of himself and became much more self-confident whenever he was around Williamson, even though he didn't know it at the time. He just knew it felt good when he was in his presence, and after a while, he also started mimicking him—sort of absorbing Mr. Williamson's personal style and his quick-witted humor. He liked having a man of this type in his life—someone he could trust.

Little Ken seldom went directly home after school, preferring to stay at the RC even after most kids left in the evenings. Mr. Williamson noticed this pattern and often told him to go home and get some supper or just check in with his parents, but Little Ken usually made up some excuses why he wanted/needed to stay. After noticing this pattern over time, Mr. Williamson tried to learn more about Little Ken beyond his experiences with him at the RC. So one day when Little Ken was still at school,

Williamson walked over to 4139 Martin Court to talk with his mother, Hilda, about her son. It was a very brief talk. Rather, it was a listening session for Mr. Williamson. "Aaah . . . can't make d'at boy do any'ting . . . don't even try anymore . . . he's got a mind of his own just like his asshole fad'er . . . if he don't want ta' come home after school, no sweat off my brow," Hilda said as if she were referring to a dog that continually breaks off its leash and runs away, knowing it always returns when ready, not before.

He had gotten a better understanding of Little Ken's home life with just one brief interaction with Hilda Callahan. He had spent only a minute or two listening then thanked her for her time. That was all he needed. However, when Little Ken got home later that evening, she was waiting for him. Hilda not only yelled at him using her most "colorful" language, but she also used her seasoned extension cord on him because, as she said it, for "sending d'at man ta' see her wit' out tellin' her beforehand."

This was something Little Ken hadn't done or would ever do. The very last thing he wanted was for Mr. Williamson to meet his mother. She continued, "Why . . . just a nudder' step and he cud'a been in da' house wit' me alone . . . alone . . . what wud' da' neighbors have thought d'en? . . . he cud' a dun' any ting' he wanted wit' me." That was the reason she gave Little Ken later that day, just before she also gave him a beating with her extension cord. "Ya' shud'nt sent him here," she said, even knowing he never did such a thing. Little Ken was more embarrassed than physically hurt by this specific beating just knowing that Mr. Williamson now knew about his mother and his home life. In those days, feelings of shame just seem to hurt him much more and lasted longer than the rips and bites from her extension cord.

Mr. Williamson never discussed the details of that visit with Little Ken. He told him that he had just run into her accidently and said hello. But for the next year or so, Mr. Williamson asked his wife to pack an extra sandwich in his daily lunch bag. He would give it to Little Ken saying he needed some help with the huge lunch his wife had packed. And since Mr. Williamson had keys to the soda machines and both candy machines inside the RC, he ensured Little Ken got at least one of his favorite drinks (a grape or orange Nehi, Squirt, or Yoo-hoo) and one of his favorite candy bars (Zagnut, Milky Way, or Snickers) every day he volunteered and worked at the RC. It was the least he could do for a boy who gave so much yet asked for so little.

Little Ken really liked working and playing at the RC and came to like and respect Mr. Williamson even more with every passing day. He was really fascinated by him. Little Ken watched and learned how he related to everyone, even local gang members. Mr. Williamson never seemed to get angry with any kid even when they deserved it. And Little Ken never saw him raise his voice when correcting bad kids who broke the rules. He had a smile for everyone including the real jerks—kids as well as their parents. Being exposed daily to such adult behaviors was a good thing for Little Ken—a real good thing. Yet, the most fascinating thing about Mr. Williamson involved something far more interesting than just his abilities and knowledge.

Mr. Williamson was a black man.

As a matter of fact, he was the first black man Little Ken ever knew. And, he also turned out to be the very first man (male) he came to respect and admire in his life. He was the John Wayne of Little Ken's world—always doing right, always there to help, and always a good guy. Yet, many of the fights Ken had throughout the Projects were because he was defending his relationship with Mr. Williamson. "You, nigger lover . . . Williamson has got you doing his nigger work for him . . . you can't even see it" was a message he got on many occasions, not only from classmates and neighborhood kids, but also from many of their parents across the Projects. Such messages eventually made their way throughout the Projects and to Hilda's ears. So she felt compelled to "correct" him for being so "chummy" with the nigger man. "Listen . . . ya' stay away from da't bugger man. He's up to no gud' I tell ya' . . . probably just usin' ya' ta' get ta' me, I bet. Ya' know how d'ey are about women. Or worst, he's probably tryin' ta' open da' door for more blacks to come live in da' projects. So stay away from 'em, ya' hear, boy." As usual, Hilda made the issue all about herself.

Little Ken certainly feared his mother's wrath, but he always ignored anything she said regarding Mr. Williamson.

He also hated such words coming from her and other people about him and felt compelled to fight whenever he heard such names as bugger man and nigger expressed to him—even when the kids were bigger or even when he was outnumbered. When Mr. Williamson saw bruises and cuts showing up routinely on Little Ken's face, he asked what was happening, but Little Ken didn't tell him the truth at first. As time went on, however, the fights subsided somewhat and he'd then talk openly about it with Mr. Williamson. That's when Little Ken learned that he should never fight on this topic—violence wasn't the solution. Rather, he guided and encouraged him to merely walk away whenever possible. "Listen, Kenneth, you have to just walk away . . . never run away, just walk—there's a difference. Those kids and their parents are just ignorant . . . they're really afraid, not mad . . . and it will take much more than fists and fights to fix such things in them. It will take time." His words were not only wise, but also comforting for Little Ken.

Mr. Williamson never called him "Little Ken", "Ken" or "Kenny"." Rather he always addressed him as "Kenneth." He believed a man's name and title reflected who he really was and who he would become. To be called Little Ken would likely keep him little, not only in the minds of others, but in his own eyes. Little Ken didn't fully understand what "ignorant, afraid, and angry" really meant (a phrase Mr. Williamson used many times), but he trusted him and tried to follow his guidance. And on several occasions, he was able to walk away from fights, but most of the time he was not allowed to do so. He was compelled to fight.

Living in the Projects of Brooklyn in the late 1950s and 1960s was "exclusively," not predominately, a white experience. There were no black residents living there at that time, and no people of color working in the offices or maintenance buildings of the Projects either. Mr. Williamson was the very first black person to do so. Little Ken didn't fully understand or appreciate just how unique and significant Mr. Williamson's presence in the Projects was at the time in America. He was just glad he was there.

Mr. Williamson was a friend, a trusted friend, someone he respected, admired, and liked. Even though he didn't realize it at the time, Mr. Williamson had become Little Ken's first male role model, someone he wanted to be like when he grew up. Unfortunately, he never got the opportunity to tell him how positively he had impacted his life in so many ways. When Little Ken returned from his second tour in Vietnam, nearly a decade later, he learned Mr. Williamson had passed away.

He was gone, but he would never be forgotten by . . . "Kenneth."

Getting into the Victory

Another "safe" place for Little Ken was the Victory Theater located on Patapsco Avenue, between Tenth and Eleventh streets. In those days, the price of admission, twenty-five cents, allowed a person to stay as long as he wanted—all day if desired. Little Ken could watch the same movie over and over as many times as he wished. His favorite movies were any Triple Horror Feature (especially Hammer Films starring Peter Cushing and Christopher Lee). He also enjoyed double feature, John Wayne movies. Any flick that took him far away from the Projects in his mind especially places such as Africa, Asia, or the Pacific islands, were most appealing to him. For some reason he loved the heat, the jungle, rivers and lakes, and animals. The movie theater not only served as a great escape from the realities of life at 4139 Martin Court, but also provided a comfortable and safe place to be. There was only one downside to the Victory movie theater; he couldn't do his homework there. Without lighting, it was impossible to read or write anything. Each week, Little Ken would also have to collect at least thirteen empty soda bottles (six to twelve ounce size). He'd cash them in at Giles Grocery store in order to pay for all day at the Victory Theater on a weekend day. Most empty bottles were worth two cents in those days ("2 cent'ers," he'd call them). The larger soda bottles, "26 ounc'ers," were the grand prizes in the bottle scavenging world. Each was worth a whole nickel. Collecting bottles was another routine for Little Ken—a good one. The weeks when he couldn't get enough bottles saved, he used two other "creative" backup methods to gain entrance into the Victory:

1. He would wait at the rear exit of the theater until kids came out from watching their movie and then he would scamper in before the exit door closed.

2. He would occasionally take a more direct, bolder route and go directly up to the cashier at the front entrance and provide a sob story such as, "There's been an accident, and my mother sent me to get my older brother to come home . . . he's inside now. May I go in and get him? I'll only take me minute, really . . . got to get him home, please . . . oh please . . ." Little Ken then would be allowed to go inside to find his make believe brother, but would never come out. He'd stay until the evening.

Surviving Mother

Meanwhile, back at his mother's bedroom . . .

Hilda had just turned off the stove herself, took Little Ken by the hand, and then headed up the stairs. They entered her bedroom together.

She turned and "partially" closed the door behind them. Little Ken instinctively and immediately applied one of his most well-developed skills learned growing up in the Projects—scanning the environment. He was searching for any of the four following things:

1. Potential or real threats
2. Number and physical size of the people present
3. Objects that could be used as an instant weapon, if needed
4. Any barriers to a quick escape.

By the age of twelve, this quick "survival scan" process had already evolved into a well-disciplined, natural reflex of sorts. He applied it without hesitation whenever entering a potentially threatening situation or environment of any kind. Throughout his subsequent teenage years in the Projects, at Sparta High School, and as a young man in Vietnam, this routine would prove to be one of his most reliable personal assets. Unfortunately, at this young age, he also was just too immature to manage this routine very well; it was getting a little out of hand. That is, he didn't know when it was really needed and when it wasn't. And he seemed to be going into "survival scan" mode even during normal, everyday situations, whether real danger existed or not. When in doubt, Little Ken would error on the side of applying it. And each time he did, it became more emotionally draining and taxing.

This routine began serving as his personal warning system seemingly linked directly to his nervous system. It alerted him to potential danger. Little Ken likened it to the warning cries of "Danger, Will Robinson!" that bellowed out of the Robinson family's likeable robot when an alien threat arose in episodes of the 1960s TV series *Lost in Space.* As a result, he began seeing and anticipating unexpected threats everywhere—at school, walking to the store, at the RC, in a neighbor's house, and even sitting alone in the dark of the Victory movie theater on Saturday afternoons. There always seemed to be an unknown, ever-present enemy of some kind in his mind, somewhere nearby . . . just beyond sight . . . just out of reach . . . just around the corner . . . just waiting . . . for him.

As such, he had to be ready, on high alert, all the time.

For good or bad, survival scans had become a permanent part of him. This silent, hidden process was unknown to those around him because he learned how to naturally disguise and view such a personal insecurity as "preparedness." This "always being prepared" mind-set came with a high price; it was not only emotionally draining, but it was also mentally time-consuming because real threats, those that could actually do harm, seldom if ever, came about. They existed only in his mind, not in reality. But at this moment in the bedroom, it was "reality." Her bedroom was the one place where this specific routine always came in handy . . . always proved helpful . . . always paid off . . . and always made a difference. It was the most dangerous place on earth for Little Ken Callahan. He was walking into such reality at this very moment, with his mother at his side.

As they entered Hilda's bedroom together, all his skills, senses, and emotions were on high alert. That's when Little Ken executed his "survival scan." Immediately he noticed there was only one man in the bedroom. The man was sitting in his mother's plush cushioned chair at the foot of her bed. He was a stranger. Little Ken was hoping for a familiar face this time, just made things a little more predictable. And predictability was his friend. In the first few seconds, Little Ken sensed this man was not going to be a physical threat to him, if it came to that. Most of the time during "high times" in her bedroom, things only became confrontational, not combative. It appeared this was going to be one of the non-combative times. The top of his mother's vanity was covered with a variety of perfume bottles in all shapes. An ashtray on her vanity was molded in the shape of a large fish and was overflowing with cigarette butts. A single cigarette was still burning. The tail-fin had two sharp tips pointing in opposite directions and its head had a huge, toothless mouth open wide as if about to swallow a fisherman's lure. Little Ken was very familiar with this specific ashtray because its pointy tail-fin could be easily used for protection, if needed. It was an effective, handheld defensive weapon—an "equalizer," as his mother called such emergency fighting tools. "Just makes t'ings a little more fair when y'ur up against a larger fella. Just never know when sometin' simple like d'is can come in handy. Take d'is fish for example . . . it's hard, pointy, fits easy into y'ur hand, and it's strong as a pipe. And see d'at hanger in the closet . . . why just unwind its neck and wrap the rest around yur' hand and ya' can take out a man's eye wit' it in a flash—he won't even know what hit 'em. Even d'is here pencil can be a gud' weapon . . . if sharp enough ya' got a knife dat's good for at least one jab. Look . . . ya' only need a second or two ta' get away from a bigger fella . . . and d'ese t'ings can give ya' dat extra time if needed'."

She taught this to both Little Ken and Butch, his older brother, only weeks earlier. Hilda would instruct them occasionally on similar things in life. She would do so as clearly and expertly as any math teacher instructing eighth-grade algebra students in formulating a simple ratio. Little Ken also knew this bedroom well and where all the potential weapons were hidden in plain sight. There was a small stool in front of her vanity that had a huge mirror hanging above; it made the room appear much larger than it really was. A small lamp was sitting on top of the wooden stand next to his mother's queen-size mahogany bed. Country music was also coming from a small radio on the far side of the bedroom floor. There was only one window, a five-foot-by-four-foot lift style that was covered by a single pull shade identical to every other window treatment at 4139 Martin Court. The pull shade's purpose was for concealment, not decoration. There were no other window treatments, just the pull shade.

However, the most predominant feature in Hilda's bedroom was a golden-framed life-size portrait of Elvis Presley—the King. It was a towering portrait hanging above the bed's headboard. Actually, it wasn't a portrait at all—more like a shrine that dwarfed everything else in the room. From the doorway, Little Ken could see Elvis's reflection in the mirror above his mother's vanity. No matter if she was lying in bed or putting on her makeup at the vanity, she could have direct eye contact with the King.

Hilda Callahan worshiped Elvis.

A single beam of late afternoon, gray light was streaming into the room through a tiny crack between the shade and window frame. This ray of light was cutting directly through the dull orange haze emanating from the bedside lamp and the thick fog of cigarette smoke that formed above everything. As such, the bedroom felt more like a poorly lighted peep show booth in an adult bookstore rather than a mother's boudoir. The room also smelled as it usually did—a sickeningly sweet combination of cheap perfume, Seagram's 7 whiskey, and cigarette butts. Little Ken had grown accustomed to this unique mixture of scents by now and was even beginning to find it comforting in a strange sort of way. Then Hilda said the following words to her son in a very slow, deliberate manner, reserved only for her most important messages to him: "Ken, d'is is Mr. Penn. He owns Downton's bar down on Patapsco Avenue . . . ya' know da' one where I work now and d'en. He's a gud' friend of mine, darlin' . . . and he wants ta' be yur' friend too." She had slowed her speech, placing emphasis on every single word, especially . . . *friend*.

Little Ken got the message. He did not have to reply or respond in any way. At twelve, he was a seasoned veteran observing "high times" no matter with whom or where in the house it occurred. Once again, he glanced over at the man sitting near his mother's bed. The man was smiling at Little Ken and pulling back his greasy black hair over a receding hairline. He was a short, fat man with bulging eyes rapidly going back and forth behind thick-rimmed glasses. He had dark eyebrows and a marshmallow body—a Peter Lorre look-alike if there ever was one. He was almost a twin of the Dr. Bedlo (Peter Lorre's character in the 1960s version of *The Raven* also starring Boris Karloff and Vincent Price.) Most important, Little Ken knew the man was not a physical threat to him or his mother. He was just too fat to be a threat.

Mr. Penn leaned forward in the chair and just began staring. He seemed hypnotized at first and then started a weird, sneering laugh. To Little Ken, this Peter Lorre-man's laugher reminded him of the carnival scene from Walt Disney's *Pinocchio*, when all the bad kids of the world were transforming into working donkeys. Their loud and chaotic laughter gradually turned into half-human, half-mule hee-hawing screeches as realization of what was happening to them became more apparent. But just as the boy-to-donkey laughter slowly changed over time in *Pinocchio*, so too did Mr. Penn's sarcastic sneers turn into something altogether different.

Hilda took another swig of Seagram's 7 and slapped Mr. Penn on the shoulder. She then grabbed a pillow from the head of the bed and quickly removed its pillowcase and placed over Little Ken's head. Whether this simple pillowcase routine was designed to protect him from all the horrors of "high times" or merely for her selfish needs, Little Ken would never know. So, he just closed his eyes and allowed his listening skills to go on alert as "high times" began unfolding once again.

Butch Callahan (Butch)—Older Brother

Little Ken always had been afraid of suffocation—of being smothered. He could tolerate almost anything his mother or brother Butch would do to him but couldn't bear to be confined in small spaces, bounded or covered. Anything that came close to obstructing his ability to move or breathe was a nightmare for him. Later in life, he came to learn such irrational fear was called claustrophobia. But at this moment, he didn't care what it was called.

He feared the fear.

Little Ken never conquered this fear growing up despite surviving so many "noble" attempts made by Butch, who intentionally administered what he fondly called suffocation "practice sessions" on him. These skirmishes occurred anytime and anywhere, most often happening when Butch and Little Ken were at home at 4139 Martin Court . . . alone. As brothers, they shared the same bedroom but had separate single beds. Butch would often pretend to be asleep, just waiting for Little Ken to doze off. Then he would sneak out of bed, jump him, tie his hands behind his back with a belt, wrap a pillowcase around his head, then leave him there for hours, struggling and crying. Butch moved fast, real fast, and Little Ken usually never knew what hit him until it was too late. And it took a long time for him to eventually break his bonds and regain normal breathing and self-control. Even though Butch was only about two years older than Little Ken, he was much bigger and stronger, weighed more, and was faster. More important, Butch knew everything about Ken—his likes, dislikes, habits, strengths, weaknesses and fears—all of which he used to his advantage.

When it came to fighting, Butch knew Little Ken was not an easy pushover even though he never lost a fight to him—not once. He viewed fighting as play and never seemed to tire of it, but Little Ken chose to fight only when his back was against the wall, as a last resort. Little Ken never feared any of his mother's boyfriends, fully grown men, as much as he did Butch simply because he knew so much about him. Butch's knowledge was far more dangerous than his brute force, meanness, and cruelty all combined. And that's exactly what Little Ken feared most about him. This type of awareness about his brother, unfortunately, also shaped his attitude about other people. As a result, Little Ken seldom, if ever, allowed others to get too close to him—even other family members, longtime friends, colleagues, or wives throughout the remainder of his life. He would let them in, but only so far. He also would not allow himself to get too close to others either. "There's safety and security in 'distance'." This mind-set was to become one of his long-term values and principles—a deeply embedded psychological, emotional, and behavioral routine. Unfortunately, he wouldn't come to recognize how counterproductive this was for several decades.

Butch found many "creative and fun" ways to exploit knowledge of his little brother's fear. For example, he discovered that dragging Little Ken into the bathroom and forcing his head into the toilet was a barrel of laughs. He'd submerge Little Ken's head into the toilet bowl then flush, thus causing the water level to recede, giving him just a few precious seconds to catch a single breath. The water level would then rise again, and his head would be re-submerged. Butch repeated this hysterically fun "practice session" until he got bored or until Little Ken passed out. "Dunk, flush, breathe . . . Dunk, flush, breath . . . Dunk, flush, breath," he would say aloud as his little brother struggled for air. Butch also had his own set of well-developed routines, too.

Little Ken's greatest fears about suffocation and being physically constrained didn't decrease as Butch thought would happen via such "practice sessions." Instead, his fear increased in intensity over time. Unfortunately for Little Ken, this routine of Butch's became one of his most favorite pastimes—playing suffocation with his little brother which continued for years.

Another little playtime activity Butch delighted in was placing all his weight on Little Ken's chest and arms in the middle of their living room. This was a real hoot for Butch as he kept him pinned solidly to the floor facing the ceiling, wrapping a towel or shirt around Little Ken's face, and then just holding it there. This was the best of the best. He knew suffocating was Little Ken's greatest fear, so he wanted to take him there, to the brink, as often as possible, while also keeping it as real as possible. After all, he loved his little brother so much and wanted him to get the most out of each and every precious "practice session." And to add even more fun for everyone, Butch created his own personal chant to go along with it as Ken was pinned down grasping for air. "Suffocation, no air, can't breathe, Ha-ha . . . Suffocation, no air, can't breathe, Ho-ho . . . Suffocation, no air, can't breathe, He-he."

Butch's desire to torment and torture seemed to be an extra chromosome he had somehow inherited from his mother while still in her womb. He just enjoyed it too much, just as she did. Hilda, too, took pleasure in watching it unfold from the comfort of her living room sofa as she watched TV. And having a "live" audience added an extra dimension to Butch's own personal joy, even though it also added more horror for Little Ken. Hilda Callahan viewed such "practice sessions" as her boys merely playing together. She would often laugh along with Butch as Little Ken was pinned on the living-room floor, face and mouth wrapped in towels, immobile from the waste up with his feet flailing in all directions. She also heard his muffled screams and pleas for help made directly to her as Butch worked his magic: "Help me, Momma! Stop him. I love you. I'll be good, I promise. Stop him. Please. I'll massage your legs in that special way you like it. I'll rub your feet for as long as you want too . . . and everything else . . . just help me. Just make him stop, please. I'll be good. I love you. Please, Momma." Little Ken's futile pleas were always heard by his mother; they just were never responded to, except with laughter.

Eventually, each of these living-room routines would come to an end, but only when a TV commercial finished or when one of Hilda's favorite shows came back on. Of course, these special moments naturally stopped each time Little Ken passed out from sheer terror, physical exhaustion, or both. During the summer, Butch or his mother had to close the living room windows to keep the neighbors from thinking Little Ken was actually being killed or something. They were afraid someone would have called the cops.

No one ever did.

Butcher-Bird—"The Impaler"

Little Ken was always tense whenever Butch was near, especially when in the house alone. Together, they could take on any five kids their age in the neighborhood. But one-on-one, Little Ken was no match for the "Butcher-Bird"—the nickname given to him by his mother and many neighborhood kids. It was a very appropriate identity for him, and one he liked a lot.

In the world of Audubon, there are many types of "butchers" (as seasoned birders call them)—Blacks, Greys, Pied, Hooded and Tagula. This carnivorous bird's large, distinctive bill has a pronounced hook at the end used to skewer its prey (insects, lizards, small vertebra, helpless new-born baby birds). As such, they are also called by more accurate names, including—"The Skewer", "The Spear", and, of course, *"The Impaler."* The reputation of Little Ken's brother fit nicely with the reputation of this raptor. "Butcher-bird's" own temperament and predatory character was perfectly in sync with this specie's fine plumage. Even the first seven letters of his real name illustrated this natural affinity—<u>Butch</u> <u>E</u>rrol Callahan.

Despite the hostility and distrust, Little Ken and Butcher-Bird had not always been at odds. At an earlier time in their life, they were best friends, caring brothers. That was before they moved into the Projects of Brooklyn while in the second and third grades. They used to go everywhere together and do things side by side. Little Ken was Butch's sidekick. They played together, bathed together, ate together, and slept together. They were inseparable at that age. And Butcher-Bird and Little Ken also shared a special routine of their own when they were about ten or so—stealing food.

Butcher-Bird called it "raiding a nest."

When there was absolutely no food in 4139 Martin Court (except for their mom's precious, ever-present M&Ms that could never be touched even if her boys' flesh was falling off their bones from hunger) . . . they "raided a nest." Both boys worked in tandem. They'd enter neighborhood grocery stores together, including Giles Food Market, and then they'd head off in two different directions. Little Ken would quickly find the store clerk, and Butcher-Bird would dart down one of the food aisles. Then Little Ken would approach and distract the clerk or store owner by asking a series of well-practiced questions about food items. He'd do so using his most proper, most respectful manners: "Excuse me sir, my mom wants to know if you carry Tang, and if not, where we could get it?" Or, "Please, sir, what day do you have raw hamburger or hot dogs on sale?" Or, "Sir, can you help me figure out how much two pounds of potatoes would costs?"

While the clerk was answering such fine questions posed by a polite, good-looking young boy, Butcher-Bird would be frantically flying down food aisles filling his pants and shirt with as many items as could be inconspicuously carried out. However, the only items he really could fit underneath his clothes were "squashable items," things like bread, Hostess cakes, or packages of ground hamburger. He'd always skip by canned goods or boxes of any kind—such items were just too obvious under clothing. The key to successful "nest raiding" was the ability of Little

Ken to pull off a deceptive diversion with a clerk just long enough for Butcher-Bird to soar through the nest. This approach worked well most of the time but could only be repeated once in the same store before the clerks would become suspicious.

Ken originally got the idea about stealing food from local grocery stores after seeing an early Elvis Presley movie, *King Creole* (1958, Hal B. Wallis Production). This movie had a scene where a teenager living in New Orleans entered a drugstore with a guitar and began walking around singing, entertaining patrons and clerks. This was a distracting maneuver that allowed other gang members to casually stroll through the aisles filling their clothes with store items. They then departed without being detected. Elvis continued playing his guitar and singing, then gradually departed as well. By the time the clerks realized their store had been robbed, Elvis and his gang were long gone.

Butcher-Bird and Little Ken were caught only once during their many raids on local grocery stores across Brooklyn and South Baltimore. To be exact, only Little Ken was caught. On this particular raid, the store owner saw Butcher-Bird in action as Little Ken was engaging the clerk. Neither boy noticed the owner's presence when they arrived. Usually, if more than one employee was present in the store, they would just skip it and move to another store. The owner yelled, and Butcher-Bird flew the coop out a nearby door with only one or two items under his clothes.

But Little Ken wasn't so lucky or so fast that day. He didn't make it out.

Ken was held, interrogated, and slapped around by the clerk and the owner. Butcher-Bird flew the coop and never looked back. When a policeman eventually arrived, Little Ken just started crying loud and long, feigning victimhood, youthful ignorance, and the compelling force of hunger. In retrospect, Little Ken would come to understand that he wasn't "feigning" it at all. Eventually they let him go, but not before the owner gave him a few more kicks in the ass. When Little Ken got home later that day, Butcher-Bird had already eaten everything. Butcher-Bird's overall predatory reputation was beginning to spread and take wing around that time. The legend of "eater of others' eggs" was taking root.

It wasn't until Hilda's third divorce, coupled with moving into the Projects, that the boys' relationship started to deteriorate. And then around 1960 or so, everything in the Callahan family seemed to really fall apart. Specifically, the following changes took place about the same time turning brotherly and motherly love into domestic fear and distrust:

- Hilda had to go to work every day and many nights.
- There was no permanent man around the house.
- There was no predictable income coming into the house.
- Food became scarce, and they fought over it regularly.
- Their sister, Sandy, was born and entered 4139 Martin Court.
- Their oldest brother, Walter, ran away from home.
- More and more men were entering and leaving their home.

But the thing that really set things off between Little Ken and Butcher-Bird happened around the time Little Ken turned eleven. Butcher-Bird failed the sixth grade—not just because his poor grades compelled teachers to keep him back a year at PS 244 (Overlook Elementary School), but also because of his attitude and behavior. Actually, Butch failing the sixth grade in itself was not a real problem for him; he didn't care about that. The thing that got his feathers permanently ruffled was he was placed in the same sixth grade homeroom class as his little brother, Ken, who had just completed the fifth grade and was also entering the sixth grade. PS 244 was located at the top of Tenth Street just beyond the Projects. It was a small school consisting of a series of scattered Quonset huts rather than brick or wood buildings. And it had only one sixth-grade class.

Little Ken and Butcher-Bird were stuck in the same sixth-grade class in 1960.

This was just too great an embarrassment for the Butcher-Bird; he needed his wing space as well as to be the only Callahan in the flock. Having his kid brother potentially "out flying" him within the classroom was just too much risk to take. That's when the full wrath of Butcher-Bird's claws was unleashed on Little Ken and any other kid who said a word about it. No kid was beyond striking range of the Butcher-Bird.

That's also when the nickname "Butcher-Bird" stuck to him like chewed bubblegum on the bottom of a shoe. And, he liked it.

A Wicked, Sinful Ride

Meanwhile, back in the bedroom . . .

The betrayal of her son, the abnegation of sacred motherly obligations, continued as Little Ken's fully naked body and pillow-cased head remained motionless, yet fully alert. This too, was just another routine unfolding at 4139 Martin Court in 1961. Through this unspeakable behavior, she could be assured more working hours at Downton's Bar (Brooklyn's number one drinking establishment at the time.) Hilda was becoming the town's most popular, most sought-after barmaid, and she liked that so much she'd spare no expense achieving it, including giving away the innocence of her son.

When it was over, Hilda and Mr. Penn collapsed on the floor.

At this moment everything in the room became hauntingly silent, still and sullen. Even though the radio could still be faintly heard in the background, not another sound or movement was apparent. And the only motion that could be observed in the bedroom was a thin stream of lifeless smoke drifting from a lit cigarette on the vanity. This slow and steady motion of gray smoke was hypnotic, forming an endless trail of shadows circling the bedroom, crawling up the mirror, rolling along the wall, and casually coming to rest on the floor, then somehow lazily making its way back up to the ceiling above. All three human bodies in the bedroom were motionless, cadaver-like, really; each in a state of obvious physical collapse as well as in an unknowable state of emotional exhaustion and surrender. Even though the bodies were only inches from each another, they were not physically touching in any way. Each was alone and would be detached forever even though they just had shared the most intimate, most compromising clash of souls possible. Their motionless bodies (including Little Ken's) remained perfectly stationary. Even though humans could be seen, only empty shells of lifeless humanity were actually present at this moment—forever bonded by unspeakable shared sin. This was parental betrayal of the highest magnitude, an eternal destruction of innocence that could never be restored. Through a camera's lens, this bedroom scene appeared more like a black-and-white, photograph taken on the set of a B-rated horror film depicting the aftermath of a psychotic killer's butchery of a family. The only thing missing from the picture was the presence of blood. Everything else had the look and feel of an actual horror movie snapshot.

At this exact moment, time was meaningless . . . time was empty . . . time was endless . . . time was worthless.

Yet, this was not a horror movie at all. It was just another routine being played out at 4139 Martin Court in the Projects of Brooklyn, Baltimore, in 1961. The participants would soon rise, go their separate ways, and life would continue as usual. Just like the ringing of three o'clock school bells, rides on yellow buses, and completion of homework assignments, this too was just another after school "routine."

Inside the Pillowcase—a Fair Exchange

Little Ken had remained perfectly still, yet fully alert, throughout it all; he was just waiting for things to finish-out as usual. Everything physically happening to him beyond the pillowcase was never of importance to him. And, since he couldn't "see" anything anyway, his attention always stayed laser-focused on what he could "hear" instead—listening was the most important sense he had during high times. Little Ken always concentrated on the dialogue, the talk, the words being exchanged between Mr. Penn (and anyone else) and his mother. Voice tones, language and volume were critically important because without sight, his ears became his eyes. Fortunately, his capacity to listen had become very well refined over time. He was already on high alert, attentive to every word and sound around him, and his ability to analyze voices and words had evolved into a foolproof, early warning system of sorts that always seemed to telegraph to him one of two things:

1. Imminent threat and likely violence, or
2. Peaceful, friendly coexistence.

Possible scenarios usually fell into one of these two situations. If violence did break out, he wanted to be ahead of it, instead of responding to it. He hated surprises; they made him more vulnerable. As such, Little Ken had developed another important routine during such times, a process that stayed with him for decades. This was the step-by-step process that became ingrained in his mind:

Step 1: Remove the pillowcase quickly and scan the room.
Step 2: Assess the people situation.
Step 3: Dodge immediate blows and find firm footing.
Step 4: Locate any possible weapon (an "equalizer," as Hilda called it).
Step 5: Aid his mother, if needed.
Step 6: Search for and make a "clean getaway."

Incidents requiring this complete routine had been needed less frequent lately. But Little Ken knew the probability of something happening was always present during "high times." The combined ingredients of whiskey, men, sex, money, country music, and Hilda always represented a potentially explosive situation—anything could happen. Therefore, his ability to stay laser-focused on every sound, every word, and every noise in the absence of sight became a key survival skill—another valuable routine. Fortunately, this afternoon's "high time" didn't evolve into violence. He had sensed it right away when first seeing what type of man Mr. Penn was—a nonphysical threat. Little Ken knew his role and what was required during "high times;" he just didn't understand the "why" of it all; one day he would, just not this day.

After a few minutes, Hilda Callahan rose from the floor and told Little Ken to leave the room. She then walked to the far side of the bedroom next to the window, lit a cigarette, and inhaled deeply. As usual, she held the smoke in her lungs for as long as she could, then allowed it to lazily crawl out of her nostrils. She just stood there staring outside even though the shade was pulled all the way down to the window's sill. While her body was inside the room, her mind seemed far away in that very distant, unknowable place and time where all woeful thoughts, feelings and memories eventually end-up.

Little Ken made his way to the door and was about to leave the bedroom. Then he stopped, turned around facing in the direction of his mother.

Then he asked from across the room, "Mom, can I have that money you promised, you know, so I go to Central's Restaurant to get something instead of eating those naked pancakes downstairs . . . remember you said you would earlier?" She slowly turned around from the window and took another deep drag from her cigarette. She just stood there staring at him, her son, her lover, her fantasy, her past, her future—at what she had nurtured.

Hilda Callahan was in no hurry to answer her son; she already knew what her answer would and had to be. More important, she knew "how" to answer him at this moment. Slowly and deliberately, she began another one of her motherly routines. "Listen, I thought ya' said ya' already had pancakes a-goin' on the stove downstairs. Well, don't ya'? Just finish d'ose up and maybe next time ya' listen ta' me when I say go over da' Johnsons or Jacksons and get sometin' ta' eat after school. Now . . . just go and leave me and Mr. Penn alone. We got some business ta' finish up."

When giving instructions of this kind to her son, she always maintained long, direct, intense eye contact. Even though it was not the answer he desired, having his mother's attention, even for such a brief moment, made Little Ken feel important, needed, and loved. He liked having eye contact with her a lot. To him, it was the closest thing to a warm hug he could expect to ever get from her. It was just her way; he came to understand and accept it. And she knew he understood it. Giving attention to Little Ken through personal eye contact was her way of rendering rewards and punishments, rather than using it for genuine mother-son communications. This was one of her most effective routines with him. Hilda viewed ten seconds of pure, direct, nonverbal connection with him as an investment—a down payment for future deeds, favors, and obedience. Additionally, it served as a subtle yet perverted kind of thank-you for having done his "fair share" in helping his mother keep her job. To her, that should be reward enough.

"And don't turn on d'at damn TV . . . I'm goin' out later tonight and want ta' get a little sleep after Mr. Penn leaves."

With that, she slowly turned and continued her insolent stare into the deep nothingness of the drawn window shade. Little Ken stood there for a moment disappointed, but not surprised. He responded. "I won't turn on the TV, I promise." His reply was genuine and he did so quickly because he now had a "clean getaway" opportunity in sight. So he put his pants on, pulled the door further open then walked out and headed downstairs to finish cooking his naked pancakes. They were gone in seconds after cooking them; chewing and tasting only seemed to slow him down during such times. But, for the first time since leaving school at three o'clock, Little Ken noticed his feet and hands had finally warmed; back to normal body temperature, that is. Even though he felt empty and hollow inside as a result of so many routines this day, at least he was no longer cold, and his belly was full of something.

At 4139 Martin Court in 1961, "routines" always seemed to find a way to balance things out.

For Little Ken Callahan, it was a fair exchange.

CHAPTER 2
High School and Army Induction
(1965-1967)

KENNETH CALLAHAN GRADUATED FROM ANNE Arundel High School (AAHS) on June 10, 1967. He entered the US Army less than three weeks later at the age of eighteen. Ken (no longer Little Ken) originally wanted to join the army to go-off and fight in the Arab-Israeli War of 1967. He wanted to do so, not for deeply held religious beliefs, but rather because his favorite TV series was *The Rat Patrol* (about a team of jeep-bound army commandos fighting Germans in the desert of North Africa during World War II). As history clearly tells, the 1967 Arab-Israeli War was not only the most decisive war ever waged in modern times, but also the shortest. It came to be known as the Six-Day War (June 5 to June 10, 1967).

Sometimes timing is everything.

Obviously, Ken never got to fight in the desert sands of North Africa. As a matter of fact, that war ended well before his head was shaved at army boot camp in Fort Bragg, North Carolina, on June 27, 1967. As noble as his original motives were, the truth was he joined the army as soon as possible after graduating from high school to flee the memories of his upbringing. It didn't matter to Ken on which continent, country, or planet he eventually landed as long as it was far, far away from the Projects of Brooklyn.

For Ken Callahan, entering the US Army was more about "escaping" than joining.

The Asphalts and Sparta High School

A lot happened to him from fifteen to eighteen. One of his biggest lessons was getting "into" high school—it was far more difficult and complicated than getting "out." Ken made a key mistake early on. He just assumed attending tenth grade at Sparta High School in Baltimore City would be a piece of cake, just another different type of violence to overcome—nothing new. However, he didn't anticipate the scope of relentless violence he would have to face along the way; it was very different from the hostility he faced in the Projects and within his own home.

First of all, Ken had to take a public bus every day from Patapsco Avenue in Brooklyn, through the Cherry Hill black community, cross over the Hanover Street Bridge straddling parts of Baltimore's Harbor, and then navigate through the endless asphalt neighborhoods of South Baltimore—all this before even stepping inside a school. Even though it was only a seven-mile trip, it took nearly forty-five minutes one-way because of all the stops the bus had to make. Additionally, Ken then had to travel another three blocks on foot before even reaching the Sparta's school grounds.

What transformed this two hour, roundtrip jaunt into "the school commute from hell" was not just the distance; it was also because of the Asphalts—one of the city's most pervasive teenage gangs. They made each trip even more challenging. The Asphalts owned the streets of South Baltimore in those days. A short, three-block walk from the bus stop to the school grounds would normally take a couple of minutes for Ken (or any other healthy fifteen-year-old boy). But he learned on the first day of school the obvious, most direct route from the bus stop to school was also risky, very risky.

The Asphalts found Ken easily and quickly on his first day. He stuck out like a wounded antelope on the Serengeti of Africa. As such, he was easy prey, fresh meat, and low-hanging fruit ready for picking by members of the Asphalts. The first time he was spotted and caught, they just kicked him in the balls a few times, tap-danced on his head, and told him never to come onto their turf again without paying a "twenty-five-cent toll."

This was something Ken could never do. Twenty-five cents was his bus fare each day, and he couldn't give that up. The second time he was caught, they not only took his bus money but also his lunch, and they continued to perfect their tap-dancing skills. After years of growing up in the Projects, Ken had learned how to take such blows and take them well. But he wasn't going to allow himself to be caught a third time. He didn't know how far they'd go the next time. So Ken stayed late after school one day to survey several neighborhoods surrounding Sparta High School. He waited on the school grounds until night and then stealthily checked out alleyways, back paths, and possible clean getaway routes he could use coming and going to school. It took several hours of hiding and slow exploration, but he learned quickly. Unfortunately, his surveying time took him late into the evening that night, and he missed the last public bus back to Brooklyn. So he had to jog the entire route home in the dark.

Ken learned how to avoid the toughest streets and sidewalks on which the Asphalts had lookout sites. So instead of taking the shortest route after getting off the bus each day, he began using back alleyways and cracks between buildings to move about. It was challenging at first, but it actually became fun over time. He was moving through the Asphalts' turf right under their noses without being seen or heard. Having grown up in the Projects, Ken was very comfortable traversing back alleys. It took him a little longer to get to school each day, but at least he was able to make it with his bus money intact and lunch in hand. More importantly, he was able to keep his front teeth in his mouth and his balls safely tucked away where they belonged. Sometimes he wondered which was most valuable to him—his bus money, his lunch, his teeth, or his balls. He decided "lunch" was most important, with bus money running a close second. Bruised balls and lose teeth would eventually heal (a lesson he learned well in the Projects). But, food and money were far more vital to him now at the age of fifteen. Once he carved out a few unique routes after getting off the public bus in South Baltimore, he was able to get to and from school virtually unscathed, most of the time but not all of the time. The major downside of this daily trip was the possibility of having his bus fare stolen. Without it, he would have to walk, jog, or hitchhike back to Brooklyn after school, no matter how bad the weather was.

It wasn't the length of the trip back home that was so bad; rather the toughest part was getting over the Hanover Street Bridge. He was also told that being a white boy, making it through Boogy Land (the name his mother called Cherry Hill) in one piece would be a problem. "Don't get caught d'er boy . . . dos' boogies will jump ya', beat ya', strip ya' naked, and throw ya' into a big boiling pot dey' got set up behind their community swimmin' pool . . . d'en d'ey eat ya'. D'ey will. So stay out of d'ere."

Just as a hot branding iron leaves a well-defined symbol on a steer's rump, such racial stereotypes were also deeply seared into Ken's mind by his mother and some neighbors while growing up. Fortunately, when Ken was younger, he also came to know Mr. Williamson, a black man. He knew him very well, and such racial stereotypes never found a permanent resting place in Little Ken's mind or heart. These feelings were reinforced on several occasions when he had to make his way through Cherry Hill on foot from school. He was never attacked or molested there by anyone. Never. To the contrary, Ken was personally helped once by a kind, elderly black man who gave him a dime on a cold snowy day so he could catch a bus out of Cherry Hill and get back to Brooklyn. To Ken, compared to the Asphalts and many residents of Brooklyn's projects, the people of Cherry Hill proved to be a blessing, not a curse.

After months of this routine, Ken realized he had to stop going to and coming from Sparta High School every day. While he did learn ways to survive during these commutes throughout the tenth grade, he knew his luck would run out one day. Two more years of this seemed like an eternity to him, and he sensed it would be impossible to maintain such luck.

He had to find another way to graduate.

Anne Arundel High School (AAHS)

So Ken became a transfer-in student at Anne Arundel High School in 1965, but it didn't come easily. He transferred during his junior year and became a good student, not a great student (number 52 in a class of 250). Ken made the honor roll once or twice, and that surprised even him. Nevertheless, he always studied hard and played hard, wanting badly to fit in and be a part of a normal high school culture. So he participated in many aspects of AAHS school life. Specifically, Ken became a varsity letterman in baseball (all-county, first baseman), a member of the AAHS Varsity Chorus, and a Thespian.

Becoming a part of something bigger than himself was what he silently desired, perhaps because doing so was such an uncomfortable part of his family and community life growing up in Brooklyn. His self-image did not seem to evolve positively during those years, and he wanted to prove to himself that he could fit in and be a part of bigger whole. As such, he learned how to appear to others as an outgoing, self-confident, gregarious boy. But deep inside, he silently felt like a loner, a loser really—never as good as the other kids, simply because of his upbringing.

AAHS was a suburban school neatly snuggled within a well-kept, middle-class neighborhood of Anne Arundel County, Maryland. It was located between the towns of Glen Burnie (the county) and Brooklyn (the city) only a few miles from Friendship International Airport, which later evolved into Baltimore Washington International Airport (BWI) in 1973.

Ken really liked the school. He especially enjoyed his classmates, the teachers, and the school's many extracurricular activities. Having transferred from Baltimore City's notorious Sparta High School, where gang violence was ever present, Ken quickly came to appreciate just how "civilized" AAHS was. He quickly learned to savor the warmth of this school's social, academic, and athletic environment. The friendly and colorful hallways, warm classrooms, and caring faculty became very special to him. He even liked the smell of his assigned school locker. All these things helped him quickly adjust and easily adapt. Additionally, Ken also appreciated the school's well-kept grounds, athletic fields, and facilities. It was just a good place to be. If he learned anything academically while there, he felt it would be a welcomed bonus.

Ken was also made to feel welcomed by the girls at AAHS. At the end of many school days, he would go to his locker to drop off the books he wouldn't need for homework, and there he'd find handwritten, folded notes inserted into his locker. Such notes were written by girls (he assumed) in his class expressing how good it was to have him at AAHS.

They also complimented him on his good looks and friendly ways. But of course, these notes were never signed, so he never knew from whom they came. Even so, such little gestures went a long way in helping Ken feel even more welcomed.

Equally important, he came to appreciate the safety and security the school offered—a stark contrast from Sparta High School. Ken no longer had to keep looking over his shoulder or behind him while coming and going between home and AAHS. And he no longer had to do "head counts" in cars slowly passing him by on the streets. At Sparta High School, one or two people passing by in a car were manageable, if they jumped him. But three or more was no match, and he knew it. When that happened, he had to have a quick, clean getaway. Fortunately for Ken, he was fast on his feet, real fast; and with just a few steps advantage, he could out-run any group of kids who were bent on doing him harm. At AAHS, this athletic agility was not required, nor did he feel compelled to carry a hidden weapon of any kind (an "equalizer" as his mother so fondly called a stealth weapon such as a knife, pipe, or fist-ready rock). He just felt safer there and no longer worried about such things. From the first day at AAHS, Ken sensed school life was going to be good in the eleventh and twelfth grades.

However, since he lived in the Projects of Brooklyn, which technically was located within Baltimore City limits outside of Anne Arundel County, he was required by law to attend Sparta High School during the tenth grade, even though AAHS was much closer and far more convenient. He'd have to complete his eleventh and twelfth grades there, too, if he couldn't come up with a way around it.

So here's what Ken did to get into AAHS.

The Great Escape

All through the tenth grade at Sparta High School, Ken dreamed of finishing his last two years of high school at AAHS. In his mind, going to school at AAHS would be like living on the set of *The Mickey Mouse Club*—a caring, fun, exciting, educational, safe place to learn. In contrast, staying two more years at Sparta High School would be like being trapped in a movie such as *West Side Story*, *To Sir with Love*, or *The Blackboard Jungle*—a teenager's nightmare. In short, Ken had to find a way to become a "mouseketeer," if he was to finish high school and get out of Brooklyn altogether.

This was the only option he had short of dropping out of school, running away from home like his two older brothers did, or joining the US Army before his time. So he had to devise a plan to escape his current circumstances and break free from what he knew would only lead to more trouble, limited opportunities, continued pain, and a poor education. Graduating from high school was the difference between getting out of Brooklyn and being stuck there for the rest of his life. Therefore, an escape plan from Sparta High School to AAHS was critical. But just having a simple plan wasn't going to be enough; Ken needed a great plan—a "great escape" plan.

In the past, he always found ways to avoid bad things and times, including evading Butcher-Bird's many traps, eluding his mother's biting extension cord attacks, circumventing gang maneuvers, and discovering new food sources. Yet, such actions and plans were always short-term, tactical fixes needed just to get through a specific tough moment in time. Nothing like the kind of solution he needed now. To get out of attending one high school in the city just to get in another high school in the county was far more tricky and complex than anything he had devised in the past. And then sustain it over two years made things even more challenging. It was going to require much more thought, broader creativity, and true ingenuity. Getting into AAHS was the key to everything, to his future. To fail meant he'd likely be stuck in Brooklyn the rest of his life—his biggest nightmare.

So, he had to think this through.

During the first month of summer vacation after completing his tenth grade at Sparta High, he kept failing to come up with a plan. He was getting more desperate with each passing day, and then he recalled a movie he once saw. It was called *The Great Escape* (1963) starring James Gardner and Steve McQueen. He tried to reconstruct every part of this movie in his mind but only could recall bits and pieces at first. The movie was about a group of American, British, and Canadian soldiers being held in a POW camp deep within Germany during World War II. Many men escaped the camp safely. However, many were caught and were returned to the camp, or they were executed on the spot while trying to cross the vast German countryside. Much of this movie focused on "how" the POWs devised creative ways to break out and flee Germany. What impressed Ken the most was not the ideas they generated (which were many) but rather, how they thought through each idea. Their planning process was "great." That is, the way ideas were analyzed, drawn-up, modified, practiced, and then executed was always fascinating to Ken. Their ultimate escape strategy had two key dimensions in Ken's mind—first, was to build a single underground tunnel, and second was to flee in multiple directions using multiple disguises.

If Ken was to come up with his own "great escape," he knew his strategy had to be at least two-dimensional and equally creative. Then an idea hit him between the eyes as hard as a Jim Palmer fastball nailing an irate fan in the front row at a Baltimore Orioles home game. The POWs knew they couldn't escape individually; they had to work together or none of them would have a chance. That was the biggest lesson Ken took from that movie. This implied that Ken could not pull off such a "great escape" of his own by himself—he needed an accomplice. So he decided to pull his estranged Uncle into his plan. And, in July 1965, he paid him a visit. His name was Daniel Harrington, an older brother of Ken's mother, Hilda.

Uncle Dan and his family lived at 223 West Arundel Road within Brooklyn Park, not far from the high school. Ken wanted to convince his Uncle to allow him to use his address (a "county" residence) as his permanent address for two years. Even though Ken would still actually be living within the Projects along with his mother, he would be using his Uncle's address on paper only. If his Uncle allowed it, Ken could then be officially viewed as a "county" resident, not a resident of Baltimore City. This could make him eligible to attend AAHS at the start of the new school year (September 1965), only two months from the day he called on his Uncle.

Who would ever know? Who would even care, really?

And even if AAHS staff discovered his deceptive address, Ken was related by blood to his Uncle; he was "kin." He was simply living at the address of his Uncle could be easily explained—a serious illness, divorce, or death in Ken's own family forcing him to move in temporarily with his Uncle. After all, Ken was just a helpless little sixteen-year-old kid who needed adult supervision during this time of personal family crisis. And that would be it. At least that's how Ken had thought it through.

He was also confident that no one in their right mind would ever check things out by going inside the Projects anyway. Who would choose to go there unless absolutely necessary? So, Ken concluded that pulling off such a "great escape" could actually work but only if his Uncle Dan became an accomplice—if he would go along with it. He also knew it wouldn't be easy because his Uncle had a bad relationship with his own sister. But it was still worth a shot. So he paid his Uncle Dan a visit knowing there was nothing to lose and everything to gain.

At first, Uncle Dan was reluctant and skeptical when Ken explained things. As a matter of fact, he didn't even recognize Ken when he knocked on his front door; it had been a long time since the Callahan and Harrington families had gotten together (even though the two families were separated by only a mile or two). And his Uncle didn't want anything to do with sister, Hilda. Ken never understood why they no longer got along because he could only remember good times when both families were close. He recalled a period of time when their families attended birthday parties together, went to the beach and even shared picnics regularly. But something had happened over the past few years that Ken was unaware of. Whatever it was, things were never resolved between the families and as a result, they kept their distance. That's all Ken knew when he knocked on his Uncle's door that day.

Nevertheless, Uncle Dan listened as Ken explained his plight and his unique request. When he was finished, his Uncle seemed genuinely impressed that a boy sixteen years old (especially a boy with Callahan DNA flowing through his veins) could be as creative and resourceful in devising such an idea on his own. "What does your mother think about this, Ken?" his uncle asked sternly. Ken hesitated then responded directly; he wasn't expecting such a question. "Sir, she doesn't know anything about this; just haven't told her about it yet."

Ken noticed a slight smile appear on his Uncle's face (the first and only time he saw his Uncle smile during the visit). But the smile lasted only a second or two then it disappeared as fast as it came.

"You mean she didn't put you up to this?"

"That's right, sir."

His Uncle then took Ken into the kitchen and made sandwiches for both of them. He had a few more questions for Ken, most of which he remembered not having answers to. Even so, his Uncle eventually gave permission to do so. Ken was elated. But his permission came with two strings attached:

1. He must do well in school (and show this Uncle each report card).
2. He must never allow his mother near his Uncle's house.

Such conditions were more than acceptable to Ken, who was now bursting out of his skin with joy. But before Ken left his Uncle's house, he asked him why their families didn't get together anymore. He really missed spending time with his cousins and his Uncle and Aunt and asked, "Was it something that I did?" Ken always thought such things were his fault, something wrong that he did or caused, but never was aware of. "No . . . not at all. You had nothing to do with the way things are today between your mom and me. And yes, we really did have some good family times, including with your other Uncles and their families. I'm glad you remember those times, Ken. They're worth remembering. Try not to forget them."

Ken was glad to hear this.

Uncle Dan then continued, "But, your mom and I just don't see eye to eye on a lot of things, many things happened after her many husbands divorced her and when you all moved into the Projects—that was a bad place, a real bad place for you kids. During those times your mom's behavior became too . . . too unpredictable. She was just crazy to be around. I'll just leave it there, for now."

Ken didn't fully understand what his Uncle was implying and didn't need to pursue it further. Yet, he clearly understood his use of the word *unpredictable* as applied to his mother. It seemed things became very "unpredictable" around the time they moved into the Projects, that was for sure. Nothing seemed stable or reliable after that point, not just for the kids, but for her too. With his mother's constant drinking, having different boyfriends around, Butcher-Bird's constant crazy behavior, coupled with never having enough food to eat or money for anything, Ken always felt unsettled; he really never felt at home while at home.

"Unpredictability" was a good word to describe life at 4139 Martin Court. As his Uncle continued explaining things, Ken's mind flashed back to a specific example of such unpredictability and his mother. It was a time when he and Butcher-Bird were in the sixth grade together. It was also an unforgettable moment when his mother's unpredictability became very well known throughout the community as well.

Déjà Mother / Déjà Pain

During this time, Ken and Butcher-Bird were in elementary school, PS 244, located atop of the highest hill in Brooklyn. The school was called the Overlook Elementary School in those days because from its vantage point, Baltimore City's full skyline and harbor could be clearly seen. Also at that time, he and Butcher-Bird were in the exact same class. Butcher-Bird had failed the year before and was forced to repeat the sixth grade. Little Ken had caught up with him and Butcher-Bird didn't like that one bit. They were not only in the same grade, but they were also brothers in the same classroom.

On this bright, sunny spring afternoon, their young teacher decided to take the sixth grade class on a field trip. It was really just across the street from the school in a huge open field where several baseball fields were situated. Never the less, the teacher called it a field trip anyway. The students were going to learn how to measure the size of a full acre. They learned how to measure it inside the classroom, but now the teacher wanted them to see how really big an acre actually was. She hoped the kids would retain much more by seeing an acre than by just doing the math. So they broke away from the classroom and headed over to the baseball field with lots of string and several wooden stakes in hand on this sunny spring afternoon.

Ken loved field trips, but Butcher-Bird didn't. He was just looking forward to the end of the school day, nothing more. If this trip would speed things up a little, that would be OK with him. But he wouldn't participate unless the teacher made him. It was just the Butcher-Bird way.

Most of the kids in class started their individual assignments immediately upon hitting the field. They were almost finished outlining a full acre when a girl stopped what she was doing and began pointing down the hill at something in the distance coming their way. She didn't say anything, just stood there staring and pointing. Then all the kids, as well as the teacher, stopped their activities and turned to see what was so interesting. The kids were stunned, but Butcher-Bird was *not*. He immediately recognized what (who) the object was, quickly turned, and headed off in the opposite direction without saying a word. His wings were fully expanded as he flew through his classmates, by his younger brother and teacher, leaving them all behind in a cloud of his dust.

Because of Little Ken's lazy eye, he just stood there trying to focus in on the fast-moving object coming their way. He had been born with a medical condition called amblyopia (lazy eye), which resulted in poor, blurry vision in his right eye. This physical incapacity (more about brain development than eyeball functioning) hindered him from processing motion and three-dimensional images normally in that eye. If this visual deficiency had been addressed before he turned five, it could have been corrected. But at eleven, it was just too late to fix. However, since Butcher-Bird's vision was superior, he quickly recognized the moving object coming up the hill and decided not to be around when the inevitable "fireworks" went off.

The object was a woman—Hilda Callahan, the mother of Butcher-Bird and Little Ken.

She was nearly undressed running frantically up the hill waving and screaming something the kids couldn't make out. Even though she was

Little Ken's mother, he still couldn't identify her as she approached because of his poor vision. Hilda was wearing only a half-slip, bra, and a pair of slippers. Her hair was so wild it seemed to be on fire, and her makeup was even wilder. The closer she got to the kids, the louder her screams became. "Where's ma' babies . . . where's ma' babies . . . where's ma' babies . . . where's ma' babies?" Her eyes were desperately searching the vast landscape for her ultimate targets—her two boys. As she neared the group of terrified kids, she began running through the crowd going right up to individuals, grabbing them and examining their faces, close up. That's when most of the kids panicked and started running in all directions.

The young teacher didn't really know what to do about this wild woman at first. So she just pulled some of the kids quickly together and then she headed over to intercept the woman with hair on fire before she scared the hell out of her entire sixth-grade class. She didn't recognize the woman, but Little Ken's vision had finally focused and then he knew who it was. He also recognized her by her smell—she was reeking of beer, whiskey, cigarettes, and thick perfume. Hilda Callahan was drunk, out of control. And, he knew she was in a very unpredictable mood; anything could happen.

Seeing her in her underwear was nothing new to him; however, seeing her in her underwear "outside" with his classmates staring at her, was something very new and very humiliating. However, Little Ken was not nearly as embarrassed as the recently departed Butcher-Bird obviously was, but he was about to become so once his classmates and his teacher discovered the crazy lady with hair of fire was his mother.

"School" had been one of Little Ken's safe sanctuaries—a place where he could go without having to be constantly looking over his shoulder, a place where he could let his guard down at least for a while, a place where he could be secure knowing others were unaware of the truth about his home life. It was a safe place for him, like the Victory Theater and the recreation center, but no longer. The cat was out of the bag. And that's when Little Ken became frightened "for" her rather than frightened "of" her. He now was beginning to think something really, really bad had happened to cause her to be acting this way "outside, in public."

Normally, she reserved her most bizarre behavior for moments inside 4139 Martin Court. Seeing her in a drunken state inside their house was one thing, but being out in public was something so new—it actually frightened him. That's when he began crying and running from deep inside the crowd of kids directly to his mother.

As a matter of fact, he and the teacher reached his mother at the same time. Hilda immediately scooped up her son and began kissing him all over his face. Her lipstick was already smeared beyond her lips, and it then spread even further as she began feverously kissing his face and head. All the while, her bloodshot eyes were darting back and forth obviously in search of her other son. "Ya' alive . . . ya' alive . . . I love ya', I love ya' . . . ya' really okay? Where's Butch . . . he okay? D'ey told me ya' both been kilt' . . . had ta' find ya' . . . where's Butch, where's the Butcher-Bird?" Her voice was high-pitched, loud, and erratic as she continued searching for Butcher-Bird. She then stumbled and fell, taking the teacher and Little Ken to the ground with her. Now, all three of them were in a chaotic pile in the open field and were also becoming entangled within the large mass of string the teacher still held in her hands. They were trying to get back on their feet, but it took some time because Hilda kept holding her son close while also frantically searching for Butcher-Bird. They appeared like three helpless moths trying to frantically escape a spider's web. The teacher was then able to dislodge herself and free Ken. Hilda immediately took Little Ken by the hand, turned around, and started marching back down the hill at a brisk pace with fragments of string still hanging from her. She didn't say a word as she left the teacher and her kids behind; everyone was in disbelief at what just happened.

Because Hilda was very tall, her pace and strides were much greater than Little Ken's—he just couldn't keep up with her no matter how much he tried. She was now dragging him behind her keeping an iron grip on his arm and picking him off the ground each time he fell. This mother-son sprint continued all the way down the hill, across a lower field, through the alleyway on the outskirts of the Projects and then directly to 4139 Martin Court. Once back in their house, she darted straight into the kitchen with Little Ken still in hand. There, several men were drinking and laughing hysterically. The kitchen table was full of beer bottles, and the whole house smelled of cigarettes and cigars. As usual, loud country-western music was blaring away as one man yelled to her, "Christ, Hilda . . . we were just kidding you. Your kids are fine, right guys? We didn't think you'd take us so seriously. Wow, that was really something to watch." With that, all the men continued laughing.

Hilda Callahan had been drinking with her boyfriends. She also had been in the process of putting on her waitress uniform in her bedroom when they yelled up the stairs that her kids had been killed at school. She reacted immediately to their words. She became wild with panic, totally out of control and headed directly for the school even before putting on the rest of her waitress uniform. It was around two thirty in the afternoon, and she was scheduled to work the three-to-eleven shift at the Downton's Bar. She didn't make it to work that day.

Little Ken would never forget that event. And he was certain his classmates and teacher would never forget it either.

Listening to his Uncle Dan described his mother's unpredictability was clearly understood by Little Ken. They finished their sandwich together and Ken thanked him once again for giving permission to him. He promised to meet all the conditions including doing well in school and not doing anything to discredit himself. Most importantly, he promised to keep his mother away from his Uncle, away from his house, and away from his family. Ken would never forget his Uncle's kindness for it could not have come at a more critical time in his life.

After returning to his house in the Projects later that day, he finally explained everything about what he was trying to do to his mother. She didn't seem to care one way or the other, and the following week he dragged her to AAHS to become officially enrolled in the 1965-1966 school year. She used the false address of 223 West Arundel Road, Brooklyn Park, Maryland in doing so. The only thing Hilda had to do was act like a "mother" and to sign one form. Still, she did it reluctantly even though she knew it could mean her son would have a better chance of graduating from high school (a "first" in Callahan family history). The "great escape" strategy called for him to keep a low profile regarding his personal life while simultaneously keeping a high profile regarding his academic and extracurricular activities. This approach replicated the two-dimensional approach he learned from *The Great Escape* movie:

Dimension 1:   One little deception, a false address was his "tunnel."
Dimension 2:   A two part execution: (1) keep a high profile via good grades and fitting in with classmates and (2) keeping a low profile via avoidance of close interpersonal relationships. This was his "multiple" disguise part.

Even though he was still a loner at heart and didn't share much personal information with other students, his classmates and teachers appeared to like him, and after a while they came to accept him as one of their own. The "great escape" strategy seemed to work . . . at least for a while. With all this in place, Ken was able to attend Anne Arundel High School during his eleventh and twelfth grades. He also was able to keep each commitment he had made along the way to his Uncle Dan.

Mr. Francis Jackson

Throughout the two years at AAHS, Ken thought all his teachers were just terrific—they knew their stuff and taught it well. However, one of his teachers, Mr. Francis Jackson, the music and choral director of the AAHS in 1965, had the biggest impact on Ken's learning as well as on his life (even though Ken didn't fully understand it at the time). Mr. Jackson was a good man, a great teacher. He was also a tall man about thirty years old at the time in 1965. He was a handsome, distinguished-looking teacher who had a full head of premature graying hair. He also had a slight southern drawl that Ken found interesting. And his personable, casual style was well complimented by always being well dressed and impeccably groomed. To Ken, Mr. Jackson was professional and businesslike, yet approachable and fun to learn from. He would always recall one specific incident that occurred with Mr. Jackson. He had asked Ken to stay after class one day to help him rearrange the room's chairs in preparation for the next class. As they were moving chairs and desks around, they began talking about many things. That's when Mr. Jackson casually asked him the following question—a question that would change his view of himself and his future forever, "So, Ken . . . what college are you planning to attend once you graduate from here?" Ken was very surprised at the question, not because a teacher had taken a little interest in him, but rather because it was something that never had entered his mind, not once until then. The two words *college* and *Ken* had never been used in a single sentence before. So he was somewhat taken off guard. For Ken, just getting "into" AAHS was the single greatest feat of his life, and now getting "out" of AAHS without his cover being blown was the only important thing to him. A high school diploma was his ticket out of Brooklyn, and there really was no further option or acceptable direction for him to take. As such, "college" never even entered the picture because college was the place where only the rich and smart kids got to go, anyway.

At least that's how he viewed things.

So he didn't know how to respond to Mr. Jackson's question; he was somewhat embarrassed about it. Ken had come to admire and like Mr. Jackson from afar, not only because he was a great teacher, but also because he made him and all the students feel special and important in his classroom. He never criticized or put down any student, even those kids caught daydreaming in the midst of music practice (like he had been caught on a few occasions). He felt Mr. Jackson also had a good sense of humor and always seemed to find a way to make even a boring subject such as "music appreciation" as interesting as possible. For example, he'd weave classical painting, architecture, and history into his lectures on music, which brought more meaning to the subject. He also made music come alive and much more relevant. Half notes and quarter notes started to have a real purpose and place in life—not just on a sheet of music. Not only that, he often integrated practical application of social and interpersonal skills (e.g., how to dress, how to eat food in public, how conduct social conversations) within his own classes and during various field trips he would lead with students. In short, he helped kids "broaden" their minds, not just "fill" their minds.

Mr. Jackson's—"music journeys" as Ken viewed them were great. He saw his very first opera, *Carmen,* at Baltimore's Lyric Theater along with his classmates in 1965 with Mr. Jackson supervising, tutoring, and mentoring all the way. And Ken and his classmates saw several other live productions of contemporary musicals, including Rodgers and Hammerstein's *Oklahoma* and *Carousel* throughout the county as well as at other high schools in the city. In short, Mr. Johnson always found a way to help his students learn, not just about music, but about much more. And in the process, they also learned about themselves too. Ken felt very fortunate to be one of his students.

So when he asked him about college after class that day, Ken didn't feel it was unusual, only a little embarrassed about not having an adequate answer, but he was glad just to talk to Mr. Jackson about it. "College? . . . well . . . I'm not going to college, Mr. Jackson," Ken said while looking directly at him. Mr. Jackson immediately replied, "Oh . . . why not?" This question (why) was far more challenging and even more revealing than his first question. Again, Ken was direct and honest, but somewhat embarrassed at not having an answer. "Well . . . I just . . . can't," Ken said. "You . . . *can't?*" Now, it was Mr. Jackson who was the surprised person in the room. And he wanted to learn more about Ken's reply. "You mean you can't because of your . . . grades?"

"No, sir," Ken replied.

"Oh, Okay then . . . is it because of the money needed to attend college?"

"No, sir."

"OK . . . is it because your parents have other plans for you?"

"No, sir."

Mr. Jackson was now even more curious than before. So he stopped what he was doing at the far end of the classroom and walked over to Ken, sat down, and gestured to Ken to sit for a moment to talk to him. His causal question to a student suddenly transformed into the quest to discover the holy grail of Ken Callahan. He was curious to learn why Ken seemed so adamant and embarrassed by talking about this. He needed to get to the bottom of it.

So he continued questioning Ken, "Well . . . help me understand this . . . is it that you just don't want to go to college . . . is that it, Ken? Look, it's OK if you don't, really . . . most kids choose not to go to college . . . there isn't anything wrong with that."

"No, Mr. Jackson . . . I'd really like to go to college, who wouldn't?" Ken said sincerely.

"I'm really sorry, but I just don't understand." Mr. Jackson was now genuinely confused.

"Well, I thought you knew already . . . being a teacher and all."

"Knew what, Ken?"

"You know . . . I'm GE." Mr. Jackson had to think quickly; he was still missing something big time. So he asked Ken to explain and he did, "You know . . . GE—General ED . . . General Education . . . I'm not allowed to go to college. You got to be in the academic track (AT) to go to college. I'm in the GE track. Everybody knows that, right?"

He was stunned at Ken's perception as well as at his innocent ignorance. Actually, Mr. Jackson was genuinely moved by it. Then he realized this could be the way "college" appeared to many kids like Ken. The way the education system was set up could lead to such conclusions, especially to kids who didn't have people in their lives to guide them through such deep waters. So he went on to explained that it didn't matter which curriculum he was in; attending college is kind of a right that he had once he finished high school. Being in the GE track or the commercial track (CT) didn't exclude or prohibit students from going to college if they wanted to do so.

This was a revelation to Ken.

Once Ken learned about this, he had a ton of questions about college—all of which Mr. Jackson made time to answer for him over the following weeks and months. He was so moved by Ken's interest in college, that he actually took Ken to a real college campus in Maryland—Towson State

College. He wanted Ken to see, feel, and touch "college." He wanted him to talk to college students as they moved between classes on a college campus. He also gave Ken a personal tour of the Towson State College by going into classrooms, watching live classes being conducted by professors in lecture halls, walking around athletic fields, and even visiting dorms to see students (most of whom were not much older than Ken) as they actually lived and played while at college. From then on, Ken's view of what he could become changed forever.

College had never been on his radar screen, not even close. But now, it was a vision that he would carry forever and achieve one day. As a result, he also viewed Mr. Jackson differently, not only as a fine teacher but also as a caring and kind friend. It would take him many years after completing high school, including two years in Vietnam, but Ken would graduate from college with an undergraduate degree—a Bachelors of Arts. Even though Ken would never get a chance to actually live on a college campus within a dorm or be invited to join a fraternity (things he always wanted to do), he did graduate; it was a proud moment in his life. Specifically, it would occur thirteen years after moving chairs around a classroom and having a brief discussion with a kind and caring music teacher from AAHS.

Later on in Ken's life, he would see two movies that automatically refreshed those positive memories of Mr. Jackson's wonderful lectures and lessons of life through his mind and heart. The first was 1995's *Mr. Holland's Opus* starring Richard Dreyfuss. This was a great movie about a music teacher who also touched the lives of many students in many ways beyond music—just as Mr. Jackson had touched him. And the second movie was the 1986 comedy *Ferris Bueller's Day Off* starring Matthew Broderick in the title role. This flick always seemed to jolt Ken back to memories of Mr. Jackson. There was one specific scene in this very funny movie that showed many bored (very bored) high school students unsuccessfully trying to stay awake during an American history class being given by Ben Stein. "Unsuccessfully" being the key word here. Mr. Jackson's classes were never boring; they were just the opposite.

He and Ken would maintain a genuine friendship and mentor relationship for decades after leaving AAHS. Ken even remembered receiving a few letters from him while serving in Vietnam, which he appreciated so much. All of Ken's teachers were good people and genuinely interested in how well their students learned inside and outside the classroom. He enjoyed being taught by all of them, but Mr. Jackson will always have a special place in Ken's heart.

Only a couple of kids knew Ken when he arrived at AAHS; one of them was Suzie Dennis. She also had grown-up in Brooklyn as a younger child before her family moved to Brooklyn Park. That happened when she was ten or so. That's where she and Ken originally met years before. Suzie not only knew Ken before he came to AAHS, but she also knew his brother Butch, and had even been in his home at 801 Herndon Court (the second address he had within the Projects). It was good to have one or two familiar faces around, but that was enough for Ken. He didn't want others to know about his background, and Suzie never let on throughout the entire two years he attended AAHS.

She and Ken shared several school activities together as members of the AAHS Varsity Choir. There was one event Ken and Suzie shared together that he would remember for the rest of his life—a very good memory. They both were seniors at the time. It started with a simple question Suzie asked him one day when they accidently ran into each other in the AAHS hallways while walking between classes. "Hey . . . you want to become famous?" she said to Ken out of the blue as they were passing each other.

He didn't know what she really meant but stopped and talked to her. Suzie was a petite girl, very cute with long blonde hair; she was friendly and very well-liked by her classmates, including Ken. So he replied to her right away, "Sure . . . I'd like to become famous, who wouldn't . . . as long as it doesn't mean I have to leave my brain to science to become famous!"

Suzie's s sense of humor and quick wit always seemed loaded for bear, and Ken was a very easy target for her on that day. "Ken . . . I don't think you ever have to worry about becoming famous in that way . . . I'm sure modern science already has an ample supply of monkey brains with similar IQs as yours; so don't worry about that."

Ken didn't know whether to be relieved or insulted. Either way, he sensed whatever Suzie had in mind would at least be fun. "Ha ha . . . everyone likes a little ass now and then, but nobody likes a smart-ass anytime." The "Brooklyn" side of Ken was coming out, but she could handle it. "Yeah, yeah, yeah . . . listen, do you want to be on television or not." She moved the conversation quickly along, and Ken became immediately excited at the thought. "Sure . . . what's up? Are they looking to replace Little Joe on *Bonanza*? If so, I'm sure I could take over that role without a problem." Ken was really overcompensating now.

"Now you're really dreaming, boy. But anyway . . . I've got two tickets for the *Kirby Scott Show* next week, and I need a dance partner. You want to join me, or would you rather stay home and watch me dance with another guy and become famous without you?"

Ken was surprised and delighted at the opportunity; he accepted her invitation right away. The *Kirby Scott Show* was Baltimore's version of Dick Clark's nationwide *American Bandstand*. It was a live, locally televised teenage dance program that aired on weekday afternoons. Kirby Scott was the name of the host, and he was a big deal throughout Maryland in the late 1960s. Of course, Ken wanted to be on the program; what teenager wouldn't? Being Suzie's dance partner was just the cherry on the cake—an extra bonus.

So they went on "the" Kirby Scott Show together the following week. Suzie and Ken had a great time—they danced, smiled and sweated while also constantly maneuvering between the double mobile cameras that were gliding around the floor. It made for a great shared memory. What made it even more memorable was they also made it as "finalists" on the program's dance contest; ended up losing but got a lot more face time on TV for the entire school and community to see.

"It was because of you, Suzie . . . you were *hot*. That's why we were selected," Ken said to Sue. Of course she downplayed her looks, insisting it was because they were among the best dancers. Ken quickly rebutted her, "Nope . . . TV cameras always follow the *hot* chicks even if they can't dance, and your great dancing ability only added to things. That's why we were finalists." Ken was adamant about that.

And, they never agreed on that point. Suzie and Ken had shared fifteen minutes of fame together, which would never be forgotten. Equally important, Ken then knew he was going to love AAHS even more. It truly was becoming the "civilized" place that he hoped it would be. Being at AAHS had come at a critical time in his life. He was beginning to feel good about himself and much more secure just by being in a stimulating, safe environment. Ken was learning and growing faster than he ever expected, and there was a side of him that wished high school could go on forever.

Sometimes wishing for something can be a good or bad thing. And, Ken Callahan was about find out which.

Caught

About a month before Ken's graduation from AAHS in 1967, he was called to the school Administrator's office. In the two years since arriving at the school, he never entered any of the administrative offices unless he had to; no normal student wanted to be called there, really. Ken was no different. As he walked in, he sensed this was not going to be a very good day.

He was right and wrong. As he walked into the office, he was told to take a seat by the school's Administrator and he then came right to the point without any chitchat. His question to Ken was simple and clear, "Where do you live, Ken?" Ken's heart dropped to his stomach immediately. That's when he knew the Administrator also knew. Why else would such a question even be asked? While Ken always thought it might be possible to get caught, he just hoped it wouldn't happen. And since graduation was now less than a month away, Ken's dream of getting a "clean getaway" without doing anyone any harm turned into a full-blown nightmare in a matter of seconds.

He stumbled and stammered as he tried to answer the Administrator's question—all the moisture in his throat had instantly evaporated. Instead of words coming out of his mouth, a slew of stutters and ums found their way to the Administrator's ears. Nevertheless, Ken knew what he wanted to say because he had practiced for this moment so many times over the past two years, just in case. Even though his heart was pounding and his mouth felt drier than a ravine in Death Valley, his confidence and preparation seemed to automatically kick in. So the Administrator asked the question again. "Where do you live, Ken?" This time Ken replied very slowly, very deliberately, just like he had practiced, "Well sir . . . my address is 223 West Arundel Road."

And that's all Ken said. He told the truth.

Even though he did not answer the exact question asked, he stated the truth. That's why he could do so with a straight face. And he thought his practice had paid off. However, his confidence waned when he noticed the Administrator's eyebrows rise quickly forming huge wrinkles across his forehead. And then after a very long sigh, the Administrator leaned forward in his chair and said, "Ummm . . . I don't recall asking you about your *address*, Ken. I asked 'Where do you live?' Now, please answer the question." Ken's preparation hadn't included answering such a precise, laser-focused question as that. He was planning on dancing around all questions for as long as needed without actually telling a lie. But Ken knew telling "a lie" could be worse than the act of falsifying his actual address. So he told him the exact truth. "At 3555 Hanson Avenue, sir. I was living in the Projects the first year I came here. Then my mother and I moved to Hanson Avenue." He also admitted that he had never lived in Anne Arundel County. He was only using his Uncle's address so he'd be eligible to attend AAHS. Ken had come clean.

The Administrator paused for a moment then replied, "Well . . . I'm glad to hear that from you, Ken. As you may have guessed, we know exactly where you live. We also know your real address as well as your false address."

There was a long silence in the room.

Ken didn't know what he was feeling—embarrassment, shame, guilt, fear . . . maybe all at once. But he did know one thing, it wasn't anger. He didn't blame anyone, but himself.

This had been his idea all along. He, alone, was responsible. It had almost worked; instead, it backfired. At that moment, he also had to admit to himself, surprisingly so, that he was also feeling somewhat "relieved." This was over at last—the façade had ended. Ken hadn't realized just how heavy a burden he had been carrying over the past two years until this moment. And, he didn't know how to react either. So he just dropped his head and looked down at his lap. Of course, he didn't want to cry, after all he was a "senior" now (at least for the moment). The thought of being kicked out of school with graduation so close was just unbearable. But then he couldn't hold back the deluge of slow-rolling tears that began crawling out of both eyes. His tears continued and started rolling down his face, to the tip of his chin and then ultimately forming a puddle the size of the Pacific Ocean on the front of his shirt.

The administrator didn't say a word either. There was a longer silence.

Then he handed Ken a tissue from the box always kept on his desk for just such personal emergencies. Ken quickly dried his tear-stained face without making eye contact with the Administrator. After a few more moments of silence, the Administrator continued, but now with a little more tenderness and empathy than before. The sharpness and directness in his voice had changed to compassion. "It's Okay Ken . . . let it out. This whole thing must have been a burden to carry around all this time. What we don't know is . . . why? Why did you feel so compelled to do this in the first place? What was driving you? I'd personally like to know just how you maintained this façade for so long and still maintain such good grades and also contribute to our school as you did in so many ways. That's why I really wanted to talk with you in the first place, before you graduated—just to learn about this, not for anything else."

Ken then started looking at the Administrator in a different way as he continued, "And Ken, I also want you to know you will still be graduating with your classmates, so don't worry about that. Just please help me understand your reasons for doing what you did. I would really like to know. Okay?"

Ken was so relieved.

That's when the "boy" Ken versus the "senior" Ken opened up. For the next thirty minutes, he shared his story, his history, his motive, his fear regarding the realities of growing up in the Projects at 4139 Martin Court, his home life, the violence, and the abuse, including his experience at Sparta High School. The Administrator listened to every word, never interrupting Ken as he continued. And when he finished, the Administrator seemed genuinely moved by what he had heard; Ken had been so detailed and very personal. His story was so different from what the Administrator was expecting to hear. That's when he knew it all had to be true.

Ken thanked him many times for his understanding and most importantly, he thanked him for his forgiveness. He never learned how the Administrator actually discovered his little secret, his little white lie, his big burden. It was then that Ken was glad his very first impression of Anne Arundel High School turned out to be quite accurate—right on target. This school and its people were very, very "civilized" after all.

Ken graduated from Anne Arundel High School alongside his classmates on June 10, 1967.

"Five Spaces Should Be Enough"

The Vietnam War was moving at full speed the summer of 1967. It was a time of great change and even greater unrest. Hippies were blossoming; drugs (especially marijuana) were making their way onto the scene; burning draft cards and making beelines to Canada were in vogue for many young men; the women's lib and gay rights movements were finally getting off the ground; the Beatles, Beach Boys, Rolling Stones, Smokey Robinson, and the Animals were on top of the charts and all politicians were at the bottom of the bird cage. And the Vietnam War was featured on TV news every night. Yet, none of this really mattered to Ken at the time.

Vietnam was just a faraway place in TV land and had nothing to do with him. He was still determined to fight in the Arab-Israeli War. The North African desert was calling to him now that he had just graduated from AAHS. But deep inside, he also knew joining the army was more of a desperate escape than a desired destination. Immediately after graduation, Ken Callahan walked proudly through the doors of the US Army Recruiting Station in Brooklyn. Of course, the recruiter was very happy to see him come in, especially carrying his freshly minted high school diploma (even though such a credential was not required to join the US Army in those days). In the summer of 1967, military recruiters were in the midst of ramping up their numbers by taking any young man who met the minimum requirements and could do all the five following things:

1. Walk through the recruiting station's doors standing up.
2. Remain standing for at least one minute without falling over.
3. Breathe without the use of any device.
4. Spell their name accurately on the "first try."
5. Speak at least one sentence in English using one noun and verb.

If so, they would easily get by the initial recruiting phase.

Completing the paperwork was usually done quickly by most young men, but not for Ken. His major stumbling block was filling in the personal information section (normally the easiest and fastest part for new recruits). However, Ken struggled with it. It wasn't because he was stupid; he was just overwhelmed with all the personal background information needed on the forms. He kept requesting more blank forms and new pencils because he was constantly wearing down the lead, the erasers, as well as the personnel forms provided to him.

Seeing Ken's obvious, painful process from afar, the Army recruiter walked over and asked about the problem. Ken looked up from the paperwork and replied genuinely, pointing to the spaces provided, "Well, sir, these forms don't have enough lines for all my past addresses. Plus . . . I'm not sure of the correct spelling of each of these addresses anyway."

There were five spaces to place his addresses, normally enough writing space for any typical eighteen-year-old. "What do you mean? . . . Five spaces should be enough," the recruiter replied, getting a little frustrated with the amount of time and paper being needed for this single recruit. Then the recruiter reached into the trash where Ken had discarded previous attempts and pulled out several crumpled forms. Ken's penmanship had always been excellent throughout school but not now. On each of the discarded forms, the recruiter noticed scratch marks, cross outs and overwrites galore. Some entries appeared more like emotional outbursts abandoned in mid-thought than actual words and numbers. Also, a couple of crumpled sheets actually had holes where Ken's erasers had bored through the paper in his futile attempt to get things perfectly correct.

With this, the recruiter sensed something was going on with this boy beyond his writing ability or penmanship. So he sat down with Ken and tried to provide a little more help than usually needed with new recruits. "Tell me son, how many addresses are you trying to put on this form anyway? After all, you're only eighteen, right . . . so how many more can there be?"

Ken hesitated for a moment and then explained he was only stuck on the fourth, seventh, ninth, and eighteenth addresses. He had the other addresses nailed but just couldn't recall these four specific street numbers. It seemed to Ken the farther back in time he went the more things got jumbled up in his mind.

The recruiter was somewhat confused with what he was hearing from this boy. Then his confusion quickly escalated to bewilderment. "Do you mean to tell me that you have lived in nineteen different places before even finishing high school? Is that what you're saying?" the recruiter asked with obvious incredulity.

"No, sir . . . it's closer to twenty-one or twenty-two at the most . . . I'm sure of that. But don't worry, I'll get them all . . . just need a little more time and a few more blank forms." Ken immediately went back to writing without waiting for the recruiter's response. He then showed the recruiter the list of addresses he was trying to "get right." The list ran from 1953 (when Ken was about four) to 1967 (when he was eighteen). It had a lot of blanks and empty spaces, but it was the best Ken could do from memory.

The list looked something like this:

1. _____ Fort Meade, Maryland, May 23, 1949
2. 833 Patapsco Avenue, Brooklyn, Maryland, 1951
3. 3704 Saint Victor Street, Brooklyn, Maryland, 1952
4. _____ Market Place Street, Glassboro, New Jersey, 1953
5. 4158 Wilkens Avenue, Maryland, 1954
6. 411 Laura Avenue, Arbutus, Maryland, 1954
7. _____ Sycamore Drive, Maryland, 1954
8. 1511 Popland Street, Curtis Bay, Maryland, 1955
9. 4139 Martin Court, (The Projects), Brooklyn, Maryland, 1955/63
10. 111 Nann Avenue, Pumphrey, Maryland, 1963
11. 1128 West Jeffrey Street, Brooklyn, Maryland, 1963
12. _____, Ballman Avenue, Brooklyn Park, Maryland, 1963
13. 1648 Hanover Street, Baltimore, Maryland, 1964
14. 113 West Fort Avenue, Baltimore, Maryland, 1964
15. 229 East Montgomery Street, Baltimore, Maryland 1964
16. 1408, Poplar Avenue, Curtis Bay, Maryland, 1964
17. 1621 Spruce Street, Curtis Bay, MD 1964
18. 801 Herndon Court, Brooklyn (The Projects), Maryland 1964
19. 952 Stoll Street, Brooklyn, Maryland, 1965
20. 929 Jeffrey Street, Brooklyn Maryland, 1965
21. * 3555 Hanson Ave, Brooklyn, Maryland, 1965/67

(* 223 West Arundel Road, Brooklyn Park, Maryland . . . address used while attending AAHS. Ken did not place this address on the list).

The recruiter was amazed at what he saw. "I never seen such a thing . . . and I've recruited hundreds of boys your age around the USA over the years." His amazement continued as he paused and just stared at Ken, observing the boy's genuine determination, sincerity and positive attitude. Ken sensed the recruiter was also thinking about what the real impact of such constant instability could have on any young person. He probably had kids of his own, and being a career military man himself likely had to relocate his own family many times as well, but certainly nothing close to twenty times. More importantly, Ken also sensed the recruiter was now looking at him in a different way. He just hoped the recruiter didn't think he was crazy or deprived because of such constant transience at his early age. And he didn't know if it would somehow disqualify from serving in the Army. On the other hand, perhaps the recruiter felt any kid who could adapt so well, so often, and still have his shit together enough to actually graduate from high school would also possess the caliber of resilience compatible with life in the US Army.

Ken just didn't know what the recruiter was thinking but soon found out. "That's OK, son . . . why don't you just go back through your high school years and also list where you were born . . . that should do it for now." With that, the recruiter brought him another blank enlistment form. Ken worked on it for a while, even more diligently this time. However, Ken then had to ask the recruiter for another form. "What now? What's wrong?" he asked. Ken replied quickly, "Well, help me with this, sir . . . regarding my father's name . . . there's only one space. I'm not really sure what to put here." The recruiter was now becoming more confused and frustrated than he had been. How complicated could this simple piece of information really be, even for Kenneth Callahan?

"The only thing that goes in this block is your father's first name, middle initial, and last name. That's it, really. I'm sure you only have one father, right?" asked the recruiter in a sarcastic manner.

But now, he knew to expect the unexpected from this young man. Ken replied after some hesitation; "Well yeah . . . of course I have only one *real* father like everybody. But my problem is this . . . my mother was married five times and I'm just not sure which name to put on this form. Should I use my biological father, my adopted father, my current father or all five? You see, that's my real problem. Also, my real name is not Callahan, either. It's Kenneth Archer. My two brothers and I were adopted when I was about four. So I'm not sure which "father" name to use . . . Lang, Archer, Mytus, Callahan, or Smith. Here, take a look."

Ken then pulled out his birth certificate and showed the recruiter. By this time, it was nearly six o'clock, an hour past normal recruiting office hours. The recruiter who had been as supportive as possible decided to just submit Ken's current paper work as it was and just hope for the best. He was sure that everything would be straightened out over at the Army Enlistment and Entrance Station in Fort Holabird in Dundalk, Ken's next administrative step in becoming a soldier.

Ken thanked the recruiter, collected his papers, and then ran happily out of the recruiting station, knowing he was one step closer to leaving Brooklyn. The recruiter then locked the door and placed the closed sign in the window. He was probably glad this day had finally come to an end, especially after listening to and learning about Kenneth Callahan. Yet, the first thing this veteran recruiter was likely to do when he arrived home that evening was hug his kids, long and hard.

"Great News—You're 4F"

A couple of weeks later on June 27, 1967, Ken entered the Armed Forces Enlistment and Entrance Station at Fort Holabird. It was located directly on the other side of the Baltimore Harbor Tunnel connecting Brooklyn and Dundalk with the rest of Baltimore City. At this station, Ken joined dozens of other boys who were also undergoing mandatory mental and physical examinations before being sworn into the US Army. Ken, being a natural athlete, thought passing the physical exam for the army was going to be as easy as downing a cheeseburger-sub at the Chicken Roost—the after-school hangout of AAHS seniors. And it was.

The math, English, and general intelligence tests proved to be more fun than work for Ken. He especially liked hearing and responding to the unique sounds of Morse code. That was more of a game than a test. Both, the physical and mental exams passed by rather quickly, but because there were so many boys being processed, it took nearly all day for every recruit to complete. Ken was now eager to hop aboard the waiting buses destined to take new recruits to Fort Bragg, North Carolina, for army boot camp. It just couldn't come fast enough. Getting a "clean getaway" out of Brooklyn was in sight, a mere bus trip away. He was about to become a soldier in the US Army and was already beginning to feel even more proud of himself. He was also very relieved because he was finally getting out of Brooklyn. While he'd certainly miss the students and faculty of AAHS (the only good thing about his first eighteen years of life), he was also excited and eager about moving on with his life.

Around 7:00 p.m., the physical and mental testing had finally been completed, and all the recruits were officially sworn in the US Army. Ken was ecstatic. He couldn't contain his emotions . . . felt like an excited puppy going crazy at the feet of its owner while watching a bowl of puppy chow being prepared at the sink.

He was ready to go.

All the recruits were outside waiting to board buses that would transport them to army boot camp in North Carolina. Each boy was carrying a small bag of personal toiletry items—the only personal possessions they would need for the next two months of life while at Fort Bragg. Then a slick-looking soldier in a well-starched, army uniform gathered everyone together and began taking roll call. They were about to be assigned a bus for their trip south. "Listen up . . . when you hear your name called, reply 'here' . . . then grab your personal belongings and get on the bus I direct you to. Most important, if your name is *not* called, head back to the examination building . . . and do it right away." With that, he proceeded to yell out names alphabetically. But when the C's were addressed, the name Kenneth Callahan was *not* called. Once the slick soldier finished reading the list, Ken was one of only three boys left standing on the patch of grass near the parking lot.

None of them knew what to do then, including Ken. "What are you three guys standing there for . . . head on back over to the examination building as instructed. And, do it, now. Move it!"

Ken, still stunned by this unexpected turn of events, joined the two other two guys and headed into the building. About fifteen minutes or so passed without receiving any instruction after entering the examination building. It seemed like hours to Ken because his eyes had been solidly fixed on the idling buses outside the window, just watching as everyone got aboard—everyone but him. Not knowing the reasons for this big "mistake" by the military, his panic started to grow. Those buses represented his ticket out of Brooklyn and to a new life, to a new beginning, yet he didn't have a seat in any of them.

This couldn't be happening.

Then a young man holding a clip board and wearing a long white jacket approached his group. Ken just assumed he was a doctor but didn't know for sure. The man called Ken's name and was directed to accompany him to a small room on the far side of the building. They both entered then the man closed the door behind them. He looked at Ken and said, "Callahan, I've some *great news* for you. After further review of your medical paperwork, I noticed your visual examination indicates you have a condition called amblyopia, sometimes called a lazy eye. It could have been corrected by wearing a patch over your good left eye during your younger years. If this had been done, your right eye would have strengthened by now, but apparently your parents failed to do this for you. As a result, your vision is now below acceptable military standards, and it is not correctable with glasses—even with the strongest prescription lenses possible."

Ken was trying to grasp all this medical stuff but was unsuccessful. The man, sensing his confusion, decided to cut to the chase. "Callahan, what all this means is . . . you're about to be classified as 4F. That is, you're *physically unsuitable for military service*. It's your ticket out of the army even before becoming a part of it. Most important, there will be *no Vietnam* in your future. That's the *great news*, of course. All you need to do is sign right here and you can *go home*."

Ken didn't say a word as the man continued, "You know how many boys your age in America today would give their right arm for this little piece of paper . . . a lot of them. It's really your lucky day, Callahan. Congratulations!" To Ken, the man's voice was joyful, close to celebratory, just the way he thought any doctor would likely be giving the news of an impending pregnancy to a young couple. Ken felt the doctor's attitude didn't fit this situation somehow. Something was wrong, dreadfully wrong. Ken was stunned, confused, and now he was becoming very scared. His panic was intensifying rapidly. All he could feel, see, or imagine was his life passing before his eyes within this little closet of room in of all places—Dundalk, Maryland. At lightning speed, he began picturing himself staying in Brooklyn the rest of his life—endless poverty, hunger, continual violence, and a sense of never-ending dread.

Ken's worst nightmare continued in his mind; he was now envisioning the following actually happening to him—fathering kids but never being called "Dad" by any of them; he saw himself as a husband that was never around for his wife and when he was present he was beating her; he saw himself never keeping a steady job; he saw himself standing in endless unemployment lines; he saw himself moving from apartment to apartment forever; and worst, he saw himself as a punk criminal from the streets of Brooklyn circulating in and out of prison and becoming every bad man's boyfriend. His mind continued racing in every direction without the benefit of a map or a compass. Each of these visions far exceeded any horrors he could ever imagine happening in the jungles of Vietnam or the desert of North Africa. Not even close. Such images were flying through his mind faster than starlight passing through deep space.

Then Ken's physical appearance started naturally reflecting his feelings and emotions as the man witnessed the following transformation unfold in a matter of seconds. Ken's throat dried instantly as if he had just swallowed a handful of sand. He felt his face turning a deep shade of red while his body temperature and heart rate changed in lockstep with his increasing rate of breathing. He not only sensed his heartbeats increasing but also felt his pulse begin to throb in his neck and fingertips. Ken's eyes also started to fill and burn with a substance that couldn't be normal tears—just too intense to be real tears. Ken's anxiety and overwhelming panic at the thought of having to remain in Brooklyn reached peak intensity as a deafening silence engulfed the small room.

Somehow, time itself seemed to stop for Ken Callahan.

The man had never seen such a blinding transformation right before his eyes, especially considering this was such *"great news."* He was perplexed and alarmed at Ken's reaction. He was now sensing something was seriously wrong and gently touched Ken on the shoulder to help settle him down. They both then sat down at a small table in the room. Neither of them said a word. Normally, when boys receive the 4F *great news* message, their reaction is great excitement, elation and relief. Getting a 4F rating from any doctor at any US Army enlistment center in America in 1967 was like a prisoner on death row receiving a governor's last-minute stay of execution—pure ecstasy, happiness, unbridled relief.

Not this time. Not for this boy. Something else was going on here, something much deeper and far more impactful and the man had to discover what it was. After catching his breath, Ken finally looked over at the man and stared deeply into his eyes, holding it for some time without saying a word. Ken's eye contact was much more personal, much more intense than he had ever had with anyone except his mother. He wasn't sure where he learned how to apply such penetrating eye contact but sensed it was needed now. He also sensed this could be the only chance to alter a great wrong. It was one chance in a thousand, but he had to try.

That's when Ken began sensing a genuine concern swelling inside this man. So he just began telling his story, the full story, about his life in the Projects and explaining his reactions to such *"great news."* More important, Ken felt he had to convey exactly why this was a life-and-death decision and why it was so very critical for him to move away, to move ahead with the US Army. He also explained why it was so critical to do at this moment in time.

So Ken shared every detail, every event, every account, everything about his life, just as he'd done with the Administrator about month before at AAHS. When Ken's story ended, he finally broke eye contact with the white-coated young man but for only a second or two. He had been listening attentively, fully engaged with every word coming from Ken's heart and mind. It was the most compelling, genuinely conveyed story, the young doctor ever heard from a recruit. He was not only emotionally moved by what he learned, but he was also very, very angry.

Now it was the man's eyes, not Ken's, that were full of that same burning liquid. Now it was the man's blood pressure that was raising sharply, not Ken's. And now, it was the man, not Ken, who was emotionally exhausted, physically drained just from listening. Ken had just taken the man on a quick private tour, a very personal journey deep inside the Projects of Brooklyn . . . only 2 miles away. And equally important, Ken was also able to return the man back to the safety of this little room in Fort Holabird's examination building . . . in one piece. Once the man regained his own composure, he touched Ken on the shoulder again and merely nodded.

He seemed to understand.

Ken didn't know if the man was truly surprised, shocked, or just depressed at what he just heard. But it was also clear to Ken the man was also very angry at something. He just hoped his anger wasn't directed at him (for taking so much of his time with his personal story). Nevertheless, Ken did know one thing—the man had just learned something so ugly, so unreal that it just had to be the truth. He continued looking at Ken but didn't say a word. The clinical connection the man had with Ken at the beginning of his story had slowly transformed into a softer, more empathetic bonding. It was a natural and honest connection, not one driven by professional courtesy alone but rather formed through the effort of two people trying to genuinely relate and understand each other.

With that, the man looked down at his clipboard then back at Ken several times before speaking. He sensed a boy with the caliber of motivation to join the US Army for the reasons just conveyed, would not only do a fine job for his country, but also would likely evolve into a leader of men—even under the most severe combat conditions. And that was something he knew the US Army vitally needed in 1967.

The man had been so moved he decided to take a step that may have been legally and medically wrong, but in his mind, was morally right—humane thing to do for this boy in this unique situation. He then said the following to Ken in a slow, methodical, deliberate way just to ensure every word was articulated with the precision of a surgeon's scalpel: "Thanks for being so open, so forthright, Callahan. I know it must have been hard for you to share that with me and I just want you to know I understand where you're coming from . . . I do get it. Really, I get it." He then hesitated for a while before continuing. He needed to ensure his next words were clearly understood by this recruit. Ken was bracing for the worst—the "death blow" to his future.

But, it didn't come.

The man then continued, "And I want to help. You've been through a lot already in your life, haven't you? Can't imagine how you survived as you did. But I feel if a boy like you can survive in the environment you just described to me, you can do the same in Vietnam or anywhere the US Army sends you." The man now seemed more reflective and far more thoughtful than before. He then merely slipped a pen out of the front pocket of his white jacket and with one swift movement, Ken's life was changed. The man's quick hand movement flew across the paper on the clipboard as easily as an English teacher correcting a simple spelling error on a term paper. With a single hand gesture, a split second in time, the future of Kenneth Callahan was profoundly altered forever.

Ken was so surprised and so very grateful that tears continued filling his eyes. Once again, Ken was speechless and very grateful. That's when he looked deeply into the man's eyes one more time (all the way into his soul this time), shook his hand, and genuinely said, "Thank you, sir. I promise I'll be the very best soldier I can be. I promise." The man sensed Ken's genuineness and knew he would do exactly what he promised. A second later, the man's face, voice, and overall demeanor changed quickly. He seemed to become a US Army officer as he reverted back to the more authoritative command voice and presence that Ken had noticed when they first met. That's when Kenneth Callahan received his "first" official military order (without even recognizing it as such at the time). "Okay then, now get yourself together, Private Callahan and go get on a bus. I bet one seat still has your name on it. And that's an order. Move it out, soldier!" Ken didn't know whether to salute him, shake his hand, bow to him, or give him the biggest hug he'd likely ever get from any other recruit. So, he merely said, "Yes, sir!" With that, the white-coated man opened the door and they both walked out of the room together. Then Ken immediately broke into a sprint. He had never run so fast to catch a bus in his life.

And he made it—a 'clean getaway.' He jumped into the first bus he saw and took the first empty seat available, sitting down next to a big guy who was obviously as anxious to get going as well. The big guy immediately said to Ken, "Hey, man . . . what took you so long? Did the doctors discover you were really a girl or something?" With that, they both laughed as the bus slowly pulled out of the parking lot.

Ken's mind was still racing, still thinking about what had just happened and what could have happened. He was tired now, very tired. Kenneth Callahan was now officially in the US Army, off to boot camp, on the way to a brand-new life. More important, he was heading away, far away, from Brooklyn at last.

Five hours later, when all the recruits got off the buses at Fort Bragg, North Carolina, he looked for the other two guys who reentered the examination building with him back in Fort Holabird—neither one of them had made it back on a bus.

Ken felt sorry for them.

Boot camp turned out to be fun, not work, for Ken. It was not the ball breaker that it was rumored to be. He actually loved the physical aspects of boot camp and wasn't challenged by them at all. However, what he liked most was eating three meals a day—three. To him, the food alone was worth every push-up, pull-up, and long march he was made to do throughout the entire two months of boot camp. As such, time passed quickly without a hitch.

Because he had done very well on the Morse code competency testing back in Fort Holabird, he was classified as a radio operator (05B) and scheduled to attend advanced training at Fort Dix, New Jersey, after completing boot camp. Ken had always assumed he would be classified as an infantryman (11B) and was even somewhat disappointed at the classification as a radio specialist. He viewed himself as a grunt, a ground pounder, but that wasn't to be. He also had fun in radio operator's school, even more fun than at boot camp. He graduated among the top of his class, so he was then selected to complete a more complex communications course at Fort Gordon, Georgia—as a radio teletype operator (05C). This training was quite lengthy, very complex, and much more challenging for Ken. But he successfully completed it and was promoted to E-4 (specialist four) in the process. All in all, he received nine months of basic and advanced communications training in the US Army. And eight months from the day he joined the army, he landed in Vietnam.

It was March 17, 1968. And, it was hot, very hot.

CHAPTER 3
Phu Loi, Vietnam (1968)

KEN STEPPED OFF THE FLYING TIGERS airplane and was immediately greeted by an overwhelming, suffocating heat. From that moment on, everything seemed to go downhill for this well-trained, highly motivated communications specialist from Brooklyn. Before coming to Vietnam, he and his peers were told Vietnam was hot, but the description did not come close to the reality of this smothering heat. The endless blasts of thick ripping winds in Vietnam shamed even the hottest days in the swamps of Fort Gordon, Georgia. Within just a few minutes, Ken wanted to turn around and jump back inside the air-conditioned Flying Tigers cabin and continue staring at the stewardesses, just as he had done throughout the entire eighteen-hour flight from the United States to Wake Island, to Manila, and then Vietnam. He, along with all new arrivals, were left standing on the airport's tarmac for some time, just waiting and sweating. Eventually they were trucked to a processing center in Long Binh, a city outside Saigon. In military terms, Saigon was located in III Corp, just above the Mekong Delta region in the south central part of the country. The Mekong Delta was the most southern part of Vietnam and was branded IV Corp. Long Binh was the primary personnel processing center for newbies being assigned to units in the south. Ken discovered he was being assigned to the First Infantry Division (the Big Red One) of legendary fame. Not being trained in advanced infantry tactics (only advanced communications), he was somewhat concerned at first about becoming a part of an infantry unit. But he quickly learned that he would not be required to go on active patrols searching for the Viet Cong. Rather, he was to spend most of his time supporting First Infantry Division Artillery from a base camp called Phu Loi, twenty miles north of Saigon.

Phu Loi

Phu Loi was a relatively large camp, shaped like a triangle. It was barren of any foliage whatsoever and had a two-square-mile defensive diameter. It also had a three-thousand-foot airstrip running through its center and was the headquarters for several US Army units, including the Division Artillery Headquarters of the Big Red One. Phu Loi was carved out of Southeast Asia's prime jungle real estate, and had been a POW camp run by the Japanese during World War II. Throughout the year, Phu Loi was either 100 percent dirt and dust or 100 percent rain and mud. There were really only two seasons: very hot and dry and very hot and wet. No variations existed between these extremes. Construction and reconstruction were going on everywhere, all the time, inside and outside the base camp's perimeter. It was very well secured against ground attacks, but not as secure against mortars and rockets. Phu Loi was surrounded by a complex system of steel picketed, concertina razor wire, land mines, claymores, and foo gas barrels (a special mixture of explosives and napalm stored in fifty-five gallon drums), all strategically placed along Phu Loi's inner and outer perimeter. Artillery units were placed at each point of Phu Loi's triangle with large ground bunkers and thirty-foot towers established every hundred yards or so along the perimeter. The land immediately surrounding most points of the base camp was also cleared by Rome plows in combination with Agent Orange defoliants. This provided greater visibility and a good field of fire for several hundred yards in all directions. Highway 13 (more commonly called "Thunder Road") ran north to south along the village of Phu Loi and the base camp.

Ken's major concern was about incoming mortars and rockets, not ground attacks. He didn't know why he feared mortars and rockets having never encountered them before, but just the thought of being blown apart, or even worse being buried alive under the rubble of steal, sandbags, and earth crept into his psyche early on. While Phu Loi received both mortars and rockets regularly, attacks occurred mostly at night—mostly. Even so, Ken considered himself lucky and somewhat safe despite being in the midst of a combat zone surrounded by an elusive, lethal and ever-present enemy force.

The mission of his communications team was to send and receive encrypted, highly classified messages via teletype among field units and other military units within the First Infantry Division's area of operations. Encrypted messages about field conditions, enemy movements, interrogation results, logistical requirements, intelligence analysis, operational emergencies, and body counts would be sent or received, encrypted or decrypted, then delivered to the various commanders for action or further analysis. However, for the first several weeks, Ken wasn't assigned directly to a communications team. As a matter of fact, the unit didn't seemed to know what to do with Ken, nor did he feel anyone cared. This had a profound impact on how he viewed himself and his value.

Even though he had begun feeling very positive about himself as a result of the first 9 months of training in the army, this set back caused him to once again begin doubting himself even as a member of the Big Red One.

With the exception of the time when Ken was a student at Anne Arundel High School, he never felt safe within a structured environment. Yet even in the safe, nonthreatening surroundings of that school, he still felt compelled to overcompensate, to go that extra mile, to prove to others (to himself, really) that he was an OK guy. As a result, some people at school thought he was somewhat arrogant and conceited—and rightfully so. They didn't understand just how much effort he was expending every day to keep the secret of how really insecure and fragile his personality and self-view really were. Ken didn't fully realize it either, especially the degree of emotional effort he was expending daily just trying to mask it from others. Such thoughts about his ability to adapt and be integrated into the First Infantry Division caused him to flashback in time to his high school days at AAHS.

"To Conquer Conceit"

Annette was the most beautiful and talented of the AAHS cheerleaders in 1967. She stole Ken's heart without even knowing it. He began going to school sporting events just to watch her cheer, not to watch the games. While he felt all the cheerleaders were gorgeous, his eyes were always on

Annette. Actually, the only sport Ken was really interested in was baseball, where he had excelled as a varsity first baseman for AAHS. However, there were two huge downsides playing on AAHS's baseball team – cheerleaders never came to baseball games to work their motivational magic and Annette never got a chance to see Ken in action because she was always cheering at other sports after school hours, which really meant he never got a chance to impress her with his athletic ability. Nevertheless, he went to as many other sporting events as he could so he wouldn't miss a single jump, split, stretch, tumble, dance, or smile of Annette's. Ken never even knew what the score was at any moment during games nor did he care who won . . . he was too busy focusing on her. He wasn't a stalker—just a love-struck teenager infatuated with a very beautiful, very popular girl.

It was the first time in his life he had been bitten by the "love bug." Annette had the cutest smile he had ever seen. And she kept her beautiful light brown hair cut very short, high above her shoulders. Ken liked it that way even though he never told her so. She also had a natural twinkle in her eyes that always disarmed him, making him babble and stutter like a disoriented preschooler attempting to answer a teacher's question on the first day of school. If Annette merely said hello or threw him a casual glance when accidently passing in the hallways, he'd crumble emotionally inside but would never show it on the outside. Additionally, his emotions always seemed to morph into a liquid mush whenever she neared—just like Bashful did in Walt Disney's 1937 movie *Snow White and the Seven Dwarfs* whenever Snow White even glanced his way. And like Bashful, Ken became instantly oxygen-deprived whenever Annette came near his vicinity. Nothing like her existed in the Projects of Brooklyn that was for sure. Eventually, he and Annette started dating and continued for some time throughout their senior year. They enjoyed each other's company and liked being seen together as a couple.

Then their breakup came.

Ken could never recall what it was that drove them apart, so he concluded it had to be his fault. Ken always felt insecure around girls and around most adults for that matter despite his well-practiced persona and demeanor. But later on, Ken sensed their breakup may have been because he felt Annette was getting just a little too close for him (or, he was starting to feel too much for her). Either way, it was something he couldn't allow to happen with anyone. In his mind, it just wasn't safe.

Yet, he never could tell if she was really hurt, mad or indifferent because of their breakup. Each time they found themselves accidently together at school, she would appear to be either hurt (like a little girl sent directly to bed after dinner for not eating her vegetables) or really pissed (like a kitten being forced to take its first bath in the kitchen sink). Either way, Ken never knew how she really felt.

He would soon find out—big time.

Until that point in his life, the only long-term experience he had with women or girls was with his mother—Hilda. And with her, there was never a question, not one ounce of doubt, about how she felt about anyone. He always knew where he stood with her despite her many moods. But Annette was different, much different. She was goodness, far more caring and complex, or Ken was just more naive than he viewed himself. To him, she was one of the "cheerleaders." To be a cheerleader also implied she had to maintain her poise and composure at all times—never overtly showing how she really felt about anything unless it was positive in nature. Cheerleaders were the "smile" of the school, and that smile had to be present at all times, no matter how bad she felt on the inside. In retrospect, Ken viewed it as the secret cost of having cheerleader fame—the price of school celebrity measured in a currency called congeniality. Annette carried it well.

Breaking up was a good-bad news thing for him. First, the good news—being mad at Ken was a short-term thing at least in his eyes and from the view of other students and faculty members—it was over as fast as it started. The bad news (very bad news)—Annette found a very creative way to transform a short-term relationship into a long-term blow that would follow Ken the rest of his days. She was not only a great cheerleader, but she was also a very smart, resourceful, cleaver girl who contributed to the school in many ways, including being a thespian, a member of THY, and a staff member on two school publications—"AAHS Star Review" and "The Headliners."

And after their breakup, she wanted or needed "payback"—and it had to be a precise, devastating, everlasting blow. So Ken sensed Annette mustered all her creative juices to devise the perfect plan.

And it was a doozy.

In hindsight, Ken actually felt it was pure genius—the perfect payback.

This is how it evolved into such historic stature within his mind: Like all graduating seniors from AAHS, Ken had the opportunity to include his "ambition" within the school's official 1967 yearbook. Only one third of the seniors actually choose to do so, and Ken was one them. His classmates had listed a variety of ambitions in this yearbook including the desire to one day become a clerk typist, city planner, commercial artist, Peace Corps member, champion swimmer of the Atlantic Ocean, and millionaire. A few much more interesting and way-out ambitions actually listed in his 1967 yearbook included becoming a seller of guns to Indians, Australian cowboy, and even a resident of "Never Never Land." Ken thought the most difficult of these last three ambitions had to be becoming a resident of "Never Never Land." But considering the use of recreational drugs was quickly becoming commonplace within his own generation, getting to "Never Never Land" could prove to be the easiest and likely the most fun ambition of them all.

After all, it was 1967.

Ken's own ambition seemed to fit somewhere in the middle of these noble aspirations. From 1958 to 1961, Ken became hooked on swimming and scuba diving simply by watching weekly episodes of *Sea Hunt,* a TV series about an ex-navy frogman's (Lloyd Bridges) aqua adventures. Ken would watch him discover underwater treasures, fight off sharks and eels, and explore sunken pirate ships. He really liked the concept of being able to breathe underwater the most; to him that was the coolest thing ever. So becoming a frogman, a "sea hunter," who explored and played in the oceans of the world became a real dream of his. And later in life, he accomplished just that by becoming a very proficient scuba diver officially certified by the National Association of Underwater Instructors (NAUI) and the Professional Association of Diving Instructors (PADI), simultaneously. Therefore, it seemed only natural for him to submit his official ambition in the 1967 yearbook to become an oceanographer. And that's exactly what he submitted to the AAHS yearbook staff:

"to become an oceanographer."

Annette must have seen this choice as a golden opportunity. Using her resourcefulness and imagination, and likely a few solid connections on the yearbook staff, Annette was somehow able to change Ken's ambition. She made it shorter. And being such a small change, she must have thought it could be done without the risk of ever being noticed in the yearbook's final editing phase.

She was correct. No one noticed the change until it was too late.

When the yearbook was finally published and released to all students, parents, faculty, and the world, Ken's official ambition listed immediately below his portrait in the yearbook read as follows:

"to conquer conceit."

The change was simple yet devastatingly effective.

Even the official spelling of his last name in the yearbook had been misspelled, but he never associated that "mistake" with Annette's ingenuity. Her idea was sophisticated. It was meaningful, and it must have been quite satisfying to her as well. His ambition was now there for everyone to see, read, and laugh about forever. Equally impactful, it could never be changed; it was permanent. She must have known that no high school in the world would ever consider funding the republication of an entire yearbook just to make such a correction. Interestingly enough, it never really bothered Ken when he read it. He was stung at first, but it didn't last long. Actually, he was more surprised than hurt.

A year would pass before he came to truly appreciate the "genius" of her plan. That's when he came to admire just how creative Annette's plan to enact "lasting revenge" really was. And as Ken matured over the decades, he often reflected on her "creativity" from time to time. She had come very close to capturing and conveying the real truth about him, but came up just a little short, slightly off target. Ken wasn't "conceited" at all (i.e., having an unwarranted high opinion of one's self). "Conceit," however, was never at play during their relationship, nor at any time in his life as a matter of fact. Annette would have been far more accurate if she had used "narcissistic" (i.e., having an inflated sense of importance about oneself) instead of conceit. Certainly, either word would still have been adequate for other seniors at AAHS to get the message she really wanted to send: "Ken is full of himself." But that's if they even took time to read the information about the other kids. Ken just sensed most seniors were equally full of themselves. After all, teenagers are by nature the center of their own universe anyway. Ken was no different than most in that regard.

The truth about Ken was actually along those lines, just much deeper. He never possessed an "unwarranted high opinion of himself," never. In reality, it was the exact opposite—he always felt quite inferior around her and the other kids at school. He had a very poor self-image and self-identity well before arriving at AAHS, primarily because of his background and upbringing. Actually, he viewed his classmates as "normal" or "superior" to him. That's why he always tried to compensate (overcompensate, really) in order to hide his own sense of inferiority and insecurity from them—even from Annette, especially from Annette. The embarrassment would be too much for him to bear if anyone ever discovered where he had come from, who his family was, what went on in the Projects, and how he lived day to day growing up in Brooklyn.

In his mind, he came from "the other side of the tracks." At least that's what he felt at that time in his life, and that's what drove much of his behavior, feelings and perceptions. He just sensed that if his classmates knew, they would make fun of him, disparage, harass, or shun him. In retrospect, Ken never experienced that kind of behavior or attitude from anyone in AAHS, never. But it was constantly on his mind. It wasn't until decades later that he would discover *Leave It to Beaver* and *Father Knows Best* family environments of the 1950s and 1960s—those he so often longed for and valued from afar growing up in the Projects—were actually more of an exception than the norm. No family was perfect, really. Every child growing up during those times likely had secrets of their own when the front door of their own homes were closed. While his home environment may have been extreme, other kids had likely experienced somewhat disturbing things at times, too.

He certainly was not alone. But at the time, his sensitivities and insecurities could not be understood well enough to be extended beyond his immediate situation. That's why he always felt compelled to overcompensate socially for his own perceived personal inadequacies while trying to fit in at AAHS. On the interpersonal level, Ken later sensed that Annette must have experienced some of his insecurities up close and personal as they dated. He sensed that was likely what really drove her to do what she did. And that's also why he never blamed Annette for enacting such a "lasting revenge" plan on him. And besides, Ken had often experienced very similar types of deception, while growing up, so it wasn't anything new to him or as severe as other things done to him by people who also seemingly cared. That's also why he was not hurt right away when it appeared in the yearbook. If anything, he felt a little sorrow for her because he sensed to have done such a thing in the first place meant she likely had experienced similar hardships somewhere in her own life. Such feelings, thoughts and behaviors just didn't magically appear in anyone; they were most often nurtured consciously or unconsciously over time through direct experiences.

After all, he and Annette were both teenagers, just teenagers. And at such a time in life, there are no real rules guiding a teenage heart—only hormones. If Annette was given a chance to go back in time (just like Kathleen Turner had in the 1982 movie *When Peggy Sue Got Married*), and change his ambition in their yearbook by removing "conceit" and replacing it with "insecurity," he'd be quite comfortable with it. After all, "to conquer insecurity" would have been far more accurate and much closer to the truth.

Nearly a year after graduating from AAHS, the creativity and inspiration of Annette's "lasting revenge" would serve to spark a flame of revenge within Ken—the first (and thankfully, the last) act of vengeance he would ever perpetrate on anyone throughout his entire life. And it was to be devised, designed and fully executed from the most remote place on earth—Phu Loi, Vietnam.

Fitting In / Fitting Out

Meanwhile, back in Pho Loi, Vietnam . . .

Fitting in as a member of the US Army, especially being a part of the Big Red One was important to Ken. Doing so would be a real confidence booster in strengthening his self-image in a wholesome, mature way. After so many years of confusion, doubt and insecurity growing up, he was beginning to feel far more secure about who he was as a man and who he was destined to become. Having "structure" in his life was the key. He didn't understand the full impact of just how his out-of-control family structure had on his emotions, relationships, values, and view of himself but he subtly learned over the years that he could never depend on family or anyone close to him. In short, Ken wanted and needed a "second" start in life. Getting such an opportunity in South Vietnam, of all places, and during a war, was going to be just another additional challenge, especially regarding the establishment of lasting, trusting relationships.

That's why he couldn't wait to start applying his communications skills as a part of a professional team. He figured since his job was not going to be hunting Viet Cong or NVA every day, he would then do his best to help those whose job it would be. This made him feel even better about himself. He couldn't wait to jump in, get down, get dirty, get up and get ahead. Unfortunately, when he arrived at Phu Loi in March 1968, his assigned communications team was very well staffed, overstaffed to be precise. Normally, being overstaffed was a very good thing for any combat unit, but it was not good for Ken Callahan. As a matter of fact, it was the worst news imaginable. For the first several weeks, no one seemed to know what to do with him, nor did he feel anyone cared. And, there was no sense of urgency to get him involved in the unit's operations right away either. All the shifts were well manned, and no backups were needed because everyone's tour of duty in Vietnam was not coming to an end for some time. In short, Ken Callahan wasn't needed—at least that's how he saw things shaping up.

And this devastated him.

As a matter of fact, it would take several months before Ken would be permanently integrated into operations and allowed to do the job he was so well trained to do; the job he wanted to do, what he needed to do. Instead, Ken's daily routine consisted of doing work details throughout Phu Loi. He had already obtained the rank of E-4 (specialist fourth class) while in training because of his academics, but that didn't buy him any special privileges when it came to work details. Digging ditches, leveling roads, moving equipment, driving jeeps, repairing and upgrading perimeter defenses, and burning human excrement (literally) were among such daily activities. Most details didn't require much thought or problem-solving abilities but did demand a strong back, legs, arms, and hands. It wasn't the work itself that began getting Ken down. Rather, it was the ceaseless heat, endless mosquitoes and insects, constant mortar attacks, and the timelessness of it all. Such day-in day-out, mindless activities were at the heart of everything. In Vietnam, there were no calendar days of the week (no Mondays, Tuesdays, Wednesdays, etc.) only dates, hours, minutes, and seconds. Friday and Saturday nights were nonexistent. Sundays were not days of rest, and holidays meant nothing in a combat zone. Every day was like the previous day, and the next day was the same.

It wasn't actually boredom that got to Ken; there was always some kind of work that had to get done. It was more about not having anything to look forward to. It was the sense of hopelessness, helplessness, and endlessness that was ever gnawing at his soul. He learned quickly there was a big difference between having something to "look forward to" versus something to "anticipate." For example, Ken "looked forward" to the end of each day's details, to eating (anything), and even to the early morning hours because to him it was the coolest time of the day and the mosquitoes seemed less hungry. And of course, he "looked forward" to mail calls. All these things were highlights in his day. And they were worthy of "looking forward" to. They helped keep him going, moving ahead inside and outside his mind. On the other hand, there were also those daily activities he "anticipated." These were not good things—only the inevitable realities about living in a base camp within a combat zone, including—mortar and rocket attacks, countless mosquito bites, heat, dirt-filled nostrils, heat, sweaty clothes, heat, sandbags, mud, shovels, lively little scorpions, slow moving hairy tarantulas, stinging ants, heat, and the nauseating stench of human shit and urine burning deeply within his dirt-filled nostrils. And . . . more heat.

Unfortunately for Ken, his ability to minimize the effects of "anticipated" events and maximize the effects of positive events became more difficult with each passing day. Facing the realities of such life was a key part of everything, and everyone had to adapt. But not being able to apply his military expertise contributed to his feelings of worthlessness, and that he had not expected. In short, Ken was spending more time and emotion "anticipating" than "looking forward." This was a very counterproductive state of mind for him.

When Ken arrived in Phu Loi, he was somewhat relieved to discover he would not have to go on patrols or leave the relative safety of the Phu Loi base camp. However, after countless mortar and rocket attacks, he began thinking that as a member of an infantry squad on patrol, he would at least be camouflaged at times as he covertly moved through the boonies. This also implied he would be a much smaller target, much harder to locate, and therefore much more difficult to kill. And while on patrols, he would also have the capacity and opportunity to fight back when confronted—he could defend himself. Just the act of doing something in his own defense, even minimally, would be psychologically and emotionally healthier than constantly assuming the role of helpless victim walking around in a base camp or sitting and waiting on the parameter with a big bull's-eye on his head every day and night.

Working in a base camp had its obvious advantages, too. But three big factors also made him feel far more vulnerable and less of a soldier there than being in the boonies:

1. A base camp was a bigger target; easy to hit.
2. A base camp was permanently placed (enemy could find it anytime).
3. At base camp, most soldiers could not "fire back" at the source of the incoming rounds; they could only run, hide or take shelter.

(Over time, this felt like cowardly behavior and it began taking its toll on Ken's self-image.)

Because of these factors, he sensed he was far more helpless and vulnerable inside the base camp than outside the perimeter. At least while on patrol, he had mobility, and could attack—fight back in some way. Ken didn't really know how sound this logic was or what the real impact of not being able to fight back had on him. Maybe he felt this way because it was just a natural part of him to always fight back while growing up in the Projects. To him, fighting back was an expected part of life. It was as much emotional as physical. It was an automatic reflex and a "right." Without it, Ken just wasn't himself.

Sandbags & Pillowcases

Ken also had another big concern, a big secret, about his daily work details—they seemed to always involve sandbags. Filling so many sandbags each day made him feel like his entrenching tool (portable shovel) was far more important than his M16 rifle. And for some hidden reason, he also developed a "sandbag hang-up" that had become deeply embedded somewhere in the darkest recesses of his mind. He disliked the look of sandbags, the feel of sandbags, the smell of sandbags, transporting sandbags, touching sandbags, filling sandbags, tying off sandbags, and stacking sandbags. And since he only had seen them up close and personal for the first time while at boot camp, he couldn't understand where this hang-up was coming from. Yet every time he walked away from a new pile of freshly packed and stacked sandbags on a bunker, along the perimeter, or in a ditch, he would catch himself looking back over his shoulder to ensure they were staying put . . . and not following him to his next detail. He knew such thoughts and feelings should have freaked him out, but they didn't. Ken even began doubting his own sanity on this subject.

He knew sandbags were inanimate objects serving a vital protective purpose. And although sandbags really did freak him out, he was also glad to have them overhead during mortar attacks. Yet, he still kept an eye out for them all the time because they were naturally evil things in his mind. He also noticed whenever working closely around them, his breathing became much more difficult, as if a pillowcase was being pulled down over his head and tied around his neck. Ken felt compelled at times to stop what he was doing and walk away from the sandbags until he felt better. Yet the feeling would just start up again once he resumed his work. Ken never considered sharing these feelings with anyone. He sensed if someone found out he was thinking like this, he'd end-up inside a military psych ward somewhere counting flowers on wallpaper, managing cockroach races, or talking to his new imaginary friends who also feared sandbags. So, he just kept his thoughts to himself. Little did he know at the time, both sandbags and pillowcases were destined to be important symbols throughout his life.

Ken shared a "hooch" (a small make-shift dwelling) with about eight other soldiers, all enlisted men, each working in different areas on different shifts throughout division artillery. His hooch was an open-air, tin-roofed structure with no walls, just wooden pylons at each corner holding up the roof. The hooch was also surrounded by three-foot, fifty-five gallon drums fill to the max with dirt, and by stacks of sandbags barricaded on all four sides. When he was not on details or within his hooch at night, Ken was usually assigned to man a bunker on the perimeter of Phu Loi. It was usually, but not always, shared by at least one other solider. Shifts varied but usually ran about three to four hours. Having never been trained to use M60 machine guns or M18A1 Claymore Mines, which were standard weapons inside perimeter bunkers, he had to learn them quickly. Fortunately, the Viet Cong seldom tested this sector of the perimeter at night.

After each shift, Ken usually slept in his hooch during the early morning hours while others went about routine work around him. Ken liked sleeping during early daylight because there were fewer mortar attacks then, and the Vietnam heat didn't really hit full force until later in the morning. Such moments were tolerable.

The command made a noble effort to rid Phu Loi of mosquitoes, but it was a futile, endless chore. And the natural shade and shadow casted by the hooch in daylight seemed to magically attract every kind of spider, scorpion, and nasty insect seeking refuge from the relentless sun. Sometimes Ken would awake in his cot to find himself eye to eye with creatures brazenly determined to share his pillow. Cohabitating with Vietnam's variety of life forms was a natural part of life in Phu Loi.

At first, Ken was eager to help anyone anytime at Phu Loi. After all, he was now a soldier in a foreign country, representing the good old Stars and Stripes alongside other fellow Americans. In his early days in Phu Loi, he also felt good about himself just by being a part of the war. He pitched in with everything assigned to him starting in early afternoon and continuing nonstop until dusk. He took on all his assigned duties with passion and diligence. Then he would have dinner in the evening and be assigned to a bunker on the perimeter for several hours at night. Occasionally, very occasionally, he would fill in for another member at the communications station—a joy for him. The communications equipment was housed within a windowless Quonset hut not far off the southern perimeter of Phu Loi. It was heavily fortified with several layers of sandbags, encircled by endless barbed wire straddling seven-foot mesh fences.

He enjoyed working his MOS (Military Occupation Specialty) whenever he got the chance within the Quonset hut, but that seldom occurred because of excess personnel as well as "seniority" (which really meant one's time-in-country, not one's rank). He felt he belonged there all the time, not just now and then. After all, that's why he was so well trained and shipped-off to Vietnam in the first place. So Ken's daily life continued as follows—work details, dirt, mosquitoes, sweat, mud, bunkers, sleep, and then more work details, more dirt, more mosquitoes, more sweat, more bunkers, more mud, and less sleep. Two meals were provided at a nearby mess tent, which helped Ken get through some of the day's worst moments. He did appreciate the fact that he did not have to eat out of cans or from his helmet like soldiers on patrol—that was a big plus.

This was Ken's daily life at Phu Loi during the early months in Vietnam. He was turning into the dreaded *"guy in the rear with the gear and beer"* in his mind—it didn't feel good. It also didn't fit well with his own perception of himself because he knew deep inside that he could make a difference in more meaningful ways if just given a chance to prove himself.

But this was not to be at least for the time being.

And, this crushed him.

Got Attitude?

After a couple of months of this routine and mind-set, Ken's self-esteem began to deteriorate. The more body bags he saw passing through his sector coupled with increasing mortar attacks, the more his optimism also waned—turning to doubt, frustration, anger, and depression. That's when he started becoming paranoid about being overrun by the Viet Cong and being taken prisoner (something that was very unlikely to happen at a base camp the size of Phu Loi in 1968). But, it still became ever present in his mind.

Nevertheless, such thoughts were becoming more real to him—a permanent slice of his psyche. He could not seem to shake it. In the process, he also began distrusting everyone. Whenever he saw local Vietnamese who were working inside Phu Loi, he gave them a wide berth without taking his eyes off them. He also started avoiding other soldiers within his hooch and while on details. They too, noticed Ken was changing. His behavior and attitude were becoming more negative, sarcastic, and defensive. In turn, they began avoiding him as well. Unfortunately, Ken was starting to like it that way too; he was becoming more and more comfortable within his own self-driven exile and personal isolation.

Darvon

One afternoon before heading out on another detail, he noticed a small envelope in the corner of his hooch. He picked it up and noticed it contained lots of pills. He looked around and saw no one was present, so he kept them. As his work detail began that day, he took a few pills just to see what would happen, even without knowing what the pills were for. To Ken, they were pills. And pills were supposed to help people feel better. He was feeling worse about everything and about everyone more each day, so he thought the pills could help. He needed something, anything, to give him a break from the routine of things and just to get a little freedom from all his thoughts. He sensed drugs would help him get through the day faster and easier.

The pills did just that.

He had never taken drugs before even though they were plentiful in the Projects during the sixties. He would try a beer now and then at home but didn't like the taste. He also tried gin once but became sicker than a dying dog on a leash. He never touched gin or any liquor afterwards. And even though alcohol was a permanent piece of his mother's household furniture no matter where they lived in the Projects, he always avoided it. So trying pills of any kind was a risk for him, but he felt he had nothing to lose. "What were they going to do . . . send me to Vietnam?" Such was Ken's attitude, not only about drugs but also about everything. In his mind, things couldn't get worse.

He was wrong.

The pills turned out to be Darvon, an opiate derivative—a pain killer. He didn't know about drugs or the difference between sedatives, stimulants, or psychotics. And he didn't care. He began by taking a couple at a time before work details and was beginning to feel different, somewhat better, not physically better because he didn't have any real pain to start with, but the pills did seem to help him relax. He liked the feeling; it was body numbing and took the edge off things. Ken also found Darvon seemed to help him through his daily work details by producing a somewhat different, short term mind-set towards things. Yet, he realized his stamina and physical strength also decreased quicker especially during prolonged and demanding tasks such as laying barbed-wire, moving fifty-five gallon drums or lifting heavy ammunition boxes and crates.

But, feeling good was good enough to get him through such moments.

Doing a quality job just didn't seem to be as important as it used to be. Most often, he would take the pills with Coca-Cola, but often he took them with a beer if he could get his hands on one. That's when he felt the most relaxed. While his daily and nightly routines didn't change much, he was focusing more on himself than on work, the environment, or even the war. His desire to get back to the States (not necessarily back home to the Projects) had become his obsession. His thoughts were now directed on only two things—getting out of this hellhole called Vietnam and looking forward to mail calls, the only tangible joy he had during his "drug days."

Pills were second on hit parade; mail calls and letters from his fiancé were first.

"Dear John Letters"—Weapon of Cowards

When Ken wasn't thinking about getting out of Vietnam, his thoughts were on his fiancé. Right after graduating from high school, he met a city girl on a blind date. She too, had just graduated from high school in 1967, however she attended a school in the city, not AAHS. They liked each other right away. Shortly afterward, they started distance dating throughout Ken's boot camp and advanced training days—nearly nine months. She was a beautiful girl with long black hair and deep blue eyes.

Her name was Martha Elaine Slumberger.

She wanted to become a doctor one day and was heading off to college to pursue her dreams. Martha Elaine started writing him letters every day as he moved among his training assignments the summer they both graduated from high school. They shared at least one long-distance phone call per week (Saturday evenings at 7:00 p.m.) and would reunite each time Ken earned a three-day pass during his training. They eventually fell in love, and just before Ken left for Vietnam, he proposed to her. Martha Elaine quickly accepted.

While they never had serious sex together, they did fool around at every opportunity. They wanted their honeymoon to be exactly that—a real honeymoon—so they decided to wait until he returned from the war. During Ken's first month or so in Vietnam, her letters came every day, sometimes multiple letters on the same day—"double headers," Ken would call them. Letters (from anyone) were goodness, for sure, but letters from her were the best rewards in Vietnam.

Martha Elaine would also scent each letter with her own special perfume. To Ken, her unique fragrance was the essence of femininity—the most precious commodity on earth. Just one sniff generated a dozen memories of her which lasted for hours. Therefore, a single scented letter from her was much more than a piece of paper in an envelope. It was an oasis of pure fantasy in the midst of a horrid land. Whether Ken's hands were laying barbed wire on the perimeter or filling sandbags, his mind and heart were constantly burrowing deep into her letters as he dreamed of getting out of the country. Each sentence was a miracle. Each paragraph a delight, each page a marvel, and each letter a joy. Even though Ken didn't know it, her letters were actually helping reduce the amount of Darvon he was taking daily. More letters meant fewer pills.

Her letters seemed to be his anecdote to the virus called Vietnam.

Ken suspected that most men in Vietnam would agree with him about the importance of letters, but they would never articulate it openly, nor would he. It was just too "un-soldierly" to admit such vulnerability and sensitivity. Nevertheless, such feelings were real even though seldom admitted. He recalled getting a letter from his mother once during his first year in Vietnam. She asked him to send her some money—nothing more, nothing less. He did. Actually, Ken was sending her a portion of pay every month for her to place in a savings account so he'd have money upon his return. He hoped she wasn't spending that too.

Such hopes along these lines would not be fulfilled as he'd find out upon his return. Ken seldom received letters from anyone else on a regular basis besides Martha Elaine, so letters from her were jewels, far more important than food. For food, once eaten, was gone forever. But, a letter once read, kept giving back—a never-ending source of nourishment for the heart.

Her letters also helped him get through the days and nights in Phu Loi. Rereading the same letter in a day was the norm. During guard duty in the bunker at night, where light of any kind was prohibited, he would merely take out her letters and sniff and sniff. With each slow, deep inhalation of her written words, her voice and special touch came alive. Without having the ability to see inside bunkers at night, he relied on the motion of his fingers scanning across each page while lip-syncing her written words in perfect order as he had memorized them. Just as a blind person uses brail to read, Ken's scanning touch on unseen words also served the same purpose. Each finger stroke on her written words evoked a steady stream of her image. A single letter made a difference, a big difference. He wrote back to her as often as possible, for it was the only way to stay in touch with her and the "world" (the USA). Letters from her became his only reality—everything else was just a passing blur in the dirt and duty of Phu Loi.

However, about two months after arriving in Vietnam, Martha Elaine's letters suddenly stopped.

With that, days seemed to turn into weeks. Not hearing his name yelled out during mail call was like a death sentence. And this too started taking its toll on Ken Callahan. He didn't know what was happening, so every unimaginable scenario entered and stayed in his mind day and night. He continued sending her letters but without replies. With each additional letter he wrote, his fear of losing her intensified.

Adding to this growing frustration, there was no way in Vietnam in 1968 to connect with people back in the "world" except mail. There were no phones, no faxes, no Internet, no tweets, no Facebook, no Skype, no video conferencing—nothing. She was a pretty girl and a beautiful woman. And he knew "Jodie" (the symbolic name soldiers gave to every real or imagined wife-stealing, girlfriend-abusing, low-life guy) was looking for a "short time" (a one-night stand). Every soldier knew Jodie would be right there sniffing and waiting for one vulnerable moment to pounce on their girl back home. Ken's thinking was no different than every soldier in Vietnam. Deep inside the duffle bag of their minds, all soldiers brought this ever-present demon with them to Vietnam. And without having information about what was actually unfolding in the "world," Ken's panic and imagination kicked into high gear.

Unfortunately for Ken, his imagination turned into horrid reality. A couple of weeks after Martha Elaine's last letter, Ken then received a letter from a schoolmate. His name was Ted Hardy. He was also the person who originally set up the blind date that brought Ken and Martha Elaine together in the first place. It was the first and only time Ted wrote to Ken while he was in Vietnam, and it turned out to be the most devastating letter of all.

He explained that Martha Elaine had met another guy, a manager at a local Woolworth Store in Brooklyn Park. They were planning to get married once he got divorced from his current wife. Ted apologized for having to write this, but he felt compelled to do so. He also said Martha Elaine was returning Ken's engagement ring when he got back from Vietnam. With that, Ken's fears and insecurities started clawing their way out of his stomach, scratching their way up and across his chest, then wrapping totally around his face. Such suffocating anxiety dwarfed even his worst nightmares of sandbags, scorpions, and the Viet Cong. He was now drowning in a sea of his own emotions. If given the choice, Ken would have preferred an incoming mortar land directly between his legs splitting his body in two, rather than getting a letter with such news about Martha Elaine.

The most debilitating and frustrating part of this whole nightmare was that, once again, Ken could not fight back. He was a soldier who could not defend himself or counterattack because he had no weapons for this type of battle. Ken couldn't even make his case, couldn't appeal, persuade, or even plea; he could not fight back. Actually, he couldn't do a damn thing—except to accept it. This very real paradox was the number 1 unspoken, dirty little secret shared among of all soldiers in Vietnam. A secret—commonly experienced but uncommonly discussed. Dear Johns were really just another type of enemy US soldiers had to deal with even though this foe was thousands of miles away versus across a barbed-wire perimeter. No bullet manufactured could reach an enemy so far away.

As such, it was an unfair battle to fight. The helplessness it caused had a devastating effect on every Dear John recipient in Vietnam, not just Ken. He felt there should be a federal law enacted to prohibit any woman from sending a Dear John letter to a man in combat. Period!

Didn't women know the US Army never developed a flak jacket thick enough to protect a soldier from such a vicious, penetrating bullet as a Dear John letter? How stupid, how uncaring, how ignorant, how cruel could a person be to even think of doing such a thing at the most vulnerable time in a soldier's life? How much empathy or just basic human compassion would it really have taken for Martha Elaine (or any women falling "out of love" with a soldier in war) to just wait until her man returned?

To Ken, Dear John letters were weapons of cowards.

Anyone who would do such a thing was no better than the Viet Cong. Actually, the Viet Cong had more credibility and far more honor because at least they faced the US soldiers they were trying to kill. The same couldn't be said about Dear John letter writers. What was more cowardly, Ken thought, a Viet Cong's Punji stick pit or an American woman's Dear John letter? While both were designed to only maim (not kill) soldiers, the Dear John letter was far more debilitating and longer lasting. The Geneva Convention banned the use of biological weapons decades before Vietnam but still allowed a far more destructive, disabling weapon to be used in time of war—the Dear John letter. Ken believed the 1968 evening news back in the "world" should have also included, right alongside the daily body count of US soldiers killed and wounded in Vietnam, the exact number of soldiers maimed by—Dear John letter. He wanted to show the names of every woman caught sending such a letter on TV and published in local newspapers. The only thing a US soldier who received a Dear John had to do was merely forward the letter to their home town newspaper or TV news station—that would make it official and truthful. The women would be caught in their own handwriting. Case closed! Justice served! The routine practice of sending Dear John letters to US soldiers in time of war could be totally eradicated shortly after the first list of women's names was publically shown—guaranteed.

Ken wanted to go even further.

The terms *treason* and *Dear John* should also become synonyms in English language dictionaries. He knew how it could be done, too. Though fictitious, the practice of placing an *S* (for Scarlet Letter) on the clothing of promiscuous/adulterous women in the seventeenth century sent a strong message throughout colonial society. As a result, adulterous behavior declined significantly. In the same way, Ken believed placing a

"DJ" on the clothing of any contemporary woman caught sending a Dear John letter in time of war would also have a similar effect on the writing practices of future generations of women contemplating such a deed.

Obviously, Ken was hurting in a big way now. He was becoming unglued: "weapon of cowards," "US women equal to Viet Cong," "public listing of all Dear John writers," "Dear John synonymous with treason," "DJ monograms placed on women's clothing." Such thoughts and images were from a heartbroken solider, not a sane man.

Obviously, Ken Callahan was now becoming border-line, pyscho-crazy-nuts.

Lasting Revenge

What was more unsettling than becoming crazy, Ken was also getting angrier and angrier. Without a means of venting his sadness and anger, coupled with no possible source of relief in sight, all his feelings and rational thoughts just seemed to collide at once, exploding with a magnitude that shamed Hiroshima. His heartbreak quickly transformed into remorseful self-pity, and this sadness turned into a burning desire for revenge—but not just normal revenge. Ken needed and craved "lasting revenge." Nothing short of lasting revenge would even come close to alleviating the level of pain he was experiencing.

But, how?

He struggled and struggled finding a commensurate revenge alternative. Each day that went by without an answer seemed to make him sicker and sicker, angrier and angrier. His thirst for "lasting revenge" became an obsession, blinding to him to everything else in his miserable life in Phu Loi. Then one night on guard duty it came to him. Ken recalled how very effective Annette (his ex-girlfriend at Anne Arundel High School who changed his ambition in their senior yearbook) was in creating and executing her own ingenuous "lasting revenge" plan on him just the year before. Now, Ken wanted to taste that same kind of bittersweet satisfaction as Annette.

Her plan had been simple (only three words); it was emotional and personal (directly focused on his ego and self-esteem); it was simple and clear; it was uncorrectable (long-lasting/forever). Ken thought it was so thorough that doing so must have been very satisfying for Annette— well worth her vengeful effort. He wanted and needed to taste the same satisfaction, anything less than "lasting revenge" would be unworthy and frivolous.

Then it came to him. His vengeful logic went this way:

Writing more letters directly to Martha Elaine certainly was out of the question. No matter what words or appeals he used or how many letters he wrote, they would continue to come up short. Besides, he knew each of his letters was either discarded immediately by her, or even worse, shared with her new love along with lots of laughs. These images alone sent Ken over the edge with every thought. So writing directly to her was no longer an option—a waste of time. However, since writing was still the only tool at his disposal to fight back with in Vietnam, he sensed a precision letter written directly to her parents could have a much higher potential for "lasting revenge." His strategy took shape over several days and nights in between relentless mosquito bites and incessant mortars. He then realized it could work and possibly work extremely well.

Yet, instead of pleading to her parents for support or asking for a family intervention of some kind to get their daughter to return to him, he was going to do the very opposite. Ken was going to hurt them just as much as their daughter hurt him. Since Martha Elaine was engaged to him, her parents had to know all along about this whole thing with the other guy (a married man), however, they never contacted Ken to warn him. Their daughter was now engaged to two men; they had known about it. As such they were complicit. They deserved equal punishment and it added even more oxygen to Ken's flaming mind.

So, he explained to Martha Elaine's parents "in explicit detail," how he and their daughter had fooled around together right under their noses in their own house every night before he left for Vietnam.

"Yeah, that should really hurt," he thought to himself.

The more explicit, descriptive, intimate the illustrations of sex with their daughter (including all the lies he could conjure up), the more pain they would likely feel. After all, that was his goal—to inflect long distance, long lasting pain. If he couldn't hurt Martha Elaine directly, he was going to hurt the next closest thing—her parents. Painting the picture of their perfect daughter as a slut, whore, and sex-toy could prove effective. And, describing how she eagerly and passionately participated in the "sins of the flesh" would be additional icing on his cake of revenge. Her parents, being staunch Catholics, would certainly appreciate knowing that all their years of religious tutelage, so faithfully administered to their daughter, had failed miserably. After all, it was her parents who presented him with a Saint Christopher medallion on the day he left for Vietnam—a medal he had worn faithfully (and foolishly) every day since he arrived in Vietnam. "It will protect you from harm, Ken. This will also bring you peace during your most troubled times over there. Please take this with our love, support, and prayers," they said to Ken just before he boarded the Flying Tigers Airline to Vietnam.

He had never forgotten their words. Having never seen such a medal, he was impressed with their conviction and belief in a greater power—one that would be watching over him.

His letter could clearly show this "medal" certainly worked in protecting him from Viet Cong, but failed miserably protecting Ken from a more deadly enemy—their daughter, Martha Elaine. Ken hoped the level of pain they would experience by learning about their daughter, the family slut, would greatly exceed what he was feeling now and would likely be feeling forever. Martha Elaine was his first real love; she had been destined to be his only love, but no longer.

So he wrote it.

He then placed it in an envelope.

He then sealed it.

But, he could not mail it.

Rather, he carried it around for several days. The letter contained the worst language and best descriptions he could ever imagine and put in writing—all of which were lies, of course. Simple petting sometimes can be taken to extremes especially in the mind of a desperate, isolated, and scared young man, such as Ken. But, he didn't care about the truth at that time and in that place; he just cared about his revenge—his lasting revenge.

Then he mailed it.

The moment it left his hands, he regretted it. And he would regret it for the rest of his life. Ken eventually learned that revenge should be restricted to battlefields, politics, poker, and athletics, not love.

He never heard back from Martha Ellen or her parents.

Over subsequent weeks and months in Vietnam, Ken came to realize his letter to Martha Elaine's parents was just as bad as any Dear John letter sent to any soldier. He came to despise himself for doing so. His letter was the work of a real coward (just as cowardly in nature as the behavior of those same stupid women who sent Dear Johns to soldiers). By seeking his revenge in that way, he became no better than Martha Elaine or any of those other selfish, cowardly women.

Now, it was Ken who was the selfish one; he was the coward.

This vicious cycle of fear and thirst for lasting revenge had been completed, and he discovered the real target of his own lasting revenge was himself. He had to live with this shame and guilt forever. And, it all added more confusion to Ken's already chaotic, fragile state of mind in Phu Loi, driving him deeper into depression and even deeper into his pills.

Darvon was becoming his only friend, his only love.

He was now a true loner, an isolated soul, in the humanity of Phu Loi. That's when he used the same process and skills he had so well mastered growing up in Brooklyn: avoiding people and commitments, keeping his head down and eyes open, suspecting everyone of everything, trusting no one, running, hiding from everything, even himself. Since he had no real personal friends in Phu Loi, he couldn't talk to anyone about his Dear John feelings, his revenge, or his use of pills. So the best way for him to get through all this was to use more pills. And that's what he did.

Darvon had become his best buddy. And now, Ken blamed the absence of her letters for pushing him further along his path of addiction. The continual mortar attacks certainly didn't help things, but it was the Dear John coupled with his vengeful act that really accelerated his downward spiral into despair and drugs. In the past, he had always prided himself on staying awake in the bunker because falling asleep while on duty was a big no-no. He recalled this from boot camp - sleeping on duty was considered a court-martial offense in a combat zone. But now he didn't seem to care about that. The nights just seemed to pass easier with more pills. So, he took more and more. He would fall in and out of sleep as the mosquitoes continued their feast on the exposed parts of his body. The guys assigned to his bunker changed regularly, and they didn't seem to care one way or another about what he did. Besides, being court-martialed and being sent to Leavenworth Military Prison couldn't be any worse than where he was. So what was the real downside, anyway?

During the mornings, Ken would take more Darvon just before hitting his cot since it was his official downtime anyway. When he awoke, he would take more pills just before work details and again before bunker duty the next evening. This routine was well entrenched during his third month in Vietnam. Then one day he noticed he only had a few pills left. So he headed over to the medic's tent to get a refill. All he had to do was feign continuous headaches or eye aches and the medics would give him more pills. It was that simple in Phu Loi, Vietnam, in 1968. "No problem, let me know if these don't help, we can get you something stronger if needed" was the usual reply given by the medics.

Eventually, his work on details even began to deteriorate. His apathetic attitude evolved into prolonged lethargy concerning everything and everyone. And since his communications team still had not worked him into a permanent schedule of operations, his self-worth was now decreasing at an accelerated rate. He started showing up late and leaving early from work details and avoiding everyone in the process. Soldiers forced to work with him started avoiding him as well—they just didn't like him and even worse, they didn't trust him.

Steam and Cream

Since Martha Elaine no longer wanted him, he was determined to continue showing her how much he no longer wanted her. He still wanted to punish her somehow even long after the letter was sent to her parents. Ken was still angry, bitter, hurt, and betrayed. To get further satisfaction, he decided to lose his virginity. Ken was going to give it up fast and as many times as physically possible (not knowing what that even meant).

"That will show her," he kept saying to himself (even though deep inside, he was still broken in half just thinking about having sex with anyone but Martha Elaine—unimaginable just a few weeks before). To him, he was nineteen years old now, and it was time to give it up anyway. So, he began frequenting the local "steam bath" located right in Phu Loi Village. He had seen the single-story mud-and-brick building from a distance during work details but had never entered. The establishment was run by local Vietnamese. It was a safe place for soldiers to wash and bathe themselves after long patrols and field assignments. It cost only a few piaster (Vietnamese currency) or military payment certificates (MPC—official military currency in Vietnam), and soldiers could get a complete body shower and steam bath. And there was no time limit—soldiers could stay as long as they wanted. While showering or bathing, the Vietnamese would also wash uniforms and clean boots, if needed. It was a one-stop deal. "Come in filthy with a frown, go out clean with a smile" was the establishment's motto.

Once a soldier entered, he would be required to take off his boots and uniform and hang them on one of many poles in the dressing area or have them washed while he bathed. The soldier would place his personal possessions (wallets, money) into a plastic bag and carry it throughout the various sections of the steam bath house.

Weapons were not allowed in the steam bath house.

Such an establishment was more popularly called a "steam and cream" by seasoned patrons. Once showered and steamed, a soldier could then enter a small personal room where a young Vietnamese woman would render a "complete" body massage. While this would cost a little extra, it was well worth the investment because the girls would ensure "every part" of a soldier's body received the attention deserved. Additionally, if the soldier wished, he could have sex with the woman—a "short time" (the name given to describe the brevity and efficiency of getting aroused and getting off in record time). Of course, such extra services would cost a few more piasters or MPCs.

Ken had always been curious about "steam and cream" houses but never went inside primarily because of the many training lectures received that touted the variety of exotic venereal diseases running around Vietnam. Besides, at that time, Ken was still saving himself for Martha Elaine. He just wasn't interested then. However, in a very short period of time, Ken became a frequent visitor to Phu Loi's "steam and cream." He would make time to do so between noon and the start of his afternoon work detail. Because of the Darvon, his appetite diminished significantly, and he didn't require or desire lunch any longer. So he began using this time for visits to the "steam and cream" instead. His transition from virgin to "veteran lover" (if such sex could ever be called that) occurred fast and repeatedly after getting his Dear John letter; and even though Ken never had actual intercourse with the young women in the "steam and cream," he did encourage them to be as creative with their massage skills as possible.

He was never disappointed.

Anything to pass the time and get back home became the rule of the day. This was just another way to do so.

Nothing else mattered.

A Well-Deserved "Sucker Punch"

Then one evening while he was in his hooch, an older, much bigger soldier confronted him. His name was Harvey Lund, and he was entering the hooch when Ken was just leaving for that night's bunker duty. No one else was around. As usual during those days, Ken tried to walk around him without making eye contact or acknowledging him in any way which was a mutual ritual with anyone coming close to Ken. Instead of Harvey Lund just passing by, he stopped Ken by putting his hand on Ken's chest, holding him by his fatigue shirt. As Ken recalled, he was startled at the physical contact at first. And considering he had just taken a few more Darvons a little earlier, his reactions were much slower than normal. So Ken just stopped and faced him, still trying to figure out what was going on.

Harvey Lund then said, "Listen, Callahan, we've all had enough of your shit, you hear. What the hell do you think you're doing? You're just a parasite around here. If you haven't noticed, no one likes you, no one trusts you anymore . . . especially on bunker duty. You're going to get someone killed if you don't knock off the shit and get with the program. Stop taking those drugs and join the fight or you'll likely find yourself coming up on the receiving end of a bullet much sooner than you think." Lund's distain and anger at Ken were obvious. He had confronted Ken several times over the past few weeks but never as strongly and directly as this.

Ken, still a little foggy from the pills, was trying to process what was really going on. Once he did, he merely slapped Lund's hand from his fatigue shirt and took a step back. Ken didn't say word at first, still trying to formulate a proper response. Then he paused a little longer, and with a dismissive smirk, he said very simply, "Go fuck yourself . . . you asshole." Harvey Lund had had enough, especially after weeks of taking Ken's crap. He was actually hoping Ken would react in such a way as to give him a reason to crack him wide open. And that's what Lund did. He quickly drew back his right fist and let it fly. It landed squarely between Ken's chin and nose. It also came so fast Ken didn't even see it coming—didn't know what hit him. Besides, his reflexes had become so slow because of the Darvon; it's unlikely he could have stopped the blow even if Lund first yelled out the following warning in the slowest, most staggered speech allowable in a fight: "Hey, moron, it's coming now . . . you may want to duck right about now."

Ken was unconscious before he hit the floor. Harvey Lund looked down at him, stepped over his body, and walked to this cot at the back of the hooch. He dropped off his field equipment and exited the hooch, leaving Ken exactly as he had fallen. All this happened in less than a minute.

Eventually, Ken came to.

His mouth and nose were bleeding, and his jaw was throbbing. Two of his front teeth were loose, and his upper lip was so puffed out it was hard to see the lower part of his nose. Ken then staggered over to his cot and landed hard. Needless to say, he was late getting to his bunker that evening, but his bunker mate didn't seem to care one way or another. The only thing he said to Ken was, "Man, you look like shit."

It was the longest night of guard duty Ken ever had. This was when he realized he had to get out of Vietnam, and do so fast, thinking the next encounter likely would be much worse. He wasn't worried about mortars any longer; the threat from other soldiers now assumed top priority in his mind.

Adorable Little Copy Machine

Later that night, he looked over at the guy next to him in the bunker. He was snoring away, and Ken knew he wouldn't be missed if he left the bunker for a few minutes. So he snuck out and slowly made his way over to the headquarters administrative tent about three hundred yards away. It was around midnight, and he knew no one else would be there at that hour. He remembered seeing a copy machine in the tent a few days earlier when on work detail, so he pulled back the flap on the tent, entered, and closed it behind him. He located the copier and powered it up. After a minute or so, it was ready to go.

Ken then hit the Copy button but kept the lid open, thus allowing the bright light to flash across the glass top. He hit the Copy button a second time and the light scanned once again . . . only this time he leaned over and placed the right side of his face directly upon the glass, keeping his lazy eye wide open. Ken then pushed the button again and again and again, counting up to one hundred flashes before stopping. With each flash, his bad eye, his infamous lazy eye, was directly exposed to a searing beam of bright light as it whipped by. He was hoping prolonged exposure to such repetitive, highly intense beams of light, directly focused on his bad eye, would significantly degrade his vision more than it already was. Thus, his condition would be viewed as so bad that it would compel the army to send him back to the USA—out of harm's way.

"They're not going to keep me in this shit hole if . . . I can't see", was his rationale—his hope. Losing the full vision in one eye would be an easy thing to explain, especially since they already knew about his official amblyopia (lazy eye). He would say it just got worse since arriving in Vietnam. This was an easy, believable story. All he had to do was claim he had been having severe headaches over the past several weeks, and it had spread to his eyes; the medics could attest to this part, that's why he was taking so much Darvon. His visual deterioration combined with severe headaches was probably caused by all the hours of direct exposure to the sun. Since amblyopia couldn't be corrected (that's what the young doctor had said at the enlistment center in Dundalk), they would have no choice except to reassign him out of the combat zone.

It was full proof. He'd become just another unfortunate casualty in this crazy war—another statistic on a chart. Case closed. Ken gone.

He finished the last direct light exposure to his eye and turned off the copier. Naturally, Ken was temporarily blinded and somewhat disoriented, so he just sat for a few minutes trying to regain enough sight before heading back to the bunker. The next day, he planned to go see the medics and complain about his loss of sight and the continuation of painful headaches and eye aches. He would explain things had just gotten worse, and he was no longer able to see well while doing his work. With that, Ken thought he would be out of Vietnam within a few days, a week at the most. He was still only nineteen years old and had the rest of his life ahead him. With a medical discharge which was a honorable discharge, he could even receive the gratitude of a grateful nation for his service. This was his story, and he was going to stick to it.

The next morning, he decided to get a couple hours of sleep before heading over to the medic and making it official. He felt he had to be mentally alert to make his case and a few hours of shut-eye might help.

So he awoke around 10:00 a.m. He began making his way through the myriad of hooches, across the airstrip, and along the northwestern perimeter to the medic's station. He felt somewhat rested, but his jaw, mouth, and nose were still throbbing from the previous night's encounter in the hootch with Harvey Lund's right fist.

As he was making his way along the airstrip, he noticed a small group of soldiers gathered closely together on the ground. This was something he seldom saw in open spaces within the base camp because a grouping of soldiers gathered together in such a tight space made a great target for the Viet Cong—a lot of KIAs could result with just one single grenade or mortar. So this struck him as peculiar and it interested him. So he changed his direction slightly and moved a little bit closer to the group of men to check things out. He stopped about fifteen yards away and leaned against a parked deuce-and-half truck to observe things. Even though Ken's face ached and his head was exploding, he felt compelled to watch, if only for a few minutes.

Most of the soldiers were either kneeling or sitting on their helmets. Their weapons were on the ground next to them, and they were dirty and tired looking, obviously just getting back from patrol. There was one soldier standing above the group looking down on them and talking in a soft voice, so softly Ken couldn't make out what was being said. The standing-man was also gesturing over them with movements unfamiliar to Ken. So he inched a little closer along the truck to hear better. That's when he noticed the standing-man was not only wearing fatigues but he also had a colorful scarf of some kind around his neck hanging down to his waist from both shoulders. Also, Ken noticed his eyes were closed for extended periods of time, yet he was standing and speaking aloud.

The way this small group of men was drawn together had no formal military structure Ken could recognize. Rather, each man was on the ground sitting in random yet personally comfortable positions. They also seemed drawn together by some unseen yet common sense of purpose. They were listening intently to the standing man, and some men had their own eyes closed while moving their lips in sync with the words of the standing-man. Ken was now about ten yards away just watching and listening, even more curious than ever.

As the standing-man continued, Ken could only make out separate words, not full sentences. There were no military commands being yelled. There were no military instructions or operational plans being conveyed . . . nothing of the sort. The words he was now picking up sounded something like "everlasting," "kindness," "eternity," "forgiveness," "love," "faith." Ken thought to himself these were strange words in combat. A gathering of this kind felt somewhat familiar to him, but he couldn't recall exactly how.

As he continued listening and watching while still leaning against the truck, Ken's mind gradually drifted off to another time and place of his own. It was far away from Vietnam—a safe, warm place somewhere deeply hidden in his memory. He didn't feel his eyes close, but they did. The sun was not fully present in the day's sky, and the heat had not peaked yet, creating a moment that was surprisingly comfortable and comforting for Ken. It was a moment he could not resist or control.

So he just flowed along with the moment in time.

The endless stream of noises coming from helicopters, convoys, and distant artillery fire just seemed to magically fade from Ken's awareness. Actually, all the sounds of war that had been constantly bombarding his senses took a backseat to something much more familiar—something was now rapidly unfolding in his mind and he couldn't stop it; he didn't want to stop.

A Quick Trip Back Home—(Maryland, 1954)

While leaning on the side of the truck with his eyes closed, he could still hear the soft, gentle voice of the standing-man from afar. It was then that a peaceful stillness, a personal abandonment, engulfed Ken. He was falling into an emotional state that was deeply calming and relaxing. Then an ancient memory zoomed to the forefront of his mind, which seemed to generate an endless barrage of more memories. A flood of thoughts, feelings, people, and events, long buried, were being gently unearthed. His mind and body were now in two different places at once. Ken then gave himself permission to let go; allowing his mind to gently drift back in time, and far away from where he was actually standing at the moment.

It was a Sunday.

Ken's parents had taken him and his brothers, Walter and Butch, to church. He could recall this vividly because it was the first and the last time they ever went to church as a family. He was about five years old, and he could remember how warm, secure, and loving it felt inside a church. And he liked it.

His mind continued drifting through other times and places seemingly without meaning or direction. He then saw himself playing in a large field of grass on another summer day. He was with a dozen other little kids who were laughing and running around wildly as if finally freed from a long, boring school day. In the background, he heard another church bell beginning its slow, repetitive ring, which he tried counting. Little Ken wanted to test himself to see just how high he could count before he had to stop. On this day, he made it all the way to the twelfth ring and felt good about himself. Ken's focus then shifted to another scene on an equally beautiful summer day. There he saw several picnic tables, each overflowing with sandwiches, potato salad, Kool-Aid, cakes, pies, and fruit of all kinds. His mother and father were standing together, holding hands and talking with other parents. This was the only memory Ken had of his mother and father laughing and smiling together. A mild breeze was lazily making its way through the surrounding maple trees trying to ensure every leaf stayed in natural rhythm with the wind's unseen path. The sun was warmly embracing everything and everyone in sight while the unmistakable smell of freshly mown grass made everyone's senses fully appreciate life. It was just another one of those wonderful early summer days in Maryland.

To be precise, it was May 23, 1954.

Near the picnic tables was a small beach front area nestled alongside the slow-moving Magothy River in east Maryland. All the kids running around were in bathing suits so excited about finally being allowed to jump back into the river on this perfect day. A water hose, turned sprinkler and water fountain, was being generously wielded by one of the kid's parents. He was keeping them preoccupied until enough time had passed for them to safely reenter the river. Because of the "water hose turned water sprinkler," not a single kid was dry even though they were in the middle of a large grassy field. "Hey, kids . . . only fifteen minutes more to go then you can get back into the river. If any of you go in before then, you'll certainly get cramps and you'll drown. Then we'll have to take you to the hospital where you'll likely die. Then we'll have to have a funeral. Then we'll need to bury you in the ground," said an overly cautious mom as she yelled out to all the kids.

Then she continued, "You don't want that, do you? Do you? Well, neither do we . . . so stay out of the water until we say it's okay, OK?" Of course, the kids believed every word and obeyed. After all, it was 1954—a time when kids actually listened to adults, especially to parents. Ken was ready to jump into the water with or without permission. But he too obeyed. Being totally soaked from the "water hose turned water sprinkler," his mother called him to the picnic area to dry him off. She also had another motive for calling him over to her.

He came running immediately wearing his brand-new bathing suit. Little Ken was drenched to the bone as he leaped into her waiting arms which were filled with the biggest, fluffiest white towel ever made. She quickly scooped him up, gave him a very long and firm hug, and then began drying him off until he was "bone dry" (as his mother would say). He enjoyed being held by her in this way, especially when being wrapped so helplessly in her loving arms. It reminded Little Ken of a spectacular picture he had recently seen painted on the church ceiling. The painting showed hundreds of cotton clouds billowing their way through a crystal blue sky. In the midst of the clouds stood the most beautiful angel ever created by God. She was wearing a long white gown that seemed to magically blend into the surrounding clouds. The angel was also holding a plump little baby boy close to her breast in her strong arms while staring down into his eyes. The baby was returning her obvious love with the biggest smile ever to be planted on a human face. In the background, thousands of other angels were focusing their attention on both the angel and the plump little boy as they floated peacefully and joyfully along.

While Little Ken savored those close, caring moments with his mother, such memories would be few and short-lived. His carefree romps through water sprinklers, eating food whenever he was hungry and receiving warm embraces from his mother were fond memories soon to be relegated to a distant place in his mind and dusted-off only on the rarest of occasions. But for now, he was being genuinely loved by her. He didn't want to leave her warm embrace, and she wouldn't let him go.

His mother, Hilda Callahan, needed Little Ken to stay put for the moment because it was now time to show off his special birthday gift. It was his fifth birthday—May 23, 1954. She then called all the other kids and parents to the picnic table area. When everyone was gathered, including Ken's two older brothers, she had them sing "Happy Birthday" to him. Ken loved the attention and felt very special and loved. What he didn't know at that time was this would also be the last birthday party he would ever enjoy as a child. Hilda continued holding him tightly after his birthday song finished even though Ken was eager to get back to the "water hose turned water sprinkler." Then she said to the crowd, "Does anyone know what makes Ken's new birthday bathin' suit so different?" So all the parents and kids gathered closer and looked at him but didn't notice anything special at all. Seemed like a typical little boy's white bathing suit covering all his vital parts. It also had an animal design on the rear. "It's a nice bathing suit, Hilda, but what's so unique about it . . . looks like any other boy's bathing suit to me," one of the fathers yelled out from the crowd.

With that, a big knowing smile covered her face, and she quickly turned Little Ken around with his backside facing everyone. On the rear of his bathing suit was a picture of Yogi Bear's big smiling face. There was continued silence and puzzled looks everywhere. "I still don't get it," yelled another parent. His mother didn't give up her secret so quickly. She was savoring the innocence of such intrigue. Finally, she spilled the truth, "Well . . . wherever he goes today, ya' be able ta' not only see his 'bare' behind but also his 'bear' behind, too. Get it, now?" With that, everyone busted out laughing and kept pointing at Little Ken's little butt.

Little Ken didn't get it, but he started laughing along with everyone. He finally broke from his mother's arms and ran across the grassy park back to the "water hose turned water sprinkler." He and his friends were jumping up and down getting wonderfully soaked on this hot summer afternoon. That's when his friends started teasing him about his bathing suit. They busted out singing the following song to the melody of "Mary Had a Little Lamb"—"Kenny has a bare behind, bare behind, bare behind. Kenny has a bare behind, with skin as white as snow." This made him laugh even more.

These were Ken's fondest memories of his early childhood, long forgotten until now.

Chaplain Butta

His mind was still dancing through the "water hose turned water sprinkler" along with all his friends on his fifth birthday in 1954 when he suddenly felt his shoulder being grabbed. He also thought he was hearing a man's deep, bellowing voice coming down from parting clouds in the Vietnam's sky above, "Hey, soldier . . . soldier . . . you Okay . . . you Okay?" Ken continued struggling in his mind for a moment. He was still deeply implanted in Maryland, but somehow he was being pulled back to Vietnam . . . back to reality. He didn't want to leave the grassy field, his friends, or the water-hose-turned-water-sprinkler. For the first time since arriving in Vietnam, he had been truly at rest—an inner peaceful state that he didn't want to leave. But the man's voice got louder, dragging him reluctantly into the present. As his eyes slowly opened and his vision began to focus, he saw a man standing directly in front of him, no more than a foot away. He was shorter but much older than Ken. He also had dark features. Ken also noticed the man had a kind, gentle look about him, definitely not a military face. With further examination, he also noticed the man was an officer—a captain. This snapped him back to reality even more quickly.

When Ken finally regained his full senses, he nearly fell while trying to come to military attention. The group of soldiers who had been gathered together listening to the standing-man had since disbanded without Ken even noticing. His daydream visit back to the grassy field next to the Magothy River in Maryland must have lasted much longer than he realized. He was now at attention (kind of) facing an army officer; the standing-man he saw earlier with the group of soldiers.

Ken then tried to answer the captain's question the best way he could under the circumstances. "Yes . . . yes, sir, I'm Okay . . . was just getting a little rest, that's all . . . sorry, sir . . . it's been a long night," he said, obviously embarrassed as he continued scanning the captain's uniform.

Ken noticed the man belonged to the US Army Chaplain Corps assigned to the First Infantry Division—his patches and branch insignia screamed out this information to him right away. His name was Butta and had been conducting a religious field service with the group of soldiers; that's what Ken had stopped to observe. The service was an official military practice that Ken had never seen before. It all was making sense to him now as he continued to rid the fog and cobwebs from his mind.

Chaplain Butta looked Ken over very slowly from head to toe, primarily focusing on his bruised and battered face. After a few seconds of silence, he stated, "Well . . . you say you're fine, soldier, but you sure don't look Okay to me . . . what happened to you?" Ken's lips were still swollen, and the area around his left eye was covered by a deep purple bruise the size of Kansas. A sucker punch squarely hitting a person's face would have such an effect. Ken knew telling the truth about his confrontation with Harvey Lund would only lead to more trouble, so he lied.

Instead, he told Chaplain Butta it was caused by a nasty fall while on guard duty the night before. Chaplain Butta, being an astute observer of human behavior, immediately noticed Ken's nonverbals and verbals were significantly out of congruence when answering this simple, straightforward question. So he just nodded, even though he sensed something was truly troubling this soldier. That's when he decided to spend a little more time getting to know him—perhaps he could help somehow. The Chaplain didn't have another religious field service until noon and suggested Ken accompany him back to his office at the division artillery headquarters, have a Coca-Cola, chat awhile, and most importantly, get some ice placed on that "nasty fall."

Ken was stunned at the offer for many reasons.

First of all, it was a "suggestion," not an order, coming from an officer (an unnatural thing in Ken's mind). Second, he was an officer and Ken was an enlisted man (having a Coca-Cola together was fraternization, a no-no). Lastly, and most important to Ken, since arriving in Vietnam, no one, *no one*, had ever extended to him such a simple, kind gesture as this. All these thoughts raced through Ken's mind in nanoseconds. Little did he know at the time, but a single Coca-Cola coupled with a personal conversation were about to change his life forever. "Okay" Ken said cautiously.

His trip to the medics would have to wait a while.

With that, they both walked together to the First Infantry Division artillery headquarters. Chaplain Butta had a small office in the massive camouflaged tent. It housed the artillery commander, S1, S2, S3, and S4 as well as the command sergeant major (CSM). Each of these operational leaders were supported by a huge team of administrative specialists, two of whom shared Ken's hooch. Chaplain Butta's office was a small transient space that all chaplains shared. Since religious services required constant travel between field locations, sharing office space made sense for the command. No chaplain stayed in one place long enough to have his own office anyway. They walked through the headquarters' massive tent. On the way, Ken directly passed by the infamous copy machine that he had embraced so intimately just the night before. Seeing the copy machine's natural, provocative beauty close-up in daylight, Ken then knew why he "couldn't keep his eye off it."

After Chaplain Butta got some ice for Ken's face, they had a Coca-Cola together and casually talked about a variety of things—everything "except" the war. It was a personal conversation. Their time together lasted for nearly ninety minutes, a very long time in a combat zone. He asked Ken where he grew up, how well he had done in school, what sports he liked, if any girl was waiting at home for him (a sensitive subject that Ken politely avoided), what his plans were after Vietnam, what he missed most about the United States, and several other nonmilitary, non-war, non-Vietnam questions. Ken reciprocated with questions of his own for Chaplain Butta, including what it was like to be a chaplain—a man of nonviolence in a world as violent as Vietnam. Also, Ken was genuinely interested in why he had become a chaplain in the first place.

The Chaplain responded openly and genuinely to every question Ken asked. Ninety minutes flew by for Ken even though he wanted it to continue. It wasn't until well after their talk that Ken realized Chaplain Butta never brought up the subject of his "nasty fall," not even once. Most importantly, he realized it was the first real interpersonal conversation he had in nearly three months. Ken knew it was likely his own fault. He didn't know just how much he needed genuine interpersonal contact until now.

Over the past three months in Vietnam, Ken somehow lost touch with an important part of himself that he had discovered at Anne Arundel High School—a sense of self-worth. He never felt it growing up in the Projects and certainly not within his own home or family . . . but he did at that school as well as during first nine months training in the US Army. Both times were important for Ken. But in Vietnam, he didn't really know if his loss of self-worth was caused by drugs, bugs, dirt, weird sex, Dear John letters, mortars, rockets, long work details, or bunker duty at night. Or maybe it was just Vietnam in general. He didn't know, perhaps it was everything. Regardless, a simple conversation over a Coca-Cola with a stranger, a caring man, seemed to help him temporarily snap out of his long miserable, downward spiral into the depths of self-pity and remorse.

After their talk, Chaplain Butta offered to get together with Ken again on his subsequent visits to Phu Loi that occurred about twice a month. Ken said he would like that, and then he thanked Chaplain Butta for everything. It was then he realized that Chaplain Butta, a man of God, also never once spoke about religion, faith, or spirituality of any kind during their entire time together—or maybe that's exactly what he was doing, but in a way he knew Ken would understand. Most of the time, Ken forgot he was even talking to a captain or a chaplain in the US Army. It was more of a man-to-man, person-to-person, father-to-son conversation. And yet, somehow he was beginning to feel a little different about things.

As Ken was about to leave his office, instead of exchanging salutes, Chaplain Butta reached out and shook his hand. Ken was shocked. He had never shaken an officer's hand before—didn't know if enlisted men were even allowed to do so. But the quick, physical touch of a simple handshake felt good to him, real good.

It was now about noon, and the relentless heat from Vietnam's sun was forcing every living creature to seek shelter underground. Ken knew that he had to seek shelter too, but shelter of a different kind. He had a big decision to make now. He could turn north and finish his trek to the medic's tent. Or, he could head east and go back to his hooch. If he chose north to see the medic, he knew he'd either end up stateside with a medical discharge or in Leavenworth Prison with a dishonorable discharge. Even so, at least he would be out of Vietnam. And, that would still be a very good thing.

If he turned east, Ken would be going back to his hooch to prepare for another day of endless, mindless work details and another night in a mosquito-infested bunker. And there life in Vietnam would continue as usual. The alternatives were crystal clear to him. But his choice was not. He had never had a more critical decision to make. So Ken stood outside the headquarters for some time just reflecting on the day. That's when he felt something he had in his pocket. He reached in and removed the empty container of Darvon.

It needed a "refill."

At that split second, Ken Callahan realized that he, too, needed a "refill" of sorts; one for his soul and his mind. That is, he required a replenishment of pride, hope, self-esteem, and self-confidence. But it was a prescription that couldn't come from medics. It was then he also realized he needed to take personal responsibility and control of his life. That was the "refill" he truly needed. And that could only come from within—it was all about character. Then he knew what the chaplain had been doing all along. Chaplain Butta had intended to help Ken "rediscover" his own spirit—the essence of his true character. When placed in an environment like Vietnam, a bad man's character will become tarnished quickly and easily, even lost to him forever. But the core of a truly good man's character in the same environment will only be tainted for a short time, but never lost. Chaplain Butta sensed Ken was becoming a good man, a very good man. He was no different than all the boys on the edge of manhood. He only needed a little more help, support, and nurturing at this critical time in order for his true character to blossom.

And that was exactly what Chaplain Butta helped Ken discover.

The Turnaround

Ken slowly walked away from the headquarters tent with a different attitude. And when he came to the place in Phu Loi where he had to go either east or north, he chose to go east, taking him back to his hooch, back to his life. It wasn't a good life at the moment, but it was his. Only he could turn things around, and when Ken was crossing the ditch alongside the airstrip on his way back to his hooch, he threw the empty container of Darvon away. He wouldn't need any more pills. He had just gotten the best "refill" ever prescribed.

A few weeks later, Chaplain Butta returned for religious field services at Phu Loi. He and Ken met again and continued their discussion where they had left off. Eventually Ken started attending a few Catholic field services even though each session was conducted by a different chaplain. Ken liked it, and he began looking forward to attending such services whenever they became available to soldiers. After about five services, Ken expressed interest in learning more about Christianity. Chaplain Butta was honored to guide Ken on such a journey. And nearly two months later, he completed all his catechism lessons and received his first communion. Throughout his lessons, which consisted mostly of self-study in his hooch and talks with Chaplain Butta on his return visits to Phu Loi, Ken began changing his view of things even more, not only about war but also his place within it. His attitude also changed. And with that, his relationships with other soldiers quickly improved.

While the frequency of mortar attacks hitting Phu Loi did not decrease, Ken's fear and paranoia did. Coinciding with his own internal changes, he was also finally assigned to the division artillery communications team within the Quonset hut. He no longer had to pull bunker duty at night (which was a blessing in its own right), and he began evolving into a contributing member of the team. He felt his self-confidence and outlook improve every day. Ken was now applying the communication competencies he acquired in nine months of training—and it felt good. Additionally, Ken started to seek other ways to help his team. To him, keeping busy by doing important work seemed to be a key missing ingredient in his recipe for emotional survival in Vietnam. The more he worked, the more his self-esteem and self-confidence improved. Ken then volunteered to work extra hours and longer shifts when needed, even when not needed. In his off time, he usually found himself back in the communication Quonset hut, not in the "steam and cream." And when newbies from the States rotated into the unit, he was the first to volunteer to mentor and coach them. His superiors also started noticing and appreciating Ken's new contributions.

They began trusting him.

Ken felt he was finally a part of the team now. He was growing and contributing in ways he never thought possible just a few months earlier and now realized it took hitting rock bottom, coupled with giving himself permission to accept the kindness of a chaplain, that made the difference in his turnaround. Being in control of his life and accepting those things he could not control made a difference as well. In turn, this also allowed him to start placing more trust in the soldiers around him. His fear and paranoia diminished significantly (not completely) as well. Ken felt good about himself and even better about his chances of getting out of Vietnam in one piece.

Whether or not his personal and professional turnaround was ignited by a long overdue, well-deserved "sucker punch" to his face, didn't matter to him. He also didn't care if recovering from the negative impact of his Dear John letter was what really snapped him out of it. Kicking Darvon certainly helped, and learning how to tolerate thousands of mosquito bites while simultaneously swallowing tons of dirt likely made a big difference. Many things contributed to his transformation. However, Ken never seemed to get accustomed to the constant threat of mortar attacks; that would take more time. Perhaps his turnaround really just came down to a simple ninety-minute, Coca-Cola conversation with a kind man that triggered his journey back to humanity.

Regardless of the exact trigger, it was all good. The coming of age in Vietnam held no secret formulas for anyone in 1968. Each soldier had to find his own way. And there was no easy way out, no "clean getaway," this time for Ken.

He had to do it the hard way.

———◈———

CHAPTER 4

Lai Khe, Vietnam (1968-1969)

IN SEPTEMBER 1968, HE REACHED the six-month mark in Vietnam—a major milestone for him since he never thought he would ever last that long. Like all soldiers completing six months in country, he too was eligible for a little rest and relaxation (R&R)—a weeklong vacation in virtually any location within the Pacific Rim.

Ken chose Sydney, Australia. He was nineteen.

R&R

It was the perfect location and time for him. He was excited about being in a big city, meeting girls, wearing civilian clothes, and eating whatever, whenever, and wherever he wanted. This was also the "first" time in his adult life when he was actually on the town with money in his pocket. But the most significant thing he looked forward to was just a basic comfort of life—a bath. Ken wanted to take a long hot bath, in a real bathtub—one with as much hot running water as he wanted. After six months of showering once per week underneath an outside, makeshift shower made from a jet's discarded fuel tank with water warmed only by the Vietnam sun, Ken dreamed of having his own private bath at least for a while. Most importantly, he wanted a bath that wasn't also shared with a hundred men.

This was a simple pleasure he had truly missed. Ken was also looking forward to a few other "little" things that made a "big" difference, including:

- Walking on anything solid like a floor, sidewalk or paved street
- Flushing a toilet (what a luxury)
- Eating ice cream (anything cold would do)
- Putting on shoes without first emptying out alien life forms
- Going to a movie (heart be still)
- Watching TV (even commercials would be good)
- Wearing dry socks and dry underwear
- Eating a meal on a tablecloth using real silverware
- Feeling air conditioning blow on his face (just leave it on)
- Shaving his face with hot water
- Drinking anything out of a clean glass
- Driving a car (even though he still didn't have a driver's license)
- Seeing, smelling, and feeling a woman
- Talking with girls in English (even Australian accents would do)

He also wanted to listen to the Beatles over and over again. Ken heard they had just come out with a new song "Hey Jude" and wanted to hear it. There was also another thing Ken wanted to hear—someone, anyone calling him by his first name instead of "Callahan," "soldier," "specialist," "Hey you," or "asshole." In short, he just wanted to be human again.

All his wishes would come true (at least for a few days).

Once he arrived in Sydney in September 1969, along with dozens of other soldiers, he checked into the hotel assigned to him by the US Army. He didn't leave his room for the first two days on R&R. While some guys he met while traveling to Sydney wanted him to join them on the town that first night, he turned them down. He wasn't interested, not yet. All he really wanted to do was just stay in his hotel room, order room service, drink beer, watch Australian TV, and listen to music.

Alone.

Above all, he wanted to take that long, hot bath. And he did exactly that over and over again. He took a hot bath in the morning, at lunch, just before dinner in the evening, and once again before going to bed late at night. After forty-eight hours of this routine, his skin below the neck became so waterlogged and wrinkled, he thought he looked like the inner meat of a freshly steamed crab. He didn't care. He was no longer hungry. He was dry. He was safe. And he was not constantly looking over his shoulder, behind him, under his cot, or listening for incoming mortars. And that was good enough for Ken Callahan.

On his third night in Sydney, he finally ventured out. Ken and some buddies went to Kings Cross, the entertainment section of Sydney especially for US soldiers on R&R from Vietnam. He met a lot of girls, drank a lot of beer, and partied for the remainder of his time in Sydney. Ken also went on three tours during the daytime. The first tour was of the entire city of Sydney, the second was a harbor cruise on Sydney Harbor, and the third was into the countryside on the outskirts of Sydney. He met many local Australians on his tours who felt he talked funny because of his crazy Baltimore accent. Ken thought they sounded strange too, but he drank a lot of beer and laughed a lot as he discovered Australians' great sense of humor. And he discovered they loved Americans. It felt good to be admired.

The time flew by in Sidney and he was sad to leave. But strangely, there was a side of him that missed his work and his friends back at Phu Loi. And because his new role involved sending, receiving, encrypting, and decrypting messages from headquarters, he knew the First Infantry Division Artillery (his unit) was going to be redeployed from Phu Loi to Lai Khe (a village in the midst of a rubber tree plantation about twenty miles to the north). The move was going to happen around the time Ken was on R&R, but he didn't know exactly which date.

Ken hoped his unit didn't move out without him.

Just the thought of not being a part of his own unit's redeployment sent painful memories rushing through his mind about another "move" that took place without him—one that happened growing up in the Projects around 1962. That's when the fear of abandonment became a permanent part of his insecurities.

This is what happened.

Summer Breakaway Camp

Little Ken had done well academically in the seventh grade, and because he lived in the Projects (an underprivileged, low-income family neighborhood), he was selected from PS 239 to attend Summer Breakaway Camp for two weeks—free of charge.

The camp was located in rural Maryland (about twenty-five miles north of Baltimore). At this camp, Little Ken found trees, lakes and ponds, frogs, fish, snakes, horses, two swimming pools, and many other things so alien to the daily life in the Projects—where asphalt, brick, alleyways, clothes lines, and trash cans ruled the landscape. He was so excited about going to summer camp he couldn't sleep for several nights leading up to the temporary "parole" from 4139 Martin Court. His excitement was primarily driven by two personal reasons:

1. He heard kids were fed three meals each day, "every" day.
2. He would be spending fourteen fewer nights in his own home.

There were no other kids coming from the Projects because only one free slot was allocated by the school that summer. The only thing his mother had to ensure was Ken arrived at the departure point in downtown Baltimore on time and picked up on the last day of Summer Breakaway Camp two weeks later. That was it.

Little Ken's mother couldn't pass up such a deal.

So Hilda Callahan asked one of her boyfriends to drive Ken to the departure site in downtown Baltimore because she did not own a car. On departure day, Little Ken was ready to go at 6:00 a.m. even though the bus didn't leave until noon. Kids were not required to bring anything along with them, nothing at all—no change of clothes, no overnight bags, no toiletry items, no writing materials. Everything would be provided to them by the camp once they arrived. This fit into Hilda's plans perfectly since she did not have any of those items for Ken anyway. Plus, having him out of her hair for two straight weeks was a vacation for her as well. Her boyfriend picked up Little Ken and got him to Baltimore just in time. There were already about fifty kids (all boys ranging from ten to fifteen years of age) boarding two green-and-white buses as he arrived. Each kid came from other underprivileged, low-income neighborhoods across Maryland. There was another Summer Breakaway Camp just for underprivileged girls too, but it was operated at a different location in Maryland. The city didn't want to mix boys and girls.

Hilda didn't make the trip with her boyfriend to drop him off that day. She had other plans but promised to write him and would be there when he returned in two weeks. She had lied.

When Ken arrived at Summer Breakaway Camp, the camp counselors had him and the other kids turn in their clothes—shirts, shorts, socks, and even underwear. They could keep their shoes, but if they didn't have shoes or if they were too tattered and worn, shoes were provided. Their own clothes would be washed, stored away, and returned to them on their final day of camp. Each child was then given fresh "everything." Their used, dirty clothes were exchanged for clean clothes every other day, and they were given a personal toothbrush to use throughout the two weeks. Toothbrushes were also allowed to be taken home after camp if desired. Tubes of toothpaste were shared by groups of kids throughout two weeks and replaced immediately when it emptied.

Ken loved everything about Summer Breakaway Camp. There was a pool where he received swimming lessons; they played baseball and went on nature hikes. They also built campfires at night and sang songs until they were made to go to bed in their assigned, small wooden cabins. Each cabin housed about ten kids as well as one camp counselor, and the cabins were named after a famous Indian tribe as well. Ken's cabin was called the Apaches. During competitive games, kids competed on teams under the name of their Indian cabin. Ken especially enjoyed any water competition—in the pool, lake or river. His Apaches won first place in every distance swim event, and as a result, each Apache team member received extra marshmallows during evening campfires. Ken especially loved competing when food was the prize . . . just seemed to motivate him a little more. Out of all the wonderful things about Summer Breakaway Camp, Ken most enjoyed three "special" events that happened each and every day like clockwork. The first event was called breakfast. The second event was called lunch, and the third was dinner. At each of these special events, he was always the first kid in line and the last to leave the table. These special events were held in a place called the Chuck Wagon dining hall. There, Little Ken ate and ate and ate. Hot food always caught his attention, but Kool-Aid (called "Bug Juice"), coupled with peanut butter and jelly sandwiches were his favorite things to eat. If the counselors had allowed him to do so, it was the only thing he would have eaten at breakfast, lunch, and dinner. And during hikes through the lush woods of Maryland, the counselors also gave out candy bars and snacks along the trails. Ken would eat anything given to him, anything, anytime except one thing—M&Ms. His aversion to M&Ms was in the essence of his being. He'd have no part of them even when the counselors freely gave them out. It was the only thing he politely declined throughout the entire two weeks at camp.

Each day immediately following lunch, the counselors settled the kids down in their cabins for a rest period. That's when the kids were provided with paper, pencil, and envelope for writing home. Ken had never written a letter before and found it to be fun. The counselors would then collect the letters from the kids and take them to the main office at camp. There, each letter received a stamp and was mailed out in bulk. All incoming mail from parents or friends to the kids would be distributed during the after-lunch rest period as well. Little Ken wrote a letter home every day just like all the other kids, but he never received a letter during the entire two weeks. He was somewhat disappointed, but not really surprised and never let his disappointment be seen by the other kids—never. After several days went by without getting a letter from his mother, one of his new friends offered to share with him one of his own letters. At first, Ken was hesitant, but then he and his friend began reading letters together. He really liked that. And from that point on, they became the best of friends—Apache-friends.

In the evenings just before bedtime, each cabin of boys would also be required to shower in the Kids Clean-up Cave, the name fondly given to the shower area by the camp counselors. It was necessary for removing all the crud and crap the kids naturally acquired during a long day of play and competition. There, they would take showers and brush their teeth as a group. Each cabin had a specific time slot every morning and night, which meant they had to get there, get in, get wet, get dried, get brushed, and get out fast twice a day. The Kids Clean-up Cave consisted of a small wooden structure on the edge of the woods with a large mesh screen wrapped around it, which allow for cool breezes and open ventilation to naturally occur. It was divided into two sections under the single roof. First, there was the shower area where ten kids could easily get wet, soap up, and rinse off. At the far end of the room was a huge circular washbasin with multiple jets around it enabling all the kids to brush their teeth at once.

The "cave" had been designed for efficiency, but the kids were never, never efficient when it came to washing themselves; just too great an opportunity for more fun. They always stretched things out over as much time as possible. As such, no cabin of kids ever stayed within their assigned time slot—it was impossible.

This Is a Toothbrush

One evening at the "cave's" washing basin, Little Ken's new Apache-friend noticed he was having some trouble handling his toothbrush and toothpaste. It appeared to him that Little Ken didn't know how toothpaste was placed on a toothbrush without having it all fall off. Little Ken had missed the brush part of his big red toothbrush on several attempts but eventually got it to stay on during his last try. He also noticed Little Ken seemed unsure about how or where to start brushing in his mouth. His Apache-friend had become somewhat concerned and wanted to help him, just as he did by sharing his own letters from home. But he didn't know how to approach him. So his Apache-friend, seeing Little Ken struggling even more, just moved over a little closer to him at the washbasin and whispered,

"Let me show you how to use that thing . . . it takes a couple of tries at first really . . . . took me a couple of tries when I started brushing . . . here's how it goes . . . you'll get the hang of it in no time."

He said it in a way trying not to draw the attention of the other kids.

Even though Little Ken was now twelve, it was the first time he had been taught how to use a toothbrush, and since he never had owned one, this was all new to him. "Well . . . I've seen it on TV, but I haven't gotten a toothbrush of my own yet . . . so yea, show me more . . . thanks," Ken replied quickly and eagerly and was not embarrassed at his lack of experience in this area. He just assumed all kids his age were also learning how to brush and was quite thankful for the help. Because it was so busy and loud in the "cave" with ten kids yelling, playing, slapping, and screaming, no one was paying any attention to the personal instructions Little Ken was getting from his Apache-friend.

After a few more tries, Little Ken had brushing down pat. He liked it too. It tasted a little weird at first, kind of a burning sensation, but it felt good.

Little Ken's next big brushing challenge was learning how to hold the toothbrush in a way that would allow him to reach each tooth, especially the back ones. At one brief moment in his process, Little Ken was using both hands at the same time to hold his toothbrush handle while brushing. When his Apache-friend saw this, he quickly reached over and stopped him. He glanced around to see if any of the other kids were looking (they weren't) and then showed Little Ken how he could get to the bigger teeth in the back by either switching hands or by tilting his wrist slightly. "Either way works for me, Ken . . . most of the time all I do is just change hands . . . it's just quicker."

Little Ken was a fast learner and got it right away. However, when his mouth was full of toothpaste foam, he swallowed it instead of spitting it out and rinsing afterward. His Apache-friend intervened once again after seeing the expression on Little Ken's face as he responded to the taste of dissolving toothpaste going down. Ken was so appreciative learning that final little step; he didn't want to repeat it ever again. And he wouldn't.

Hilda Callahan never invested the time to help her kids learn the basics about brushing or about any other personal hygiene necessities for that matter. Two of Little Ken's teeth had to be extracted before he was ten simply because she waited too long to take him to a dentist. Little Ken complained to her about his teeth hurting for quite some time; she just ignored him, hoping the pain would just go away. Both teeth could have been saved, but they became so abscessed and infected, they just had to come out. Even worse for Little Ken, his teeth had abscessed so badly that the Novocain administered was not effective at all; and since he was also so young, the dentist was afraid to use anything to put him to sleep, fearing the worse could happen. Therefore, he had both teeth extracted without any real anesthetic at all. After a lengthy and very painful experience in the dentist chair, both teeth were finally extracted. The good news was Little Ken passed out from the pain halfway through the procedures while still in the dentist's chair. When he came to, he was at home with a hole on both sides of his jaw the size of watermelons. Ken avoided dentists from then on and never again complained to his mother about subsequent toothaches, no matter how much pain he was in. And he didn't see another dentist until he joined the US Army years later.

He was sorry when Summer Breakaway Camp came to an end. It seemed he was just settling-in when it was time to leave. He was especially sorry about leaving his newly found Apache-friend, from whom he learned so much and who he came to trust in such a short time.

However, Little Ken would be even more disappointed when he arrived home.

Abandoned Or Just Temporarily Misplaced?

The green-and-white Summer Breakaway Camp buses pulled into Baltimore City's downtown area, not far from city hall. It was around 6:00 p.m. on the final day. A large group of parents and families were waiting there as their sons, brothers, and friends scampered out of the buses. Even though only two weeks had passed, the reunion-like atmosphere was as festive as a military transit ship pulling into New York City harbor after World War II.

It was a controlled chaos of joy, laugher, chatter, and fun.

Two weeks was just too long for some families to be separated, even under such pleasant circumstances. It took over thirty minutes for all the kids to say good-bye to each other and to thank their wonderful counselors whom they had come to know so well. Then each kid ran into the waiting arms of their loved ones and were hugged, kissed, and quickly hustled away to loving homes throughout Baltimore City and across the state of Maryland. As loud and crazy as these family reunions started, they ended with an equal silence and calm. One of the two buses had already departed, heading back to Summer Breakaway Camp to get ready for the next bunch of kids scheduled to arrive in a few days. Only one bus and two camp counselors remained. They were waiting for the final parents to arrive and collect the last kid who was patiently waiting on the curb behind the bus.

It was Little Ken Callahan.

"Hey, Ken, where are your parents?" one counselor asked with genuine concern.

Feeling embarrassed, Little Ken didn't know what to say. He knew deep inside that his mother either forgot him or just chose not to come. Either way, he sensed it would be a long, long wait. So he just shrugged his shoulders without directly answering the counselor. Another thirty minutes passed with no one arriving, so the counselor had to make a decision. "We're sorry Ken, but we've waited as long as we can and we have to go. Is there anyone we can call to come get you?"

Again, Little Ken merely nodded his head and shrugged his shoulders. He knew he'd have to find his own way home—nothing new for him. As the counselors went back to figuring out what to do with him, Ken slowly turned and silently walked away without the counselors noticing his departure. Being unfamiliar with the inner city of Baltimore at that age, Little Ken really didn't know where he was heading, but knew he couldn't stay there. He was very comfortable on the streets of Brooklyn and even more comfortable in the asphalted alleyways of the Projects, but this part of the city was different, really different. It was unknown to him and a little scary because it was so very big. Even so, he sensed that moving was better than staying put . . . thinking he'd be an easy target out in the open, so he was going to rely on his mobility and "survivor scan" skills to stay safe.

So he headed out . . . somewhere . . . anywhere . . . nowhere.

After a while, he found himself walking among the tallest buildings he had ever seen. The endless traffic, hustling people, and deafening street noises were foreign to him, yet kind of exciting too. While staring up the side of a huge brick building that reminded him of the *Daily Planet* newspaper building where Clark Kent worked in the 1950s *Superman* TV series, Little Ken recalled a singular memory from his past. He had been sitting atop a huge building similar to these when he was about four years old. His two brothers, Walter and Butch, were with him along with his mother. There was also a man present taking a photo of them atop this building. He thought the man was his father but couldn't be sure and he didn't know what his family was doing there or how they got atop such a big building, but did remember it was a good feeling of being secure and loved. It was the Empire State Building in New York City. And he was not afraid.

It was a very good memory.

So Little Ken continued his aimless walk through Baltimore City. Eventually he passed the last of the tall buildings. Then he realized he was entering a neighborhood with long row houses aligned on both sides of the street. Even though it was now early evening, the intense heat of the day was still being released from the asphalt sidewalks and tar streets of Baltimore's inner city. This neighborhood seemed somewhat familiar because there was a lot of activity, chatter and noise all around him, just like the Projects. And, the friendly smell of asphalt also made him feel at home. Every house also looked exactly like the other, and each had similar white asphalted porch steps as well. And all the houses were linked side by side just like his neighbor in Martin Court. But despite all the similarities, this was not Brooklyn; it felt different, smelled different, and looked different in some unfamiliar ways. And the people were different too—real different.

They all were black people.

Little Ken was in a black neighborhood of Baltimore City.

A group of kids were in the street playing a game. He couldn't tell, but it seemed like baseball. Several families were gathered outside on their porches just talking, laughing, and listening to a kind of music Little Ken didn't recognize; it certainly wasn't any music he ever heard before. However, he soon recognized the familiar smell of whiskey and cigarette smoke whiffing into his nostrils from some unknown source as he continued making his way through this strange neighborhood. Even though it was different from the Projects, he was more curious than scared. Then he wondered if it could be Mr. Williamson's neighborhood. He was a black man too and lived somewhere far from Brooklyn, maybe they knew him, Little Ken was thinking to himself. He then was about to cross the street to ask one of the adults if they knew Mr. Williamson, and if so, perhaps he could help him get back home to the Projects of Brooklyn. But before he could do so, he heard a single voice yell.

It came from the group of kids who had been playing in the street: "Hey look!"

It was such a loud scream, even Little Ken stopped and looked to see where the kid was pointing. Unfortunately, the kid was pointing in his direction. With that, all the other kids in the street and the families on nearby porches stopped what they were doing. Everyone was now looking at Little Ken. He didn't understand what was happening or why he had become the center of attention, but he then felt a rush of heat quickly engulf his face and rush through his brain. It was the same type of feeling he got every time Butcher-Bird and his mother pinned him on the ground or trapped him in one of his tight escape places at 4139 Martin Court.

That's when Ken panicked.

So he started running back toward the direction of the tall buildings but now he was sprinting down the middle of the street, not on the sidewalk. His feet were trying to keep pace with his panicking mind, but he was failing miserably. Ken was nearing the end of the neighborhood when he heard the pounding footsteps of the kids closing in. The first group caught up to him and held him as the others formed a circle around him. Ken was surrounded; there was no "clean getaway," not this time. Then one of the bigger kids came right up to his face and said, "What are you doing here? What do you want?" Little Ken didn't know what to say or do. So he just started telling the big kid his story about getting lost and was just trying to find his way home. His words were rapid and endless as his eyes kept darting among the many other faces that had surrounded him; each face appeared to be angry, smiling, or just curious. He just couldn't tell. That's what confused him even more. Little Ken also didn't know if he had to fight them, cry or just laugh along with them.

Meanwhile, the circle of kids was tightening.

Then in the middle of his explanation, the loud screeching sound of grinding brakes rose from behind Little Ken and the group of kids. They all jumped, including Little Ken—everyone was frightened out of their wits at this surprise, startling noise. Little Ken turned and saw the green-and-white Summer Breakaway Camp bus coming to an abrupt halt only feet from the circle of bodies gathered in the center of the street. Its doors flew open and out stepped a Summer Breakaway Camp counselor. Without hesitation, he glided through the sea of kids as easily as a wave breaking through rocks on a beach and marched directly up to Little Ken, grabbed him by the arm, and started scolding him without even acknowledging the presence of all the other of kids. "Ken . . . there you are. We've been looking an hour for you; we didn't even notice that you wandered off at first then we didn't know which direction you went. Never do that again. So now get your butt back on the bus; we got to get you home . . . your parents are going to be worried sick about you." He then dragged Little Ken by the arm and put him back on the bus.

The counselor then turned and said the following to the group of kids in the street, "Hey thanks kids. Thanks for helping us find him. If you weren't having this big party in the middle of the street, we would likely had driven right by and missed him. You've all been a big help, thanks again."

The kids were stunned; no one responded, not even the bigger kids. They just watched as the door closed and the bus slowly pulled out and continued on its way. Little Ken took a seat without knowing if the counselors were angry, scared, or relieved. He really didn't care at that very moment how they felt; he was just glad to be heading somewhere.

The counselors then asked Little Ken how to take him home, but he couldn't give any directions because he still didn't know where he was. Yet there was one thing he knew quite well—his address, 4139 Martin Court, the Projects of Brooklyn. That was all the two counselors and the bus driver needed to know; they would figure the rest out shortly.

And they did. Twenty minutes passed before the bus hit Tenth Street and Patapsco Avenue in Brooklyn. The Projects was only a few blocks from this major intersection, quite close to the Victory movie theater—one of Little Ken's most favorite, familiar places. He could make it home from there even wearing a blindfold if needed. Little Ken thanked the counselors and the bus driver. They let him out, turned the bus around, and headed back to Summer Breakaway Camp. They were well behind their time schedule for sure, but they also likely felt a lot better knowing the last of the kids got home safely. Little Ken watched as the bus turned and pulled away, then he headed up Tenth Street to the Projects, to *his* Projects and to a very familiar place. He never thought seeing the Projects would be such a wonderful sight, but it was on this day.

Unfortunately, he'd soon wish he had stayed on the bus.

Mrs. Baumann

Little Ken sprinted up Tenth Street and headed directly for the Martin Court alleyway in the Projects. When he saw his unit he ran up to the back door; it was locked (nothing new). Not only was it locked, but also all the lights were off. He quickly noticed the window shades had been removed. It was about 8:00 p.m. on this balmy summer evening, and the day's light was still slowly transforming itself into shades of purple and gray. That's when he pressed his face and hands on the windowpane to get a closer look. He noticed there was no furniture inside, none. The kitchen and living room were as empty as an abandoned warehouse. The Callahan family either had been evicted, or they had just simply moved out quickly and efficiently. Ken couldn't be sure. So he just sat on the back door steps wondering what happened and what to do. After a while, he walked to nearby neighbor's unit at the end of Martin Court to ask about his family.

The neighbor, Mrs. Baumann, was a kind elderly woman who lived alone. She had known Ken for many years and liked him, but only saw his little sister occasionally and didn't know her well. However, she didn't like anything about his brother, Butch, or his mother, Hilda.

Mrs. Baumann took him in for the evening—he stayed for several days. She didn't know exactly what had happened to his family, but she remembered seeing them with a couple of men moving things out of their unit a few days earlier. She didn't know where they went, but she promised to find out. Mrs. Baumann reassured Little Ken that his family was fine and they would surely be coming for him soon. In her heart, she didn't really know but she lied to him anyway.

Having come to know Hilda Callahan well over the years, Mrs. Baumann knew anything could have happened. Yet, she didn't want to burden Little Ken with such things now, not this evening. He just looked too tired, beat and hungry. So she made him a late dinner and they ate together. That's when he told her every detail, everything that happened at Summer Breakaway Camp. He told her about the swimming pool, the competition (and all the extra marshmallows he won), the hikes through the woods, and the many animals he saw. Of course, Little Ken also told her everything about the Chuck Wagon dining hall—his favorite place of all at Summer Breakaway Camp, especially about being able to eat three times a day, each and every day. He also spent quite a bit of time telling her about his Apache-friend from whom he learned so much, including brushing teeth and writing letters. He wanted to share with her how he felt about not getting a letter from his mother while all the other kids did. But he didn't. Instead he said, "And I've got something to show you, Mrs. Baumann."

With that, he reached into his back pocket, took out a long slender object wrapped in toilet paper with a rubber band tied tightly around it. Mrs. Bauman was anticipating what it was as he slowly, very slowly unveiled it for her. First, he gently placed it on the table as if he was placing a baby bird back in its tree after a long fall. Then he scooted his chair back, stood up, and just looked down at it for a moment. He started carefully removing the rubber band without disturbing the loosely wrapped tissue surrounding the contents. And with both hands, he began softly unfolding layer after layer of tissue just as methodically and disciplined as a mother surgically removes pins from a baby's diaper. When the final layer of tissue was removed, he stepped back to just admire the special contents. Little

Ken then looked over at Mrs. Baumann, whose excitement had begun rising in anticipation just watching the formal unveiling ceremony of Little Ken's Summer Breakaway Camp prize.

There was a long period of silence. Neither one of them spoke a word; they both just stared down at the wonders he unveiled. When she finally got a full glimpse of the prize, Mrs. Baumann's look of amazement and excitement quickly turned into curiosity, then to puzzlement.

It was a toothbrush—"his" toothbrush!

Little Ken looked at her and started his presentation, "See . . . they gave it to me . . . to keep . . . said it was mine if I wanted it . . . really. I didn't steal it . . . was a gift . . . they said I earned it . . . so I kept it. Really . . . isn't it beautiful, Mrs. Baumann?" Little Ken was as excited and proud as any athlete showing off their first victory medal. He was beaming with pride.

Mrs. Baumann was genuinely confused but only at first, then came to understand—fully understand. She looked over at Little Ken who was still standing there staring at her with the biggest smile she had ever seen on this boy's face. In all the years living so close to him in the Projects, she had never seen him so happy and proud. It was amazing to her that this was a side of him she never knew existed.

She then replied, "Oh, Ken . . . that's the most beautiful toothbrush I've ever seen . . . and I especially like that bright red handle too." Little Ken continued to beam. He then leaned down and began spreading the tissue back even further from his red-handled toothbrush, making it appear like a beautiful colored egg nestled snuggly at the bottom of an Easter basket. "Yea . . . she's a beauty, huh." Ken couldn't seem to take his eyes off of it as he continued, "And . . . YOU can use it too, Mrs. Baumann . . . anytime you like, really . . . just ask me . . . I promise . . . anytime you like."

With that, Mrs. Baumann's eyes filled with tears. She didn't blink for fear of making a scene. So instead, she just walked around the kitchen table and gave him a long and very warm hug. Then she thanked him for such a generous offer and told him no one ever offered to share their toothbrush with her, never in all her life.

She was genuinely moved.

Little Ken went on and re-explained that he was allowed to keep it; that he hadn't stolen it. The counselors said it was a gift from the Summer Breakaway Camp and that any kid could keep the toothbrush he was given. They said that on the first day of camp, and they kept their promise. Little Ken just couldn't understand why the other kids just threw theirs away on the last camp day.

But he had kept his.

Mrs. Baumann enjoyed hearing about all Little Ken's experiences at Summer Breakaway Camp as much as he enjoyed sharing it with her. She hadn't had such a long conversation with a young person for quite some time. They both laughed and talked together for hours that evening—it was the first and only sit-down meal Ken ever remembered having in the Projects. And he'd bet that if Mrs. Baumann had known beforehand that he was going off to Summer Breakaway Camp for two weeks, she would have written a letter to him, maybe twice. When they finished their "dinner party" together, she went to her bedroom and returned with a pillow, sheet, and blanket. She put it on the sofa in her living room for him; he was spending the night. Later, Mrs. Baumann was washing the dishes and cleaning off the kitchen table but couldn't help and watch Little Ken's routine of getting ready for bed. She became very curious as she watched him from a distance. First of all, he had to brush his teeth. He just had to. Little Ken spent a very long time in the bathroom just brushing and brushing; she could hear him doing so for quite a while. Then he came out of the bathroom with a smile beaming so brightly it seemed to dim every light in her house. She could tell he paid close attention to his Apache-friend's tooth brushing lessons.

Mrs. Baumann noticed how he approached the sofa where his bedding had been placed. At first, he just stood there staring down at it. His joyful, playful mood seemed to quickly change to something more pensive, something different that she couldn't identify. Little Ken then slowly picked up the pillow, holding it at arm's length from his body, like a stinky pair of underwear. He then separated the pillow from the pillowcase and walked over to the far wall and placed the pillowcase on the floor. He then came back to the sofa and picked up the blanket and sheet and wrapped it around him from head to toe while still standing, the way he saw Indians do on TV westerns. Then he laid down, placed his head flat on the pillowcase-less pillow, and kept one arm fully exposed outside and above the blanket; a second later he was fast asleep. As Mrs. Baumann was getting ready for bed herself, she walked by him and couldn't help but notice his toothbrush was still being held firmly in his exposed hand on top of his blanket.

Little Ken spent the next three days and nights with Mrs. Baumann. Then on the fourth day after leaving Summer Breakaway Camp, he was reunited with his mother, brother and little sister. They had moved in with Hilda's new boyfriend, Butch Hanley. He owned a trailer on Bell Grove Road in Pumphrey, Maryland, which was adjacent to Brooklyn Park only a few miles from the Projects in Brooklyn.

Hilda Callahan never explained why she didn't pick up Little Ken at the end of Summer Breakaway Camp in Baltimore City as she had promised she would do. And she didn't explain to Mrs. Baumann or to Little Ken why she didn't come looking for him until three days later. She didn't have to explain a thing to anyone. After all, she was Hilda M. Callahan.

She merely said to Little Ken, "I knew ya' find your way home, boy . . . ya' always did." And that was that.

When Little Ken finally got settled in Butch Hanley's trailer, he started looking for his clothes and things. He went through several boxes but couldn't find anything. Then he saw a small storage compartment located in the back of the trailer. There, he discovered something he'd never forget—a stack of envelops—each written to her in Little Ken's handwriting with identical return address—Summer Breakaway Camp.

She had received and saved every letter he wrote to her. However, not one letter had been opened, not one had been read. Even so, Little Ken felt a little better about one thing—at least she did not throw them away. In his mind, he hadn't been totally forgotten or totally abandoned, after all.

He had just been "momentarily misplaced."

Lai Khe

After returning to Saigon from R&R in Sydney Australia, Ken hopped on a C-130 and flew directly into Lai Khe, Vietnam. His unit had, indeed, moved without him, but he didn't feel abandoned, forgotten or misplaced, not this time.

Ken Callahan never set foot in Phu Loi again. He remembered passing by the base camp about a month after R&R while on a convoy from Lai Khe to Saigon. He was traveling along Highway 13 (Thunder Road) when he saw the strong perimeter defenses, solid bunkers, and vast open fields surrounding the base camp. So many memories also flashed through his mind about his early days there as his convoyed passed. He recalled . . . Darvon, Dear John, dirt, rain and mud, mosquitoes, spiders, scorpions, "steam and cream," mortar attacks, bunkers, sandbags, rocket attacks, barbed wire, foo gas, sucker punches, night guard duty, Quonset huts, chaplains, and catechism. So much change, so much pain, yet so much growth too. Even though he sensed he would likely never set foot in that place again, he knew somehow his memories there would be a part of him forever.

He was right.

Ken was looking forward to Lai Khe as the C-130 approached the landing zone, and secretly hoped to find at least one functioning bathtub there. He would be very disappointed. Even though both Phu Loi and Lai Khe were only twenty miles apart, Lai Khe was unique in so many ways. First of all, it was located about forty miles north of Saigon, making it far more greener but also more remote. As a matter of fact, Ken's unit was now located in the midst of thousands of rubber trees—a former French rubber tree plantation that decades before had employed local Vietnamese villagers to produce raw rubber. It was still a very hot place, but a little cooler than Phu Loi because the presence of all the trees and foliage just made it feel that way. Ken quickly noticed even the slightest difference in temperature worked miracles on his attitude and outlook. His communication unit was now housed within a large bunker within the rubber trees versus in an old Quonset hut in the middle of a dust, dirt and mud wasteland of Phu Loi. And it was located closer to the division artillery headquarters and to the mess tent as well. Wooden pallets and planks formed walkways between facilities and bunkers, allowing quicker and easier foot travel. And Highway 13 ran through the center of the basecamp with the village of Lai Khe (local Vietnamese stores and homes) actually situated inside the parameters—a rare exception for any US military installation in Vietnam. Ken quickly discovered his new hooch wasn't new at all. It actually was an old, traditional army canvas tent likely held over from the Korean War. But it housed fewer men, about six. That was good because even though there was less space overall, when it came to one's personal privacy, the tent was considered a prize.

After his R&R in Australia, he settled into a routine operational schedule at Lai Khe. Ken was now on a rotating shift within the communication unit's operations area, and he was given more and more leadership opportunity, which he now gladly accepted. And in October 1968, he was promoted to buck sergeant (E-5) in charge of an entire team of communication specialists. This meant he worked the day shift and his life improved even more. Ken was now dealing with people he trusted; they trusted him and he continued gaining the respect of the senior enlisted staff and officers alike.

He was growing and changing for the better. Equally important, he was off the pills altogether. Ken was also finally getting over the loss of his fiancé, Martha Elaine, and his personal faith in something bigger than himself had helped change his attitude for the good. When each day shift ended at Lai Khe, he also had a little more personal time on his hands and even though he no longer was taking Darvon, he did start experimenting a little with marijuana.

Ha` Pronounced Wa'

He was first introduced to marijuana in Lai Khe Village. This was the place soldiers would go to grab a few beers, kick back in the bars and relax while listening to American pop and soul music being "almost" played well by local Vietnamese bands. And of course, there were young women to help soldiers unwind. One day, when Ken was in the hooch of a beautiful Vietnamese woman, she asked him for a cigarette after sharing a little affectionate pushing and tugging together. Ken never smoked cigarettes and told her so when she had asked. She looked surprised and questioned him with credulity, in perfect English, "I see . . . then Ken tell me, what is it that do you do with your monthly cigarette rations from the army?" Ken was immediately impressed by her knowledge of the US Army but not surprised. Even though she was a young woman, about Ken's age—nineteen, he knew in "Vietnamese years" that meant she was also much older and more mature than her chronological age. She had gotten around; she also liked and trusted US soldiers.

Her name was Ha` (pronounced as "Wa").

Little did Ken know at the time, but the meaning of her name would become a lifetime memory for him. In short, he'd never view another "river" the same after knowing Ha`. So he told her he didn't get cigarette rations often, but when he did he just gave them away to other soldiers who did smoke, or he traded them for cassettes, books, beer, or anything else he needed yet couldn't afford. Hearing that, she smiled and then made him a proposal. If he brought to her any of his cigarette rations, he could exchange the tobacco in each cigarette for marijuana. That is, she would physically remove the tobacco from each individual cigarette without damaging the cigarette paper, filter, or the package. She would then replace the tobacco with well-cut, highly refined marijuana. In doing so, each cigarette in each pack would be repackaged and resealed perfectly and flawlessly—appearing on the surface as just another pack of regular cigarettes. He was very surprised and said, "No way . . . it's impossible to replicate a cigarette like that. It would be so obvious people would know it was fake or it had been tampered with."

In the past, he saw guys trying to roll a simple joint using regular cigarette paper and it always turned out to be a mess, even though they could still smoke it. Yet he was still impressed at the concept and wanted to see one. If she could actually do this, it would prove to be the best hiding place for grass ever imagined—right out in plain sight of everyone, including any MP, NCO, or officer.

"*Genius,*" Ken thought to himself, if it proved to be true.

Ha` accepted his challenge. She quickly pulled a single pack of perfectly sealed cigarettes from under her bed. Ken examined it. It was untouched, just like any pack of manufactured cigarettes purchased in a PX (Post Exchange). She then broke its seal and opened it. Instead of tobacco, it contained twenty "grass cigarettes" perfectly packed just as she had said.

He was astounded.

Ken learned from Ha` that Vietnamese people prized American tobacco above everything, except money, food, and family. American tobacco was highly sought because it was much milder and better tasting than tobacco grown anywhere in Southeast Asia. Local tobacco was harsh tasting, fast burning, and, to Ken, it stunk—always smelling like deep-fried tennis shoes. That's why this deal made sense and why it was such a fair exchange: Vietnamese grass (which she had plenty of) for American tobacco (which Americans had plenty of). No money involved at all—no piasters, MPC, or dollars needed. It was a straight-up exchange—one commodity for another commodity. The longer he thought about this, the more he knew it would be a good deal for anyone who liked to smoke grass. Unfortunately, he did not smoke and had never tried grass even though he had been around it when other soldiers fired-up. He just wasn't interested but thanked her for the offer anyway.

Ha` was an attractive, smart young woman who spoke three languages fluently—Vietnamese, French, and English. That's why Ken was attracted to her in the first place even though there were far more beautiful girls in Lai Khe Village. And Ken was soon to learn something else about her that he would come to admire. She was also very, very persuasive, relentlessly so. "Ummm, so you're telling me, Ken, that you're a 'cherry boy' when it comes to smoking grass?" (Confirming he was a "virgin" about inhaling smoke from the wacky weed).

She then continued, "I see. Well then, why not just try it once to see if you would like it or not? Grass won't hurt you, I promise. Everyone smokes—Vietnamese smoke, Americans smoke, French smoke, Japanese smoke, the whole world smokes grass, really. There's no harm, only lots of fun and good feelings, believe me. I only smoke now and then myself, and look at me, I'm no nut. I'm not sick. I'm not addicted. I'm no boogeyman—like in your American movies. I can take grass or leave it. Most of the time, I'm just too busy to smoke, anyway. But other times, when I'm just relaxing by myself or with friends like you right now, I don't see any problem with it. It's just like drinking a *'beer in the can without the can, man'*, right, except it's cheaper and no hangover. So . . . you want to try, just once? Come on."

She made a very strong case. But Ken was still thinking it through. Then he sensed he didn't want her to view him as a wimp (a "cherry boy" in her words). So he gave in and said yes, "Okay, but just this once."

With that, Ha` leaned over and gave him a quick kiss on his cheek in a gleeful, childlike way, and then quickly produced a ready-made joint. She lit it herself, inhaled deeply, and then handed it to Ken. He took it but wasn't sure how to even hold it. She showed him. He then took a big hit while also trying to inhale. But it was disastrous. This was the first time he had ever felt smoke of any kind in his mouth, no less feeling it rush down his throat into his lungs (except, of course by accident via constant secondhand smoke he breathed in daily from his mother's cigarettes at home in the Projects). He also recalled the one time as a child he tried to light a cigarette he took from his mother's pocketbook. He had burned himself so quickly, he never tried smoking anything again, until now.

Ken's face turned red quickly, his eyes started to tear uncontrollably, and he started a series of deep coughs trying to rid his lungs of the awful stuff. So she handed him his beer and he took a long deep swig. It didn't help. His coughing continued. Once he regained his composure, they hugged and she encouraged him to take just one more puff, but smaller and quicker this time. He did so but it still had no effect. Ha` took another hit herself and passed it back to Ken. This time he politely refused. Since it had no effect on him, he felt he didn't need to try again. Ken just assumed he was immune or something so they went back to talking and resumed a little sex play. However after a few minutes, Ken found himself taking another hit from the grass cigarette—this time on his own. He was now starting to feel a little more relaxed and somehow becoming more interested in everything around him, especially the little things—the floor, the light, the bed, the hooch walls, and many outside sounds as well. Everything seemed to be coming alive all at once.

The Chocolate River

There was a small rotating fan sitting on a nearby table. It kept the air moving throughout the hooch making the temperature inside feel relatively comfortable even though outside it was ninety degrees. For some reason, Ken started focusing on the fan's rotating motion and the subtle sound it made as it moved from left to right then back again, over and over, never breaking its repetitive cycle. He had been in her hooch for well over an hour now, but it wasn't until this moment that he even noticed the fan at all. But now, he was really "getting into it."

Ken also began seeing Ha` in a different way too. She was so very, very beautiful, more so than ever before. They began embracing each other naturally, automatically. No signal, nods, or permissions were needed. Sex with Ha` was now different. It was also becoming fun, funny, and fantastic at the same time. This was somewhat delightfully weird for Ken. They both then burst out in laughter for no reason as they continued their close embrace. Ken never knew he could have fun while having sex. He was beginning to accept that he may be getting stoned after all but wasn't quite sure. He kept thinking . . . was this "stoned sex" he had always heard about? Was there even such a thing? He didn't know, but his mind seemed bent on resolving this eternal question even though he was in the midst of such deep embraces with Ha`.

He thought that "steam and cream" sex in Phu Loi couldn't be considered real sex now. It was closer to "revenge sex" because he was still withdrawing from Martha Elaine at the time. And sex in Sydney Australia during R&R didn't count as real sex either because he was still in his mourning period for Martha Elaine. So that, too, was technically a kind of "revenge sex." Before this moment, his only view of sex was, "Get it done as fast as possible—get down, get in, get off, get up, and get out."

What else could sex really involve anyway? Of course, any real man knows this already, right? These types of unanswerable questions ruling the universe of all men kept dancing through his mind in the midst of loving Ha`. Suddenly, the mental wrestling match he was having with himself (and losing) turned into an endless barrage of intense cravings and sensations—both physically and emotionally. His mind and thoughts (versus his body and feelings) were no longer players in this game called sex.

Something was changing.

The fragrance of Ha`s hair was now becoming intoxicatingly sweet to him while the taste of her sultry lips and tongue had already become excitingly electric and paralyzing at the same time. *Was this even possible*, he thought. Their mutually shared body oils, moisture, and sweat were now entwined as one, making him feel as if they both were snuggly wrapped in the softest bed of elephant leaves floating lazily down a river of warm milk chocolate on some exotic South Pacific island. And each time Ha` touched him (where only a well-practiced woman can touch a man so naturally), his body responded in ways he never thought possible.

Was this feeling the real difference between sex and intercourse? Love verses sex? Surrender versus submission? Was this the way it was meant to be? If so, why right now? Why Vietnam? Why war? Why this woman? Why me? Why? Why? Why? So many new thoughts, feelings, and unanswerable questions were now exploding constantly throughout every part of Ken's mind and emotions. Even so, his body was still able to ignore each question without missing a single ripple along his milk chocolate river with her totally wrapped around him.

Ken was stoned for the first time. And he didn't even know it.

The next evening he eagerly brought Ha` three packs of Lucky Strikes. She gave him a quick embrace when they first met, then took the packs. She then gave him one "grass cigarette" in return, along with the following instructions, "Now . . . go for a slow, leisurely walk around Lai Khe village. And on this walk I want you to think only about where you are right now in your life at nineteen, really think long and hard. Look around and see my people, hear the sounds of my village, and smell its smells. Let yourself go and give yourself permission to see, hear, and smell—for the first time. Then return to me in thirty minutes. I'll have something for you."

He had come to trust her now, so that's exactly what he set off to do.

Along his walk, he took a couple tokes from his "grass cigarette" and began thinking and seeing Lai Khe village in a different way. He was now noticing and appreciating things that had been around him all along but never noticed before, including Vietnamese people going about their daily work; the sound of a steel hammer striking an anvil; the wonderful rich smells and aromas emanating from many families' cooking fires; the wide variety of animal squeals, yaps, clucks, and barks constantly ricocheting throughout the village; and the youthful sounds of kids playing aimlessly in instant puddles formed by a surprise downpour. Even the overhead screeches of jets and the thumping of helicopters seemed different to him now. Collectively, everything that was happening around him magically minimized the full impact of the day's scorching, intense heat—everyone's common foe. He was beginning to better understand just how Vietnamese people seemed to cope with the intense climate and endless war. By collectively acknowledging and accepting the natural order of things, everything just seemed to balance out. Death was balanced with life—hot with cold; old with young; love with hate; worry with tolerance; friend with enemy.

Ken had always been a little paranoid in the presence of Vietnamese, especially when he didn't have his weapon with him, like at this moment. But he now felt comfortable and relaxed. He didn't know if it was the grass making him see and feel things this way or if he was just maturing. He would never know for sure, but if he guessed, he'd say it was the grass. After all, how mature can a guy at nineteen really be? But he did realize for the first time just how lucky and privileged this kid from Brooklyn, Baltimore, really was. At this very moment in his life, he was in the middle of an old French rubber tree plantation, walking around a small country village in the southern part of South Vietnam on the South China Sea in the late 1960s. He was eighteen thousand miles from home and he was in good health. At that moment, Ken Callahan realized he had a lot to be thankful for.

Ha` had planted that thought in his mind before he started his walk through Lai Khe village that evening. And it stayed with him, not only through his walk but also for the rest of his tour of duty and the remainder of his life, even though he didn't know it at the time. When Ken returned to Ha`s hooch, she handed back to him three packs of grass cigarettes perfectly resealed. Her "grass transfusion" had been completed with surgical precision just as she promised. He was amazed at how quickly and efficiently she had done so. He had a month's supply and it would likely come in handy for trading.

Good deal.

Before heading back to headquarters, they took another leisurely ride together down the warm chocolate river, a memory that would be solidly stored in Ken's mind forever. That's when he came to fully understand why the meaning of Ha`s name suited her very well.

In Vietnamese, Ha` means "river."

The Smoke Tent

There was no way Ken could smoke all that grass each month. He, like Ha`, didn't smoke that often, so he just started trading his grass for other things—Coca-Cola, toothpaste, books, socks, or whatever he needed. However, when he did smoke, he discovered quickly there was also a big downside; he was always hungry and always wanted to have sex until the buzz wore off. Considering where he was and what he was doing every day, Ken thought this was just another fair exchange.

He learned to live with it.

Ken was working the day shift now, and in the evenings from time to time, he would join a few other sergeants and soldiers from other units in the "smoke tent." This remote, special place was located on the edge of the division artillery's sector in Lai Khe. It was only a small army lean-to tied to a couple of rubber trees—not an actual tent. But it was a great getaway from the daily grind of things. He and the guys would quietly get stoned together or just smoke and reminisce about home while listening to the Stones, Beatles, or Motown on a battery-driven cassette player. Most often, they just talked about their plans once they were back in the States. Sometimes, one of the guys would read a letter from home to everyone. That's when the guys were very quiet, listening intently and fantasizing about home. Ken was one of the dedicated listeners since he seldom received letters from anyone anymore and never from Martha Elaine.

He was slowly getting over her.

Very seldom was work or war discussed in the "smoke tent" area. It was time off and a good way to leave the war behind. Ken never smoked grass when on duty and never in the presence of his own team members, even though he knew many who smoked grass, too. Lai Khe was mortared and rocketed much more frequently than Phu Loi because it was located more remotely. During the TET Offensive of 1968, Lai Khe was given the dubious name of Rocket City because of the constant incoming rockets received during that time. The Viet Cong usually focused their mortars where the largest concentration of soldiers would be and at the ammo depots, artillery units, and along the airstrip.

Since the "smoke tent" was in a remote area of thick rubber trees and vegetation, Ken and the guys felt less like a target. Even though their logic was sound, they also were proven wrong far too often. Every guy would still instinctively grab his helmet and hit the ground immediately upon hearing a rocket jet by overhead or when they felt a nearby thud break the silence (which usually was instantly followed by a mortar exploding). While rubber trees did make the temperature feel somewhat cooler (as compared to the heat in the dust and dirt bowl of Phu Loi), the bad news was incoming rounds often exploded in treetops, spraying its lethal shrapnel "down and around" versus "up and across" the landscape. That was a real disadvantage to not being close to sturdy bunkers during the attacks. The lean-to in the smoke tent area provided no protection, except from the rain. All and all, it still provided a kind of escape from the routine of long days and helped provide Ken with a distraction when memories of Martha Elaine or the Projects came rushing back to him.

Then in mid-October, Ken was called into command sergeant major's (CSM) office at headquarters. An operational necessity had arisen that required a communications expert. This soldier, not only had to be able to handle complex communications systems, but also do so while flying aerial missions throughout the entire First Infantry Division's area of operations—a vast region of South Central Vietnam (III Corps) from

Saigon and the South China Sea to the Mekong River running along the Cambodian border to the west. Additionally, this soldier had to work closely with the command staff, even more closely with the commander of the First Infantry Division Artillery, Colonel Britton (06). Usually such positions were "assigned" to soldiers via direct verbal or written orders, but not this time. The command was looking for a "volunteer" in this case. Not only did this soldier have to be proficient in technical systems and procedures (voice and Morse code), but also had to receive the endorsements from his direct supervisors and then be interviewed (something Ken had never done) by several field grade officers. Ultimately, he would also have to meet personally with Colonel Britton. "Well, you want to be considered for this position or not, Sergeant," the CSM said without even looking up at Ken from his desk in the headquarters bunker.

Ken had finally become comfortable in his job, new location, and new life after nearly six months in country. He had become quite effective working in operations and came to trust and like all the soldiers on his team. Yet he also thought such an opportunity would finally allow him to get into the war more directly—he'd finally be able to "fight back" instead of constantly being on the receiving end of mortars and rockets. Ken also sensed this opportunity could greatly accelerate his combat experience as well as help make the second half of his tour in Vietnam pass much faster.

He only had to think about it for a few seconds before replying directly to the CSM, "Absolutely."

Ken passed all necessary interviews with staff officers and received the endorsement of his direct supervisors in the communications unit. He knew they remembered Ken's earlier months in Phu Loi, but they never brought it forward during the command interviewing process. They just attributed his bad behavior and attitude to being a new guy adjusting to the combat environment of Vietnam, nothing more, nothing less.

Ken was so grateful for their support. So in October 1968, Ken became the First Infantry Division Artillery commander's radio telephone operator (RTO) and would stay in this role until he departed Vietnam in March 1969.

His life as a soldier was about to change, big time.

Finally into the Fight

As the commander's RTO, he became a member of an elite six-man team, consisting of two helicopter pilots (lieutenants and warrant officers), two door gunners (Specialist 4s), one commander (full bird colonel), and a radio operator (buck sergeant). This was Colonel Britton's "command and control" flight team. While in the air, their primary mission was to oversee all artillery elements during major infantry operations and enemy engagements throughout the entire First Infantry Division's area of operations. Ken's specific role was to ensure the commander and the team could always be able to communicate with any unit or person within his command, on the ground, in the air . . . at any time. Additionally, he had to ensure communication security. He was required to maintain the communications equipment on board and keep it in good operating condition, manage the traffic coming into the commander, execute authenticity procedures and codes—especially ensuring any Vietnamese military units engaging the Huey were who they said they were.

His primary communication mode was voice, but he had to be ready to send and receive Morse code whenever required as well. Even though the communication system in the commander's Huey was new to him at first, he learned quickly. His personal call sign during his first month was Spicy Rattler 8. Colonel Britton was, of course, Spicy Rattler 1. During his time on the flight team, he was also taught by the door gunners how to load, fire, and reload the M60s while flying at one hundred miles per hour in their HUD-1 Huey helicopter. However, the pilots did not teach him how to fly the Huey.

That was a wise decision on their part.

The commander of the division artillery directed all major fire support base (FSB) movements and redeployments, including the establishment of new FSBs. Most of them were 105 mm and 155 mm artillery units strategically placed and/or tactically dispersed north and west of Saigon along the Saigon River running all the way to the Fishhook region near Cambodia.

Each FSB was given a familiar and friendly name such as FSB Holiday Inn, Howard Johnson, Marriott, and Hilton. Ken liked that because it brought a little bit Americana to Vietnam. On a typical day, Colonel Britton and Ken would be picked up from the headquarters and driven by jeep through the rubber tree plantation area to Lai Khe's airstrip and then to the helicopter takeoff and landing zone (LZ) located in the middle of the base camp. Most often, the pilots and door gunners would already be there prepping the Huey for takeoff. Ken and the commander would get aboard and head to various FSBs to do spot inspections, observe planning and training exercises, oversee FSB movements, evacuate personnel as needed, call-in artillery support, and directly participate in joint field operations with infantry units. They averaged about three missions per day throughout the operational area, which also included the Iron Triangle (the region that had one of the largest enemy underground tunnel complexes in South Vietnam).

While in the air, Ken felt relatively safe because command and control missions assumed higher altitudes than low-flying, tactical aircrafts. He also felt safer because he was now a constantly moving, highly flexible mobile target (versus being a huge, stationary target at base camp). Also, his team could "fight back" when directly engaged by the enemy or when direct artillery or air support was requested from ground forces. However, it was always the takeoffs and landings in the field that caused Ken the most concern. The Huey would receive mostly small arm fire and usually during arrivals or departures at remote LZs or FSBs. When hit, he could feel and hear bullets impact the Huey and watch as tracers flew by. But on most missions, such incidents were the exception because the commander's Huey was seldom required to land or enter live fire zones unless under extreme emergency conditions.

This was Ken's logic, his daily rationalization when flying, but many other soldiers felt the opposite. One of his "smoke tent" buddies told him so, "You're nuts . . . flying in helicopters in Vietnam is the most vulnerable place a guy can be in country, second only to walking point on patrol. No thanks, I'm staying at base camp. At least I can duck here." Ken understood his point.

The Bunker

One day, around the time Ken finally reached his "double digit midget" status (the magical milestone that came when ninety-nine or fewer days remained on a soldier's tour of duty), his team landed about ten miles southeast of Lai Khe at a relatively large FSB—Holiday Inn. A huge staging area was being formed nearby consisting of infantry and mechanized units as well as a contingency of ARVN (Army of Republic of Vietnam). Holiday Inn was a semi-permanent artillery site that hadn't moved from its location in some time, which meant extensive defenses were in place, including a couple of well-fortified bunkers strategically placed on its perimeter. The fire control center (FCC), another bunker, was located in the center of the FSB about thirty yards from the helicopter's landing zone.

The pilots were ramping down the Huey's engines after landing because Colonel Britton's visit was scheduled to go much longer than normal. Most often, the Colonel's pilots kept the engines running just at a slower rate without turning them completely off when landing in remote field locations. This allowed the team, not only to conserve fuel, but also stay ready for an emergency takeoff, if needed. Colonel Britton left the Huey immediately when it touched-down, and headed directly for the FCC. After recalibrating and securing the Huey's communications equipment, Ken grabbed his M16 and also headed to the FCC to catch-up with the colonel.

When Ken was just outside the perimeter, an incoming mortar round exploded. It impacted about one hundred yards north of the FSB in a open area. It seemed a little odd to everyone because it was so off-target, well away from the main staging area and FSB Holiday Inn—where most of the troops were actually concentrated. So everyone, including Ken, just stopped, hit the ground, looked and waited. A few seconds later, the first of several more mortars started landing about seventy five yards out but were now clearly "walking" toward the FSB and the staging area. That's when everyone started darting for nearby bunkers and ditches—the Viet Cong were now adjusting their fire. So Ken ran directly toward a bunker that was about fifteen yards away along the FSB perimeter. He was just about to dive inside when the impact of a mortar struck, collapsing the bunker's front entrance. Unfortunately for Ken, much of the wall collapsed directly on top of him. He was instantly pinned to the ground beneath a huge pile of dirt, debris, and sandbags—lots of sandbags. Fortunately, he was only dazed, not seriously injured by shrapnel. That was the good news. But after some time, he realized he could not move his body, or anything.

He was buried alive. And, that was the bad news.

The massive weight of dozens of solid sandbags rendered his arms and legs useless. He couldn't move. His eyes were struggling to open in a frantic search for anything, but instead found only a wall of thick brown darkness and shadows. Additionally, he couldn't hear anything except a constant high-pitch ringing sound in his ears. Ken didn't know if his eardrums had been busted by the blast or if the wall of sandbags had just sandwiched both sides of his head blocking out all sound.

He just didn't know.

Without being able to hear or see anything now, coupled with his inability to move at all, an uncontrollable panic overcame him. It was a suffocating, smothering kind of mental paralysis that intensified with each futile breath he attempted because each gasp turned into the taste of burning dirt flying into his lungs. Compounding all this, Ken had become maddeningly disoriented. He didn't know if he was facing down, up, right, or left. It was as if he had been blindfolded, gagged, tied from head to toe with the heaviest rope ever made, and set aimlessly adrift across the darkest parts of space, alone. The only conscious thought he had was to scream and keep screaming. However, his disorientation and paralysis kept him from doing even that. He tried anyway. It was then he realized he couldn't even hear his own cries for help. His lips and mouth seemed to be moving, but he only heard distant echoes reverberating somewhere in a deep tunnel of his mind and couldn't tell if his cries were even reaching those around him, over him, or under him. He didn't even know if anyone was out there at all. For all he knew, everyone could have been killed, or even worse, they were buried alive just like him.

His panic continued.

Then a frightening thought whipped to the forefront of his mind, "*What if nobody knows I'm here? What if they can't hear or see me? I could be here forever . . . buried alive . . . never to be found . . . left face-to-face, nose-to-nose with hundreds of rats, insects and sandbags.*" Ken Callahan's biggest nightmare had come true—slowly smothered to death by sandbags. And at that moment, all time and reason faded from reality. This was the horror of all horrors for him. He was never really sure where his fear of suffocation came from, only that it had been with him since he was a kid. Nevertheless, this was real, and it was here right now, and he knew he couldn't handle it for even another second. That's when he felt his mind slipping away from him—actually it was rushing away at supersonic speed toward some undefined destination, an unknowable place and time. He didn't know where he was headed but now had no choice but to follow and go along with it. Ken was hoping he'd soon see that notorious, comforting "light at the end of the tunnel" he had heard about—at least that would be worth running ahead to.

But that was not in the cards for Ken Callahan, not even close.

Instead of running "ahead" to anything, Ken was about to find himself jumping "back" in time. He was about to reenter a place and moment that would make his current bunker nightmare feel like a fun, kiddie ride at Disneyland. It was also the same place and time he had revisited many times in his dreams since 1961—the last place on earth he ever wanted to be. It was the place from where he "escaped" two years before vowing never to return—Brooklyn, the Projects, and 4139 Martin Court—to his mother's bedroom.

Mother's Bedroom "Revisited" (1961)

In this sandbag nightmare, Ken's mind quickly becomes a kaleidoscope of emotions and memories all dancing around like Ping Pong balls in an air machine. As he enters his mother's bedroom, all his senses are on high alert, as usual. Immediately he notices that a man is present in the room with his mother. The man is sitting in a plush-cushioned chair next to the foot of the bed and she is standing next to him. He is a stranger—a fat, Peter Lorre look-alike man. As usual, her bedroom is thick with cigarette smoke and stale perfume. A single beam of late afternoon light is streaking between the window frame and the drawn window shade. He notices his mother's vanity is still covered with a variety of perfume bottles of all shapes and sizes. However, the "fish-shaped ashtray" is no longer just sitting on top the vanity. Rather, it has come alive before his eyes and is now flipping and flopping on its hind fins on the floor. The fish's mouth is also rapidly opening and closing as its dark lifeless eyes keep staring directly at Little Ken as its dancing continues. The large painting of the King over his mother's headboard has also come to life and Elvis is now singing and gyrating his hips and pointing directly at Little Ken with one hand while holding a microphone in the other. He is singing Hank Williams' "Your Cheatin' Heart" while a full orchestra is playing in the background. The music is loud and so out of rhythm, it's disorienting to Little Ken. As he continues to scan the bedroom, he also notices all the pillows on the bed are standing upright doing a sort of a striptease dance in slow motion to Elvis's crazy melody while removing their own pillowcases inch by inch in a sensuous, sexy manner.

A walking-fish ashtray, strip-teasing pillows and an out-of-rhythm Elvis were making the bedroom come to life in the most bizarre way right before his eyes. In the middle of the bed, sits a well-polished, leather saddle with a single spotlight shining on it showcasing its well-kept curves, big horn, soft seat, cinch straps, and stirrups. At the foot of the bed, Ken's mother and the man are smoking, drinking, and laughing together then they notice Little Ken standing at the doorway. Immediately they stop laughing and, in unison, turn and look at him. The man begins gesturing for Little Ken to come over to him. His mother is wearing her signature red flamingo bathrobe and she begins patting a spot on the bed where she wants her son to come and sit.

But Little Ken is now frozen in place.

Suddenly the bedroom door slams shut behind him; he is so startled he can't move. Little Ken is feeling like the room just swallowed him whole and he didn't know whether to run to his mother's arms or turn and run through the door all the way out of 4139 Martin Court. But he is unable to do either because his feet are now solidly stuck in a deep mud pocket that had just magically formed beneath him. Actually, the entire bedroom floor is now transformed into a massive soggy swamp. The more he moves, the deeper he sinks in the mud pocket. He can no longer move his legs, and his arms are now being bound by a set of creeping vines that magically sprouted up and wrapped around him. A constricting paralysis is taking over Little Ken's body and mind. He's helpless in the muddy swamp called his mother's bedroom. That's when he tries to yell for his brothers, Butch or Walter, to come and help him, but his lips and tongue have just morphed into a mouthless, strip of flesh. The only sounds he can produce are muffled moans that he alone can hear.

His nightmare continues on—Elvis Presley's singing keeps getting louder and louder while the pillows and fish ashtray continued their enticing motions. Together, his mother and the man start pulling Little Ken and his mud pockets closer to them by some unseen lasso at the end of their ever-extending, out-stretched arms and hands. With each lasso tug, he is pulled closer and closer to the bed and he is so close now that he can smell the man's horrid breath and his mother's thick, stale perfume. That's when his mother pulls the saddle from the middle of the bed and wraps the cinch straps around Little Ken and begins . . .

Back to Reality

Meanwhile, back at the bunker where Ken was still buried . . .

Ken's emotions and mind were still somewhere between his mother's bedroom and FSB Holiday Inn. Then he began hearing human sounds and voices coming at him from all directions, but he couldn't make out any words or language. He was also still unable to move or even cry out. His only prayer was the language he ultimately heard would be English, not Vietnamese.

Ken couldn't tell how much time had passed since his burial in the sandbag coffin—could have been minutes, hours, or days. He was going to try to yell out once again when suddenly he felt a strong force on both feet, and the next thing he knew bright sun light was penetrating his closed eye lids. Light was everywhere now but he still couldn't see a thing. Then he began inhaling mountains of fresh-flowing, wonderful air directly through his mouth. Ken never thought he'd value the Vietnamese weather in such a way as he did at that moment. The soldier who pulled him out of his sandbag nightmare then sat him up, did a quick survey of his body, and asked if he was okay. Ken nodded without saying anything and the soldier stayed for a few seconds before heading off to help others. That's when he realized the language the man spoke was English, not Vietnamese.

Three additional mortars had landed on FSB Holiday Inn following the first that was so far off-target. One of the three directly hit the bunker Ken had just reached, sending him back home Brooklyn for an unexpected visit. Then, the mortar attack stopped as quickly as it started. All in all, the attack lasted only a few minutes from start to finish. What seemed like several hours in combat time to Ken who was pinned inside his sandbag tomb, turned out to be minutes in real-time.

After he had been pulled-out, sat-up and checked-out by his rescuer, Ken tried standing in order to head back to the Huey. But, he did so too quickly, lost his balance, and had to sat-back down. He stayed seated a little longer and glanced around the staging area to see things were returning to normal. Then, he tried standing and walking again. Ken made it a few steps this time but then had to sit back down once again to regain his bearings as well as his composure. Ken's head, hands and fatigues were totally covered with dust, dirt, sweat and mud when he realized he was without his helmet and rifle. So, he rose slowly and went back to the pile of rubble, dug around a little, and saw the butt of his M16 sticking out from some sandbags. His helmet was next to it. He grabbed them and tried, once again, to head back to the Huey; it was his fourth attempt.

He made it this time.

Ken entered the Huey and the team was preparing to leave. When the first mortar landed, the Huey had taken-off right away which was standing operating procedure under such conditions and circled the area lending fire support in retaliation, then returned to the FSB. After a few minutes, Colonel Britton came jogging out of the FCC and quickly made it back aboard. That's when he and Ken reunited. Something big was about to unfold elsewhere and they had to be on their way immediately. "Sergeant, you look like an elephant just took a dirt and sand crap on you . . . you Okay?" the colonel asked. Ken said he was fine and didn't feel required to explain anything further. He was still somewhat stunned by everything. Once they were airborne and new flight orders given, the Huey leveled off and headed west. In the meantime, Ken acquired a secure channel and established communications with FSB Marriott—their next destination.

He then settled back and looked out the right side of the Huey as he continued clearing dirt from his nostrils and fatigues. As the Huey continued on course, Ken also began staring at the horizon and the Vietnam countryside below. He watched as his new world kept magically appearing and disappearing beneath him—scattered villages with surrounding open fields and rice paddies, patches of dense jungle and wild brush running along-side the ever-changing dark brown waters of the Saigon River, and an endless montage of B52 craters in all shapes and sizes seemingly sprinkled across the earth like freckles on a little girl's face. This was his world and for the first time since arriving in Vietnam he was thankful for it. That's when he began fully savoring the spacious expanse of open sky as well as the constant stream of fresh air whipping through the cabin and rushing into his welcoming nostrils and lungs. That's also when he knew just how very lucky he had been at FSB Holiday Inn.

No one on his team ever said a thing to Ken about his personal ordeal at the bunker, and he never brought it up either. Things had unfolded so fast at FSB Holiday Inn that it was likely his team never even saw what had happened to him, especially considering they had taken-off to engage the enemy during that time themselves.

And, that was okay with him.

Ken had not been seriously injured, just shaken up pretty good physically and emotionally. He had survived many incoming mortar attacks on the ground at Phu Loi and Lai Khe as well as small arm fire in the air, but this was the first time he felt his life was going to be lost. He didn't know if this experience was going to haunt him the rest of his life and he didn't care to know at the moment. Ken only knew that he and the members of his team were safe.

That was all that mattered.

A Butcher-Bird Sighting

One early evening in January 1969, about a month after Ken's intimate involvement with the bunker at FSB Holiday Inn, the Vietnam sun was racing to the horizon as Ken's flight team was returning to Lai Khe. He always savored return sorties to base camp at that time of day because the heat was starting to wane a little. The early evening hour at dusk seem to be giving all forms of life in Vietnam a well-deserved reward for making it through another boil in the lobster pot. Ken's headsets in his helmet shut out most (not all) of the ambient noises generated by the Huey's powerful engines, the endless radio traffic, and the seventy-five mile-an-hour winds. Ken enjoyed these moments flying without having to be on high alert every second. Flying back to Lai Khe at this time in the early evening was just one of those times.

The silence and relaxation didn't last long. "Spicy Rattler 1 this is Spicy Rattler 7. Spicy Rattler 1 this is Spicy Rattler 7, come in." Ken seldom heard the call sign Spicy Rattler "7" on live radio traffic but immediately knew it was the command sergeant major (CSM). So he replied on behalf of Colonel Britton (Spicy Rattle 1) who was on a different frequency with another commander at the time and couldn't take the CSM's direct call anyway. It was very rare for the CSM to be contacting Colonel Britton just before landing in Lai Khe since they would soon be together anyway at the headquarters. The Huey was only seven minutes out of Lai Khe at the time.

So Ken responded, "Spicy Rattler 7 this is Spicy Rattler 8 . . . be advised Spicy Rattler 1 is not available, can I help?" There was a long pause then the CSM responded, "Spicy Rattler 8 please ask Spicy Rattler 1 to contact me on a secure channel prior to landing. It is critical he do so *before* landing . . . *before* landing."

"This is Spicy Rattler 8, will do. Are you sure there isn't anything I can do for you Spicy Rattler 7."

"Affirmative—just do what I told you to do or I'll have your stripes! Got it! And, advise Spicy Rattler 1 this is a confidential call and no one, especially you, Spicy Rattler 8, are to be on it. Is that clear? Please confirm."

"Roger that . . . Out." With that, Ken terminated contact.

Ken was now somewhat concerned that such a secure channel message was required but didn't include him. Normally, he was on every communication with Colonel Britton during operations. And since they were landing in a just few minutes anyway, he was even more curious why the CSM would risk sensitive communication over the air, even on a secure frequency if they would be face to face shortly. Also, the way the CSM said "especially you, Spicy Rattler 8" made him feel even more suspicious. Something big was up and he didn't know about it. Every scenario rushed through his head at lightning speed—major attack on Lai Khe pending; trouble at a FSB; emergency meeting in Saigon . . . or, maybe someone found his perfectly camouflaged "packs of grass" in his tent wasn't camouflaged so perfectly after all. He didn't know, but he was now thinking the worst.

As soon as Colonel Britton was finished with his other communication, Ken informed him of the CSM's request and asked if he needed help establishing a secure frequency. "You say that was the CSM and he needed to talk now? Must be important, he never contacts me like this." Colonel Britton had just magically echoed Ken's own personal thoughts aloud.

"Yes, sir, that's what he said," Ken replied.

"OK, thanks."

With that, Ken got Colonel Britton a secure frequency, established the authentication codes, and immediately hopped off the channel, leaving the colonel and the CSM talking without Ken knowing what was going on. During his somewhat lengthy conversation with the CSM, Colonel Britton kept glancing at Ken now and then. Ken couldn't read minds, but he sure could interpret facial expressions and attitude pretty well having grown up around his mother and brother in the Projects—it was a matter of survival, knowing what was going to happen before anything really happened. Reading facial expressions and listening with his eyes, became a survivor skill at a very young age. It was a competency he prided himself on refining over the years. Now, he was certain the message from the CSM involved him in some way, but how? Just before terminating his conversation with the CSM, Ken noticed Colonel Britton's face broke into a huge, knowing smile just like a father accidently discovering a hidden scratch on his car after their child's first solo drive. This look perplexed Ken even further.

The Huey was about to land when the colonel finished communicating with the CSM. Ken could clearly see the landing pad area at the Lai Khe airfield and also saw two jeeps pulling in preparing to pick up the team and take them all back to headquarters. The Huey landed without incident. Ken secured the communication equipment, and the door gunners and pilots secured the rest of the Huey. Just before departing, Colonel Britton said to Ken, "Sergeant Callahan, let the crew take the first jeep back this time and you and I will take the second for a change. There's something else we've got to do before heading back."

"Yes, sir," Ken replied without hesitation, even though this just added to the suspense about something big coming, but what it was he did not know.

Usually, Ken and the commander took the lead jeep but not this time. Ken just thought they were going to stop at another place on the way back to the headquarters or something, or maybe he wanted the crew to get back as soon as possible and catch up on some well-deserved rest after a long day. Colonel Britton was always looking after the welfare of his men in such ways.

The propeller blades came to a slow stop; the crew exited the landing pad and jumped into the first jeep and headed back. A few minutes later, the colonel and Ken walked over to the second jeep and driver. They dumped their equipment in the backseat as usual and he was about to jump in the back with the gear but Colonel Britton stopped him and said he wanted the backseat this time and directed Ken to get into the front.

He said so without giving any explanation. Ken was surprised but did so immediately just as the colonel hopped into the back.

Ken loved army jeeps.

Once he mastered a clutch (which was a challenge because he just couldn't sense the correct pressure/play feel using his foot), it became second nature to him. From then on, Ken loved jeeps especially the ones without tops; driving those made him feel like he was racing a sports car convertible. Ever since he saw the opening scene from *State Fair* starring Pat Boone and Ann-Margaret, he wanted his own convertible. This scene depicted a young Pat Boone driving a candy apple Spitfire convertible along a long winding country road through the low-rolling hills of Texas in the early 1960s. He was driving by himself on a beautiful summer day with the air rushing through his perfect hair. He had one arm resting atop the driver's door and the other hand steering the car effortlessly. All the time he's singing the theme song from *State Fair* as cameras captured shots of him from above, from behind, from both sides from every angle. He was not only driving a car, but he was also dreaming of winning the fair's sports car competition while also stealing the heart of the most beautiful girl in the world doing so. Of course, Pat Boone was able to win a race and win a heart . . . in just ninety minutes.

But Ken just wanted a car—a convertible, any convertible would do. He'd even settle for an army jeep, at nineteen that's all he deserved anyway. To get one, he had been saving most of his money since entering the army. And since he was in Vietnam, he was also getting combat pay in addition to his base pay, so he could save even more. He was going to get that car sometime between the time he left the army and started college. The military had a relationship with several major car manufacturers during the Vietnam War that discounted the price of cars for Vietnam veterans. These dealers would have a car waiting at home for soldiers returning who participated. He had already saved nearly $1,600 in his first two years in the army, sending nearly $75 to $100 per month home where his mother said she was saving it for him in a special bank account. However, when he returned from Vietnam, she told him, "Well, I needed da' money for some ting's, darlin'. You understand, don't ya' . . . right?" He discovered this after his first year in Vietnam. He didn't send money home during his second tour.

Once he and the colonel were in the jeep, the driver slowly pulled away from the landing pad. They were heading down the airstrip to the rubber tree plantation when halfway through the dirt trails of rubber trees, the driver turned away from the headquarters and started heading in the opposite direction. Ken hadn't been paying that much attention since this was just a routine jaunt he had done every day for months. His mind was focused on processing all the day's activities and looking forward to relaxing in the smoke tent for a while after catching some chow. That's when Colonel Britton tapped Ken on his shoulder and said, "Where the hell we going, Sergeant? This driver seems lost or something, get him back on track. Who's this guy they sent to get us, anyway?"

With that, Ken looked over at the driver, whose helmet was low on his head; he also was slumped forward close to the steering wheel looking straight ahead focused on the road. The driver was like a man possessed by the Lord to get to the pearly gates before they closed. So Ken tapped him on the arm and gestured to him to turn around. He had missed the trail to headquarters. *"Just must be new guy or something,"* Ken thought to himself. But the driver disregarded Ken's direction and kept driving straight ahead. Ken was surprised at this big discount coming from a driver. He glanced quickly back at the colonel who also had a puzzled look on his face. Then he directed the driver to pull over and come to a stop. The driver did so. When the jeep finally came to a stop, Ken leaned over and got face-to-face with the driver, getting ready to chew this newbie a brand-new asshole, and then he stopped in mid thought. Ken was momentarily disoriented at what he thought he was seeing. Then he forced his eyes to drop to the name on the newbie's fatigue and it read—Callahan. He then pulled the driver around to face him directly. That's when Ken's mouth dropped.

Ken couldn't believe his eyes, it was his older brother Butch—the Butcher-Bird.

He was stunned and just leaned back in his seat, just staring at what could not be. Then finally he said, "What the shit?" Ken questioned aloud and apologized to the colonel for his language. "Hi Little Terd, how ya' doing? Oops, I mean Sergeant Terd, right? . . . Please forgive me," Butch said with a playful, yet genuine smile.

This could not be happening. Ken thought it had to be the marijuana he had been smoking last night. Maybe Ha` had been lying to him all along—smoking grass was really dangerous to the mind, after all. He had to be hallucinating at this moment. Or maybe this was all a dream. Maybe he had been shot down and killed, and now he was in hell with the Butcher-Bird in a jeep next him for eternity. His mind kept spinning. It just couldn't be Butch. This was Southeast Asia, South Vietnam, III Corps, Lai Khe, and the First Infantry Division Artillery. There was no way he could be here, but he was.

Ken was speechless. That's when Colonel Britton began to burst out laughing from the backseat. Butch also started laughing and reached over and gave Ken a big bear hug, crushing Ken's chest—Butch still had all his strength, that's for sure. "That was the best trick we pulled off all year. I didn't think the CSM could really do it, but he did. Can't wait to tell him his mission was complete," Colonel Britton said in the midst of his laughter.

Ken then embraced his brother, touched his face to be sure it was him and not a dream/nightmare. But once Butcher-Bird smiled and Ken saw the gaping space between his two front teeth, then he knew it had to be him. He just stared at him; no words were spoken by anyone. Butch then took off his helmet and held it in his hands, then said, as he kept looking back and forth from Ken to the colonel, "Christ . . . how can you guys wear these things on your head for so long; feels like I've got a second head on my shoulders."

The colonel replied, "Yea, I guess after wearing that sissy Navy Popeye hat for so long, this helmet must feel like a bowling ball between your ears. So now let's turn around, take that right about twenty meters back and let's get home."

Butch and Ken quickly swapped seats. It would be easier and faster since he knew the way. Ken started the jeep, did a quick U-turn, and pulled away. He kept one eye on the path and one on Butch all the time. Ken had so many questions but didn't say a word; he didn't know what to say. Neither did Butch. That's when the colonel started explaining how things unfolded, "When the CSM contacted me just before landing, he explained that somehow your brother made it to Lai Khe about an hour ago. The CSM wanted to surprise you, so he took your brother to your tent, got him out of his navy uniform (bell-bottoms and all), and gave him a set of your fatigues. He got him a helmet and some boots over at the supply tent, too. It was the CSM's idea to have him pick us up at the landing pad by acting as one of the drivers. His name was Callahan too, so he guessed it was OK for him to wear your uniform anyway. That's when he decided to pull this trick on you. From the look that's still on your face, I guess it worked. Wait till I see the CSM and tell him his surprise was a success."

Ken continued to be speechless and kept staring over at this brother in between the potholes, mud pockets, and the colonel's explanation.

Butcher-Bird's R&R

Butch was in the US Navy, serving on the USS Hancock (CVA-19), an Essex Class aircraft carrier off the coast of Vietnam. He was a naval weapons specialist. The USS Hancock's mission was launching aerial bombing missions in North Vietnam and conducting aerial operations in support of military operations in South Vietnam. Butch had been stationed aboard the ship for about six months. "I told you I'd try to come visit you if I could, little brother. Well, here I am. Bet you thought I was just bullshitting you, didn't you?" Butch said proudly.

He vaguely recalled Butch writing he would do so, but had discounted it, knowing it would be virtually impossible to do. Butch proved him wrong—for here he was now in Lai Khe. Getting to Vietnam also had proven to be the easy part; locating Ken was in the midst of a rubber tree plantation deep in the jungles of Vietnam was the hard part. "How did you pull it off? How did you locate my unit? How did you find Lai Khe? Did you travel in your navy bell-bottoms all the way here? If so, you were a great target for the VC! Why did you want to step foot in this shit hole, anyway? How did you even get permission? You are on orders, right? Was permission actually granted for such a trip?"

Ken's series of questions didn't stop until they arrived back at headquarters. There, they dropped off the colonel where Ken knew the CSM would certainly be waiting to brief him on the arrival of aircraft weapons specialist—Butch Callahan. Butch and Ken then walked to his tent together. There, Ken secured his weapon and gear, and they both headed over to the mess tent to grab some chow. Ken introduced Butch to a few guys who were also getting a late bite to eat. They were interested and amazed at Butch's journey. He was kind of a celebrity already—no one ever came to Lai Khe just for a nice visit. Not anyone in their right mind, that is. "You're on R&R? Really? Get out of here you dumb fuck!" one soldier screamed hearing Butch's story.

Come to find out, Butch took his scheduled R&R time to come to Vietnam instead of going to some exotic vacation spot like Ken did in Sydney, Australia. He had his R&R orders on him as he was traveling. First he caught a direct hop off the USS Hancock on a fixed-wing craft that went directly to Saigon on mail runs. There, he explained what he was doing to a flight operational officer who helped him catch a C-130 flight into Phu Loi and then he jumped on a helicopter that just happened to be going right to Lai Khe. Getting to Lai Khe was also easy according to Butch. Finding his little brother was much more difficult. He explained what he was doing to the flight control center operations sergeant at Lai Khe who tried to find Ken out of all the various units within the First Infantry Division. Butch didn't know Ken was in the artillery (didn't even know there was a difference between infantry and artillery). And of course, that was the last place the control center sergeant looked. Butch kept saying, "He's in the First Infantry Division in Lai Khe, Vietnam, that's all I know." But eventually he radioed the CSM in division artillery HQ who drove out and personally picked-up Butch.

All this had happened in less than twelve hours after leaving the USS Hancock around 6 a.m. that same day. Butch explained all this to Ken and several others who gathered around his table in the mess tent to hear his story. "It was a little weird when I landed in Saigon. Everyone kept pointing and staring at me because I was wearing my white bell-bottoms and my Popeye hat. That's all I had. Must have been as strange as seeing a white elephant in the jungle or a hard-boiled egg in a bowl of green pea soup. But everyone was cool and very helpful once I explained what I was trying to do. They really wanted to help me get to a place called Lai Khe. And they did."

"How did you get permission to do this?" Ken then asked.

Butch took a long pause before "whispering" his answer to Ken. "Well, I'm not really supposed to be here, I guess . . . you see, I don't have official permission. I'm actually supposed to be in Bangkok on my R&R."

And then he showed Ken his official military travel orders. That's when Ken was floored. "What? You're telling me you're AWOL—absent without leave?" Ken also whispered this back to Butch in amazement, above all not wanting to alert the others to this "slight" military infraction. Butch acknowledged it by slowly nodding his head, and then continued his story. "My R&R orders are for Bangkok, not Vietnam. But, my unit commander could not officially authorize me to set foot in Vietnam unless it was mission critical, so he refused my request. But once I explained things in more detail—what I needed to do, what you were doing in Vietnam, and being less than one hundred miles away, and also since it could be the only chance I would ever get to see my little brother ever again, he was more understanding."

Butch went on, "However, he kind of said it to me Unofficially-like, that is . . . 'look Callahan, this command isn't responsible if you get 'lost' temporarily during your R&R. As long as you get back here onto the USS Hancock on time, that's all that matters. And 'off the record,' I feel that any man, who freely chooses to go to Vietnam for any reason instead of going to Bangkok for R&R must be either confused, stupid, or really nuts. I don't know which of these you are but I could easily see how any stupid man could get lost and a little confused traveling in Southeast Asia during a time of war. It's that kind of explanation that could just come in handy if such a 'stupid' man did get caught. Get my drift. So remember that. Also, such a stupid man's commander could also officially say he had never approved such a venture and never would do so, especially for such a 'stupid' seaman under his command. Get my drift again, Callahan? So just let me say, good luck on your 'R&R to Bangkok' and by the way, if you do accidently run into any family members (especially a little brother) during your 'R&R to Bangkok,' tell him to kick your butt and send you back here in one piece. But only do so after a few good days of catching-up together and after about hundred beers or so. Now get out of here.'"

Butch told an amazing story. Ken didn't believe a word of it of course, but enjoyed it anyway, and so did the other guys. However, Ken was never more proud of his older brother than at this moment. Actually, it was the only time Ken could ever remember being proud of Butch at all. And as history would ultimately prove, it was the first, last, and only time Ken would feel that way throughout the remainder of his brother's life. Butcher-Bird was in Lai Khe and Ken was glad to see him. Doing such a thing was the most unselfish thing he ever saw Butch do. He was beginning to view him differently. After all the years of torment, torture, and bad times he gave Ken growing up in the Projects, he had thought they would just end up hating each other forever. The toughest time was around 1963 when his little sister was sold for $200 and they had moved at least six times in a single year. It was also when their relationship was the most painful, spiteful, and hurtful. Ken had always come up on the short end of Butch's wrath during those times. And it was during the period when teenagers really needed a mother the most to get through the emotional roller coaster of life.

In those days, Butch and Ken received just the opposite from her—more of "attraction" than "attention."

Home Sweet Home ("Bird-Eating Spiders" and All)

They walked over to Ken's tent located on the inner part of the compound in the midst of the rubber tree plantation. It was nothing special; just a standard, military-issued, large green water-repellent canvas tent—the heavy kind used in the Korean War. It was designed for harsh environments and was quite hot and stuffy inside most of the time. There were no window slits or mesh screens, so the only breezes came in from either the front or back entrance. Fortunately, electricity was finally provided to the tent a month or so after Ken arrived in Lai Khe. So if a soldier had a fan, it could be very useful in moving the thick, dry air around inside.

Ken had a single, army-issued cot with mosquito netting suspended by a few nails above his bunk. He also had a strong wooden box with a metal latch the size of a footlocker to store some of his clothes and secure his M16 when not flying.

He had about an eight-by-ten-foot area in total, but the ceiling of the tent was nearly nine feet high which made it feel less confining. Ken always felt pressured and tense in confined areas, so the height helped a lot. He also cut a two-by-two-foot hole through the tent's heavy canvas just below the foot of his cot. No one could see the hole because he left a flap over it, but he knew it was there just in case he ever needed a "clean and fast getaway" out of the tent. He got the idea from a TV family show series where the family's pet dog had a small entrance in the back door of the house that swung both ways, allowing the dog to come and go freely. He thought the idea came from *My Three Sons*, or *Father Knows Best* but he wasn't sure. Anyhow, it was there if he ever needed it.

The tent was about thirty-by-twenty feet and could hold up to fifteen or twenty men if needed. There were about a dozen such tents in the area and Ken was fortunate because only six to eight men were actually sharing this tent in Lai Khe at the time. The floor consisted of a wobbly collection of wooden pallets connected with rope, wire, and anything else available that could bind them. It gave the semblance of a real floor. And it also kept the soldiers off the ground, above most of the scorpions, ants and spiders. Equally important, during the rainy days it kept them out of the mud. That was important. This huge mass of durable, heavy canvas was held up at the corners and on the side by about ten wooden poles. Two light bulbs were suspended inside above it all and provided additional light. His tent was also surrounded by twenty—fifty-five gallon drums filled with dirt and sand. To Ken these drums were like huge metal sandbags. This was an attempt to minimize the impact of incoming mortars that landed nearby. That is, from mortars actually making it to the ground. But all too often mortars would hit the treetops of the rubber trees and explode above the tents, spraying deadly shrapnel down versus along the ground. Butch was not impressed with these surroundings but he just needed some place, any place, to kick back for a day or two, and this would do. One of the soldiers in Ken's tent just happened to be on convoy to Phu Loi so Ken placed Butch in his bunk area, which was adjacent to Ken near the front entrance. Butch hadn't brought anything with him except some toiletries, so Ken gave him some extra socks, underwear, and a towel. Butch had always been a fussy, detailed kid. Everything had to be in its place. His shirts, shoes and pants couldn't be touched. If it belonged to Butch, it was his—period. Butch would beat the crap out of Ken as a kid if he found something of Ken's made its way into his imaginary area. Everything had to be neat, clean, and in its correct place, especially when it came to his personal possessions as well as cleanliness. In Lai Khe, Butcher-Bird would quickly discover that he had to adapt and adjust. That's what war in the jungle was all about.

Ken was about to find out just how much Butch was willing to "adapt and adjust" to his new temporary surroundings.

"Hey, where's the head?" Butch yelled across the tent. Ken didn't know what Butch was asking so he asked, "What's that? The last I saw your 'head' it was between your ears, should still be resting on your shoulders at least that's where I think most other peoples' heads are. What the hell are you talking about anyway, Butcher-Bird?"

"You know . . . the crapper, the shitter, the toilet, the latrine . . . where do you go when you got to go? The 'head,' man." Butch then paused. "Sorry, my mind is still on navy time, aboard the USS Hancock."

Ken laughed when he finally caught on.

"Okay . . . follow me; you're really going to love our 'head', Butcher-bird," Ken said with a knowing smile. He couldn't wait to introduce Butch to a new way of crapping. He sensed Butch would not be pleased. So they left the tent and Butch followed him along a trail of pallets winding through trees and brush coming to an opening of a small isolated section in the rubber trees. There, a small patch of land had been cleared and in the middle of it stood a small wooden shack—a make-shift latrine about six feet high and eight feet long. Two long planks jetted out from behind it on the ground. At the end of one plank was a sawed-in-half, fifty-five gallon drum with dark black smoke rising from its insides. "Here's your 'head,' sailor. It's been waiting just for your special ass to pay it a visit;

it can't wait to say hello to you. Go in and do your business," Ken said, pointing to the latrine proudly.

Butch hesitated then looked inside.

There was a single, long horizontal board running left to right. It had two butt-size round holes about three feet apart. Rolls of toilet paper, old copies of the Stars and Stripes, and a few Playboys and Sex to Sexy magazines were scattered around the latrine. The sound of hungry flies and curious mosquitoes buzzing around in concert had become symphonic to Ken but repulsive and threatening to the Butcher-Bird. He slammed the door before even taking a step inside. Then he turned and looked at Ken and said, "What the fuck . . . you got to be kidding me. I can't crap in there. And what's up with that smell? Don't tell me, is that what I think it is . . . behind here . . . in that half barrel . . . is that burning shit and piss?" A big smile came over Ken's face, knowing his brother's need for orderliness and cleanliness. He immediately confirmed Butch's astute observation.

"Yep."

Pouring gasoline over human waste and keeping the burn going all day was the most effective and most sanitary way to minimize (not eliminate totally) disease. Ken always laughed to himself when he heard an officer refer to this sanitization system as helpful in "minimizing diseases." But since there was no running water and no real sewerage system anywhere in Lai Khe, this was as good as it got—state of the art. With that, Butch held his nose with one hand, leaned into the latrine and quickly grabbed a toilet paper roll off the bench. He then turned and started walking away into the nearby brush. He wasn't going to sit inside that "shitter" for a second. At least that's what he said at the time.

That's when Ken tried to dissuade him from going into the brush to do his business, "Hey, where ya flying off to Butcher-Bird?" Ken asked, already knowing what his answer was going to be—had to be. "To take a real American shit, not a Vietnam shit, man, you have just been here too long to like to shit in that thing," he said without looking back as he continued heading off into the brush. Ken let him walk away but only for a short distance before he tried to change his mind about doing such a silly thing. Butch didn't fully appreciate the luxury of being able to sit and crap. Most grunts would give their left testicle for such a convenience in the field. So he yelled at him to stop and listen for a second. Then Ken started his presentation and hoped his soon-to-be-departed brother would listen to it—something Butch never did growing up. He didn't know if he would listen, but he had to try anyway.

"Listen, Butcher-Bird. I wouldn't do that if I were you. Within the latrine, you will less likely be bitten by a snake. Can't guarantee it, but you're chances are less. You see, cobras don't like fire, they stay away. And you wouldn't want to kick over a rock or a log where you're heading because you could easily disturb a nest of resting scorpions . . . wait a minute, forget that. Since the sun is about to go down and things are cooling off a little, they should already be out looking for their evening dinner anyway. So ignore that—they're not resting at all right now."

That's when Butch finally stopped, turned and looked directly at his little brother. He was actually beginning to listen. If so, it would be a first for Ken—his brother was actually listening. So he couldn't let this once in a lifetime opportunity pass him by. Ken continued his presentation, "Yeah, you may also want to keep an eye out when you're squatting, especially watch for anything that has six or more legs than you—eight to be exact. If you see something like that, it will likely be a Vietnamese jumping spider, lynx spider, or wolf spider. Don't worry though, they're not real poisonous. But if you're real lucky, you could actually run into one of Vietnam's largest tarantulas, instead—the 'bird-eating tarantula.' They're a blast, really. You'll make a perfect snack for them too . . . you being a Butcher-BIRD and all."

Ken continued to savor this educational moment with his older brother, "And by the way, don't go looking for any webs to signal their presence when squatting or when wiping yourself . . . those guys don't use webs for hunting their prey . . . they prefer to prowl the ground, to stalk and then to strike instead. Webs just seem to slow them down. Oh by the way, you should also know that 'Butcher-Bird-eating-tarantulas' . . . ooops, I meant 'bird eating tarantulas' will actually run right at you. They're much bolder and far more aggressive than other Vietnamese spiders. Just remember, at least they're not poisonous, so don't worry, their bite won't kill you. But, they do leave a hell of a welt on your butt, one the size of the Empire State Building.

Butch was listening closely, very closely to every word as Ken unloaded his final emotional appeal on him, "So go right ahead. I'm going to wait over here for you, if you don't mind. We really don't get any entertainment around here so I'm just going to watch the show from here, nothing personal, Butch."

Ken's presentation had caught Butch's attention. He stopped where he was and looked down at his feet and around the ground closest to him for a couple of seconds. Then he scanned back and forth between the latrine and the bush a couple more times, going through his obvious Butcher-Bird decision process. He then decided the latrine may not be such a bad choice after all.

Ken thought he had made a wise decision. "Christ, it stinks so bad in here my eyes are burning. I can't hold my breath long enough to get through this. Where do you flush, anyway?" But he somehow was able to hold his breath long enough to finish his business, and he didn't even have to flush. "You're not going to make me burn my own shit now, are you?" Butch said in a pleading manner rather than a request. "Nope, a papa-san [a male Vietnamese] routinely cleans and burns things around here for us. But we have to do it ourselves on special Vietnamese holidays when they don't work. So this is your lucky day, Butcher-Bird, you don't have to flush. You're one lucky Butcher-Bird today."

After Butch did his business, they headed back to the tent, cleaned up a little, then walked over to the "smoke tent." It was an exceptionally mild evening in Lai Khe—only eighty degrees in the evening, and for some reason, mosquitoes were not as hungry as usual.

It was going to be a good evening.

"Going Deep"—Sigmund would be Proud

Butch had never smoked grass.

He told Ken that he had tried it once before in San Diego but didn't like it. So that night under the stars near the 'smoke tent', he just drank beer and talked with the guys. Mostly, he explained what life on the USS Hancock was all about and discussed the latest news from the States. As the night drew on, eventually Ken and Butch were the only ones left. That's when they started reminiscing about Brooklyn, the Projects, Cottage Grove Beach, the recreation center, Camp Canoy, and the Baltimore Orioles and Baltimore Colts. Butch was never much of a sports guy like Ken was, but it was fun to talk about those teams with anyone, even with Butch. After some time, and after a few more beers and a couple of joints, they started getting "closer to home"—discussing the plight of their little sister, growing up in 4139 Martin Court, the Projects and other things of a more personal nature. It was inevitable that such one-on-one catch-up time include such things.

Butch still hated and despised his mother for giving up their little sister, Sandy, at the age of three or so for $200. He said it was the worst thing a mother could ever do to a child and he would never forget or forgive her for doing such a thing—never. This was the only topic Ken and Butch really argued about during his three-day stay in Lai Khe in 1969. Ken's position differed greatly from Butch's. In Ken's mind, his mother did the "right thing" under the circumstances regarding their little sister. Because of her adoption, Sandy was removed from the abusive environment that was 4139 Martin Court. She was spared a childhood living in constant fear, incessant hunger, emotional instability, ongoing violence, and sexual abuse. Any long-term exposure to Hilda Callahan would have negatively impacted and touched every aspect of her life according to Ken. They didn't physically fight about it that night at the smoke tent, but they did argue and determined nothing could be done about it anyway, so they just left it at that.

Most often, parents' values and behaviors are silently passed along to their kids—by accident or by intention. Ken didn't know his mother's true intentions toward her boys but felt some things passed along were quite positive, including gaining the ability to defend themselves well, developing a drive to survive, developing resourcefulness, adaptability, and a sense of resilience so vital in bouncing back after continual disappointments, failures and ongoing traumas. And equally important, they learned how to run away, to escape and to avoid when needed. For many people, this may seem like a weakness, but to Ken, it represented strength. He had learned from his mother that surviving the moment enabled him to fight another day.

To Ken, the most important personal quality he took from exposure to Hilda Callahan was a sense of "relentlessness" in rebounding from adversity and then proactively moving ahead. It was her relentless drive (as self-serving as it was) that he quietly observed and came to strangely admire over time. That is, there was a positive side to her selfish relentlessness—it provided the personal drive, desire, passion and motivation needed in life. And, she was truly relentless. But he also recognized the negative side of her "relentlessness." That is, how she hurt people to get whatever she wanted in the process. And that was the part of her he always tried to avoid. He also sensed that both he and Butch also acquired at least four less desirable traits from their mother as well, including:

1. being more suspicious, less trusting of people,
2. being less open and honest about his feelings with people,
3. being more defensiveness and pessimistic than reality called for, and
4. being prone to first avoid and flee, rather than face and fix problems.

Such personal qualities, well hidden and permanently ingrained within both of them, would play an important part of their decisions and behaviors throughout their lives over many years. Five illustrations of such decisions and behaviors follow:

1. Both boys would be married and divorced multiple times.
2. Both boys found drugs and alcohol to be an acceptable part of life.
3. Both boys found it difficult to maintain lasting social relationships.

4. Both boys kept family members and personal relationships distanced.

5. Both boys needed highly structured environments in which to excel (i.e.: they both viewed themselves as far more autonomous, independent and confident than they really were).

And, equally important, neither boy developed a healthy, natural view of parenting. Over the years, Butch would be married at least three times during the sixties and seventies. And he also would have had at least one child, a little boy that Ken would learn about. And interestingly enough, Butch also would end up adopting his son to another family at approximately the same age (about 3) just as his mother had done to his little sister, Sandy, in the early sixties. In short, Butch would turn-around and do the exact thing that he despised all his life about his own mother—giving up a child. He acquired the exact values and behaviors he so vehemently detested about his own mother's decision. In contrast, Ken never even came close to giving up any of his kids. Not once. He would never consider doing such a thing, and because of this, he viewed himself as somewhat superior to his older brother in at least this aspect of life.

However, the truth behind such perceived superiority was quite simple—Ken would never have kids of his own at all—period. He was just too afraid, too weak and/or too much of a chicken to become anyone's father. That's how he would view himself for decades. And because of this fear, he was destined to also brand himself as a "coward"—for avoiding the top responsibility any man can possibly assume in life—fathering. To Ken, every other choice in life, except the choice to father, was "temporary and transient" in nature. That is, each of the following natural activities in life came with a hidden "escape clause" component of some kind (i.e., a way of getting out, a "clean getaway" option, a "get-out-of-jail free" card, a "second chance", "a mulligan do-over" alternative):

- Job (could always quit);
- Marriage (could always divorce);
- House (could always sell);
- Car (could always trade-in);
- Military (could always accept a dishonorable discharge);
- College (could always drop out);

- Political Office (could always resign); and
- Financial Investments (could always divest).

There was always an acceptable and honorable "way out" of everything, out of every major decision in life except one—fatherhood. The decision to "father a child" was a permanent one—no honorable way out. It was forever. It was everlasting. And this, more than any else, would scare the hell out of him throughout his entire life.

As an older man, Ken would have many discussions about fatherhood with his closest male friends, including Manny Lawrence. Manny not only had two wonderful kids of his own but after a divorce and remarriage, he found himself inheriting three more kids. He woke up one day and found himself in a real Brady Bunch scenario. And, he still did it well, very well. So his view of fatherhood was very special to Ken. One day he discussed it with him.

They gassed up Manny's outboard motorboat and headed down the Merrimack River in Southern New Hampshire. As usual, they set off to fix the problems of the world in a two-hour relaxing ride during what they fondly referred to as a "therapy lunch"—an occasional mental and physical getaway from the workplace. But mostly, the only thing they actually achieved was to relax and catch up with each other. That alone, was worth making such a trip for both of them.

On this particularly beautiful summer afternoon, they were moving leisurely south on the Merrimack when he asked Manny the following question. They were passing underneath the newly constructed bridge on Route 113 right on the New Hampshire / Massachusetts state line when the talk began. It didn't end until they docked the boat two hours later. "Tell me, Bud [nickname for Manny], after your two kids were born and you were just a young daddy, did life's decisions become easier or harder for you?" Manny didn't have to think about that question for long.

"How the hell should I know, that was over twenty-five years ago. I can't even remember what I did twenty-five minutes ago, man. Shut up, and let's have a beer or I'll make you swim back—bet that's one decision you can make easily, huh?"

Ken laughed at Manny's quick wit as well as at the truthfulness. Normally, their discussions on the river focused on sports, family, business, or politics but this question seemed to be intriguing enough for him to explore further. So after a minute or so, he replied, "Harder, much harder. From the moment of their births, every major decision I made included considering what impact it would have on the kids and I mean everything . . . from financials, changing jobs, planning, taking vacations, buying food, making medical decisions, college, travel . . . everything. My kids impacted every decision, made things more complex and challenging. But, it was good—all good."

Ken thought long about Manny's answer and saw its wisdom. During all their years as friends, Manny's approach to life had always been logical and practical, but most importantly, Ken knew him to be a truthful and thoughtful man. The day-to-day practical implications and long-term considerations of raising kids had to be a significant part in the life of any "good" father, and over time he saw Manny being among the very best at it. After a few more moments of silence, Ken replied, "Well . . . for me, it would be just the opposite, no disrespect intended, Bud."

"What do you mean?"

"I think if I were to have fathered a child, it would make my own decision making much easier—not harder."

"How so?" Manny was genuinely curious at such a view of fatherhood especially coming from a guy who had less direct experience raising children than any monkey had designing software. It was something he wanted to hear. So Ken shared his view, "For me, it would make decisions much, much *easier*, not harder. You see, there would be no complex debate or analytical thinking needed—the actual decision point would be quite fast and simple—'Is this decision going to be good or bad for my kids?' . . . period. *Yes* or *no*? Every other factor would be secondary. Everything would start and end with that. Hence, I would then be allowed to focus my attention on what was far more important—the solution . . . going about getting things done to make the decision viable. The decision would not keep me up at nights, but the solution would.

Therefore, having kids would make my decisions easier, just the solutions would be harder."

Manny had never looked at it that way but saw Ken's logic. It was then he truly knew that Ken should never have any kids—his logic just wasn't suited for the reality of raising children. And, he told Ken that straight out. After they laughed long and hard at this "truth," they realized such thoughts were getting too heavy for the boat. "Heavy talk" just didn't mix well with "boat time" on the Merrimack River. Manny then knew he had to help Ken snap out of his emotional deep dive and bring him back to the surface of the moment on the river. If not, the boat was definitely going to sink. So Manny, a man who rarely drank more than two beers in a row, had to think quickly to save his friend from drowning in his own thoughts. Then he replied to Ken, "Ken, when you eventually have your own first kid at seventy-three or so, which I think is quite possible knowing you, let's discuss this again. But for now, the only critical 'yes or no' decision you have to make is whether you should get us another beer. That should be an easy decision for you. But just know if it's the wrong answer, you'll likely be swimming back home. So think it through by asking yourself—'Is this good for me to do right now—*yes* or *no*.'"

His logic was solid on the point of beer. When the boat docked back at Manny's beach, Ken's clothes were still dry. So he must have made the right decision.

Ken had been running away and avoiding things all his life; his upbringing planted this seed about the age of twelve or so. And coupled with the lack of a solid father role model in his life, virtually guaranteed he would have no chance of ever desiring to become a father . . . unless it was by accident. Such a mindset developed at a young age would fester within him for decades.

His logic went this way: The only parental values and role model Ken possessed came directly from exposure to his mother. Since there was no permanent man in the house, she was the source of his values about becoming a parent—a father. Such values and behaviors scared him so much he never developed a mature parental view of himself as most other males do naturally sometime in their life. As a matter of fact, he was frightened to death of "fathering"—so much so that even his intense claustrophobia was dwarfed in comparison to thoughts of fathering. He was afraid that he would end up treating his own kids just as his mother had treated him and his siblings. And since he never had a good male role model growing up (a solid, permanent father figure, someone from whom he could have learned otherwise), Ken just continued avoiding people and situations that would bring him close to actually becoming a father. He had dated many girls over the years but always found ways (made ways, really) to ensure relationships never got "too close," never lasted "too long," and never bonded in trust to a level of making such a commitment. In short, he managed and manipulated personal relationships to his own personal advantage when it came to kids.

Even in Ken's first two marriages, the question of children was not a significant factor. In 1972, his first wife, Cheryl Mallory, a warm and giving woman, possessed similar views about having children at that specific time in her life. It was not a major factor in their mutual attraction to each other, and having kids wasn't a top priority for her. Cheryl and Ken divorced after five years of marriage without having children.

His second marriage (1982) to Laura Peters took place about four years after his first divorce. It also came a few years after he chose to get the "big V" (vasectomy). He was about twenty-eight at the time and had the medical procedure done just before he left the military. Laura was a well-educated, professional, and vibrant young lady who had known about Ken's "big V" before they married. Even so, she had confidence she could persuade him to reverse the medical procedure and ultimately have kids together. Her campaign was doomed from its inception. Laura and Ken divorced less than year after marrying.

Adopting a child was also always out of the question. Being "adopted" himself only added to his confusion and strengthened his negative view of "fathering." Throughout the remainder of his life and well after Vietnam, Ken would assume many roles and titles other than "father," including: husband, soldier, executive, community leader, sergeant, lieutenant, employee, brother, son, nephew, author, trainer, friend, citizen, director, speaker, athlete, adjunct professor, manager, patient, benefactor, and even lover. He easily accepted each role through his life and even proactively sought them out, excelling in most, but not all. Yet the one role he always secretly admired and prized above all was also the one he intentionally managed to elude. He kept the title of "father" very distant, well out of reach and out of temptation.

So, before he had turned thirty, Ken's anti-fathering attitude had hard-wired keeping potential fathering situations and relationships at a distance, and even choosing to make himself physically incapable of having kids (via the Big V). Kenneth A. Callahan had become virtually "Father-Bulletproof."

Yet, as he would continue to mature, Ken found himself admiring and respecting several other men as he watched them interact with their own kids. This secret observing took place at kids' birthday parties, sporting events, or just visits to their homes. During such moments, he was silently wishing he could step inside their shoes, even for a minute. But, he never shared his feelings with them until later in his life. He was embarrassed at admitting such things for some reason. Yet, such moments also represented a double-edged sword to him. On one hand, he admired these fathers and wanted to exchange places. On the other hand, his childhood fears and personal insecurities seemed to automatically resurface at each of these fleeting moments. And this frustrated him; it also positively reinforced something deep inside him that kept him coming back for more, without really ever knowing why.

Shakespeare & Officer Krupke

"To be or not to be—that is the question." Ken thought Shakespeare had it wrong—he had missed a great opportunity. This unanswerable rhetorical question was just too broad and vague for most soldiers. Even literary scholars have long argued about Shakespeare's intent regarding this passage: was he talking about life, suicide, death, responsibility, morality, the meaning of life, or existence itself. No definitive conclusion had ever been accepted by all regarding "to be or not to be." Any normal soldier who even tried to answer such a question about his own "existence" would

find it as frustrating and futile as learning how to silently swat mosquitoes without giving away his location to nearby enemy. Shakespeare should have focused on a far more practical question that all the literate men of the world (even combat soldiers) would find meaningful and useful—*"to father or not to father—that is the question."* To Ken, this type of query had real intellectual teeth and much more significant relevance to all men because it was laser focused at the true measure of a man.

Pondering one's own "replication" versus "existence" was a far more worthy quest—a thoughtful journey every man should be encouraged to take early in life. Ken often wondered if all fathers asked themselves such a question prior to actually "fathering." Did most men really think it through first, then move ahead with clear intentions? Or, did they merely give themselves permission to accidently slip into fatherhood when they finally reached the moment of physical release, the point of "no return" so to speak, giving it no extra thought at all.

Ken would never know such answers. But he did know one thing—Shakespeare really blew it with Hamlet.

He had been in a state of perpetual emotional limbo regarding this question. It would ultimately evolve into an eternal crucible, a mental stigma, a perpetual fear, and even a source of recurring remorse for years as he aged. Ken sensed he was stuck in an endless loop of emotion that began as a teenager and was destined to stay there for decades. Unknown to him at the time, this mind-set had evolved into a silent, protective barrier that kept him from taking the plunge into "fatherhood" every time the opportunity presented itself. It became safer to keep on pondering and analyzing rather than act and do because thinking about it kept him from doing anything about it.

Ken's logic went something like this over time: On one hand, if he had kids of his own, he would have the ultimate authority and opportunity to abuse them or do them harm. This thought scared him to death, and he didn't really know why. He did know however, that he would never do such a thing but also sensed he was capable—he had the potential to do so. And, this scared him to death.

After all, Ken knew what child abuse was about. He knew what it looked like. He knew what it sounded like. He knew what it felt like. He also sensed such thoughts and feelings were now a natural part of him—a far more familiar thing than the "normal" qualities of good fatherhood. He wasn't raised in a normal environment or by normal parents. Therefore, he naturally became more comfortable with the abusive versus the affectionate elements of parenting. Over time, this caused him to associate parenting "first" with such things as conflict, cruelty, and instability versus the qualities of patience, nurturance, kindness, compassion, love and protection. This mind-set was deeply imbedded within his emotional DNA by nineteen and directly prolonged by exposure to a wicked, mentally ill mother and an abusive older brother as well as many absentee fathers.

On the other hand, without having kids of his own, he would never be able to fulfill that universal, masculine obligation that all male members of his species had to meet—to bring new life into the world. He had to "replace thy self," "double up," "go forth and multiply," etc., and there was no choice in this matter. This was the absolute minimum measurement of accountability for all male *Homo sapiens*. It was binary—either a man reproduced, or he was not a man. As important as "defending the home," "bringing in the bacon," "competing and winning" were, such deeds always came up short when compared to the obligation of reproducing one's self. No matter how financially successfully he became in the world of man, "reproduction" was still the key bottom line assessment of successful manhood. And, that would elude him forever.

This was Ken's eternal dilemma. He accepted the fact that a man fathered him, but he never met this man and never desired to see him. After all, why would he want to meet his father after all these years, and if they did meet, what would Ken say or ask of him, "Thank you for bringing me into this world? Tell me, why did you abandon me and my brothers? Why did you leave us with that crazy woman in such a broken life? Why didn't you come rescue us? What was it that made you such a weak man that you couldn't even handle your wife, my mother? Why didn't you see the impact that running away would have on me and my brothers and sister? Why were you a coward? Don't you know the reason why I'm so fucked-up today is not because of my loony mom, but because of you!"

When Ken really thought about what he would do or say if he ever met his father, an entirely different view of his mother started to emerge. He began to understand why she reserved her best language, most colorful vocabulary in describing her ex-husbands, including "scum suckers," "chicken shits," "wimp bastards," "weak good-for-nothin' cowards," and of course her favorite, "hemorrhoid husbands."

Ken finally understood. She had been right, after all!

Such adjectives and descriptions were accurate! Well deserved! Spot on! His mother had been justified and correct all along! Her husbands, including Ken's biological father (whoever he was), were equal villains in his bizarre world. This whole thing wasn't just her fault, even though that's how Ken viewed it for most of his young life. Each "father" had a hand in it all. They broke their vows and commitments to her and their children. Whatever happened *to "for better or worse, in sickness and in health."*

Hilda Callahan had to do what she had to do in raising all her kids in the Projects in the 1950s and 1960s, without an education, without skills, without any source of steady income, without any financial support, without any state or local welfare assistance, without family connections . . . she had to do it all "alone."

Granted, she also mothered badly, very badly. But Ken wondered how different things could have been if there was a father's presence in 4139 Martin Court. Would it really have made a big difference in his childhood? Or, was she just so bad that her ex-husbands had to run away. If so, how could a person do so and leave their kids? That's when Ken thought perhaps his mother was right when she called them "wimps," "cowards," and "chicken shits"—not real men at all. If there had been a constant father, a real man in the picture, Ken bet things would have been better, much better. But each of his mother's husbands came up short on Ken's secret "AAAAA" rating scale. That is, he felt any credible man who intentionally or accidently fathered a child should never do any of the following "A" things:

- Never _A_bort their kids
- Never _A_ttack their kids

- Never *A*dopt their kids
- Never *A*bduct their kids
- Never *A*bandon their kids

Just one missing "A" chromosome in any father's parenting DNA and he fails, big time. All, or any, of the five "A's" was equivalent to the biggest "A" of all—Abuse. As such, they would not be worthy to retain the title "father." Perhaps the real truth was Ken didn't see himself ever becoming a father because he didn't want to be like *them* more so than because of his mother's deeds and values. As a result, Ken couldn't put the total blame on her alone any longer. In either case, questions and doubts about his own fatherhood haunted him, persisting for decades. Along this same line of thinking, he actually thought about becoming a Catholic priest—like Father Butta. At least as a priest, he would be addressed as "Father." If so, this may be the closest thing to being a father he could reasonably expect in his life. By doing so, he just wouldn't have to assume the responsibility and accountability of actually becoming a real father.

He never explored this idea beyond its initial thought, however.

Sometimes when Ken's mind started thinking about his childhood plight growing up in the Projects, he would flashback to a scene from the very first musical he saw at the movies—*West Side Story.* Ken was about twelve years old at the time. In this specific scene, members of the Jets (a neighborhood gang of white kids living on the west side of New York City), are gathered in front of a small store. They are planning a "rumble" (a street fight) against a rival gang called the Sharks (a group of Puerto Rican kids who shared the same neighborhood). A police car then pulls up in front of the store and out comes Officer Krupke. The police officer calls them "juvenile delinquents" and other nasty names before telling them to disperse. But instead of leaving, the Jets break into song and dance about being "mentally sick," "disturbed," and "misunderstood" because their childhood was based on a poor upbringing, uncaring parents, a violent environment, and a broken social and legal system. Some of the lyrics from this musical number hit close to home for Ken, especially references to:

- Parents always treat him rough,

- Ever present drugs and alcohol,
- Abusive language and vulgarities,
- Lack of dependable relationships, and
- Continually striking out on his own to survive.

As conveyed very well in the musical, Ken indeed felt he could have fit into either the Jets or Sharks cultures without any problem.

He didn't know how much impact such messages really had on him at the time, but he related to each immediately. The only difference was he seldom felt like a "victim" because of his circumstances. If anything, such understanding actually helped motivate him even more to get out of his environment faster. Nevertheless, no matter where he went after fleeing Brooklyn, his confused, negative feelings about fatherhood went with him. What it always came down to was a preoccupation with the negative side of parenting versus the good side—the joys, rewards, and personal satisfaction of having a child. And it saddened him knowing he would likely never feel the pleasures of fatherhood. He wasn't sure if fathers ever took for granted such joys, but to him it was always about the little things, the big events, and those innocent moments he only had witnessed "from a distance"—never up close and personal. For example, the following father-child experiences always touched his heart in a magical way each time he saw his male friends interacting with their own children:

- Watching their child being born
- Helping their child take their first steps
- Feeding their child
- Bathing their child
- Nursing their sick child back to health
- Tucking their child into bed after a long day's play
- Helping their child get back to sleep after a nightmare
- Changing diapers (well . . . Ken thought some things were less wondrous)
- Dressing their child
- Walking down the street holding hands with their child
- Teaching their child to throw and catch a baseball
- Teaching their child how to read and write
- Teaching their child right from wrong

- Reading a bedtime story as their child falls off to sleep
- Bathing their child and drying them afterward
- Mending their child's broken heart
- Helping their child with homework
- Holding their child in a big warm towel after a cold swim
- Having their child fall asleep in their arms
- Kissing their child good night
- Going to the movies with their child, explaining every scene
- Briefing a babysitter on their child's needs, likes, and dislikes
- Going to a parent/teacher meeting at school
- Rooting for their child during sports or other competitive events
- Watching their child graduate from school
- Walking their daughter down the aisle at her wedding

And there was one other thing, a very special fathering event always left in Ken imagination. He always wondered and often dreamed of "putting his child on a school bus" for the first time. Placing trust in others whose only purpose was to keep his child safe in his absence. This always confused yet intrigued him. The following questions always perplexed him about this:

- Could he actually let go, even temporarily?
- Could he ever "relinquish control" even for a short period?
- How does that happen with a first-time father?
- What would the child be thinking while on the bus?
- How would it feel at the end of the school day when his child came scampering off the bus and came running to his waiting arms?
- Would they kiss and hug so tightly they couldn't breathe?
- Would he sniff his child, taking in all the wondrous smells and scents of his youth?

To Ken, the simple act of "putting a child on a school bus" represented a top assessment of a real father. Had the father done all the right things during the first few years in the life of his child? If so, great; if not, shame. That's why he always held secret admiration for "good" fathers—those who stuck around long enough to at least give a child a fighting chance. "Putting a child on a school bus" was not only a "rite" of passage for the child, but also it was a "right" of ascension for a father. If the father didn't make this moment happen, to really see it through, then the title of father should be stripped from him forever.

Much later in life as an older man, Ken would see a wonderful movie entitled *Forrest Gump*. While this film won the 1996 Academy Award for Best Picture because of its epic story, wonderful characters, and special use of technology, only one scene really touched Ken's heart and caused him to watch it so many times afterward. Actually, it was the final scene of the movie. This brief moment captured a most unique and special instance when Forrest Gump put his son on a school bus for the first time; perhaps a basic activity for most fathers, but to Ken, it was a major milestone in fatherhood—Forrest was letting his son go out in the world on his own. While most people believed it was about the son maturing, Ken viewed it as an epic scene about the father. As he watched it, the powerful emotions associated with this relatively simple human event in life ignited flames of impassioned joy and a sense of fatherly pride within Ken. Yet, the same scene also released a sense of deep sorrow and remorse with him as well. He didn't know whether to smile or cry.

So he did both simultaneously, whenever he watched that scene. Along with the rising and swaying of the "floating feather" into the sky above Forrest, his son, and the school bus, Ken's tears swelled and soared in equal harmony. Despite all the outside trappings of Ken's professional, financial, and social success, this one five-minute scene exposed an eternal broken heart. Such questions, images, and feelings would haunt Ken for much of his life. That was why his secret admiration for fathers, "good fathers" that is, would always hold a strong place in his heart even though he would never experience it personally.

Both Butch and Ken were destined to carry a part of their mother's and absentee fathers' values within them forever. They shared it, but never really understood it until far too late. It was a commonality that bonded them even though they never knew it. Ken would always admire Butch for at least having had the courage to take the risk to "father," even for a short time. Butch was a "father" once. It was something Ken would never have the courage to undertake and he admired his brother for it.

Meanwhile, back at the smoke tent . . .

Ken eventually asked Butch about their days growing up in the Projects and why he was so hateful and mean to him—why he tormented and tortured him. Butch was very elusive with his answers. This was peculiar to Ken because Butch was never hesitant conveying his opinion about anything to anyone (he got that trait from his mother, for sure). Yet on this topic, he never did come out and say what he was really feeling. And Ken never forced him to do so. Rather, Butch seemed to skillfully dance around these questions and issues especially when the subject of their mother, her boyfriends, husbands and memories of those times.

Yet, he did say one thing that Ken always remembered but would not come to fully understand until much later in his life.

Butch said he tormented Ken because he didn't want him to have to go through what he had to endure himself. That's why he had always tried to make Ken believe he was somewhat weaker than he really was, especially in the mind of his mother. He knew Ken strived to seek his mother's attention, time, and affection; but Butch also knew how she could, and would, find ways to take personal advantage of that, just as she did with him. When Butch was torturing and tormenting Ken, it wasn't because he wanted to hurt him so much as to really make him stronger and tougher. That was his way of helping. Even though Butch's words could not articulate this concept clearly, Ken sensed that was what he was trying to do. They didn't spend much time exploring this further. And both seemed a little more relaxed when the subject changed to something else. The hours at the "smoke tent" that night seemed to fly quickly by.

Ken noticed that Butch had changed in many ways since he last saw him years earlier in the Projects, just before he ran off and enlisted in the US Navy. Butch didn't seem as tough as he did before. Even his language and vocabulary had improved somewhat. Butch also appeared more comfortable in his own skin than when he was in the Projects. Perhaps the US Navy helped him find himself and helped him grow in stature within his own eyes. Butch had always appeared aggressive and arrogant but not really confident and self-assured. He did now. Ken also couldn't help but feel they both had undergone similar, positive changes. He sensed that getting out of the Projects and away from the influence of their mother were key factors. Being in the military was good for both of them because it provided a kind of structure they had never had growing up. It was something solid they both could finally have to trust, to depend on—something that was always there.

Being required to manage their time, meet obligations, make commitments, work within a set of clear rules and boundaries, and to routinely have to rely on others had impacted them positively. These were very basic daily disciplines, yet each fostered a level of maturity they both needed to continually develop and trust. Even though Butch was on the water and Ken was on land and the air, the military's positive influence was the same. Different uniforms and different languages perhaps, but it all was good for both of them.

And they both were able to eat on a regular basis, regardless if it was out of can or in a mess tent or galley—food was now always available; they never had to fight over food again. That was comforting and reassuring. They both had been through a lot in their short lives, and they were adapting and surviving. This shared moment together under the stars in the jungle was good for them. They were as relaxed with each other at this brief moment in time as Ken could ever remember, and it only took one "smoke tent" deep within a French rubber tree plantation in a foreign country during a war to make it happen.

Fortunately for Butch, there wasn't any mortar or rocket attacks that night. But Ken thought Butch would have liked to have experienced that, too, in a strange sort of way. Ken also shared his recent death experience in the bunker at FSB Holiday Inn, as well as how it felt to be living constantly in life-threatening situations in Vietnam overall. In doing so, he also conveyed that it really wasn't much different from the caliber of continual tenseness, anxiousness, and dread that he felt daily while living in 4139 Martin Court in the Projects along with Butch and their mother. He went on to specifically describe how his mind zoomed right back to Brooklyn and the Projects while he was being suffocated under the bunker's rubble at FSB Holiday Inn. At that moment, he realized that he hadn't talked about this incident with anyone ever before, including his flight team members, but he was doing so with Butch. And since Ken arrived at Lai Khe, Father Butta wasn't available to talk with either.

Butch was the first, and last. And he listened to Ken; he listened well just like Father Butta had always had done when he was available. That's when Ken sensed Butch actually was compelled to come to him in Lai Khe after all, despite the risk.

He would never know for sure.

But, Butch didn't want to talk about the Projects at all. He was more interested in learning more about the bunker, the Viet Cong mortars and the FSB. That's what interested him the most. Butch had always seemed to thrive on conflict and was comfortable with it. He even initiated it himself often. This was just the opposite of Ken who avoided it and used it only as a last resort. Butch was a strong, tough boy in the Projects as compared to Ken and his peers. Ken was labeled a good kid while Butch got a very different reputation of his own during those days. Unfortunately (or fortunately), his reputation was the type of brand that skyrocketed him to street gang legendary status within the Projects. It happened around 1964 when Butch was about sixteen or so.

After a few more beers, Butch started talking about those days in the gang. It was the only thing he openly shared in detail about his memories from the Projects . . . and he had a lot to say.

"Crabs-on-Crabs" (1965)

It was another hot, sticky summer afternoon in the Projects of Brooklyn, Maryland. Butcher-Bird was returning home from a trip to "The Barges"—a mountain of old abandoned tug boats and floating debris located in the shallow waters of Baltimore Harbor's inner shore. It was in the vicinity of the Hanover Street Bridge connecting Brooklyn and Cherry Hill to South Baltimore's downtown area. This collection of waterlogged ruins and decaying boats could easily be seen from the top of the bridge. However, getting there was a challenging and dangerous trip, as difficult as crossing the Panama jungle without a machete or compass.

Several decades later, this same vicinity would be designated by the State of Maryland as a beautiful educational site providing a broad scope of environmental learning programs for all residents of the surrounding communities. It would become the Masonville Cove Environmental Education Center.

But on this day in 1965, "The Barges" was still an isolated, eye sore that most local people avoided at all costs. It consisted of a jumble of abandoned ship hulls, broken masts, boat parts, jagged pilings, and submerged flatbeds of all kinds huddled together. Hundreds of split buttresses and broken beams with jagged spikes lurked just above and below the murky waters. Most of the Barges were covered in some kind of black creosote substance that had the smell of old, tarred roads and telephone poles that had been baked endlessly by the sun. There was no rhyme or reason to the organization of these old massive components of days gone by. To Little Ken, who made the trip to the Barges on several occasions with Butcher-Bird and Walter while growing up, each piece collected there just seemed to die and stayed forever in the exact place their last boat breathes were taken. The Barges reminded him of that mythical place deep in the African jungle where old elephants went to die, as depicted in the 1950s Johnny Weissmuller Tarzan movies. This was the same kind of cemetery, but reserved for boats and remnants located on the shores of the Baltimore Harbor in Brooklyn. Yet, all pieces of the Barges shared one thing—they seemed to be slowly dancing in unison, keeping pace somehow to the lazy rising and falling of the tide. Even though waves never broke this deep within Baltimore Harbor, there was still a hypnotic, rhythmic, back-and-forth swaying of everything in its grip. Nothing was ever totally still; there was always some perpetual movement. It was like watching a fat man's big round belly expand and shrink with every deep breath while napping after downing a big turkey dinner. The ever-present breathing of debris seemed to be letting the world know, despite its apparent demise, that it was very much alive. Another thing all the Barges had in common was sharing the same filthy, polluted waters. The area had plenty of open sewers, detergents, and rotten algae blooms, caused by decades of phosphate and fertilizer deposits spewed from the many surrounding industrial sites near Brooklyn. As such, this place always freaked-out Little Ken each time he went there with his brothers. And he was always glad to leave, even though he had a great time exploring when he was there. The Projects were located less than two miles from the Barges. Yet, it was separated from the town by a fortress of thick, dense brush and woods situated just behind a Bethlehem Steel manufacturing site off Patapsco Avenue. This isolated part of Brooklyn proper consisted of thick interwoven reeds and swamp land with tunnel-like paths snaking their way to the water's edge.

Only a few people knew how to interpret these reed maps well. It was a dangerous journey. Those who tried to make it to the Barges without understanding reed paths ended up either lost or stuck for hours in well-camouflaged mud pockets located all along the paths. Even though the distance was only about a quarter mile even the most experienced traveler to the Barges needed to plan an additional hour to make it through its many entanglements and passageways. The Barges also had its own reputation warning anyone thinking about exploring them. It was one of the most deadly and frightening areas in Baltimore in the mid-1950s and 1960s that "normal" people avoided like the plague. But Butcher-Bird was not a normal person. To him, the risks and perils of getting to the Barges were well worth the treasures and rewards at the journey's end. "Crabs—the pearls of the Chesapeake," as most Marylanders called them, were the ugliest yet tastiest creatures the Chesapeake Bay ever gave up. There were thousands of them at the Barges and these were not just regular crabs; they were Chesapeake blues—*Callenectes sapidus*. And, they lived up to their Latin meaning . . . "*the beautiful, savory swimmer.*" At maturity, each of these crabs averaged at least ten inches from claw to claw and could weigh nearly two pounds. Despite the filthy waters from which they came, their meat was very, very sweet. A single claw was a meal, and two dozen of these pearls were a complete feast easily satisfying an entire baseball team of kids and their coaches in one sitting. For Butcher-Bird and his little brother as well as his mother, pearls made excellent crab cakes and crab soup. Two dozen crabs would last them several days. And since crabs were the only seafood the Callahans got during the summer months, it served as their only source of protein. Butcher-Bird would spend at least two days a week during the summer months "playing" (catching crabs) at the Barges. To him, it really was play, not real work at all. To others, it was a chore as well as a dangerous venture.

Most people who attempted the journey to the Barges also made a strategic mistake—they took a ton of crabbing equipment with them, including crab tongs, bait clips, steel baskets, several types of crab lines, rubber grabbing gloves, weights and sinkers, crab pole and net, crab measurers—most of which would be lost in the reeds or mud even before they reached their destination. And once there, just surviving became an equal challenge. Loose boards, cracked floors, rusty nails, and sharp spikes protruded from nearly every plank. One misstep and a crabber could find themselves in scum-baked, filthy water or even worse, impaled by unknown objects. Adding to the challenge, nothing was stationary. The jagged pilings and dark waters were constantly on the move, occasionally exaggerated by an unpredictable wake from passing merchant ships. Balancing one's body weight along with all that crabbing equipment quickly transformed first-time visitors into last-time survivors of the Barges.

But, not so for the Butcher-Bird; he enjoyed the Barges and really liked the trip there and back because he never burdened himself with all the equipment most people used to crab—that was his secret. And, it made things much easier for him. Actually, he would take only three things, nothing more:

1. One twenty-five-foot standard fishing line
2. One fresh chicken neck (just one was all he needed)
3. One empty bushel-size wooden basket

That was it; he needed nothing else. Butcher-Bird didn't even take along a lunch or drinking water. Rather, he relied on his bare hands for such "simple" tasks. And over time, Butcher-Bird also developed a very unique technique for catching crabs. First, he used both hands when slowly pulling the crabs up from the harbor's floor once he felt their initial "tug" on the chicken neck attached to the end of the line. When the crabs got closer to the surface, twelve inches or so, he would then begin making very slow, circular motions wrapping the line around the palm, knuckles, and fingers of his left hand rather than pulling the crab up the remaining distance with both hands. Once the crab came into visual range near the surface, his right hand would do the actual scooping from behind the crab. He was getting nearly 90 percent of all crabs that made it within visual range. Most people couldn't brag about that success rate using a pole and net.

On one of their trips to the Barges, Little Ken asked Butch, "Won't you need more than one chicken neck to catch so many crabs? It will be eaten up quickly, right? Those pearls are hungry, quick eaters, right?"

Of course, Butcher-Bird had the answer. True, a single chicken neck was usually quickly devoured in the first few tries. All it would take was two or three crabs and the big neck would be gone as each feasted on their personal elevator ride to the surface to meet Captain Butcher-Bird. When the chicken neck was totally gone, he would merely reach into his basket, rip open a live, recently captured crab, tie it to the end of line and use it as bait. This would continue until the woven basket was full. Butcher-bird really liked that part of "krabbin" (as his mother called it). "Crabs on crabs," as his mother would say.

Hilda Callahan always found a way of calling things as they really were. Butcher-Bird liked the concept of "crabs on crabs" too. Just like his mother, he got a real kick out of knowing crabs were eating their own kind. Something about the concept warmed his heart (and his mother's) in a strange way. Little Ken had gone with Butcher-Bird to the Barges on a few of his trips, but he didn't enjoy the crabbing part as much as just being able to get out of the Projects for a while. He also didn't like the taste of crabs much but enjoyed the soup. Little Ken didn't like catching and carrying them. He didn't like steaming them alive; he didn't like cracking open their backs. He didn't like breaking off their claws . . . all the fun parts for Butcher-Bird and their mother. So when Butcher-Bird was doing the actual crabbing at the Barges, Little Ken was off exploring and climbing over everything. "You'll just get in my way, anyway . . . so go away," Butcher-Bird would say to him. "Come back in a couple of hours. We'll leave when the basket gets full." Little Ken had great agility and loved the challenge of jumping, balancing, and exploring the Barges. So he'd just go off on his own for several hours.

Butcher-Bird didn't mind the crab bites he would inevitably receive during the scooping phase of crabbing. To him, without pain, where's the pleasure? It was a philosophy he and his mother totally agreed upon. For

Butcher-Bird, crab bites were no more painful than large mosquito bites anyway. However, to other crabbers, once the claw of a Chesapeake blue clamped down on their unsuspecting hand, it was like having a car door slammed on their hand. More often than not, the only way to remove the claw of a Chesapeake blue from an unsuspecting finger or hand was by breaking off the crab's entire arm. Even then, the crab's vise-like grip would not always release. Consequently, most people handled Chesapeake blues with great care and respect.

He would crab for several hours and when his woven, wooden basket was full of live crabs, Butcher-Bird locked the cover's metal latches, place the basket on his right shoulder, then call for Little Ken to return and head back to the Projects. Five dozen Chesapeake blue crabs could weigh nearly one hundred pounds but it was not a chore for Butcher-Bird to carry that weight, even while going through the mud and thick reeds surrounding the Barges. It slowed him down at times, but he felt that it was just part of the hunt. Butcher-Bird liked crabbing for several reasons: the risk, the escape, and the superiority he had over the crabs, but mostly, he liked it because he didn't have to attend summer school on those long hot, days. Hilda Callahan would give him instructions to "go hunt up some crabs" (as she would say) instead of going to summer school. He'd jump at the opportunity without hesitation.

On this particular summer day, Butcher-Bird had gone crabbing at the Barges alone. It was a very successful day and he was returning to the Projects with a full basket of Chesapeake Blues—nearly sixty-five crabs, all big ones. Butcher-Bird always threw back younger, smaller, or molting crabs along with his personal promise to each: "Don't worry, I'll be back you little suckers, I promise. You'll be in my stomach in no time when you're bigger . . . so see you then." He always kept promises made to his mother or he'd receive her wrath. And on this day, he promised her that he would bring back a lot of crabs before 3:00 PM. She was going to share them with some of her boyfriends who would be coming over later that evening. However, the mud and the reeds slowed him down longer than normal on this trip. After getting out of the swampy reed paths, he headed down to Potee Street along the back of the Bethlehem Steel works then up to Patapsco Avenue to Ninth Street. There, he stuck his head into Downton's bar—his mother's favorite "stompin' grounds," as she would call it, to see if she was still there. If Hilda wasn't working there, she'd usually be drinking there on her off time. He was just hoping she'd be there this time so he wouldn't have to hurry getting the crabs back to 801 Herndon Court—their latest address in the Projects.

His mother wasn't in the bar, which meant she'd likely be home impatiently waiting. That was bad news for Butcher-Bird; he'd have to move even faster now. So he continued down Patapsco Avenue at a much quicker pace. At Tenth Street, he took a right and headed up the hill toward the Projects. He was just hitting the top of Tenth Street when he thought he spotted a local gang of kids. This group was hanging out on the corner of Tenth Street and Herndon Court at the entrance of the Projects.

Little Ken did not personally observe the following encounter between the Butcher-Bird and the gang, but he had heard the story from many sources many times until he moved out of the Projects for good in 1965. Knowing Butcher-Bird as well as he did, Ken also had every reason to believe him. Here's what went down on this summer day— what happened that sky-rocketed Butcher-Bird's status to the status of neighborhood legend.

"Hey, look. Isn't it the simpleton Butcher-Bird coming this way?" Jimmy Wentzell said to his gang members. They all turned to see Butcher-Bird coming up the sidewalk on Tenth Street. Jimmy was the leader of the biggest gang in the Projects at the time. He earned it the hard way. The scars on the left side of his cheek clearly illustrated how he got the title. He was a short, wiry kid about eighteen, a couple years older than Butcher-Bird. His head was shaved, and he had an unlit cigarette securely fixed behind his right ear, as usual. He was the same guy who beat up Butcher-Bird's older brother Walter at the Projects' recreation center a couple of years before. Jimmy was a tough kid but would be no match for Butcher-Bird by himself. Good thing he had many of his gang members with him on this day.

The gang's standard attire included white tee shirts, dungarees, and black top canvass sneakers. Each of the gang's twenty or so members always dressed identically. On this day only five or so were actually hanging out with Jimmy Wentzell. "Yeah, that's him. What's he got on his shoulder anyway? Looks like a basket full of his mommy's underwear, I bet," said another member of the gang. Everyone laughed and started talking about Butcher-Bird's mother—Hilda Callahan. Her reputation as being the biggest, meanest slut in the Projects was known by everyone. Most of the gang's fathers could attest to this from personal experience. Another gang member then replied, "I heard his mother would do anything for a cigarette, and for an entire pack of smokes, she would do anybody, anywhere, anywhere. That bitch sure does love her cig's." Their laugher grew louder and louder as Butcher-Bird approached with his bushel of crabs on his shoulder.

He recognized the gang right away but didn't break his stride or change directions. The only adjustment he made was to move the crab basket from his right shoulder to his left, freeing his right arm and hand just in case he needed it quickly. Butcher-Bird knew he was already late getting home and he didn't want to be late for his mother. He had promised. And he knew how Hilda Callahan got when she had to wait for "anything." So, he was in a real hurry now. The crabs were clawing ferociously at the sides and top of the basket. Butcher-Bird knew the crabs were really pissed off at him for taking them from their dark murky homes, for being shoved into a small tight basket, for being piled on top of one another, and for being kept out their precious water for so long. He never fully understood why crabs didn't die right away when out of water. Butcher-Bird felt it had to be because of their hard shells or something. "Nah . . . it's cause' d'ey can hold d'ere breath longer d'en humans can . . . d'ats why ya' moron . . . everybody no's d'at. No wonder why d'ey kept ya' back a year in da' school," was his mother's answer to his excellent question.

This made perfect sense to Butcher-Bird. Butcher-Bird also knew the crabs were also really pissed off at "him" personally, more than anything else, because he caught them with his bare hands, not by a pole and net. This knowledge brought him even more pleasure.

"Let's check out the basket when he gets closer," Jimmy Wentzell said to his gang. Most of them agreed it would be fun, but not all of them were looking forward to an encounter with the Butcher-Bird. Two younger gang members quickly exchanged nervous glances. They had never messed with the Butcher-Bird before and didn't really want to, hearing he was nobody to mess with even if he was only sixteen or so. And they knew he had no sense of humor especially when it came to his "mother." The gang, like nearly everyone in the Projects, heard many stories about his temper and how he was very sensitive about any references made about his mother.

Butcher-Bird was now approaching the gang at the corner of Tenth and Herndon Court. They then stepped directly in front of him on the sidewalk blocking his way. Butcher-Bird was far more concerned about getting his crabs home to his mother in time than taking time to play with the boys, something he would truly have enjoyed given another place and time; this just was not one of those times. "Hey, Butcher-Bird, what's in the basket? Let's take a look." Jimmy Wentzell shouted as he moved out in the front of his gang directly confronting Butcher-Bird. Not wanting to lose any more time, Butcher-Bird stopped and looked directly in Jimmy's eyes and replied, "They're crabs." No emotion was reflected in Butcher-Bird's voice or face.

Jimmy looked around at his gang members and smirked. "Crabs? Why that can't be full of crabs . . . it would be too heavy to carry. So what's really in the basket, Butcher-Bird? Show us or we'll have to see for ourselves, right, guys?" The gang agreed with their leader and began moving in. Butcher-Bird, still standing with the basket on his shoulder, knew he had to deal with this now. So he took the basket off his shoulder and placed it directly between Jimmy and himself in one quick move. The two gang members who had exchanged glances earlier did so again but now in a much more revealing way having seen Butcher-Bird move one hundred pounds so effortlessly to the ground. He figured that giving the boys a quick glimpse of his pearls wouldn't do any harm, and then he'd be on his way. His mother was waiting and this would only take a second . . . he thought.

He was wrong.

Several crab claws were protruding out of tiny slits on the sides of the basket and in clear sight of the gang members. One guy bent over and actually petted one of the hanging claws. "Yep, they're real crabs alright, big one's too." Then he quickly backed off from the crabs as well as out of reach of Butcher-Bird.

"Well, I guess they are real crabs alright, Butcher-Bird . . . where did you say you was going with them?" Jimmy Wentzell said, now considering just how good they would be on his own family's table. "I didn't say, but if you must know . . . they're for my mother," Butcher-Bird quickly replied as he also picked up the basket and placed it back on his left shoulder. He didn't wait for a reply and continued walking through the gang, hoping there wouldn't be any more delay. He was almost beyond them when he heard one of gang members say, "Oh, the 'crabs' are for his . . . 'MOTHER'. Don't you guys get it? That's a joke . . . Butcher-Bird made a funny."

The gang members should have stopped at that, but they didn't. It was a mistake they all would regret for a long time.

Then another gang member jumped into the chatter, "Yeah, I thought your mother already had enough crabs of her own . . . enough for all the men around here, that's for sure. Why, she even gave my father a good case of the crabs last year, and he's still trying to get rid of them." With that, all the members of the gang began laughing and slapping each other on their backs while also brushing imaginary crabs away from their crotches.

That was the last straw for the Butcher-Bird. He stopped in his tracks, turned around, and dropped the crab basket down at his feet again. He didn't know who said that about his mother, but he would soon find out. "Who said that?" The gang stopped their laugher immediately. Smiles turned into hardened stares as they began to surround the Butcher-Bird once again.

This was what they wanted in the first place. "I said it, shit for brains. What are you going to do about it?" came from Jimmy Wentzell, even though he didn't actually say it. He wanted to take credit for such a good line in front of his gang as well as show off his bravery.

This was another mistake, a big one. Jimmy then walked right up to Butcher-Bird. He certainly had a lot of guts approaching him on his own like that, but it really showed he also had "shit for brains" even though the rest of the gang moved in too. The only thing between Jimmy, the whole gang, and Butcher-Bird was the basket of crabs. "I'm not going to do anything about it," Butcher-Bird replied without any emotion. The gang snickered and pimped around, assuming that Butcher-Bird was backing down. A sigh of real relief, however, came from the two guys who had exchanged glances earlier on . . . they were momentarily relieved. But it was too late, now.

Butcher-Bird continued, "Yeah, I'm not going to do anything about what you said . . . but my crabs *are* going to do a lot about it." Before Jimmy could even reach the blade he had in his back pocket, Butcher-Bird's lightning jab landed directly between his chin and collarbone, sinking deeply into the soft tissue surrounding his Adam's apple. Jimmy fell to his knees, breathless. Then several other members started their pitiful moves on the Butcher-Bird. One guy pulled out a long-handled, Steelman wrench that he kept down the right leg of his dungarees. He tried to separate Butcher-Bird's head from his shoulder with just one swing. But Butcher-Bird ducked at the last second, avoiding the impact and countered with a sudden and pulverizing right hook to the middle of the boy's rib cage. It instantly fractured his ribs. He dropped faster than a doughnut down a policeman's throat. Another gang member, a tall lanky boy, rushed at Butcher-Bird but he was quickly stopped by what felt like a tree trunk being thrust into his stomach. It appeared to come out of nowhere. The tree trunk was Butcher-Bird's left leg and the boy folded like a cardboard box. The other members of the gang, having finally seen Butcher-Bird in action, decided to back away. Perhaps they could talk their way out of the rest of this fight. So they took a few steps to the rear while Butcher-Bird stood his ground waiting for the next wave of attackers to come.

It never came.

Meanwhile, Jimmy had regained his breath, pulled out his blade from his back pocket, and lunge at him. Butcher-Bird intercepted him in midair and threw him back to the ground. He twisted the knife from his hand with a single turn, instantly breaking his wrist. Jimmy fell back and let out a girlish cry that echoed throughout the buildings and alleyways of the Projects and neighboring row homes. It was then that people started coming out of their houses to see what was going on; to watch the show on Tenth Street and Herndon Court.

Butcher-Bird then got face-to-face with Jimmy, who was now in agony from what was certain to be a compound fracture of his wrist. He then whispered softly into Jimmy's ear, "So . . . my mother gave your father the crabs, huh?" Jimmy didn't reply. He didn't have to say a word because Butcher-Bird could see fear and defeat setting-in Jimmy's face and eyes. That was the signal that he always looked for during conflict. Now was the time to put Jimmy Wentzell and his entire gang away for good—in a way that would assure they'd never say anything about his mother again. "Well Jimmy . . . I just can't let my mother outdo me, can I? So let me introduce you to some *crabs* of my own. I'm sure you'll find *them* bigger and meaner than the crabs my mother gave your dad . . . but I'll let you be the judge of that." With that said, Butcher-Bird took Jimmy by his shirt and dragged him closer to the crab basket. He held him there with one hand and unlatched the lid's metal locks. It flipped open with a single gesture and several crabs flew out immediately as if a spring had been released. The few crabs from on top of the pile went running for their lives in all directions. The other crabs remained in place, just staring up at Butcher-Bird. Their razor-sharp claws were fully extended, snapping away as if trying to catch imaginary flies in midair. Butcher-Bird knew what the crabs really wanted—a taste of the live bait he was holding in his hand—Jimmy Wentzell.

The crabs would not be disappointed.

Jimmy's eyes were bulging out of their sockets as he tried to wrestle free from Butcher-Bird's grip, but to no avail. He then started crying like a schoolboy being spanked by a teacher, but his gang didn't come to his aid; they were frozen in place just watching in disbelief as Butcher-Bird slowly, very slowly, pressed Jimmy's face into the crab basket. By this time, those few crabs that had escaped earlier were now scurrying in all directions across the grass, down the sidewalk, and onto Tenth Street. Several passing cars screeched on their brakes and swerved, trying to avoid what they knew just couldn't be . . . crabs this far from the inner harbor—impossible. But it was true. An oncoming car sideswiped two parked cars. Another frantic driver turned sharply to avoid the mother of all crabs standing straight up on hind legs with its ten-inch claws fully spread open in the middle of the street like a tight end waiting to catch a football. The driver just missed squashing the brave crab but didn't miss the nearby fire hydrant during his panic swerve. The head-on collision with the fire hydrant created an instant geyser of water that shot a beautiful blue-and-white spray of refreshing coolness across the block on this hot afternoon on the outskirts of the Projects.

Meanwhile, back at the basket . . .

The last thing Jimmy remembered "seeing" before he passed out were dozens of mesmerizing eyes gazing up at him—each with its own empty chilling stare. He also recalled seeing blue, black, and deep green jagged claws eagerly reaching up from their entanglement. With the assistance of Butcher-Bird's weight pushing down on Jimmy's head, the crabs' eyes and their jagged claws kept getting closer and larger as his face descended into their dark, damp nest.

The last thing Jimmy ever remembered "hearing" was a steady barrage of stereophonic snapping and hissing sounds vibrating in perfect alien unison. It kept getting louder and louder as Jimmy's head continued sinking deeper and deeper.

And, the very last thing he remembered "feeling" was the burning agony of his flesh being slashed and ripped from his face, ears, and neck. It was like a thousand hypodermic needles simultaneously puncturing and exploding every inch of his skull.

But Butcher-Bird was merciful on this day. He only allowed his crabs play with Jimmy's head for a few seconds and then quickly tossed Jimmy's collapsed body with its shredded-wheat-head onto the grass next to the sidewalk. The other gang members quickly went to him without taking their eyes off Butcher-Bird. He then replaced the lid on the basket, lifted it back on his shoulder, and continued along his journey. After about a block, he stopped and looked back to witness the chaotic scene he had left behind and cracked a little smile.

A couple of the gang members were still on the ground while others were hovering around them. Local residents who had been viewing the entire event from their windows had since come out and were now standing around gazing, pointing, and chattering about the whole incident. A police car had also arrived on the scene just as the neighbors' kids were starting to cool off under the ruptured fire hydrant's spray. The traffic on Tenth Street started getting backed up as several little crablike shadows continued scurrying all over the place in search of a suitable place to live out their newly found freedom.

Butcher-Bird then turned around and headed home. His mother was waiting.

A couple weeks later, Jimmy Wentzell recovered from his crab basket encounter, but he never regained the desire to lead the gang, leaving them leaderless. After many internal gang debates, including a few fights among themselves, the unanimous choice for new leader was the Butcher-Bird. He had never been a joiner of anything, but he accepted this offer. And, from that day on, the phrase *"clawing your way to the top"* took on new meaning throughout the Projects. Butcher-Bird retained his leadership of the gang until he joined the US Navy. He was only seventeen years old and his mother, who now was going by the name of Hilda Mytus (she once again had remarried—her fourth) was required to sign the government's official "Declaration of Consent" in order for her son to join the US Navy at that young age.

And she did just that.

Butcher-Bird left Brooklyn and the Projects three days after his seventeenth birthday. And, the legend of Butcher-Bird passed into Brooklyn lore forever.

Butcher-Bird Takes Flight

Meanwhile, back at the "smoke tent" . . .

Ken and Butch were still drinking on this mild night in Lai Khe, Vietnam. All the other soldiers departed, leaving them alone to catch up. And that's what they did until the sun came up the next morning. Fortunately, the commander had given Ken the next day off because of Butch's visit. So he got a jeep then showed Butch around Lai Khe, including the village of Lai Khe. That's when Butcher-Bird met Ha`. "You don't look like brothers. Prove it. Show me your ID, Mr. Butch . . . sorry, I mean Mr. Butcher-Bird, right?" Ha` said in her usual direct manner.

Butch showed her his ID and she was amazed. "You both come from the same mother and father . . . so how come you look so different?" They couldn't explain to Ha` their complex childhood or anything about their mother, so they just agreed with her that they indeed looked very different. She was right about Butch's looks, though. He was now twenty-one and had grown another three inches and another twenty-five pounds since Ken had last seen him in the Projects. His hair was dark and cut to meet US Naval standards. He was lean and strong.

So the three of them talked for some time, drank beer, and had a few joints (Butch not smoking though). She then asked Butch if he would like to go on the "chocolate river" with one of her friends. She explained that was how she and Ken referred to making love while smoking a little grass. He didn't get the concept since he never smoked, but he got the image and understood what she was saying. He declined anyway. "What, are you some kind of queer boy? If so, that's Okay, you can still go on the chocolate river with one of my male cousins, instead. No problem." Ha` was applying her natural skills of persuasion. She just wanted to ensure Ken's big brother, Butch, had "happiness."

He laughed and so did Ken at the thought of being with another man. But he declined her kind offer explaining how he would be in Bangkok shortly and would have plenty of opportunities to go on many "chocolate river" rides there. Ken, Butch, and Ha` talked and laughed together for another hour or so and then they showed him around the village of Lai

Khe. Butch felt very comfortable there and liked the Vietnamese people, especially their pets. They returned to her hooch where Ken and Ha` smoked some more, and Butch drank another beer. It was a good time for him. He had fun and had some firsthand experience with the Vietnamese people in the process.

That evening, they went back to the "smoke tent" and kicked back some more. Ken promised Butch he would have a great surprise if they called it a short night and got some extra sleep. Butch quickly agreed. The next morning they got some breakfast and then hopped in jeeps along with the Huey's pilots and door gunners. Together, they headed out to the airfield. Ken then handed Butch a different kind of helmet, a flight helmet.

He was very surprised and delighted.

So he accompanied Ken and the crew on a direct sortie from Lai Khe to FSB Marriott about fifteen miles north. It wasn't an operational or combat flight that required the commander's presence, so they took Butch along. The only time he had ever flown in a Huey was on the quick hop he took from Phu Loi to Lai Khe just two days before. So this flight was a bonus, a real bonus. And the pilots were going to make it a very memorable flight for Ken's big brother; they wanted to see if a "Butcher-Bird" could really fly in the skies of Vietnam.

Before taking-off, he talked with the pilots and the door gunners who were interested in how the hell Butch got to Lai Khe in the first place. He explained his story to them and before taking off, the pilots promised Butch a flight he'd never forget. In the Huey, Butch was like a little kid in a candy store; he wanted to see and touch everything, leaning back and forth looking out of both sides of the Huey afraid he would miss something. He also had to touch all the instruments and equipment in his reach even though he didn't know what they were. And he asked every question imaginable about the Huey, the terrain, the waterways, the rice fields, the FSBs, and the Viet Cong. He was a sponge, absorbing every piece of information provided. He also wanted to sit in a door gunner's seat and fire the M60 machine gun but was not allowed. He then pouted briefly, but snapped out of it when the Huey started to land at FSB Marriott. The trip went fast and in Butch's mind it was over before it even started.

On their flight back to Lai Khe, the pilots deviated from their scheduled flight plan and took Butch along the winding Saigon River. They flew less than fifty feet above the water going about seventy-five miles per hour. They swayed back and forth along the river's lazy flowing brown water with the lush green and brown jungle passing by him at lightning speed. Halfway down the river, the door gunners opened up their M60s with live fire without letting Butch know it was coming. He was momentarily disoriented from the powerful noise and the unexpected vibrations caused by the firing. He eventually settled down and came to appreciate the awesome firepower of this wonderful machine. Eventually, the Huey veered off the Saigon River and headed across the wide-open paddies as Butch watch the local Vietnamese work their water buffalo and tend the rice fields.

All along, Ken kept staring at Butch, just watching his reaction to the wonders that kept unfolding before him. During the final few minutes of their sortie back to Lai Khe, Butch became totally silent. He was just taking in everything during this experience. It was good to see his older brother in a reflective state.

Ken had always feared and hated Butch as teenagers growing up in the Projects. Such feelings were still very much a part of Ken's past memory and current reality. But now, it was no longer as severe or as intense as once was. Somehow, such feelings seemed less important simply by the choice he made to come to Vietnam to see him. Ken no longer feared Butch but he still felt a degree of anger toward him. And he still did not fully trust him as brothers trust one another. Even though he knew this was a good first step in rebuilding their relationship, he also sensed it was likely not going to last over the longer term.

Nevertheless, Ken was savoring the current moments and feelings. It was a special time with his brother that he would never forget.

When they landed back in Lai Khe, Butch was on a natural high. "So what did you think of our little flying war machine?" referring to the Huey.

"Fucking great . . . nearly got a hard-on over that river . . . was just hoping to see some Viet Cong. Can we go back later today and see if any would fire at us . . . that would be so cool," Butch said in a very serious manner. "I don't think so . . . besides, I also don't think you'd like it as much as you think you would once it started, believe me, Butch." Ken tried to change the subject by saying, "I bet watching those huge canons on the USS Hancock unleash their load is even more awesome than a mere M60 machine gun on a helicopter, right?"

Butch agreed and started explaining what it was like on the USS Hancock during firing missions. Once he finished, Ken moved Butch to a jeep with driver and sent him back to headquarters promising to see him around sunset when they returned from their final mission of the day—a trip that Butch could not go on.

He really wanted to go with Ken again and put up a fuss. Then he reluctantly acquiesced and climbed into the jeep. As the jeep pulled away he noticed Butch's head was pointing down like a scolded child who had just been corrected for acting up in class. So Ken yelled a friendly reminder to Butch as the jeep pulled away from the Huey, "And stay on the wooden planks walking through the camp and don't shit in the brush—use the latrine! Just remember that big 'bird-eating' tarantula knows you're in town; it can't wait to sink its fangs into a different kind of bird—Butcher-Bird ass, that is. So stay alert. See you around dusk."

Butch didn't respond.

That evening Ken and Butch hung out at Ken's tent, drank beer, and talked some more. Butch had to leave the next morning and somehow find a way to get back on his abbreviated R&R schedule. So they just kicked back their last night together. And, in the morning, Ken placed Butch on a C-130 that was heading for Tan Son Nhut Air Base located near Saigon. There he caught a flight directly to Bangkok and finished up his R&R in Thailand. He did make it back to the USS Hancock on time. His commander didn't ask him about his R&R and Butch did not volunteer any information about it either.

The Butcher-Bird had gotten his own "clean getaway" as well as a "clean return" while catching up with his little brother in the process. Later that month, Ken received a short letter from Butch telling him about Bangkok and his return to the USS Hancock. He didn't thank Ken for taking care of him in Lai Khe, and he didn't expect it. Ken sensed it was really he who should have thanked Butch for making such a daring decision and taking such a risk to come and see him in the first place. But he never did either.

Ken and Butch wouldn't meet or communicate again for several years.

His anger and hatred he had felt for Butch were beginning to diminish; at least now, Ken no longer feared him. While he still sensed they would never be as close as they were before moving into the Projects as little boys, he had to admit Butch had changed for the better since joining the navy. The military structure and discipline seemed to have had a positive effect on him, not only in attitude but also in his self-image.

Unfortunately, once Butch left the navy in 1970, he no longer had the strict standards and disciplines to help guide him through life and he would eventually regress back to his teenage, self-oriented, and violent ways.

The first time Ken ever openly articulated this event, Butch's visit to him in Vietnam, as well as his feelings for his brother would occur forty years later. It would take place at the Massachusetts National Military Cemetery when Ken was giving the eulogy at Butch's funeral.

The Bronze Star

From October 1968 to March 1969, Ken flew three to five missions per day—over 250 missions altogether alongside two different Division Artillery commanders. While pilots and door gunners changed frequently, Ken remain the single constant on the Huey. He even saw his original commander, Colonel Britton, finish his own tour of duty and depart Vietnam with honor well before Ken's own departure day. He was replaced by Colonel Holder.

The day before Ken was scheduled to depart Vietnam, the new artillery commander called him into his office. Ken was somewhat concerned at first, thinking his tour of duty was going to be involuntarily extended for another six months which could easily happen. Such involuntary actions were always done at the discretion of the commanders. As he walked into the commander's office that day, he quickly noticed the command sergeant major (CSM) was also present. This was a bad sign to Ken because whenever the CSM and commander were together, it usually implied some kind of punitive or corrective action was about to be taken on an enlisted man or noncommissioned officer.

So Ken braced for the worse.

But rather than corrective action, the commander, Colonel Holder, personally thanked Ken for his exceptional service rendered to him and the entire First Infantry Division Artillery Command. Then Colonel Holder and the CSM came to "attention" and officially presented Ken with six military awards including the Vietnamese Cross of Gallantry campaign medal and the Army Air Medal with four Oak Leaf Clusters.

Ken was shocked. Even though he knew his flight hours and missions earned him an Army Air Medal, such awards were usually placed in a soldier's permanent record then forwarded along to his next commander for presentation. To have a personal award ceremony, with a full-bird colonel and a CSM was a rare exception and a profound honor in Ken's eyes. The next thing that happened caused Ken, not only to be speechless for the moment, but also be humbled for the rest of his life. At that time everything that followed seemed to happen in slow motion. Ken recalled watching Colonel Holder walk over to his desk, reach into his drawer, and remove a navy blue leather box. The colonel then opened it and carefully took out the contents. The next thing he recalled was feeling the colonel pinning the Bronze Star on his chest. Even though he knew it occurred, Ken had no memory of the CSM also reading the entire Bronze Star citation aloud as he was required to do by military protocol.

It read as follows:

By direction of the president,

The Bronze Star Medal
is presented to

Sgt. Kenneth A. Callahan

First Infantry Division Artillery who distinguished himself by outstandingly meritorious service in connection with military operations against a hostile force in the Republic of Vietnam. During the period March 1968 to March 1969 he consistently manifested exemplary professionalism and initiative in obtaining outstanding results. His rapid assessment and solution of numerous problems inherent in a counterinsurgency environment greatly enhanced the allied effectiveness against a determined and aggressive enemy. Despite many adversities, he invariably performed his duties in a resolute and efficient manner. Energetically applying his sound judgment and extensive knowledge, he has contributed materially to the successful accomplishment of the United States mission in the Republic of Vietnam. His loyalty, diligence, and devotion to duty were in keeping with the highest traditions of the military service and reflect great credit upon himself and the United States Army.

Ken also remembered shaking hands, saluting, and saying farewell. However, he did not remember departing the commander's office nor did he recall catching a hop on a C-130 out of Lai Khe the next day. And he did not remember landing in Saigon. But, he did remember his flight back to the United States on the Flying Tigers Airline the following day simply because it was the same airline that brought him to Vietnam a year earlier in March, 1968.

"Are You Going to San Francisco?"

The flight back to the USA from Saigon took about eighteen hours in real time but only minutes in Ken time.

The plane was packed with about two hundred servicemen from all branches who had served in III and IV Corps (the southern half of Vietnam). Even though each soldier had a smile on his face knowing he was about to reenter the "world," many used the time to reflect on a year of great personal challenge. Boys who entered Vietnam were now returning as men. And men who entered Vietnam were now returning older and wiser. Yet everyone was silently saddened by the loss of friends as well as for the loss of their innocence, even though no one ever expressed such feelings aloud. Ken was just one such boy returning as a man.

Despite Flying Tigers being a government-chartered flight, it was still a commercial airline, which meant "stewardesses" versus crewmen would be in charge of the cabin. Just by seeing an American woman up-close, talking to them, listening to them, and watching them move about the aisle made the long trip much more enjoyable and meaningful. Since there were no movies on most airlines in 1969, soldiers just read, wrote, drank, or talked to those around them to pass the hours. When the stewardesses' service finished, they'd sit and talk with groups of soldiers. They'd answer questions about the states, TV shows, politics, sports, etc., and try to make the flight time fly by even faster. They even created a fun and festive atmosphere on the plane by holding raffles and contests among the soldiers—giving away simple yet very rare prizes seldom found in Vietnam, including little car models of Mustangs, Corvettes and GTOs. Pictures of Raquel Welch, Ursula Andress, and Jane Fonda were also big hits. (Jane Fonda was still considered a real "babe" by soldiers in 1969 because of her hot role in the blockbuster movie *Barbarella*. Most soldiers had heard about this flick, but no one had yet seen it except via posters or magazines and it was well before Fonda's fall from grace due to her anti-war protest activities that she did in North Vietnam later in 1972).

Raffles were simple and conducted by selecting seat numbers or picking a soldier's names from the flight manifest. Prizes would be given to those with birthdays closest to the day the plane would land in the USA; to the oldest and youngest soldiers onboard; to anyone who could guess the exact speed of the airplane during the flight. Other simple but highly valued prizes included such things as: Peppermint Patties, Circus Peanuts, and Little Margaret candies. But the most fun prizes of all were personal items the stewardesses themselves would raffle off—scarfs, earrings, tubes of lipstick, and even a bottle of their perfume. Such small things had a big impact on guys who had "gone without" seeing or feeling the joys of such pleasures for so long. These fun things made many soldiers understand what they had been fighting for. In return, soldiers gave stewardesses their own personal items including: medals (if they were not in their fatigues), field hats, and even boot strings tied in a nice bow were a hit for a stewardess.

Time passed fast and made for a very good transition from war to peace, from confrontation to civilization. Departing the plane once touchdown occurred in Oakland, California, stewardesses freely gave soldiers warm hugs and cheek kisses while also sincerely welcoming them back to the USA and thanking them for their service and sacrifice. Ken never forgot the genuine kindness of these stewardesses on the Flying Tiger airlines, and he wasn't alone in his gratitude.

All the soldiers were transported to a central processing center. There, they showered, cleaned up, given clean uniforms, and treated to a steak dinner (or two or three or as many as they wanted). Airline tickets were processed right there in the center to help accelerate their individual trips home to every corner of the country. Before leaving the processing center, they were also briefed on the attitude many Americans held toward Vietnam veterans. Specifically, they were told encounters with hippies or student groups in California could occur which could include direct physical confrontation, cursing, spitting, or being called names such as baby killers and warmongers.

Ken had heard these stories before but didn't believe them, wouldn't believe them. Regardless, they were told to avoid these people and do not engage or provoke them. To do so was a real lose-lose situation. Some guys took this advice seriously by putting on their civilian clothes before they left the processing center. Ken would have done the same, but he didn't own any civilian clothes so he stayed in uniform. Besides, he had more important things on this mind as he and some other soldiers made their way from Oakland's processing center to San Francisco. They wanted to see the city, walk on cement, and drink some beer, lots of beer. Ken's flight home wasn't leaving for six hours or more, so he and a few others did some quick sightseeing then stopped in a local bar and downed a few celebratory beers. Time flew by and in the midst of their celebration, they noticed a few guys were about to miss their flights home if they didn't leave right away. Ken was one of them.

Hippie Encounter

So they all made their way to the San Francisco Airport and ultimately to their respective airline terminals as fast as they could, saying farewell to each other on the way. Ken was one of the unfortunate ones; he actually he missed his 10:00 p.m. flight by only a few minutes. He had to stay the night in San Francisco. The next flight to Baltimore departed at 6:30 a.m., so he decided to just sleep in the terminal instead of getting a hotel room or going all the way back to the central processing center in Oakland. He only had a few bucks anyway, and besides, sleeping in an airport terminal in San Francisco was no big deal. Actually it was kind of attractive to him—it was dry and warm, there were no bugs, flush toilets were available, clean drinking water was only a step away, and even more important, there were no incoming rockets or mortars expected. And it was all free. Perfect.

What else would a nineteen-year-old really need in order to get through a single night (besides a young, beautiful girl at his side, but he didn't think that was going to happen). So he chose to sleep in the airport and that's exactly what he did. Ken then dragged his duffle bag to the farthest corner of the terminal away from the departure gate so he could have a little privacy. He then built himself a little sleeping area and fell asleep quickly.

Around 1 a.m., Ken awoke. Except for a man pushing a broom on the other side of the terminal, Ken was all alone. He rolled over and fell back to sleep instantly. However, about an hour later, he opened his eyes once again and saw what he thought was a hippie (a "real" hippie) standing about thirty feet away. He didn't really know if the guy was a hippie or not, having never seen one before, but he sure looked like one according to what Ken had heard—long hair, mustache, beard, bell bottoms, beads, and sandals.

He and the hippie were the only living souls in the terminal.

Ken wasn't certain, but he sensed the hippie was staring directly at him and he continued to do so for some time . . . just standing there, motionless, staring. Ken wanted to dismiss it and go back to sleep but he couldn't. His paranoia from nights in Vietnam seemed to be carrying over to the States even though he only had been back for less than twenty-four hours. So Ken just rolled over and tried to ignore him for a few more minutes hoping the guy would be gone the next time he looked. But no such luck.

That's when Ken noticed the hippie was still there and the stories and the warnings concerning hippies came rushing back to him. Maybe there was some truth to this after all. But he wasn't going to jump to any conclusion, so he just turned-over and ignored him. But the hippie stayed around and had even moved closer. In fact, he was now only a few feet away from Ken and staring at him. It was now about 4:00 a.m. and the morning sky outside the terminal window was becoming somewhat lighter. That's when Ken stood up, stretched, and took a few steps toward to the ticket counter to see if the hippie would continue his stare and follow him.

He did.

Now Ken knew something was up but didn't feel he should take any action without being absolutely sure. That's when the hippie called to him. It was a moment he would remember the rest of his life: "Hey man . . . hey man . . . is your name Callahan . . . Ken Callahan?"

To say Ken was surprised would be a massive understatement—he was astounded. The hippie was still too far away to read the nameplate on Ken's uniform and even if he could see that far, Ken's first name was not on it. He didn't know what was happening here.

A thousand scenarios rushed through his mind and here are just two:

1. This could be a scene from a 1950s horror film . . . "late at night," "empty airport terminal," "all alone," "weird human being stalking the premises," "unsuspecting soldier asleep on the floor."
2. Or even worse, the "hippie world" was actually a highly sophisticated, well-organized movement, not just a bunch of confused dropouts from society. They were an institutionalized entity that knew every soldier's name returning from Vietnam and they were out to stop them before they got home to kill more babies.

Given more time, Ken would likely have conjured up other irrational scenarios, but he didn't. He was just too stunned to respond. So he said the following "almost" answer that had no real teeth, but it was the only thing he could manage to say in the midst of a 4:00 a.m., triple time zone hangover from hell, "Who wants to know?"

Without answering, the hippie stood up and started walking directly at Ken. When he was about a foot away and just when Ken was ready to spring on him, the hippie said the following with his arms wide open: "Ken Callahan . . . right, Man . . . Anne Arundel High School . . . . it's me Man . . . Dwane . . . Dwane Laws . . . Man . . . Remember me?"

Ken did not recognize the name at first and certainly didn't recognize the face. Instead, he kept saying to himself, *Who is this guy? How did he know my name? What the fuck's up?* The hippie then approached Ken talking even louder and faster than before, "It's me . . . Dwane . . . class of '67 . . . we both were transfer-in students . . . we had lunch everyday together for months . . . it's me . . . Dwane Laws . . . Dwane Laws. I know it's you man . . . got to be you."

Then it came to Ken. He was quite relieved but also very stunned. Figure the odds of such a coincidence. Two AAHS graduates, three thousand miles away from Maryland, coming from two different places, both had been living in two different worlds, with two totally different looks—one a soldier and one a hippie. Could this really be?

Dwane then continued, "Man, I couldn't believe it was you. That's why I had to keep my distance. You know . . . all the weird things we hear about you Vietnam vets . . . just had to be careful . . . didn't want to spook you and see you going all crazy nuts on me or something . . . heard you guys explode if you get agitated . . . you know, Man."

Ken then looked closer, much closer at this guy trying to see a real face beneath all that facial hair. Then he recognized his "muzzle" (Ken always referred to the combination of a person's eyes, nose, cheeks, and mouth area as the one thing that never really change over time—just like a dog's muzzle never seems to change as it aged). People were the same in his mind. Now, they were standing only two feet apart, and Ken finally got his mind and emotions in check. That's when he said to Dwane as they shook hands and hugged, "Dwane Laws . . . no shit! Is that really you under all that . . . all that . . . fuzz? What's happened to you? What are you doing here?"

With that, they sat and talked endlessly. They both kept touching each other's face and head, making sure this was really happening to both of them. After a while, other passengers started filling the terminal, and then the flight crew also arrived. Ken and Dwane were slowly swallowed by the crowd—the hectic movement and constant noise just gradually engulfed them; they became just a part of the moment. It just so happened that Dwane Laws was heading back to Maryland to visit relatives when he ran into Ken at the San Francisco Airport in March of 1969. He had been attending U.C. Berkeley for the past two years since graduating from AAHS. He too was simply trying to catch an early morning flight to Baltimore just as Ken was doing.

They boarded the plane together, rearranged their seats, and caught up on so many things during their six straight hour flight home. They also drank until they both were cut off by the stewardess, and in the process became kind of celebrities on the flight because of their obvious differences in appearance coupled with their obvious affection. Passengers sitting nearby had overheard their conversation and joined in. Passengers also started buying endless drinks for the boys, and that's how they got blitzed so fast and why eventually they had to be cut off by a stewardess. People started asking Ken about the war while others asked Dwane about life at the "liberal Mecca of the World"—Berkeley. That's when a few arguments broke out among other passengers over the war and antiwar movement. But no conflict arose at all between Ken and Dwane—none whatsoever. As a matter of fact, just the opposite unfolded. Ken and Dwane just picked up from where they left off the last time they were together at AAHS. It seemed they both were laughing more than talking all the way across the USA.

Somewhere between San Francisco and Baltimore, Dwane took off a set of beads he had been wearing and placed it over Ken's head and shoulders. It felt a little weird because Ken knew soldiers weren't authorized to wear anything except official military garb. But he didn't care at that moment . . . *"What are they going to do, send me to Vietnam?"* he thought. That's when Ken gave one his medals to Dwane to wear. It was a great welcome home flight for Ken Callahan and for Dwane Laws.

They landed at Friendship International Airport in Maryland, just a few miles from AAHS. There, they embraced once again and then said farewell. Both boys then went their separate ways after a wonderful, unscheduled, unplanned, unimaginable reunion that took place thirty-two thousand feet above the earth in March of 1969.

Ken Callahan and Dwane Laws, AAHS graduates, never saw or spoke to each other again until August 1, 2012 (forty-three years after their chance reunion in the San Francisco airport). Maintaining close, interpersonal relationships had never been one of Ken's strengths, nor would it become so for decades.

CHAPTER 5

"All in the Family" (1980-2010)

KEN'S MOTHER, HILDA M. CALLAHAN (a.k.a. Harrington, Lang, Archer, Callahan, Mytus, and Smith) died in 1998. He was informed of her death by a member of her fifth husband's family—the Smiths. Ken then tried to contact both of his brothers, Walter and Butch, to inform them of her death, but it was difficult to do after so many years of estrangement. He only saw or heard from Walter three or four times over a couple of decades and Butch even less. All three brothers seemed to like it that way for some reason.

Ken always thought each of the brothers felt more comfortable, safer, that way. Ken was forty-eight; Butcher-Bird was fifty; Walter was fifty-three at the time of their mother's death. Sandy, who at the age of three had been adopted to another family, would be about thirty-eight. Ken had one opportunity to meet Sandy after she had been adopted as a child. This brief reunion happened in 1976 when she was about sixteen and living somewhere in Maryland with her adopted family. Ken was still married to his first wife, Cheryl, who also met Sandy. He could not recall how, why, or exactly where the meeting occurred, but Ken felt it was good to see her and to know she was okay. Sandy was a young, beautiful teenage girl with a good head on her shoulders as he would recall later. He would also recall she had the looks, but not the demeanor of her real mother—Hilda.

Ken and his little sister, Sandy, never saw each other again after this one brief encounter. While his reunion with her was short, his memory of her was long-lasting.

A Mother's Passing

Hilda Callahan was seventy-seven years old when she died of congestive heart failure. She had also suffered from severe dementia for several years prior to her death. Her fifth and final husband, Joseph Smith, died a couple years earlier and his family members felt Hilda had "put him in an early grave" because of the way she treated him while they were married. For decades, she seemed to do everything she could to keep his family separated from him. She still had to control things even in her later years, just as she had done raising her kids and managing her first four husbands. Joseph Smith was a kind, gentle, and nonviolent man; he was also a very good man. Ken was the only child of Hilda Callahan still remaining under her control in 1965 when they moved into 3555 Horton Avenue, Joseph Smith's house. Hilda met Joseph in the Downton's bar. She served him, seduced him, persuaded him, and moved in with him all within a few weeks. She was separated from Oren Mytus (her fourth husband) but still legally married when she moved. They couldn't marry so they lived in sin together. But, Ken didn't care. All he valued was the fact that he was about to have a permanent roof over his head, a real bed to sleep in, and food in his belly. Joseph Smith, being a good man, was a bonus. That was more than enough for Ken at age sixteen.

He and his mother had been living in another one-bedroom, rental apartment just outside the Projects when she met Joseph. Their address was 929 Jeffrey Street. They had been living there only a few months after being evicted from 801 Herndon Court in the Projects. Their first eviction occurred two years earlier while living at 4139 Martin Court. In between both evictions (1963 to early 1965), they lived in another ten or so rental apartments across South Baltimore and Brooklyn.

Just to have lived and survived in the Projects at any time was one thing. To move out of the Projects on one's own terms was another thing. To be "evicted" from the Projects was an entirely different thing. Yet, to be evicted from the Projects twice in a single lifetime was just unparalleled. Most families would naturally be embarrassed by such a track record, but not Ken. By 1965, he was already a seasoned veteran of nomadism and resiliency. When it came to adapting to unexpected change, accepting personal disappointments, surviving physical and emotional abuse, withstanding manipulation and betrayal, overcoming neglect and abandonment, as well as adjusting to continued instability, Ken's skin was tough, and his scars were even tougher. Therefore, something as innocuous as another eviction notice or another husband for his mother was a mere speed bump in life—he'd just slow down a little, cross it, and move on to the next thing. Time would ultimately show that Ken could easily get through and get around such things quickly. But time would also show Ken's emotions would never allow him to get over anything for too long.

At first, Ken viewed Joseph Smith as just another man in his mother's life, but he turned out to be a knight in shining armor. He wasn't like any other man his mother brought home. As a matter of fact, Ken never recalled seeing Joseph Smith until they actually moved in with him, and he had never seen him come to their apartment like her other boyfriends. That's why Ken thought this man could be different.

Ken's intuitive assessment of this man was correct.

Joseph Smith had his own home and brought up his family in the same location on Hanson Avenue where Hilda and Ken moved. He was a very stable and kind man who Ken quickly came to trust and admire. When Ken and his mother moved in, he had his own room—no longer having to sleep on the sofa or floor while his mother entertained her boyfriends less than ten feet away. Smith ensured there was always food in the refrigerator and that Hilda made dinner for him and Ken every night. This was an amazing thing to Ken—scheduled dinner time, open refrigerator with food, having his own bedroom with a radio. Smith also had a son of his own; his name was Bobby who was a couple of years younger than Ken. And he also had his own bedroom. They both got along fine, but shortly after the families merged, Bobby moved to his real mother's place. This left Joseph Smith, Hilda, and Ken in the house by themselves.

Ken never recalled having a real sit-down family dinner with his mother, brothers, and sister—not once in all the years in the Projects. That's why having dinner with his mother and a man (any man) was so special. He didn't care if she was married to him or not, and he didn't even care what food was served. This was just civilized, and he also liked it because it reminded him of all the *Leave It to Beaver* family meals on TV. There was not a single episode of *Leave it to Beaver* that didn't show at least one meal scene among Ward, June, Wally and the Beaver, actually sitting down together eating and talking together. That was Ken's favorite part of the show and always imagined himself jumping into the TV screen and joining them.

He would ultimately remain in the Joseph Smiths house until he graduated from Anne Arundel High, which represented nearly two consecutive years in the same place—a stable run in Ken's mind. He had already gained permission to use his Uncle Dan's county address before moving into Hanson Avenue with Smith, so things were working out fine for him. He had a permanent roof over his head and a positive male figure around. He didn't have to go back and forth to Sparta High School, and since his mother no longer was required to work at the Downton's bar, she also seemed to be settling down a little after such a long, chaotic, and disturbing life.

But it wouldn't last long. Hilda would eventually evoke her dysfunctional magic, even on the good hearted Joseph Smith.

When school began at Anne Arundel High School in September 1965, Ken could merely walk, jog, or take a short five-minute bus ride from 1st street straight up Ritchie Highway to Blossom Lane, where the high school was located. All of these modes were faster and much safer than going to Sparta High. Equally great, he also had a lunch bag to take with him "every school day" that contained an actual sandwich and a piece of fruit. Joseph Smith would make it for him every morning, not Hilda. She was changing now, but not that much, not fast enough to pack her son a lunch for school. Smith recognized this about her right away, and without Hilda knowing, he would not only make Ken's lunch, but he would also place some extra change in his lunch bag—a dime, nickel, or quarter. Ken wouldn't know how much, but it always gave him something to look forward to discovering, and the coinage came in handy too. "A teenager should have some carrying-around change," Smith would say.

He'd also give Ken extra change for doing chores around the house after school and on the weekends. Hilda never knew about that either. Most important, Smith never hit Ken once nor harmed him in any way. He didn't even raise his voice in anger and never insulted or abused him. While his mother still took opportunities to lay into him, the sting of her extension cord was never felt again. On the times when Smith witnessed her beating or demeaning Ken, he'd always make an effort to personally follow up with him and try to minimize the impact of her blows or tongue. He comforted him, and Ken liked that. This was new to him and Smith would also do it in Hilda's presence. Ken felt Joseph Smith was trying to teach his mother basic things such as affection, kindness, forgiveness, and even tenderness.

And she hated that.

Ken never knew why, but her beatings decreased in frequency during his junior year in high school, then totally stopped when he entered his senior year. In retrospect, Ken attributed this major sea change in his mother's behavior to the presence of Joseph Smith, nothing else. A few years after Ken graduated from high school and went off to Vietnam in the army, Joseph Smith and Hilda Callahan finally married. It was then that Hilda's bad magic was again let out of the bottle, leading to the destruction of Smith's financial, social, and personal life. Hilda's campaign began by insisting he take her to dog races and casinos. She liked gambling. Sometimes she would win, most times she'd lose. Because of this, Smith had to take on an extra part-time job while working his full time just to keep up with her needs and pleasures. With Ken gone, she began taking out her need to abuse on Joseph Smith. Eventually, her gambling caused them to miss mortgage payments and other debts, forcing them to sell the house on Hanson Avenue where Joseph had raised his kids and where he was expecting to live out his retirement days and eventually die.

But Hilda Callahan made such a pretty picture impossible to paint.

During the 1970s and 1980s, Hilda and Joseph were forced to live in many rental apartments throughout Brooklyn, Arbutus and Curtis Bay (just like the first half of her life). Hilda had now gone back to her old ways. It was inevitable. She also started building a wall between Smith and his kids, siblings, and parents. She would not allow him to phone them, never took messages when they called him, and never allowed him to visit them on holidays, birthdays, or any special occasion. The only time he was ever able to catch up with his family was when he clandestinely did so, without her knowledge. And since she had no family members of her own to harass, she could devote all her attention to Joseph Smith. Over the subsequent years of their marriage, as she continued aging, it got even worst for Smith. This wonderful man was in the clutches of Hilda with no way out. He was living every man's worst nightmare according to his own family members. And this went on for nearly two decades. Ken made short visits to them on occasions in the late 1980s and early 1990s. He even met with Smith's family to try to help out, but together they couldn't seem to break him away from her. She was his wife "for better or worse" and he was determined to be there for her, even under such circumstances.

That was just the kind of man he was—a good husband, a good man.

Then Joseph Smith passed away. He died a broken man—a shell of person he was before meeting Hilda Callahan. His funeral, of course, was all about Hilda, not him; she made it so. But everyone who attended his funeral, including Ken and his wife Dawn, knew the truth. She had driven this wonderful man to an early grave.

The good news (or bad news) was Hilda was now totally on her own for the first time. She had no kids actively participating in her life, no more boyfriends, and absolutely no friends. Her looks had faded, and even though she had plenty of siblings, nieces, nephews, and cousins, no one wanted to have anything to do with her. And, her physical health was deteriorating as quickly as her mind. Hilda could no longer care for herself, and no one wanted to care for her—she just hadn't earned genuine affection and generosity of others. Over the years she had isolated everyone around her, and in the process she had only managed to accomplish one thing—to isolate herself.

During her last year of life, she lived in a nursing facility in Curtis Bay called, Tranquil Valley Rest Home. Dementia was taking more and more of her mind every day, and thousands of cigarettes had also taken a huge bite out of her lungs and heart along the way. None the less, Hilda's true nature seemed to keep shining through until the bitter end.

The staff at Tranquil Valley was very helpful and expert at comforting her during this time in her life. Fortunately for Hilda, each person was a kind and caring professional who, at first, did not fully recognize her true nature. However, they soon came to understand who Hilda Smith truly was. Unfortunately for Hilda, these fine people were also men and women of African American descent, and this made her final days personally very uncomfortable. The kind of hatred and ignorance she spewed across Brooklyn for most of her life was now coming back to haunt her. Her racial prejudice and intolerance for anyone who didn't look like her started to be felt by the fine people who were caring for her in this facility. On several occasions, members of the Smith family visited Hilda, keeping their promises made to Joseph. He requested they look after her upon his death, as much as humanly possible. That is, as much as could be tolerated. Despite their personal feelings and better judgment, the Smith family honored his wishes. They were a very honorable, kind and generous family—just like Joseph always had been.

Ken came to visit her twice during the two years she lived in the rest home. On both occasions, he first met with the social worker and the director. They would bring him up to date on her condition as well as pass along any relevant information and observations. Consistently, they told him of her abusive language and demeaning treatment of the support staff. Hilda's attitudes and values were exposed for the entire world to experience on a routine basis and a staff member even told Ken that his mother often referred to the nursing home as her personal "black hell." It didn't seem to matter to Hilda Smith what others really thought about her or how she treated them. She was going to be herself. "Get ya' fuckin' black hands off me;" "Where da' hell ya' been, I been callin' y'ur slow ass for hours;" "Ya' koons always been slow anyway." These were routine racial slurs used even until her last breath.

Ken recalled the last time he saw his mother at Tranquil Valley. It also would be the last time in his life he would see her alive. It was in 1998, a few weeks before her death. She was tied to a chair by a white sheet that was helping keep her body upright while sitting at a table in the main dining room of the nursing facility. It was around noon time and lunch was in progress. Most of the other residents and patients were sitting together at various tables, but Hilda was alone tied to her chair across the room. When Ken approached her, she stopped eating, made quick eye contact, touched her thinning unkempt hair, gave him a quick dismissive smile, and then began eating once again. She had lost a lot of weight, and every now and then her head kept falling to the right side then snapping back. Her mouth also seemed to be sagging on the right side of her face.

Ken sat down next to her, said hello and asked her name. She quickly replied, "Hil . . . da?" just like a young schoolgirl unsure of the answer to the teacher's question. She touched her hair once again after saying her name and he sat with her sharing a very long silence. Then he asked if she knew who he was, even giving her a hint at the answer. "<u>Mom</u> . . . do you know me? Do you know who I am . . . <u>Mom</u>?" She paused, smiled again momentarily and then replied to his question along with a question of her own, "Sure . . . ya' work here . . . right?" She didn't seem to expect nor need a response from Ken since she immediately looked back down at her plate and continued eating. Hilda Harrington (maiden name), Lang, Archer, Callahan, Mytus, Smith no longer recognized anyone or anything, anymore—only a person's skin color and the food on her plate.

After some time, Ken's years in the Military Intelligence gathering and analysis community seemed to naturally take over his mind and some of his emotions. One of the most important capacities any intelligence officer or field agent routinely depended on was the use of good questions. At times, effective questioning was far more useful than even sophisticated technology, covert relationships, or one's intuitive strengths. The ability to ask great questions during interrogations lead to far more valuable information and super gatherers of timely information relied on this one skill more than anything else. It brought to mind a James Bond movie that Ken had seen in 1968—*You Only Live Twice*, starring Sean Connery. Simply by watching that movie, even the common observer could see that the majority of things that Bond said were questions—not clever sayings, not insightful statements or meaningful conclusions . . . questions.

Such "great probes" (as they were called in the intelligence community) coupled with precise follow-up questions could always reveal at least three things, if not, questions were not considered "great probes." These three pieces of information were:

1. Information unavailable from any other source,
2. Information that confirms or contradicts other sources, and
3. Information exposing something previously unknown about the person being questioned or the objective being sought.

Right now, Ken sensed he needed such a "great probe" to use with his own mother. He also knew deep inside that it shouldn't be done within these circumstances, especially considering she was no longer solidly in touch with reality. Additionally, he knew how manipulative, invasive, and self-serving such a "great probe" was, including the risk of doing so. "Great probes" always implied "great risk." The old saying *be careful what you ask for . . . you may not like the answer,* has been proven over and over again to be true. Yet, Ken sensed the opportunity to ask her anything about his life with her would likely never come again. That was the risk. And, it was worth taking.

So he slowly asked his mother the following question. He did so with great trepidation, knowing the consequence of her answer also came with a high risk of crushing him.

"Hilda (not 'mom', this time) . . . did you ever have any children? If so, please tell me about them, Okay? I would really like to know."

As soon as the words left his lips, Ken knew it was wrong; he felt shame and guilt rushing through his veins right away. Then he hoped she hadn't heard or understood the question, or just would allow it to pass. At that second, he sensed that he really didn't need to know how she truly felt about him or her other kids. Her personal thoughts and values toward them were meant to stay deep inside her memory and not shared with anyone else, including him.

Ken became momentarily disoriented trying to emotionally process what he had just done. So he just waited for time to take its course; hoping she wouldn't respond at all. There was a long silence. Hilda seemed to be thinking about it, but Ken didn't know for sure. And then a heavier kind of silence seemed to engulf them both. Her mind seemed to be travelling across the galaxy while her lifeless stare was drilling directly through Ken's body, landing at some distant point across the dining room. But, even more time went by without a response from her.

He was glad and relieved that she wasn't attempting to answer such an unscrupulous question. Then she looked at him. This was the only time during their lunch together when she actually made direct eye contact—the exact kind of intense eye contact she had always seemed to keep in reserve just for Ken on the rarest of moments while raising him. That's when an ancient feeling of dread, fear and sorrow surfaced from Ken's dark past. Eyes met and held without a word.

She then spoke.

Her words came slowly, genuinely, and quite reflectively as if she was speaking to him on her sofa in the living room of 4139 Martin Court with Little Ken safely snuggled underneath her long, extended legs, "No . . . no darlin' . . . never had da' kids of ma' own . . . wudda' liked it dough' I guess . . . I t'ink it wudda' been real nice ta' had some kids . . . I t'ink I wudda' made a real gud' mudder' I bet . . . yeah . . . a real gud' mudder' I bet."

Ken became instantly numb and speechless. At that moment, an intense heat rushed up from his chest and landed squarely across his face like a Lone Ranger mask. The top and back sides of his eyes also seemed to be ignited by a sharp liquid flame that would not cease. Ken could no longer see anything, even though he sensed their eye contact had not been broken. Several more moments passed in slow motion before he regained his composure. Ken then said the only thing any son could say to a mother at such a time in such a place: "Mom (no longer Hilda) . . . I bet you would have made a really good mother, too." With that, a few more minutes of silence passed between them. Ken had just asked the un-askable question accompanied by very questionable motives. While her answer was clear, the meaning and implications of her response would never be clear in his mind and would haunt him forever.

With "Great Probes" come "great risks."

During that timeless lunch hour, his thoughts could not help but flashback to so many moments they had shared together (good and bad), including: the Projects, 4139 Martin Court, 801 Herndon Court, Mr. Penn, canned milk and water, naked pancakes, her bedroom, his torturous brother (Butcher-Bird), Walter, Sandy, "High Times", her extension cord, the Yogi Bear bathing suit, Mrs. Baumann, his loving furnace, her boyfriends, the smell of whiskey and cigarettes, the Barges, crabs, the ashtray stand, Mr. Williamson and the RC, the Victory Movie Theatre, Summer Breakaway Camp, Camp Canoe, the Asphalts, Mr. Jackson, The Kirby Scott Show, Sparta High School, AAHS, his lazy eye, Vietnam, and of course her treasured M&Ms. Such images were now bombarding his mind so fast that Ken was becoming even more disoriented. Yet, each memory also seemed different now after so many years, and each had a single common thread forever joining them together—her.

Then his eyes began to fill with more and more wet memories. He was afraid to blink for fear of submerging the entire dining room, like the scene from *The Poseidon Adventure* on New Year's Eve when God sent the biggest tsunami to capsize the cruise ship. He was sure just one blink would drown all the residents in Tranquil Valley dining room. Ken didn't know if his swelling tears represented sadness about the loss of his mother or a strange final relief of sorts, knowing she no longer could hurt another person again. He just didn't know which was which.

Either way, he knew she would remain in his mind and his heart forever—for good or bad. She had been a part of every difficult time in his life, and deep inside he still feared and hated her to some degree. Yet, she was still his mother. Knowingly or unknowingly, she had helped (or forced) him to learn how to adapt, how to adjust, how to survive. His exceptional resilience could be attributed directly to her; he also learned how to bounce back from disappointment, heartbreak, and crisis as well as how to get-up and move-on. Even though Ken sensed such capabilities were not passed on by clear intention from her, he was still grateful. She had brought him into this world and there was part of him that was obligated to love her, but there was also another part of him that would not allow him to verbalize it. Ken had never forgiven her for all that she did, and did not do, and it wasn't until that moment that he realized she never once asked for his forgiveness for anything. He then knew perhaps the good and bad always seem to balance out in the end.

Ken was just staring at her now, not knowing it would be the last time he would ever see her alive. It was all he could manage now and knew staying any longer would not be possible. Then he stood, leaned over, kissed her forehead, and said, "Good-bye, Mom." She did not verbally respond. Instead she just looked up at him, touched her hair once again, and gave him a half-smile, because the right side of her mouth now seemed fully immobile.

Before he finally turned to walk away, Ken glanced around the dining room. He hadn't noticed how silent and still the entire room had become. But it was. No one, not one person, was eating. Rather, everyone sat just gazing at him and his mother. Several people even had their utensils suspended in midair, between their plate and mouth. It was as if their mind just skipped a beat causing them to simply forget what to do with the food heading their way. The staff was also motionless, just staring as well. Ken noticed the natural clatter of pots and pans coming from the kitchen and the soft elevator music that had been coming from some unseen source also had mysteriously ceased. At that moment, he knew each of these people knew Hilda Smith. They knew her well. It seemed to Ken as if he was standing in the middle of the final ballroom scene from Stephen King's horror movie *The Shining*. It was the moment when Jack Nicholson's mind finally snaps; hijacked by all the well-dressed, ghosts-guests who had been waiting for his inevitable transformation to occur.

Even though each patient was looking at him and his mother, no one was really connecting with them. They were sharing the same moment together, yet each person was totally isolated by a veil of secret thoughts and unknowable feelings. He then looked down at his mother once again, brushed her thin gray hair back, kissed her forehead again, turned, and slowly walked out of the room. Ken never looked back; he never came back.

Ken never saw his mother alive again.

Mercifully, she died a few weeks later—February 21, 1998. She was buried at the Memorial Park Cemetery in Hagerstown, Maryland, next to her last husband, Joseph Smith. All the funeral arrangements were carried out by the good family members of Joseph Smith, who continued to follow through with every commitment they made to him before his death. Ken and his wife Dawn were living in Massachusetts at the time of Hilda's death. They, along with Daniel Harrington Jr. and his wife, were in attendance at the funeral. No other family members or relatives came. Daniel was the son of Hilda's older brother Daniel Senior—the same Uncle Dan who allowed Ken to use his street number fraudulently in order to attend Anne Arundel High School back in the summer of 1965.

The funeral service was a simple one and conducted well by Giant Funeral Home at the intersection of Ritchie Highway and 6th Street in Brooklyn Park. There were only six people in all who actually came to pay their respects, even fewer accompanied Hilda Smith's body to the cemetery. And that included Ken and his wife. He never revisited her gravesite after she had been laid to rest. However, fourteen years later in 2012, Ken would make a trip there to "rebury" (figuratively) her. It would be the first and last time he would ever visit her gravesite. He would be sixty-three at that time.

At this private "reburial" ceremony, he would not only forgive her, but would ask for her forgiveness of him as well. And, he would tell her he loved her—something he couldn't do at the Tranquil Valley Nursing Home when he last saw her alive.

Walter

Walter Callahan (Ken's oldest brother) kept himself very well camouflaged for quite some time. He had been living in Hartford, Texas in 1985 then moved to several other places eventually ending-up in Vetton, Utah during the late 1990s. After many phone calls and Internet searches, Ken was eventually able to connect and inform him of their mother's death in 1998. There was a long pause after Ken told him. Then Walter quickly said, "Sorry to hear that. Thanks, for letting me know, little brother." Walter did not say another word about her death (or life), and Ken couldn't tell if he was sad, mad, hurt, sorry or angry. But he did sense his brother seemed more apathetic than anything . . . at least on the outside.

Before that phone call, the last time Ken saw Walter was ten years earlier around 1987. Walter was living in Hartford, Texas (a rural town just north of Houston), and he seemed to have finally settled down after years of wandering a nomadic life that took him up and down the East Coast from job to job. He was about fifty-four at that time when Ken caught up with him. He had met a nice lady named Jane and he was living with her in a mobile home park on the outskirts of Hartford.

Walter had been married at least two times in his life, once to a woman named Lydia, with whom he had at least three kids while living in the Baltimore area. But they divorced. He left her or she left him; Ken never knew which. Jane had kids of her own, but it was never clear to Ken if any were Walter's, even though one of the younger kids kept calling him Paw-Paw, which Ken sensed was closer to the meaning of "grandpa" versus father. Walter seemed to like being called Paw-Paw, and since he seemed happy, that was all that was important.

Ken recalled spending one night with him and Jane in their mobile home in the late 1980s. He had been on a business trip to the Houston area conducting a training class for Digital Equipment Corporation at the time, and he took a day off to drive to Hartford and catch up with Walter as well as meet Jane for the first time. Coincidently, they had just reconnected by phone after years of estrangement so Ken's scheduled business trip to Houston gave them an opportunity to catch up. It was a comfortable mobile home. After a pleasant dinner with them, Joan went to bed, and Walter and Ken stayed up for a while just talking about things. Nothing was said about their mother outside a quick reference, and they didn't discuss the Projects or their life growing up there at all.

Their after-dinner chat included downing a dozen beers or so and their talk lasted well into the night. They talked about what they both had been doing since leaving Baltimore. Walter never seemed to be able to hold down a permanent job, always preferring to take short-term direct labor jobs wherever he was at the time. Since he never finished high school, he was limited to such work, but it seemed to suit his lifestyle. He was very good with his hands, had a strong back, and could fix anything mechanical and anything around the house. He also really enjoyed doing yard work and landscaping. The larger and longer the project, the better it worked out for Walter financially, but he didn't stay long enough in one place to really settle into a permanent job of any kind.

Mighty Mighty

Around midnight and after a few more beers, they were sitting on the living room floor when Walter said, "Hey, little brother, I want you meet the latest member of my new family." With that, he went to another part of the living room and came back carrying a thick transparent plastic box. That's when he introduced Ken to his pet tarantula—"Mighty Mighty." "Little Brother . . . this is Mighty Mighty . . . Mighty Mighty, this is my little brother, Ken. I hope you both know the only thing you have in common in this world is—me," Walter said that in a loud and formal way as if making an announcement at royal ball or something. His simulated British accent was so bad it made Ken laugh, but his laughter quickly stopped when he took a much closer look at Mighty Mighty.

Walter thought the name was appropriate because this spider was huge—twice the size of normal tarantulas found in the Texas desert. She was also far more colorful than any tarantula Ken ever saw in Vietnam. It turned out that she was really a Mexican red-knee tarantula, not a local, Texan tarantula. Hence, her name and color were quite appropriate. Walter loved his "little girl" (as he would call her). Jane feared it and kept threatening to get rid of it, but she never did. The one-by-three-foot plastic box was strong and well-sealed. It had a series of little perforated holes running across the top, and its transparent floor was covered with tiny stones, brush, twigs, and branches simulating the southwest mountain area of Mexico. There was also a large rock at the far end of the case providing her with a nice condominium-like, spider hiding place. She was very intimidating to look at; however, she was not very poisonous to humans.

Ken then said to him, "Walter, she is gorgeous. Have you taught her how to speak English yet or has she taught you Spanish?"

He merely replied, "Si senior."

She was beautiful and playful, reminding Ken of the leading lady in the 1955 classic horror movie *Tarantula*. This flick starred Leo G. Carol as a well-intended scientist who accidently creates a ten-story-high monster spider that terrified and ate people throughout the southwest. The only difference between both tarantulas was Mighty Mighty had more color and was a few stories shorter than the leading lady.

Then Walter took her out of the plastic case to show Ken close-up. She was very hairy and had about a six-inch leg span that could cover the diameter of a dinner plate. Walter first cupped her in his own huge hands while she just sat still, two of her long hairy black and red legs were dangling over the side of his massive knuckles. That's how big she really was. She then started slowly walking up Walter's left arm, stopping momentarily at his elbow. She did so cautiously at first while he talked to her and petted her along the journey. Then she quickly hustled to his shoulder where she came to a complete stop. She was now cheek to cheek with lover boy, Walter. He found her crawling along a creek bed near the San Jacinto River just north of Houston. It was a rare find because red-knees usually do not expose themselves in open areas; it just made them too vulnerable to big birds and rodents. Someone must have abandoned her there because she was too far from her natural elements—mountains and desert. Walter knew she couldn't survive long in such an environment so he captured her—they fell in love instantly. When Walter first saw her, he remembered saying to himself, "This could be love at first bite."

Ken then reached over and petted her carefully just as Walter showed him. He never petted or held the tarantulas he encountered in Vietnam; only contact he made with them was using the heel of his boot. Mighty Mighty felt like a Brillo pad even though from a distance her hair looked soft and fuzzy. Walter also wanted Ken to scratch her belly and showed him how to do it without coming too close to her quarter-inch fangs. "She really likes to be scratched there, really." But he declined his brother's kind offer. Ken normally liked rubbing and scratching bellies, especially if they belonged to people, but he had to draw a line when it came to being so intimate with anything that had eight legs.

Walter and Mighty Mighty had been together for only a few months and considering female red-knees had a life expectancy of about fifteen to twenty years living in captivity, their future relationship could be a long one. Ken humorously thought to himself that if Walter kept her that long, it would likely proved to be the most enduring relationship he would have in his entire life. But he didn't share that kind of wit with Walter, not knowing how he would take it. And equally relevant, Ken didn't share it because it pertained just as much to him for much of his own life as well. Later he thought he should have shared that thought with Walter; they both would have likely got a good laugh out of it.

Ken hadn't been that close to a tarantula since Vietnam, and he knew no such critters were in New England either. That's when he shared with Walter the story about Butch's visit to Lai Khe, Vietnam, in 1969, nearly twenty years earlier. It had been that long since he and Walter had been together face-to-face. Hearing Ken's stories about Butch visiting him in Vietnam (e.g., his Popeye navy suit in the jungle, the jeep ride, the lean-to, the shitter, the Smoke Tent, flying low along the Saigon River) made Walter laugh long and loud. He especially broke up when Ken described Butch's reaction to the filthy shitter in Lai Khe and when he was learning about "bird-eating tarantulas." Butch was really freaked out about both. "He always was a little wuss about bugs and things. Everything had to be so neat, and everything had to be in its place for him . . . didn't it?" Walter said it in a sarcastic way.

Then they talked about Butch, who neither of them had seen or heard from in years. They both hoped he was fine but didn't know what he had been up to. Neither Walter nor Ken attempted to reach out to him during that time, and the last time Ken saw Butch was the summer after returning from his second tour in Vietnam. Butch kept his distance from them as well. Actually, keeping a safe distance between the brothers seemed natural and comfortable for them. They shared the commonality of their mother's blood (even though different fathers were involved), but they also seemed to share another secret—one that none of them wanted to discuss in any way. Ken always had felt that was what kept them apart throughout the years, but he wasn't really sure. Something happened growing up in the Projects that was so dark that each of them had been running from it ever since.

He wouldn't discover the truth about it for another twenty years or so.

Ken left Walter's mobile home early the next morning with the biggest hangover he had in years. It was about 5:30 a.m., and everyone was still asleep when he departed. But before he showered, Ken looked around the living room and bathroom floor to check whether Mighty Mighty had made it safely back to her spider-condo. His shower would be a little more pleasurable knowing she was secure. He then headed back to Houston to conduct another training session for Digital, which was scheduled to start at 8:00 a.m. It was going to be a long day with his wonderful hangover. Yet it had been good to be with his oldest brother again, and it was just long enough too—any longer would have been difficult for both of them. While Ken always felt safe and comfortable around Walter growing up in the Projects, he didn't maintain a close relationship with him afterward.

After the Mighty Mighty visit, several years would pass before Walter and Ken talked again.

Butcher-Bird's Broken Wings

In 1990, Butch had been living in the San Diego area. He had recently divorced his fourth wife after being married to her for only six weeks or so. He was about forty-two at the time. Hilda, had been contacted by a San Diego-based hospital. She was confused and didn't know what to do about Butch, who had been in a motorcycle accident and was badly hurt. So she called Ken for help. She wanted him to take her out to California to take care of "Butch's affairs" in case he died. She thought Butch had some kind of estate, which she also thought she could inherit. Immediately, his mother's intentions became clear to Ken as she said the following, "Kenny . . . Butch's dyin' in California . . . was in a motorcycle crash d'ats dun em' in . . . wasn't wearin' a helmet. Da' hospital called and said I got ta' make decisions 'bout his *estate*. Ya' gots ta' get me out d'ere so I can handle his affairs and all, darlin'. Come get me immediately." This was the message left on Ken and Dawn's home answering machine one night. It was the first time they had heard from her in years.

To Ken, the operative word in her message was *estate*, implying some kind of assets may be coming to her. It was also the first time Ken had heard anything about Butch in many years as well; he didn't know much about Butch's life or situation at all. So he calmed his mother down when he called her back, He got the hospital's number and then called them directly to learn the details about his brother—Butch Callahan. He hadn't understood what his mother meant when she said, "Butch's got da' mental health . . . da' mental health, darlin'." Ken felt compelled to find out what was going on, so he contacted the hospital and discovered Butch had a serious head injury caused by a motorcycle accident. He was in a coma. Signatures had to be received in order to continue his care, and even though his condition was no longer life-threatening, his cognitive functioning had been severely impacted and extensive long-term rehabilitation would likely be required.

With that information, Ken called his mother back and brought her up to speed on things. Once she learned Butch's "estate" was more about his debts and bills rather than assets, her interest in Butch's health deflated faster than a balloon touching the head of a pin. That's when she backed away and wished Ken the best of luck handling things from there on. Hilda retreated back to her shadows. With that, Ken then flew out to San Diego the next day and saw Butch, who was still unconscious in a coma, hooked up with breathing equipment and constraints within the trauma ward of Kaiser Permanente. The doctors didn't know how long he would be there, nor what his long-term prognosis was ultimately going to be. So Ken signed some papers on behalf of his mother then went to Butch's apartment to secure his personal property.

That took only a few minutes.

He had been living alone quite sparsely in an apartment house in San Diego around University Boulevard. There weren't many possessions in the apartment when Ken arrived; the place had been nearly cleaned out. He found out later that ex-wives and ex-girlfriends had already picked the place clean once they learned about his "impending death." Apparently, most of Butch's stuff was their stuff anyway; they just wanted it back. Ken understood.

He then flew back to New Hampshire where he and Dawn were living at the time. There was now nothing more to do for Butch except wait and hope he recovered. After another week in a coma, Butch awoke. He spent several more weeks in the hospital recovering; his body was responding well but his mind was lagging far behind. Eventually, he was moved from the hospital to the smaller rehabilitation facility just outside of San Diego where he was given more treatment and close supervision. His decision making abilities, daily living skills, and emotional control were just too inadequate for self-functioning. He was suffering from a frontal lobe injury, which likely would be permanent.

That's when Ken and Dawn decided to fly out together to see Butch face-to-face and help where they could. She had never met Butch, the "Butcher-bird," even though she heard a lot about him. It was going to be a unique experience for her. At the time, she was an executive account manager with Digital Equipment Corporation (DEC), the same business where Ken worked. She had just begun planting seeds to transition to her next career—Elder Care Services—a long-term calling she always dreamed of but hadn't acted upon it until recently. Caring for her own mother, father, and several senior members of Wrentham, Massachusetts, where she grew up had become not only a passion of hers, but was now blossoming into her new profession. She was given the nickname "Angel Dawn" by neighbors and family members long before this time because of all the personal help she so freely rendered to senior residents of Wrentham, specifically helping the elderly get through family, medical, and financial problems.

Many of these folks including her own her parents, raised their families with the help of each other during and after World War II in the town of Wrentham. Most families in the town were very close during those days and Dawn learned how to cook, ride a bike, play field hockey, and drive a car, not only from her parents but also through the personal guidance received from so many members of this fine generation of giving people. In turn, she felt a special calling to return the kindness they so freely gave her growing up. Each time she did even the smallest personal service for these wonderful people, they'd simply call her "Angel Dawn."

Over the years, the nick-name stuck.

She left DEC in the mid early 1990s, went back to college, and obtained her master's degree in clinical psychotherapy from Sacred Heart College in Nashua, New Hampshire. At the time, Ken was serving as a member of Sacred Heart College's board of advisors. They both loved the college's environment and its people who shared strong Christian values upon which the school was based. It was managed and led by a French order of nuns called the Presentation of Joan. The college's academic standards were only surpassed by their calling to serve God, the world and their community. Such values had fit well with Angel Dawn's calling. Little did she know that her early psychology and counseling education, as well as her natural instincts, would come in handy right away—with Butch. She would be put to the test during her initial face-to-face encounter with him and well before her formal credentials were actually obtained. Angel Dawn's relationship and communication skills as well as her practical problem-solving abilities were about to be well tested and well stretched, not only by Butch, but also by the "Butcher-Bird."

When they arrived at the rehabilitation facility near San Diego, the place instantly reminded Ken of the 1976 Academy Award-winning movie *One Flew Over the Cuckoo's Nest,* starring Jack Nicholson. It was a secured institution surrounded by a series of high fences and interconnected buildings spread across several acres. Its charter was to take of care of state residents who could no longer care for themselves. Since Butch couldn't be released on his own, and his mother didn't want to care for him, especially after learning there was no financial incentive for her, this facility was the best place for him until he was able to function independently.

Deadly Chewing Gum

After going through a long administrative and security process at the facility, Ken and Angel Dawn were escorted to the patient area and then to the specific room where Butch had been assigned. He shared a single, barred-window room with about five other male patients. When they entered this room, Butch was alone sitting on his bunk staring down at the floor with his head in his hands. He was wearing a one-piece, state-provided jumpsuit, and tennis shoes. Butch didn't even notice when Ken and Angel Dawn appeared at the entrance of the room. They just stood there for a moment and then Ken asked Angel Dawn to wait at the entrance while he engaged his brother.

Ken immediately noticed the natural shine of Butcher-Bird's feathers had greatly faded since he last saw him. Butch lost a lot of weight, most likely because of the lengthy stay in Kaiser's intensive care center. His dark hair had been shaved to the point that Ken couldn't really tell where his receding hairline started. To Ken, Butch's head looked like a dull bowling ball, and because of his weight loss, he was merely a shadow of the giant he used to be. He appeared distraught and far away.

Ken immediately felt sorry for his brother. Butch had always prided himself on his looks and appearance as well as being so autonomous and independent—all of which were now gone; hopefully for just a short time. But that was not to be for the Butcher-Bird.

So Angel Dawn waited at the entrance of the room as Ken slowly walked over and sat down on the cot next to Butch. "Hi, Butch . . . how are you doing? It's Ken . . . your brother . . . remember me." Ken was hoping Butch would at least recognize him. He was sitting on Butch's left side less than a foot away from him. Then Butch turned his head slowly, made brief eye contact with Ken, looked him up and down, and then glanced over his shoulder at Angel Dawn who was standing at the room entrance. He then looked back at Ken. But instead of giving him a hug, saying hello, or even answering his question, Butch sharply said the following with Hilda-like directness, distaste, and venom, while his face remained totally expressionless, and without emotion of any kind, "Spit out d'at goddamn gum or I'll stick it up ya' ass."

Ken had been chewing gum since he got on the plane from Boston earlier that day. He chewed gum whenever he became nervous about anything in those days and forgot just how much Butch had always hated anyone chewing gum in his presence when he was a kid. To him it was as a nasty habit, as bad as someone allowing cigarette smoke to roll into his space. Short of farting in public, Butch hated gum chewing and cigarette smoking the most. Ken was caught by surprise at his comment. He just wasn't expecting that from Butch, at least not that direct and certainly not that soon under these circumstances. He also noticed his brother was now talking with the same kind of accent, tone, and language that their mother used all the time (e.g., contractions d'at for "that," ya' for "you"). That's when he knew Butch must have been through a lot since he last saw him, well before his motorcycle accident and head injury occurred a month earlier.

Just one sentence, one snippet of pure attitude, and Ken's mind was taken all the way back to their days growing up together in the Projects. In a matter of nanoseconds, Ken was once again inside 4139 Martin Court running to find his safe place between the kitchen wall and the steel furnace—the only spot on the first floor of their unit where neither Butch nor his mother could directly get at him.

At that moment, sitting next Butch on the cot, Ken's tension and body heat rose so quickly and so intensely he just responded without any thought or compassion. He stood and slammed his left fist into Butch's mouth. It landed squarely and solidly. Butch fell over instantly. Ken then spat the chewing gum out and it landed directly on Butch's bloody face. He then began stomping Butch's head on the floor as his body was twitching and flailing. Butch didn't know what had hit him. It came on him so fast even Ken was surprised at his own quick reactions. Then Ken turned around and walked over to Angel Dawn. He gently took her by the arm and they left the room together. They then walked slowly out of the building, passed the security guards, got into their rent-a-car, and drove away. They never returned. For all Ken cared, Butcher-Bird could rot in that place until all his feathers fell off his bones.

That's exactly what happened on that day—*but only in Ken's mind.*

He hadn't felt that degree of "heat" rush through his blood so fast in decades. He never thought he would ever feel such rage again after leaving the Projects, but he did now. The only difference was Ken controlled his behavior this time, even though his ancient emotions were still as alive and real as ever before. In reality, things unfolded quite differently following Butch's deadly chewing gum comment.

Ken just sat there for a moment, not responding at all on the outside (even though his emotions inside were boiling). Butch and Ken's bodies were facing straight ahead on the edge of the cot, but their faces were at ninety-degree angles directly facing each other, eye to eye, only inches apart. Then there was silence; a very long silence.

Angel Dawn to the Rescue

There was no motion or sound of any kind in the room at that moment. Neither Butch nor Ken moved or made a sound—the tension was so thick it could almost be seen. Watching this quickly unfold from across the room, Angel Dawn sensed she had to act. She knew about Butch's short-fuse reputation under "normal" conditions but had no idea what he was capable of considering his recent head injury and current emotional state. She felt anything could happen. So she made her way over to the cot and stood facing both of them. She thought her presence alone, being so up close and personal, might be distracting enough to defuse any lingering thoughts or emotions associated with the "deadly chewing gum." On the outside, she appeared calm and confident, but she later admitted to Ken that she was actually as nervous and vulnerable as a male black widow spider attempting to mate with a female twice its size.

Butch then looked up at her.

She offered her hand in a feminine, nonthreatening way, trying to project an air of confidence and friendliness even though that's not what she was feeling. Butch held her eye contact, looked her up and down, and slowly extended his hand in response. She took it and without any trace of condescension or fear slowly said: "Hi, Butch. I'm Dawn, Ken's wife. I've heard a lot about you over the years and so glad to finally meet you. Tell me, how are they treating you in this place?"

Ken was surprised (and quite delighted) that his wife acted so decisively under the circumstances. Secretly, he was also quite relieved. Ken didn't know how Butch was going to react to her but was preparing for the worst, if needed. Fortunately, Butch stayed seated and didn't react physically at all, except to brush his fingers quickly over his shaved head. He then replied directly to Dawn's question, "Dawn, huh . . . well . . . d'is place sucks. Da' food sucks. Da' people are morons . . . can't do anything without permission . . . its worst d'en da' fuckin' navy. Ya' here ta' get me out a' d'is place?"

His request was delivered to her, not to Ken. It came in the form of a statement or directive rather than as a question or a genuine plea for help. Dawn understood him immediately at that point. He was mad and afraid, not angry and hostile despite his persona. That's all she needed to know and wasn't intimidated from that point on. "Well . . . we hope so . . . we're here to help any way we can, Butch. It may take a little time . . . after all, you've been through a lot . . . had a serious injury, didn't you? Can you tell me about it? I would really like to know." Again, she was just hoping to refocus his attention on himself rather than on the facility, or Ken, or the deadly chewing gum. Her education seemed to be paying off because Butch began describing his motorcycle (not his accident) and how it felt to ride on Highway 1 along the California coastline from San Francisco to Monterey Bay. But he couldn't recall or describe anything about his accident . . . nothing at all. He didn't even try. That part of his memory was seemingly gone forever. Butch seemed more concerned about getting out and getting back on his "ride" than anything else.

As Butch continued, Ken moved off the cot, removed the chewing gum from his mouth and deposited it in the huge metal waste basket at the entrance of the room. He was now watching Dawn from a far as she worked her magic. She then sat down next to Butch on the cot exactly where Ken had been only seconds before. Now Butch was talking nonstop. She was listening. She knew not to interrupt him now that he was opening up and refocusing off the deadly chewing gum. She really knew her stuff and Ken was so proud of her. He seldom got to see her in action like this and liked it. He then could see Butch starting to be "himself" (at least that part of him that he remembered). But Ken still didn't know what to expect since Butch was explosive by nature, and considering his brain injury, he was even more uncertain than ever. Nevertheless, Butch seemed to be getting comfortable with Angel Dawn, so he just kept his distance and observed from the entrance of the room.

After thirty minutes or so, an orderly came into the room and escorted Butch down the hall with Ken and Angel Dawn close behind. He was on a strict supervised schedule once he left his room, and it was now time for

Butch to participate in some physical activity with other patients. So he was taken outside to a volleyball court while Ken and Angel Dawn stayed inside watching Butch through a large glass window. There were several other families also watching from behind the glass window as their own loved ones played on the volleyball court.

The orderly placed Butch on one side of the net behind a few other patients. The ball made its way back and forth seemingly without any direction given. It was more like free-for-all volleyball game with a single ball flying around without rules or purpose. The patients were merely going through hitting and kicking motions if the ball came anywhere near them. On several occasions, the ball entered Butch's vicinity and flew right by him. Each time, Butch would reach up to swat it, but he was usually two or three seconds late with his swing. His physical reflexes were obviously lagging far behind his visual, mental, and emotional capacities. In short, he was as out of sync managing time, space, and motion, just like most of the other patients on the volleyball court that day.

If it were not so sad, it would be comical—like watching an episode of *The Three Stooges* trying to master "anything." This sad, heartbreaking activity went on for some time then the game was abruptly ended by the orderlies. All the patients then came back into the building and were heading off to lunch as a group. Butch fell right into step with all of them, walking right by Ken and Angel Dawn without recognizing or acknowledging them in any way. Their momentarily presence in his mind and memory had passed. Ken then sensed that his brother would need lots of time before he was able to get his feathers realigned and be able to fly on his own. His recovery was going to be hard and long.

In the facility's administration office, Ken signed some more papers to ensure Butch could receive the treatment he needed and then he and Angel Dawn left. They sensed Butch was at least safe and would be cared for. That's when he and Angel Dawn became Butch's conservators. Ken would not see Butch face to face again for quite some time. Dawn never saw him again at all.

Over the next couple of years, Butch would be moved from one facility to another across California because he just couldn't fit in with other patients, and he could not or would not follow any rules. Without major improvement, he would likely be required to stay within such facilities the rest of his life or until a family member or friend took him in.

The Breakout

About eighteen months after Ken and Angel Dawn's visit to Butch, a facility manager from Butch's latest residence contacted them. His behavior was becoming more and more inappropriate and unmanageable. And, he was now frightening the staff and other patients. Butch was intimidating older patients and harassing the younger ones. He placed chewing gum in the door locks of patients that he disliked the most. And he scared patients at night by making strange animal noises and throwing objects against their doors.

It appeared the "playful" side of Butcher-Bird was trying to make a come-back. He didn't like living in this facility and was hell bent on ensuring everyone knew about his discomfort and displeasure. He tried running away a couple of times but he always returned as soon as he became hungry. The staff really wanted to throw him out permanently or send him to another facility, but they couldn't do it because of state policies or something of that nature.

They were seeking any personal advice in handling Butch better when they called Ken and Angel Dawn. That's when Ken decided to reach out to Walter, who always had a unique view of Butch and knew him much better and in a different way from Ken. He was able to get a hold of him quite easily this time, and then told him about Butch's plight. And after some discussion, Walter volunteered to get him out of there; that is, "break him out" of the state of California. Walter thought it could give Butch a second chance if he came to live with him and Jane for a while in Hartford, Texas. He was willing to try and see if it could work out. Equally important to Walter, he would start receiving Butch's Supplemental Security Income (SSI) payments for doing so. Walter could use the extra income. And besides, he seemed to hate the state of California for some reason. On the surface, this seemed like a good situation if it worked. But, Walter also needed Ken's help to execute the plan.

And, he got it.

So in the early 1990s, Walter's plan to free the Butcher-bird from his California cage started to take shape. Ken would fly out to San Diego while Walter drove his pickup truck from Texas. They would meet the day before and then break out the Butcher-Bird the next morning. Together, all three of them would then drive out of California, go through Arizona and New Mexico and finish up in Hartford, Texas. There, Butch would stay at Walter's and Ken would catch a flight back to Massachusetts. That was the plan. However, the reality of it all then started to seep into in Ken's mind.

Just the thought of having all three Callahan brothers together for three consecutive days and nights (the time it would take to drive from San Diego, California to Hartford, Texas) was one thing that started to scare the hell out of him. Angel Dawn was even more freaked-out just thinking about this plan. Two specific practical realities of this plan brought her much more concern. The Callahan boys (men) would be saddled together in the very confined space of a pickup truck's cabin for a prolonged period of time. And they would be traveling across the very hot southwest desert during the midsummer without air conditioning. Angel Dawn knew this was a bad combination of factors especially considering the added danger of Butch's mental condition. She felt compelled to call the state troopers of California, Arizona, New Mexico, and Texas ahead of time. It was only fair to inform them of such impending doom well in advance. Angel Dawn loved those southwestern states and wanted to ensure the beauty of the land would not be jeopardized. And, the state troopers would be better prepared to minimize, perhaps not fully eliminate, at least some of the possible fallout that was about to be unleashed upon their unsuspecting citizens.

She and Ken discussed this for some time, and he agreed with her about the risks. But, he also viewed it as an adventure—not just a venture. Actually, in Ken's mind, it had the makings of a really good psychological thriller, a western disaster movie of sorts.

He would entitle this movie something like this:

> *"Once upon a Time in the West, The Good, Bad, and Ugly Flew Over a Cockoo's Nest."*

It was a long title for sure, but not nearly as long as a three-day road trip through hell with all three Callahan boys. If he could only get the great movie producer John Ford of *The Searchers, Tie a Yellow Ribbon, and Fort Apache* fame to direct this flick, the Callahans could become instant millionaires. Of course, Ken would never share this fantasy with Angel Dawn. Regardless, she was against the whole thing and made a strong case to Ken for stopping everything right in its tracks, "Look, Butch needs to stay-put because it's impossible he fully recovered that fast. Most of the time it takes years or decades of treatment and constant support before anyone is able to respond normally after such extreme trauma. And forgive me for saying, but Butch is nothing special—far from a superman. And considering his predisposition as well as his natural aggressive behavior as showcased in the nursing and rehabilitation facilities he's been in lately, I think it's best to keep him where he is."

Angel Dawn felt Butch needed more help and structure, not more freedom and autonomy. To unleash him at this time would not only be harmful to him personally but also to the poor unsuspecting people of the southwest as well. And the kind of assistance Walter would give, despite his positive intentions, could eventually prove ineffective, even counterproductive.

Ken understood where she was coming from. He also knew the combination of interpersonal and environmental factors of this venture were potentially explosive—as dangerous a combination as mixing Hilda Callahan, whiskey, men, cigarettes, and country music all at once. Butch's break out had an equally explosive potential. Nevertheless, Ken decided to go along with it. He couldn't help but recall the time Butch voluntarily dropped into Vietnam, a combat zone, just to find and catch up with him. It was a noble yet needless thing to do, but Butch did it just the same. It was the only good, generous thing Butch ever did for him.

Now, it was Ken's turn to return the gesture.

His biggest concern was not what would happen between him and Butch. Rather, the danger was what was going to unfold between Walter and Butch. Ken never knew why they kept a safe distance apart since the Projects, but they did. Ken was just too young at the time to know everything that went down in 4139 Martin Court, but something did. And, they both knew about it but just wouldn't discuss it with Ken. Even so, if Walter was so hell-bent on having Butch come live with him in Hartford, Texas, he was going to help him do it. Ken couldn't recall a single time in his life when Walter ever asked him for help of any kind. He kept a safe distance from Ken as well. So this was the first time he felt compelled to support Walter personally, at least this one time. Ken was actually doing this for Walter more so than for Butch.

So in the summer of 1991, they executed Walter's plan.

They connected in San Diego just as planned. It took Walter about a day and half of straight driving. Ken flew directly to San Diego from Boston in six hours. They met at the San Diego airport, got a motel room, went out that night grabbed some dinner and a few beers, and discussed the plan some more. They also contacted Butch and told him to be ready the next morning. The cavalry was on the way. Butch was excited as a kid being tucked into bed on Christmas Eve. They called it an early night because Walter was exhausted after driving so long, and Ken was suffering a little from jet lag.

It was good for Ken to have had some more one-on-one time with Walter again. He hadn't seen or talked at length with him since his Mighty Mighty visit in Hartford, Texas years earlier. But he was very glad Walter didn't bring Mighty Mighty along with him as he playfully threatened to do. Ken slept much better that night because of it. Very early the next morning, they arrived at the small, non-secure nursing facility. It was just about sunrise. They parked the pickup truck on the street and kept the engine running. It was a Sunday.

Then they waited and waited for Butch to arrive as agreed. Ken had made Butch repeat their break-out time to him severe times the night before on the phone. He didn't want to enter the facility for fear of someone catching on to them, after all this was being done without permission from the facility manager or the state. Ken assumed they would be delighted to rid themselves of Butch Callahan any way it took. Regardless, it was going to be a real "clean get-a-way" in Ken's mind.

While Butch was free to leave anytime, it was still a "breakout" according to Walter and Butch. And, once Butch was in Texas, all would be fine. He'd be taking up residence in another state while still receiving his SSI benefits, of which Walter would benefit. And, the state of California would be rid of one less crazed Butcher-bird to care for. Everyone wins. At least, that's how Ken naively viewed things "if" it could be pulled off without a hitch. In short, Butch would have merely left the State of California without saying good-bye. Another thirty minutes passed and still no sign of a Butcher-bird anywhere, then he came running out. Actually he came out "almost" running to be accurate. That is, his movements appeared to be a combination of staggering, limping, and jumping all at once. But from Ken's view, it really couldn't be called running, not even close. Butch's mind certainly seemed to be running fast, but his body somehow just wasn't willing to keep pace. Butch's physical motions reminded Ken of the way Walter Brennan's character moved during the 1957 hit TV series *The Real McCoy's*. Actually, Amos McCoy was much faster than Butch. Ken was surprised and heartbroken to see this. He was expecting Butcher-bird would have healed physically since he last saw him in the hospital several years before, but he hadn't. His broken wings just didn't mend very well, after all.

Butch was carrying nothing with him except a small bag containing a toothbrush, floss, one pair of socks and underwear. That was it. Ken also assumed that was pretty much all he owned anyway. Butch then saw Walter and Ken waving from the pickup truck across the street. When he eventually made it to the truck, he threw his bag in the back and hopped clumsily but quickly into the cabin of the pickup truck. It was then Ken noticed a Mexican man had been watching everything from the facility's main office window but he did not do anything. As they pulled away, Butch gave the "bird" to the entire facility as well as to the Mexican man in the window. Ken sensed the Mexican man was glad to see Butch leaving, but he wasn't sure. Three hours later, Walter's pickup truck pulled across the California-Arizona border. They were on their way to Hartford, Texas—all three Callahan brothers were now together for the first time since their days in the Projects of Brooklyn. Little did Ken know, but this single trip would also be the very last time all three Callahan boys would ever be together.

The trip itself was long and uneventful, despite the explosive potential that was ever present among the brothers. They had taken the most direct route—Interstate 8 out of California and Interstate 10 across Arizona, New Mexico, and Texas. Every hour or so Butch wanted to stop at the Grand Canyon. Even long after passing the entire state of Arizona he still wanted to stop there. Butch continued his pleading even when they neared the outskirts of Houston, Texas. Butch's thinking ability as well as his emotional development had not improved as much as Ken had hoped it would. Each evening they ate and drank together as brothers, without a single real fight. However, at one truck stop, Walter nearly got into a fight with a trucker for some reason, but it ended as fast as it started. They also stayed in small cheap motels on both nights—once in Arizona and once in western Texas. Ken thought the motels were three cuts below the quality of the Bates Motel in Alfred Hitchcock's *Psycho*, but each was clean and most important, each also had wonderful air conditioning.

That was good enough.

Another problem was deciding where everyone was going to sleep. They had to get two separate rooms each time which meant someone was getting a room alone while the other two shared. It was decided that Butch could not stay alone (despite his protests), so Ken and Walter swapped sleeping with him each night. When it was Ken's turn to sleep with Butch, the second night, Ken slept with one eye open at all times. He sensed Butch's love of torturing him as kid while growing up in the Projects had not been buried deep enough in Butch's memory. And considering Butch's recent head injury, Ken knew he was capable of anything. It was a long night during his shift sleeping with Butch, to say the least. But Butch slept through the night peacefully. Ken did not.

They eventually made it across Texas to Hartford with everyone making it in one piece. There were only a few minor clashes along the way. The most consistent problem turned out to be Butch's "constant need" to drive the pickup truck. But, Walter wouldn't allow it even on the long, barren hundred mile straight-aways across the southwest where there was no traffic, no signs, no intersections, no pedestrians at all—just lots of desert, cactus, and plenty of dead armadillo on the road. The other ongoing problem was Walter's pickup had no air-conditioning. Well, he actually had it, but it didn't work. Either way, it was hot, very hot and that didn't help Butch's mood at all.

When they arrived in Hartford two and half days after leaving San Diego, Ken spent the night with them and flew back to Massachusetts the next morning, leaving his two brothers together with hope things would work out between them. And, for a while Butch did get along with Walter and Jane (and Mighty Mighty). Jane was very accommodating and very kind to Butch, but the bliss was short lived.

Butch kept trying to get a driver's license but he kept failing the written test. So most of the time while staying with Walter, Butch was riding a bicycle wherever he went or had to depend on Walter or Jane to drive him where ever he needed to go. And when he finally had enough of that and enough of Walter, which occurred less than two months after arriving in Hartford, Butch hopped on his bicycle one day and just never came back. The Butcher-bird "flew over the cuckoo's nest" without even saying adios, good-bye or gracias to Walter and Jane. He just flew the coop. Sometime later, Walter heard the Butcher-bird had gone to Denver and then made it to the northwest, landing somewhere around Seattle, Washington. Butch, 'Butcher-Bird', Weapons Specialist Callahan, and/or Butch Callahan would never be seen again by either Walter or Ken. Actually, the next time Ken would come into physical contact with his brother Butch would be over fifteen years later, in the year 2009; Ken would then be holding the cremated remains of Butch in his hands.

Butcher-Bird's Letter

However, a few years after fleeing Walter's hospitality in Hartford Texas, Ken would speak once again with Butch. It would occur in 1998 around the time of their mother's death.

Several weeks after Hilda's passing, Ken was finally able to get a hold of Butch who had been moving around the great Northwest for years and ultimately landing in Salem, Oregon. Ken thought Butcher-bird's wings must have been really hurting since he made that long bike ride-flight from Hartford to Salem. They hadn't spoken to each other since Butch's "California breakout" even though he had Ken's number and address all along, or could have easily contacted him anytime.

However, this phone call was the first opportunity Ken had to inform Butch about their mother's death, despite all the effort he made to contact him after it occurred. Butch's reaction to the news was minimal, just as Walter's had been. But he was far more sarcastic and dismissive. He simply said, ". . . bout' time . . . how old was da' bitch anyway . . . 150, I bet." Ken didn't respond.

Butch had been living in the Salem, Oregon and that's all he learned about him on this call. The Butcher-bird kept all other personal information about himself well hidden underneath his tail feathers where no one could get to without first getting pass his sharp claws and even sharper beak. Ken wasn't even going to try. This would also turn-out to be the very last time Ken would ever hear his brother's voice. Their conversation lasted only a few minutes without him revealing anything significant about himself. But, at least he knew Butch was still alive and physically fine. Ken wasn't sure how well he was psychologically or emotionally, however. Butch just didn't give him enough time to discover much while on the phone call; it ended as fast as it started with Butch merely saying, "Later."

However, about two weeks later, Ken did receive a letter from him—the first and only written correspondence from him since the late 1960s, around the time Butch visited him in Lai Khe, Vietnam. Even though the correspondence came to Ken inside an envelope, delivered by the US Postal Service, and had words written on paper, Ken didn't feel it qualified as a "letter." It certainly had the look and feel of a letter, but something in Ken's mind quickly disqualified it as any letter he ever received in his life.

Rather, it was a series of fragmented thoughts, feelings, statements, and jumbled images linked together by a few commas and periods. Six highly emotional exclamation marks were also included. Butch's "almost letter" (as Ken called it) was hand-scribbled (not handwritten). A dull pencil had been used. Its format actually seemed more like a psychotic ransom letter of some sort—the kind bad guys constructed using word cutouts from newspapers or magazines pasted on the pages so police could not identify the writer. It just had that kind of structure and feel. Many words were misspelled; some letter i's were dotted, some not; periods were missing; sentences were incomplete; thoughts were more like splintered expressions fused together than completely thought out ideas; most words were printed, others were written. To Ken, the letter could have been created in a few minutes or over days. It was written on four very small sheets of perforated lined paper that seemed to have been ripped from a spiral notebook, the kind engineers or computer nerds always seem to carry in their shirt pocket. The envelope and the letter itself were encrypted with many secret messages containing complex and virtually undecipherable meanings. It had been years since Ken had heard from Butch, but in the midst of reading this letter, he sensed Butcher-Bird's psychological feathers had deteriorated even faster, more severely than his physical state.

Ken concluded this single almost-letter was Butch's response to the news of his mother's passing. It was a "written" response that he couldn't (or wouldn't) give orally over the phone to Ken when he was briefly talking with him just two weeks before. The "exact" letter (word for word, comma by comma) Ken received from Butch follows. The envelope was postmarked March 17, 1998, Salem, Oregon, three weeks after Hilda's death, and about a week after talking to Ken about her death. Coincidently, March 17 was also the day Ken originally landed in Vietnam in 1968—exactly thirty years earlier to the day.

The letter's addressee was:

'Yen Yen' Callahan
332 Sleep Hollow Rd.
Nashua, New Hampshire, 03062

"*Yen Yen*" was the name given to Ken by their little sister, Sandy, when she was about two years old. She was still too young to properly pronounce *K* sounds, so she merely said "Yen" (for Ken). And for some reason, Sandy had also always used his name twice when calling him or referring to him. For example: "Mommy, where's Yen Yen?" or "Yen Yen, come tuck me in" or "Yen Yen, I hungeee hungeee [hungry]."

Because of this, Ken knew the letter was from Butch even before opening it. Besides himself and his mother, only Butch had such knowledge of those exact words his little sister used in referring to "Ken." Walter had left the house well before Sandy was talking and since their mother was now dead, he concluded the letter could only be from Butch. There was also no way to tell from whom, or from where the letter came by reading the return address on the envelope:

J. Doe
69 Lone
Anywhere, USA

Ken immediately sensed this was Butch's way of telling him not to respond and that he didn't want to be contacted later on. The letter's contents also conveyed this hidden message but even more explicitly. As a matter of fact, it was the only message that was 100 percent clear to Ken in the entire letter. Because of this, Ken was very hesitant in opening the letter at all.

He was glad Angel Dawn was there when it arrived. As usual, she had a way of cutting through the crap and going right to the core of problems, especially when it pertained to relationships, medical, psychological, or financial issues. They had been living at Sleep Hollow in Nashua, New Hampshire, at the time of Butch's letter. And, that was where they both sat down and read it together as best they could.

His poor spelling, grammar, and penmanship caused problems right away. But, it was the encrypted emotions that forced them both to read and reread it together many times to decipher hidden meanings. The following is an exact replication of Butcher-Bird's letter—every word, comma, exclamation point, misspelling, and embedded emotion.

98

Hey, Little Shit,

The wicked witch Bitch is DEAD (AKA) taking a dirt nap forever & a day

The Devil said your mother was to ugly to go to hell!

Yes, I was a mother fucker, when I was 12, 13 on Herdon ct

It fell naked as a Bluebird on it's back shitfaced!

You'll love this one, everyone here thinks Im an only child with no family.

I like that way. Old family problems suck.

My new life & what I call a family was as nice surprize for me forever

I'm back on the Coast that's the <u>most!</u>

The lesser coast to the East sucks the most, I know it!

Loose my # or you'll have a ear drum <u>Busted!</u>

P.S.

Con—sucks

Lib is freedom

Butch, your has been BRO!

Butch's handwriting seemed more like the psychotic chicken scratch of a prisoner on death row rather than human scribe. It took Ken and Angel Dawn hours to decipher the meaning of it all, and they still fell short. While they thought the message was clear at first, it was not. Ten years would pass before they would come to fully understand the true meaning and lasting implications of Butch's letter—the real story, not only about Butch but about his little brother, Ken, as well. He would come to understand many other hidden secrets that had bonded him and his brother in so many ways beyond blood and DNA—in ways he never thought could ever exist among members of the same family. Such self-discovery would be uncovered, discovered and re-discovered during many PTSD therapy sessions within the Veteran Administration's renowned PTSD clinic in Plainville, Massachusetts . . . a place where Ken would one day become a patient himself.

Butcher-Bird's "First" Burial

Butch E. Callahan died on June 23, 2009 of multisystem failures and advanced dementia/vascular within the Greenville Recovery Hospital (a mental institution) located in the Sun Valley area about 50 miles west of San Diego. He had been a full time patient/resident there for several years, but no one—friends, family, and relatives had ever known about it. Four decades had passed since Ken and Butch's curious reunion took place in Lai Khe, Vietnam, in 1969. Those three days together in a war zone and their three-day pickup truck drive from California to Texas with brother Walter represented the longest periods of time the two brothers would be have spent together outside the Projects. While they Kumbayah'd well during their time in Lai Khe, afterwards they reverted back to being just as estranged and as distant with one another as ever. They seldom connected over the phone, never wrote (with one exception), and met face-to-face no more than a few times during all that time. Ken had reached out to him, but Butch seemed more comfortable with distance and space than with phones calls, voices or face-to-face contact.

Then in the summer of 2009, Ken and Angel Dawn were notified of Butch's death. This notification came from the State of California. They then received his cremated remains along with some official death documentation and some of Butch's previous military records. There were no personal possessions, even though he had been a resident of a state institution for several years. He had no photos, no other personal papers or letters, or any other items of his own when he died. He was living totally on the services that the State of California provided to those who were incapable of caring for themselves. Butch Callahan had been "institutionalized"—involuntarily locked in a fully secured, mental care and treatment facility without the possibility of escape. He had been there for several years and died there—in the care of the state.

After receiving his cremated remains, Ken and Angel Dawn made arrangements to have Butch properly buried at the Massachusetts National Military Cemetery on Cape Cod. This beautiful place was located fifty miles east of their home in North Attleboro, Massachusetts. Despite their strained personal relationship over the years and considering Ken's mixed emotions about him, he was still his brother. Equally important, Butch had been a US serviceman who served his nation during a time of war. He had also been discharged from the US Navy under honorable conditions. As such, Ken obtained all necessary documentation and proof needed and then provided it to the officials at the national cemetery in Massachusetts . . . including Butch's cremated remains. Then on September 11, 2009, Weapons Specialist, Butch E. Callahan, US Navy, was given a formal military burial.

Ken invited several close friends to attend the burial including Jonathan O' Donald (a former US Navy officer) and Abby Plumsworthy—Angel Dawn's longtime friend and former classmate from Wrentham High School. Additionally, Angel Dawn's nephew, Lieutenant William Fargo (US Coast Guard Academy graduate) was also present. Coincidently, William just so happened to be on active duty stationed at Otis Air Force base, located adjacent to the national military cemetery on Cape Cod. He was a Coast Guard rescue helicopter pilot who also, coincidently, had been assigned the extra duty assignment for the month of September as the official military representative at burials of all servicemen taking place at the national cemetery. As a result he personally participated in Butch's burial. The actual memorial ceremony also included the presentation of a US flag, the playing of the national anthem, and the participation of two uniformed burial guards. During the ceremony, Ken said a eulogy for his brother as well. He described the good side and the challenging parts of his brother's life as best he could.

Deep inside, Ken also wanted to say that he had forgiven Butch for all the things he had done to him growing up, but he just could not bring himself to do so, even at this opportunity. He also wanted to say how much he loved Butch, despite their relationship, but that too, he could not bring himself to do either, not at that time. Ken didn't know it then, but three years later he would find himself re-burying (virtually) Butch once again. Only on that occasion, he would be able to convey his most personal feelings and sentiments. This "reburial" would take place at Butch's gravesite on Cape Cod once again as a part of Ken's own PTSD metaphoric "reburial" ceremony for his brother. It would occur in the summer of 2012 with Angel Dawn and Jonathan O' Donald at his side once again. Butch's precise burial plot was located in the midst of a wide-open grass field deep within the center of the cemetery. There he would rest forever among thousands of other fine servicemen and servicewoman. Two huge rocks protruding above the grounds only twenty-five feet away from his burial site in the midst of vast grasslands and rolling-hills so beautifully manicured it brought tears to Angel Dawn's eyes. Even though every plot was well marked within the cemetery, it was at times difficult locating the exact location of a loved-one, even with a site map in hand. Thousands of similarly marked, ground-level grave markers were hard to distinguish, unless standing directly over each unique site, including Butch's. However, the two rocks served as a friendly beacon for locating his. Surrounding his grave site was also a very well-paved network of winding roads making way across the one hundred acres of Cape Cod's beautiful countryside. This was where Butch would spend the rest of eternity.

Specifically, his burial location (Section: 34 Site: 944) and the inscription on his headstone follows:

Butch E. Callahan
WS 2 US Navy
Vietnam
Jan 31, 1947-Jun 23, 2009
"At Rest . . . Finally"

Butch Errol Callahan, Butch, the "Butcher-Bird" was now truly at rest after such a turbulent life.

Ken

Ken left the US Army in 1980 after about ten years of active duty. He had never intended to stay in the service so long, never considered making it a career, but he wanted and needed to achieve two things prior to leaving the security, structure and "safety" of the military. He felt entering civilian life with an honorable discharge was a very good thing, but it alone wouldn't be enough to compete for jobs and sustain a non-military career. He was proud of his military record; his training and education; his two-year military intelligence assignment in Okinawa, Japan; his training expertise and certifications; his military awards including the Bronze Star, as well as being granted a top secret security clearance with special intelligence access credentials. In 1980, he still held mixed feelings about his combat time in Vietnam and how he viewed himself, the war, and the government's role in it all. He always respected his fellow soldiers who served there and always would but, overall this part of his military background would present an ongoing personal struggle for him much of his life. Yet, everything else was very positive in his mind—valuable lessons, experiences and memories.

Despite all of his personal and professional growth he experienced within the military, he believed obtaining at least two more credentials would make a big difference, not only in the civilian marketplace, but also in strengthening his own self-esteem and personal confidence. So he became driven early in his military career to acquire the following credentials before he permanently left the US Army:

1. An undergraduate degree,
2. A direct US Army Officer Commission.

When he was originally discharged in 1970 after two tours in Vietnam, he was a buck sergeant (E5). He then went to college for two years at the University of Maryland (College Park) during which time he reconnected with and married Cheryl, one of his former Anne Arundel High School sweethearts. Ken then reentered the US Army in 1972 after two years of college and was assigned to the US Army Security Agency (ASA), later to be called the US Army Intelligence Command, located at Fort Devens, Massachusetts. There he became a US Army Intelligence instructor.

With a year's direct experience with the 525 Military Intelligence Command in Vietnam's Mekong Delta already under his belt (which officially represented Ken's second tour of duty in Vietnam), it was a logical assignment for the US Army to place Ken at the intelligence training school at Fort Devens. There, he specialized in Morse Code Electronic Warfare Support Measures which included: eavesdropping, monitoring, and intercepting Chinese, North Vietnamese, and North Korean military communications activities during live operations. At the training school, he also mastered all the competencies and disciplines required within the five phases training professional cycle, including training analysis, design, development, delivery, and evaluation. He enjoyed conducting and evaluating the effectiveness of training; he liked it a lot. His passion for training grew over time and it would ultimately prove to be his long-term professional calling throughout the remainder of his military career as well as in his entire civilian career.

After a year or so at the intelligence school, he then took another overseas assignment; this time to Okinawa, Japan. This was one of ASA's most strategic listening posts in Asia at the time. He and his first wife, Cheryl, lived on the local Japanese economy from 1974 to 1976. They enjoyed the Japanese people and the island's many water-bound activities, including SCUBA diving, snorkeling, boating, and sightseeing. It was a long and enjoyable time in their marriage, but afterward, they returned to the training school at Fort Devens and eventually divorced ("irreconcilable difference"). It was a relatively simple divorce mainly because there were no children involved. They merely divided their assets, and Cheryl moved back to Baltimore while Ken stayed in Massachusetts in the army until he was honorably discharged a few years later, in 1980.

During his time in Japan and at Fort Devens, Ken continued his formal education with an unbridled fervor. He completed his associate degree and then attended nearly four more years of night school before finally obtaining an undergraduate degree—a bachelor of arts from the University of the State of New York. It had taken him much longer than he expected to obtain his academic goal, but he was committed to seeing it through. And he did.

Immediately after finishing all his academic requirements, he immediately applied for a direct commission within the US Army, something he had done on two previous occasions but was turned-down primarily because he lacked his under-graduate degree. On his third attempt, Ken also received many formal written endorsements from his current and past commanders to become a commissioned officer. Such command endorsements, coupled with his exemplary military performance ratings and performance over the years, including two tours of duty in Vietnam with one being in direct combat (First Infantry Division) and another tour in a military intelligence unit (525 Military Intelligence Command), played a key part with the commissioning board in Washington, DC. And, being a recipient of the Bronze Star added even more to his overall credibility.

Good Friend / Good Family

With all that and now including his Bachelor's Degree, he applied once again for a direct commission to the grade of captain (O3) in the US Army. And in 1980, it was approved. However, because he had no direct experience commanding an army company, it could only be approved at the level of first lieutenant (O2), versus captain (O3). Even so, Ken was still very delighted. He had finally achieved both of his goals—obtaining a bachelor's degree and rising to the level of a commissioned officer in the US Army.

There were many times throughout this long process, when Ken doubted and questioned himself about having such high goals, but there was a man who believed in him and was always motivating and supporting him throughout it all.

His name was Thomas Lancer.

Thomas had been a soldier himself at one time, even spending time within ASA a few years before Ken. He also served a year in Vietnam as well and when honorably discharged, he chose to stay in the Fort Devens area to raise his family. He had become an insurance professional helping young soldiers assigned to the intelligence training school financially protect themselves and their families while on active duty. That's where Thomas and Ken met in 1972.

They befriended each other and Ken came to trust him as a solid guy, a good friend, and a fine father. One night, Thomas invited Ken home during his earlier days at Fort Devens. He wanted him to meet his young, growing family: his beautiful wife, Wanda, and their three wonderful children—Brandon, Alicia, and Thomas Junior. Ken immediately fell in love with them. They, in turn, embraced him as just another "brother," "Uncle," and "friend." He never knew which role they really viewed him as, but he really didn't care. All Ken needed to know was they trusted and liked him; they accepted him into their lives so they could call him anything they wanted. For years, Ken found himself involved in the lives of these great kids—with sports, travel, birthdays, homework, sickness, cars, school, and pets. Ken was content just to have dinner with them, play with them, and just hang out with the family, most of time. He became just another member of "the family", sort of stray dog who came into their lives but never left. And he loved it. He loved them. It was as close to the *Leave It to Beaver* kind of domestic environment he had always longed for as a child, but never experienced it during his own upbringing. He even stayed close to them when the Lancers relocated from Shrewsbury, Massachusetts to Europe while Ken was in Japan.

They reunited in the late 1970s back in Massachusetts after Ken returned from Japan and the Lancers came back from Europe. As time evolved through the 1970s and 1980s, Ken watched as all three kids blossomed. Alicia grew up and embarked on a successful career in business and then became a beautiful mother raising a family of her own in Ayer, Massachusetts. Thomas Junior also built his own family in New York, and along the way he became a well-respected, medical doctor. Sadly, on December 2, 1984, the Lancer's oldest son, Brandon, was tragically killed in a car accident while attending Mount Wachusett Community College in Gardner, Massachusetts. Brandon had not only been a good, kind boy growing up, but he also grew into a wonderfully caring, giving young man who Ken came to love as a younger brother.

Ken never forgot the evening he got the phone call from Thomas about Brandon's tragic death: "Ken . . . we lost our boy." That's all Thomas said on the phone. That's all he had to say. That's all he could say. For the very first time in his life, Ken's heart was truly broken. Ken couldn't begin to imagine the kind of pain Thomas and Wanda, as parents, had to endure forever at the loss of their son. They could never be the same afterwards, nor could Ken. Brandon would always be a part of Ken and never, never forgotten. While Ken seemed destined never to use the word *son* when referring to anyone, he came as close as possible to doing so with Brandon. He would always feel blessed by having had Brandon in his life, even for such a short time.

A year or so after Brandon's death, Wanda somehow mustered enough strength and courage to write a wonderful book dedicated to the memory of her son—entitled: *A Mother's Heart* (Insight Books Publication, 1985). It was a series of short stories that captured many personal insights that are commonly felt by many mothers, yet uncommonly articulated. The essence of Brandon's character ran through every one of her beautifully written stories and would touch Ken's own heart forever.

When Ken finished his degree and ultimately received his direct commission to first lieutenant, Thomas and Wanda were there. They personally attended his commissioning ceremony held in the commander's office at Fort Devens intelligence training school in 1980. He was so honored by their presence. Yet, not everyone was happy about Ken's commissioning in 1980. He had quickly reached the rank of sergeant first class (E-7) in only nine years of active service, a major feat within the army during those days. To "give up" all his authority and rank as a senior enlisted man to accept a direct commission to the "lowly" rank of first lieutenant (O2) was a controversial decision, not for him, but for many of his peers. They thought it was a "step down." Doing such a thing was lunacy, "Callahan, with your accelerated advancement thus far in the enlisted ranks, you could easily reach command sergeant major [the highest rank possible in the army for an enlisted man] within only a few more years. That would be an amazing feat. Why blow it all just to become a 'lowly luey.'"

Ken heard this many times from well-intended cadre at the intelligence school. He also understood and appreciated what they were doing in dissuading him from such a course of action. But Ken had never intended to make the US Army a career in the first place, never. After all, joining the army was more of an escape than a goal for him. It just took him longer than expected to achieve the two things he sought for himself once he began maturing in the service. Throughout all this "in your face" commissioning controversy at Fort Devens, one person was steadfast in his support of Ken. Of course, it was Thomas Lancer. "Ken . . . try to stay focused on your goals. You always said the military was good, very good for you, but try to always remember . . . you were good for the army. It just wasn't forever. You've reached your goals and now you can leave with even more credibility than ever before. Stick with your dream, KB."

Thomas constantly reminded him of his dream. And, he and Wanda always called him Kenny Boy ("KB") out of affection throughout this period. In their eyes, Ken was a man for sure, but he always had that boyish, playful, less serious side of him that they enjoyed.

"It's a part of your charm, KB . . . don't ever lose it." Wanda would say.

His scheduled reenlistment was quickly approaching in May 1980. And, when it came, Ken chose not to reenlist as an enlisted man. Instead, he accepted an honorable discharge on his last day of service and the very next day, he received orders activating him as a First Lieutenant, Infantry Officer assigned to US Army Intelligence School's electronic warfare training team. And for the entire summer of 1980, "Lieutenant" Kenneth Callahan conducted electronic warfare training courses in simulated field operations throughout the wetlands of New England. Simultaneously, he was also applying for civilian jobs with many companies across Massachusetts. One such company was Digital Equipment Corporation (DEC), one of the world's largest computer manufacturers at that time. DEC's corporate headquarters was located in Maynard, Massachusetts, not far from Fort Devens. In June 1980, DEC contacted him for an interview regarding a training position. It was focused at conducting communication skill courses for employees and managers, including: fundamentals of interpersonal communications, relationship building, presentation skills, and customer engagements competencies.

Ken was excited about the opportunity and was eager to go on interviews. There was only one problem; he didn't own a civilian suit to wear on interviews. With all the changes and excitement over the past year, buying his first business suit was something that just fell through the cracks of his mind. So he talked to Thomas. It would take a couple days to get a tailor-made suit ready for him, and Thomas was adamant that Ken shouldn't wear an off-the-rack suit; it was just not becoming. So he suggested that Ken go on the interview wearing his official, army dress greens; his first lieutenant uniform, instead. Thomas thought by doing so, it could help differentiate him from all the other job candidates who would be competing for the same position. Ken's only concern was that many people in America still held a bad taste in their mouth about the military's role in Vietnam War—still viewing it, and the soldiers who fought it, very negatively. He didn't want to blow this opportunity right off the bat by his appearance. And, he certainly didn't want to make others feel uncomfortable in his presence, especially during a job interview.

Thomas disagreed and tried to convince Ken it wouldn't be a factor, not in 1980. "People have moved on, really, especially in the business world. You would likely get slammed if you were applying for a job at a college or university where liberal values and anti-military sentiments always will be much deeper, but not so much in the high-tech world of computers and business. They're bottom-line people—just get the results needed; that's what counts. And, Ken, if there's anything I can say about you is—you perform, you deliver, you get the job done, no matter what. So just let it go. It's all in your head, nowhere else." This was making sense to Ken. Thomas continued, "And besides, you can always get a business suit later on. You're good-looking in a uniform, really, and your interviewers may even enjoy it, too. It's a rare thing nowadays for anyone to show up for an interview in a uniform. Why not go for it?" To encourage Ken even further, he challenged him personally. If he actually got the job with DEC, Thomas would buy him his very first business suit—first one of his life. If he didn't get the job, then Ken would have to buy him and Wanda a dinner at the Bull Run, their favorite restaurant in Shirley, Massachusetts. This was a worthy challenge that Thomas knew would motivate and get Ken to excel even more.

Thomas was right. Ken went on his very first interview wearing his military uniform.

Thomas also helped Ken do some research on DEC in preparation for his interview. "You just can't walk into a company nowadays without doing your homework. It's another thing that may help distinguish you from other candidates for the job."

Digital Equipment Corporation was a huge, multinational computer enterprise at that time, with manufacturing plants and sales and service centers spread across the globe. It had nearly two hundred thousand employees and was growing at 20 percent annual compounded growth rates. Locally, DEC also had its own fleet of helicopters and small fixed-wing aircrafts to transport customers and employees to and from their sites throughout New England and across and the United States. It was also a very modern, progressive corporation driven by well-established business values of its founder—Ken Olsen. Little did Ken know at the time, but six years later, this same Ken Olsen would be named "Entrepreneur of the Century" by *Fortune* Magazine. Some man! Some leader! Some company! Ken was so psyched at just having an opportunity to compete for a position within such a great, reputable organization. He had to do well on this interview and hoped Thomas' advice was as on-target as it usually was.

On the day of the interview, Ken arrived in Maynard, DEC's headquarters, early. But he discovered quickly that the interviewer and the location of the interview had been changed; Merrimack, New Hampshire was the new location and Darlene Dunlap (head of the training organization) was the new interviewer.

Unfortunately, Ken never got the message about either change.

He had shown-up in Maynard only to learn about both changes on the spot. He didn't want to change the interview time, not after all his preparation, and there was no way he could drive to New Hampshire in time. So he got an idea. Instead of simply requesting another interview date, he sprinted over to DEC's helicopter flight pad that just so happened to be located on their Maynard facility property. He thought perhaps he could just catch a quick lift to New Hampshire. After all it was only 40 miles or so (10 to 15 minutes of air time). He had nothing to lose, but everything to gain by trying. In Vietnam, hopping flights was done all the time; it was habitual and easily accomplished. So he didn't think it would be a big deal to do in the civilian world, too. Besides, he just wasn't going to accept the fact that a simple administrative fluke could stop him from taking such an important step in his life. He also feared such an opportunity may never come his way again. That was what scared him the most. So, it was a risk he was willing to take.

Ken was going to make it happen, one way or another. If the helicopter was heading north "anywhere," he was going to be on it. So he hurried over to the helicopter pad, walked-up close to it, and immediately noticed two empty seats inside. So he merely hopped in and sat down. Then he asked the man next him if this was the flight that was heading north—asking in more of a "confirming" (all knowing) way rather than as a plea for information. A little self-confidence and assertiveness couldn't hurt under such circumstances. The man replied quickly, "Yea . . . it's going to Merrimack, New Hampshire." Ken was very surprised to hear that, but also very relieved. He quickly said: "Good, then I am on the right flight after all. Thanks." That's when Ken buckled-up and just sat back. About a minute later he saw another man jogging over the helicopter. A little panic rose in Ken's stomach knowing there would be no other seat left after this man boarded. As he climbed in, Ken was praying to himself that no one else followed. If so, the grounds crew or pilot would have to check the official flight manifest, then Ken would be discovered.

But, no one else approached the helicopter. That's when a ground operations guy came and quickly slid the helicopter's passenger door closed. Ken felt very familiar vibrations and heard even more familiar sounds of a helicopter coming alive. Then he watched the propellers starting their slow spin and a few seconds later they were heading north. He'd worry about how to get back from Merrimack later on—would walk back if he had to. Getting there on time was all that mattered to him.

Ken would find out later, he was not on any official manifest for that flight (no surprise), nor had he even checked into DEC's flight office at the helicopter pad before getting aboard. He'd also find out the pilots just assumed he was approved; they didn't want to question a man in uniform—he had looked just too damn official. It wasn't until half way to Merrimack that the pilot asked for his identification and confirmed that he had gotten on the wrong flight however was now required to go all the way to Merrimack. He apologized to Ken for the mix-up and for any personal inconvenience.

Ken graciously accepted the pilot's apology.

Already, Ken's uniform proved to be quite a valuable asset, and his interview hadn't even begun. He didn't know by boarding the helicopter, a private commercial vehicle without official authorization, he was breaking not only DEC's travel policies and procedures, but also breaching federal flight regulations. But such things really didn't matter to him at the moment. He was now flying eighty to hundred miles per hour, heading due north towards Merrimack. And, he now felt that his chances of making the interview were very good.

He was right.

Not in Kansas Anymore—Lost Soldier

As soon as the helicopter's skids had left the ground at Maynard, his mind flashbacked uncontrollably to the many takeoffs and landings his Huey had made in Lai Khe, Vietnam. It had been nearly a decade since his last helicopter flight, but the feelings and sounds were as real as if it were yesterday. The terrain in New England was much different of course; much more beautiful than Vietnam, especially on a warm summer day. He savored every moment of the twelve minute, interstate flight.

The helicopter landed in the middle of DEC's largest site in southern New Hampshire—the Merrimack facility. He departed the helicopter with three other people (the others were likely going further north so they remained on board). Ken then began walking on a well paved, winding walkway that ran from the brightly colored landing pad, around a sparkling pond to the back of a series of modern, two-story glass and brick buildings. The buildings' glass windows dominated the landscape and seemed to naturally reflect and magically double every image in sight—the surrounding pond, the blue sky, the rich tree line and beautiful foliage. Coupled with a carpet of well-manicured lawns and flowers of all kinds, this setting made Ken feel like he was gliding along a beautiful kaleidoscope of colors within Disney World's house of mirrors rather than walking on the grounds of a high-tech corporation. In the center of this wondrous landscape was a huge fountain shooting repetitive patterns of water droplets high into the sky and generating an endless, rainbow of sparkles that continuously floated back down into the pond.

Many DEC employees were just casually walking around the pond on the perfectly curved concrete pathways. Ken thought they were either solving the problems of the computer world or just taking personal breaks. Some people were seated on scattered benches around the pond and others within the soft grassy areas. The trees surrounding the pond were a mixture of full white pines and magnificent maples that provide perfect shade for anyone seeking to avoid the direct sun. Ken thought this was one of the most beautiful places he had ever seen. *If this is any indication of what civilian life is all about . . . count me in*, he also thought to himself.

As Ken was making his way to the main building, he began feeling somewhat self-conscious for the first time—a little out of place. He noticed people were staring at him and rightfully so, he was the only person in military uniform. It was then he realized how it must feel to be the last lit bulb left hanging on a Christmas tree after the holidays.

He stuck out big time.

Even so, he liked this environment. This place felt safe and inspiring. It was filled with all kinds of seemingly unmanaged human activity. Everyone seemed to be doing their own thing—without any apparent supervision or direction. *How* could this be? This concept blew him away. It was so foreign to him—just as if he had landed in a different country or culture for the first time. Questions began bombarding his mind faster than meteorites striking the earth. "*Where are the leaders? Where's the discipline? Where's the structure? Where's the organization? Who's in charge, anyway? What ranks are these people? How can you tell who's important and who's not? Where's the supervision? How do I address them—'Sir?', 'Mam?', 'Hey You?', What are the rules here, anyway?"*

Yet, there also seemed to be some kind of common purpose shared among everyone. He couldn't identify it or see it, but he could feel it. As he continued along the path, a huge smile began spreading beneath his well-practiced, disciplined facial expression that had been naturally etched-in after a decade of military service. He was feeling like a kid in a toy store who could only look but not touch. Ken was getting a little dizzy by now trying to see, smell, and sense everything around him at once—the people, the sparkling pond, the trees swaying in the breeze, and the fading sounds of the departing helicopter as it continued to its next destination. But what struck him the most was just how calm and peaceful it was here. It was a civilized atmosphere—one that he couldn't fully appreciate, not yet, but sensed he could and would one day.

Lieutenant Callahan was in awe.

There was no military base he had ever seen that could match such a facility. This peaceful, nonviolent world could possibly become a part of his future with just a little luck. Seeing how the other half lived and worked was worth all the time and effort just getting to Merrimack. If he didn't get this job, he still felt ahead of the game. Just being where he was at this moment was valuable in itself. So he kept following the path, looking in every direction, and smelling every "proverbial rose" he could see and touch.

"Hey guys . . . get over here and take a look at this. The United States military has just landed . . . I think we're being invaded." said a young woman to her colleagues from inside the main building.

She was on the first floor and just happened to look out the long winding window behind her office cubicle at ground level when she noticed Ken. To her, he seemed like a little Boy Scout lost in the woods without a compass—sort of like the way Dorothy must have felt after being dropped in the middle of munchkin land in the 1939 movie *The Wizard of Oz.*

She felt like yelling to him through the glass window: "Hey, you're not in Kansas anymore!" But, she didn't.

The young woman was very well dressed. She was wearing a big red feminine bow tie that accented her well-tailored navy blue skirted business suit perfectly. She appeared like a picture out of *Vogue's* business edition illustrating how to dress for success in 1980. Her thick brown hair, cute nose, greenish blue eyes, infectious smile, and engaging personality were attributes that Ken would later come to love about this woman. Then several of her coworkers came running into her cubicle to see the alleged military invasion unfolding before her eyes. "I bet he's saying to himself right now . . . 'Take me to your leader . . . I come in peace . . . The force be with you," she said in her best Darth Vader voice. And they all got a kick out of it and laughed aloud in unison. "Boy, he seems like one lost soldier. I don't know if it's an army or marine uniform—can't tell these days. But I do know it's not the navy, that's for sure. Just hope this guy left his gun at home," said one of the guys who joined her.

With that, they all laughed again and then went back to their cubicles. *"Yea . . . and I hope he gets so lost that he ends up over here in our area."* the young lady thought to herself as she kept an eye on Ken. He had just stopped a group of people and was asking for directions. One person turned and pointed directly at the young lady's building obviously showing him the way.

He went in that direction; in her direction. Coincidently, the exact place of his interview was adjacent to the young lady's cubicle in DEC's training headquarters. Not only that, she would soon find out that her lost soldier was about to be interviewed by her own boss—Darlene Dunlap. She would also eventually discover one day he would be on her training team—one of her colleagues.

The young woman's name was Dawn Earnestine Brady. Her friends, colleagues and family members just called her Dawn, for short. She had no way of knowing at the time, but six years after her 'lost solider sighting' occurred in Merrimack, New Hampshire, her name would change to Dawn Earnestine Callahan. And, she would keep that name for the rest of her life. And even further down the road, everyone in her life, including all her patients, would be referring to her by a much different, much more personal and affectionate name—"Angel Dawn."

A Wonderful Career

Ken's interview with Darlene Dunlap went well, very well. Less than a week later, he was made an offer to join her team, to become a part of the fastest-growing computer company in the world—DEC. He accepted it after first discussing it with Thomas Lancer, of course. Thomas once again touted the fine reputation of DEC and strong future of the computer industry. Knowing Ken's training and communication skills and his overall character well, he knew it would be a good fit for him. "Remember, it's not luck that got you this job at this time in your career. You're thirty, well trained, competent, a good person, and you'll be able to help them grow while growing yourself in this job. I know you, Ken. And right now there's a part of you that may be thinking you're unworthy. So let it go. It's DEC that is lucky to be getting you. It's a perfect match, man. Don't forget it." With that, he gave Ken a hug and then took him to his own tailor where he had a suit custom-made for him—Ken's very first business suit. Thomas lost their bet, and honorably kept his promise to Ken—as always.

So, Ken accepted the position with DEC and committed to start in September 1980—a commitment that would last for nearly fifteen years. He first would be working out of DEC's West Boylston training site in central Massachusetts—a facility that dwarfed the beauty of the Merrimack site. And it was only seventeen miles away from his home in Shirley, Massachusetts near Fort Devens.

The remainder of the summer, Ken completed his assignment as a commissioned officer in the US Army. He then resigned his post and left active military duty permanently. He had entered civilian life in September 1980 and closed the book on a wild, exciting, challenging and very rewarding military career. Ken would never wear another military uniform the rest of his life.

The DEC training position would be the first position he would hold in a very long, progressive training career. Over the next thirty-five years, he would find himself training thousands of people in multiple industries throughout eleven countries across the world. His scope of training and development positions ranged from communication skills trainer to executive sales trainer, to training manager, to organizational development (OD) director, to human resource (HR) and quality director, to global director of learning, and managing director of learning and development. His training experience would also be well refined and well tested in equally varied organizations, ranging from small start-up firms and medium size companies to large Fortune 100 corporations within multiple industries, including computer systems and service, telecommunication services, health care, discrete and process manufacturing, international organizational development consulting, transportation security, and mortgage banking. During his tenure with such fine organizations, he had many fun and challenging opportunities to apply his training competencies in highly diverse and challenging cultures and countries throughout the world, including Mexico, Canada, France, Scotland, Malaysia, India, Thailand, Singapore, Japan, Australia, and even on the third largest island in the world—Borneo.

His training experience never seemed limited to a single topic, a single company, or a single nation. And, he liked it that way.

9/11

Of all his challenging training assignments across the world, Ken became especially proud of one particularly challenging training position he held—a role that also came about during a very challenging time in the history of the United States. Immediately following September 11, 2001 (after the bombing of the World Trade Center and the Pentagon by extreme Islamic terrorists), Ken volunteered to join a special training team that was being formed by The Transportation Security Agency (TSA). This organization was in its infancy; formed directly in response to the 9/11 attacks on the country. One of TSA's top priorities was to bolster and strengthen an antiquated airport security system. This was not only an important goal for the nation, but it was also a very urgent one. Allied

Instructional Solutions, Inc. (AIS), the Chicago-based technology leader, was selected by TSA to help them in this important work, and training would prove to be a critical component to its success. So the TSA and AIS jointly created a highly specialized nationwide training task force composed of well-tested technical, communication, and security trainers. These individuals also had to possess government security clearances. In teams, they would be chartered to go into airports across the country and quickly assess, train, certify, and/or terminate airport personnel who were directly engaged in passenger handling and security. To put things into perspective, before 9/11, most airport employees who handled the security equipment and baggage were merely direct labor, minimum-wage workers without formal certification or education.

That had to change and change quickly.

One key factor that directly contributed to the terrorists being able to get on board aircrafts unnoticed was due to inadequate screening procedures, technologies, and standards, as well as a lack of highly trained personnel on site. So Ken and his training team (as well as many other teams put in place around the country) simultaneously executed highly intense training and certification initiatives with airport screeners via three-to-four-day sessions. What made such training "highly intense" was the fact that it also had to be conducted during "live" airport operations. That is, personal training and coaching had to be conducted in the presence of actual passengers as they were boarding and departing flights "and" without passengers knowing what was going on. In short, this type of training had to be done without being obvious, without disrupting airline operations, and above all, without causing undue apprehension or anxiety among a flying public that was already on high anxiety alert about flying anywhere. Equally intense, the training teams had to appear at the airlines "unannounced" to the screeners. Only management knew such training initiatives were to take place.

Ken found this caliber of training standards and conditions to be, not only challenging and demanding, but also among the most rewarding of his professional career. During this time, Ken and his training team were assigned to six international airports along the eastern seaboard of the United States including Bangor, Maine; Manchester, New Hampshire;

Providence, Rhode Island; Newark New Jersey; Philadelphia, Pennsylvania; and Baltimore, Maryland. All the other international airports across the USA were also assigned dedicated training teams. Airport Security Screeners who failed to meet training standards were recommended for immediate termination. Those who passed stayed. Throughout the initial phases of this emergency training at airports, thousands of screeners across the nation were terminated for incompetence, poor attitude, questionable ethics, or failing to follow the new airport security regulations themselves. Such individuals were then replaced with people better suited for the new world of airport security—life after 9/11. This new breed of individuals eventually evolved into federal employees—members of the country's contemporary TSA.

Immediately following 9/11 (within hours and days), Ken and countless other veterans quickly volunteered to do "anything" for their country, no matter what. This specific position, supporting TSA, was just where Ken landed. He was glad it worked out that way professionally. He was also glad about it on a personal level. From 2001 to 2011, Ken's subsequent training roles in business required him to travel 50 percent to 60 percent of the time, mostly by air. Each time he entered an airport, he was personally screened by TSA security employees, some of whom had been trained by him. With each screening he went through, Ken had an additional sense of pride knowing his brief, yet important training assignment had contributed directly to protecting his country once again—just as he had done in the US Army as a younger man.

Of greater importance to him was the knowledge that even though continual complaints about TSA's slowness and an increased degree of perceived personal intrusiveness existed among the traveling public, he knew not a single terrorist action had been successfully executed anywhere in US airports since 9/11.

Throughout his entire career, Ken was also able to author several books on learning, training, credibility, and occupational and individual professionalism. Many of his training sessions in corporate environments focused on the key principals reflected in these works. He had a passion for the subject of "credibility" (being worthy of trust and belief). Growing up and during his early adult years, he never felt that he possessed credibility—from others' view and even when it came to how he viewed himself. He just never felt "good enough." That's why his self-esteem was always lower than it should have been. He understood this about himself and wanted to learn more about this subject. Therefore, the more he studied and learned about "credibility"—what it was, what it wasn't, who had it, who didn't, how it was gained, how it was lost, as well as why it was so important in all walks of life—the more he wrote about it. And over the years, no matter where or for whom he worked, Ken consistently integrated and constantly relied on the basic training disciplines he originally acquired within the US Army intelligence field. Additionally, he always found a way to integrate credibility principles that he studied into all his training sessions.

As a result, Ken's ongoing professional and financial success could easily be directly traced back to the wonderful and challenging experiences he had as a member of the US Army intelligence training command and the military in general. While he still had a few lingering negative memories about the military, especially about his service in Vietnam, his overall positive memories far outweigh them.

Dawn and the "Non-Date"

When Ken began working at DEC in September 1980, he and Dawn (not quite "Angel" Dawn just yet) were just colleagues—trainers. Even though they both were in the same national training organization, they taught different courses, worked from different locations, and were assigned to different teams. Ken's office was located in West Boylston, Massachusetts, at that time. He was primarily teaching communication skills, relationship building skills, and presentation skills courses while Dawn was conducting a technical computer course out of the Merrimack, New Hampshire facility (where Ken made his maiden helicopter flight with DEC to his initial interview). The only times they were together was with other trainers during joint team meetings. In short, they were just friends and colleagues working in different states, separated by forty-five miles or so.

Then on a snowy day in the winter of 1980, Ken drove up to Merrimack, New Hampshire, from his office in Massachusetts. He was attending a daylong training course on one of DEC's computer products. By coincidence, Dawn E. Brady was the trainer this day.

Ken was delighted to learn this.

He had heard a lot about her training ability; she had a great reputation, not only among peers but also from her students as well. Dawn had been a high school business teacher in her previous life before DEC, and her comfort and teaching competencies became quickly obvious to Ken as he sat in her class while the snow gently continued to fall outside. The classroom was on the first floor of the building, and Ken recalled how beautiful it was in Merrimack as he momentarily gazed outside the window on short breaks during Dawn's class. When the course ended later that day, Ken approached her. He first thanked her for the class and then asked if she would like to go out to dinner. He briefly explained that he had a few other questions about computers and also wanted to learn more about the training organization as well. And deep inside, he knew they were colleagues and also wanted to get to know her a little better. Besides, the snow was falling harder and he had a long drive back to Massachusetts. He thought driving back later on that evening made more sense. Having dinner with her could kill two birds with one stone, so to speak. "Sure Ken. Sounds good. I don't have any plans, and besides you and your classmates worked me over pretty hard today . . . I'm really starving," Dawn said jokingly.

Ken knew it was a joke because she had managed the class very well. She found ways to have fun with everyone while they learned by incorporating humor now and then and also keeping the session moving ahead very smoothly throughout the entire eight hours. Time had passed quickly. "That's great Dawn . . . but I don't know the area around here at all, so where do you recommend we go?"

"Ummm, let's see. How about Hannah Jack's . . . its close by, only five minutes or so from here . . . and it has good burgers too. Something I could use about now."

"Sounds good to me."

Then Dawn looked at him, hesitated for a second, and said, "Just to be clear . . . this is not a date, right . . . just friends, OK?"

She had been direct with Ken, saying it more as a statement than a real question. And he got the message.

So, he confirmed that with her and would also be happy to drive them to the restaurant. Ken then helped her straighten up the training room, and they drove directly to Hannah Jack's together in his car—a MGB. He bought the MGB in 1976 in Baltimore after returning from Japan, while he was still in the army. It was around the same time he got orders for Fort Devens. He loved the car and quickly discovered Dawn did too. They both loved everything about MGBs except one thing. The heating system sucked—big time. They both agreed it was virtually impossible to get warm in those little buggers. In the summer, spring, and fall, MGBs were very enjoyable to drive, easy to handle, and with the convertible top down, just plain fun. But on winter nights like this, heat was almost nonexistent; even one's breath could still be seen on short trips. Plus, on roads like this night, handling turns was a big challenge.

Fortunately the trip to Hanna Jack's was a brief one.

During the dinner, he found out a lot about her, including her passion for sports cars. At Wrentham, where she grew up, she drove a 1966, night mist blue Mustang to and from school. Accordingly, her classmates nicknamed her Mustang Sally (of Wilson Pickett fame) because she was a sports-car girl alright. And after graduating from Boston College in 1972, she started driving a canary yellow TR-6. So gliding along the snow-packed roads in Ken's MGB just to and from Hanna Jack's brought back some fond sports car memories for both of them.

They both also had a good laugh when she admitted noticing him the day he arrived in Merrimack in the helicopter for his interview—her "lost soldier" day. She shared how everyone noticed him in his uniform and how they all noticed how out of place he looked at the time. "Boy, you were quite accurate describing me to your friends that way; I was in awe when I landed next to the pond. And you know what, I really did feel like Dorothy in the land of Munchkins just as you said. Wow, that seems like ten years ago, not three months," Ken said.

During their discussion over dinner, Ken also discovered other things about Mustang Sally besides her affection for sports cars. Before coming to work at DEC, she had been a high school business teacher at Foxboro and then taught at the very prestigious Weston Academy for several years. She would still have been driving a sports car that night too, but she had recently divorced after two years of marriage and was not only recouping emotionally, but financially as well. DEC paid much better than teaching high school and that was a very good thing for her at the time.

That's why she had joined DEC in the first place. So it made sense to Ken why she wanted to keep the dinner on a colleague basis. He understood her position perfectly, and would respect it.

Dawn lived right in Nashua, New Hampshire, the town just south of Merrimack and it only took her five minutes to drive to work each way. Like Ken, she too traveled quite a bit for DEC, conducting training courses across the states to new and veteran employees. She loved movies, traveling, and most of all, she loved birds. Dawn spent a lot of her time watching them, reading about them, and going on Audubon bird watches year-round, even in sub-freezing temperatures. But, because of her extensive travel schedule, she really couldn't keep a bird in her house. She learned growing up with birds in her parents' house just how emotionally dependent birds become on their own pets (their owners). They need and deserve regular attention and affection as much as cats and dogs. Her dream was to have her own "flock" one day.

The way she so intimately and passionately spoke about birds, the more Ken envisioned her having feathers of her own (versus skin), underneath her business suit. Unfortunately, he would not discover if that was true for at least another six years. But for the moment, he was content just fantasizing now and then about her.

Their dinner passed too quickly for Ken.

He found her to be a very open, confident, and honest woman; he was beginning to like her more and more with every new fact he learned about her. When they left Hannah Jack's, the snow had lessened to only occasional flakes and their drive back to DEC's parking lot allowed them to continue talking about everything.

She was a true New England Patriots fan; since their stadium was located in Foxboro, the town next to Wrentham, where she grew up, it was mandatory to be a fan. She was also a die-hard Boston Bruins fan, but only a fair-weather friend to the Boston Red Sox—they had just let her down too many times to be truly devoted. When Ken pulled into the huge parking lot at DEC, she asked to be dropped off at the main entrance of the building instead at her car. She had forgotten to take home something and wanted to run in and pick it up. So Ken did so and waited for her while keeping the car running. She then hopped back in and he started to take her to her car on the far side of the parking lot.

Miraculously, the heat had somehow kicked-in and the interior of the MGB was now as warm as a toaster. Dawn remarked right away as she got back into the car: "Wow . . . what did you do—get a bonfire started in the trunk or something when I was gone. It feels great in here."

It really was comfortable now, so instead of taking her to her car, they just sat there for some time talking some more. The bright light from the main entrance of the building allowed them to see the snow falling on and around them, but there was virtually no wind. The night was turning into a winter wonderland. Every now and then, Ken would hit the windshield wipers and clear their vision just to see nature's spectacle surrounding them. Then Ken asked her a question that would change the way he would come to see her forever. "Tell me about your parents, Dawn . . . do they still live in Wrentham?" Ken was just hoping her story was different from his.

He wouldn't be disappointed.

Bud and Lillian Brady

Ken's simple question turned into the most beautiful, genuine story about parents he had ever heard. She spoke about her mom and dad, Lillian and Bud Brady, in terms that described saints—not humans. It was obvious to him right away how much she loved and respected her parents. They married during WWII. During the war, Bud was assigned to the Army Air Corps in India and North Africa. He returned home safely after the war and eventually purchased Lillian's own mother's home at 313 Main Street in Wrentham, Massachusetts. It was a very small and modest house, a single-story ranch at the intersection of Main and Waters Street. It was the same place Dawn was born and was raised until she left for Boston College in 1968.

Bud and Lillian had two children—a boy and girl (Dawn). She was the younger of the two.

Bud had been a cabinet maker by trade and started his own business by building a simple workshop in the back of their yard. Actually, his workshop eventually became as large as their house. He was a self-employed cabinet maker when such skills were highly valued and much more appreciated by everyone. He was also a Master Mason for the majority of his adult life as he raised his family. He also became a member of the board of directors for the Wrentham Savings Bank along the way. Bud was a quiet man, a man of few words, but his presence and character spoke tons about him. And he was a good man, generous man, competent man, and a wonderful father.

When Dawn was a little girl, she wanted to hug her father every night, but she was always in bed when he came home from work; he worked sixty to eighty hours per week, so it wasn't easy to get his attention or real personal time. So she found one way to get his attention that seemed to work, and she told Ken about it as the snow was beginning to fall a little harder, "When I was told to go to bed some nights, I'd leave the living room then brush my teeth and head for my bedroom. But instead, I'd go to their bedroom and crawl into Dad's side and pretend to be asleep when they eventually came to bed. Then Dad would have to scoop me up in his strong arms and carry me to my room across the hallway. It would only last a few seconds, but it was like a lifetime of memories for me. My head would be resting on his shoulder, and we'd be cheek to cheek, even for a few seconds. I would be able to smell wood and sawdust on his work clothes from the long day in the cabinet shop. He'd put me into my bed, pull up the sheets to my neck, and then tuck me in. I lived for those fleeting yet wonderful moments with him." Ken could sense the affection for her dad was genuine simply by how detailed and freely she talked about him. Then she continued with her description of her father, "He was strict with us, but he was always there for us too. We knew he loved us, but he found it hard to communicate it sometimes. Nevertheless, we always were safe and secure and always felt cared for by his presence. He gave me and my brother everything that was important . . . everything."

Her mother, Lillian, was a typical housewife raising her kids in the 1950s and 1960s. She was a caring, giving mother, whose kids came "first, first, first and first" as Dawn described her. Lillian never learned to drive a car. "Why should I drive, I never want to go anywhere. Everything I want or need is right here in this house—I've got my two beautiful kids, my husband, my garden and TV . . . what else is there." Dawn knew there was some great wisdom in that answer.

But, in 1955, her parents' lives were nearly crushed. Dawn was about five, and she was playing baseball with some bigger boys during a church picnic at Rolling Acres, a local picnic area. Her tomboy nature compelled her to play, and she was assigned the catcher on the team—the only position none of the boys wanted to play themselves. And it was the only way she was going to be allowed to play anyway. She did so gladly. A boy swung his bat, accidently hitting her in the stomach. She fell instantly to the ground and was taken to the local doctor by her parents who were also at the picnic on that day. "Looks OK now. Just watch her pulse through the night, though. If it starts to go up, get her to the hospital right away," the local doctor told Bud and Lillian, both of whom had been in total panic mode.

And they did just that. Actually, Lillian never left Dawn's side that evening and well into the night. Around 2:00 a.m., she was rechecking Dawn's pulse for the hundredth time when she noticed Dawn would not wake up in the process as she usually did. They immediately contacted Dawn's older cousin, Paula, and asked her to come over to the house and babysit their son. They then rushed Dawn to Norwood hospital.

But it was too late.

Dawn's spleen ruptured on the way. By the time they arrived, she was already in a coma, and an emergency operation had to be conducted to save her life. After several more days in a coma and another month's stay in the hospital, Dawn pulled through and was finally allowed to go home.

To Dawn, her parents gave her life, and then they saved her life.

She went on to explain that both of her parents had contracted cancer. Lillian fully recovered from lung cancer but not her father. He was diagnosed with skin cancer and currently was in the midst of routine chemo and radiation treatment at the renowned Massachusetts Medical Center (MMC). They were both in their sixties then, and they needed Dawn's care more than ever, which she willingly and eagerly gave them. Her compassion for her parents nearly brought Ken to tears. It was a caliber of genuine tenderness and empathy he had never felt for his own parents, and to hear the words and emotions she used was inspiring to him. At that time in his life, his feelings for his own parents were closer to shame and embarrassment, nothing near the authentic affection Dawn possessed for Bud and Lillian.

He was truly moved by her sincerity as well as by her undying commitment to them. Dawn would continue to give such unconditional love and support to her parents for the rest of their lives. Bud Brady would die of metastatic melanoma in 2001 while sitting in the comfort of his living room recliner watching TV. And Lillian would pass away about eight years later while residing in the continuous loving care of the Dodge Newcomb retirement home in Norton, Massachusetts—only a few miles from where Dawn would be living at the time.

Little did she know then, but Dawn would actually get to see her mother live once again . . . even after her death.

A Visit from Lillian

Angel Dawn would be sitting on her well-flowered patio in North Attleboro Massachusetts. It would be a beautiful summer morning a week following her mother's death. She missed her mother so much and would often go the patio and just reminisce of their times together. She and her mother had a very special relationship—a genuine bonding love anyone could quickly spot merely by watching them interacting together. They were not only mother-daughter, but they also appeared like sisters, kissing cousins and best friends all wrapped into a single relationship.

Angel Dawn loved her so much, and missed her even more.

During her final days, Lillian had been living at the residential home. She loved it there because it was very small compared with the mega-size rest homes across New England at the time. This place had only twenty-four rooms and Lillian had one of them. The staff was very friendly, capable and professional—always rendering only the highest degree of personalized care to all residents. It was a single story residence quietly nestled in Norton's thick forest area allowing for privacy and tranquility, even during the long New England winters. What made this place even more special for Lillian was that several of her longtime friends, including a sister-in-law, also resided there at one time or another. This made her final days even more comfortable and far more special.

Lillian loved birds, especially hummingbirds. She would watch them very closely every day during the summer months by looking through Dodge's huge picture window located in central activity room. She would wait patiently as the hummingbirds arrived to have their first long drink of sugar water for the day; then she'd watch as they would fly back and forth to the feeder five to eight times per hour on some days. Their round-trips from the nearby trees to the nectar feeder were very predictable: "Just like kids going to a refrigerator" Lillian would tell Dawn each time she visited her mother. They then would sit together and just wait and watch, wait and watch. Dawn would not go more than two days without seeing her. "Mom . . . I think you're going to turn into a hummingbird one day," Angel Dawn would tell her.

Deep inside, Lillian dreamed that such a wish would come true, and she even told Dawn that exact thing many times, "Dawn . . . becoming a hummingbird would be a joy in the next life. Then I could speed along through the trees and clouds on the wind directly to your house. There I could watch you through your kitchen window anytime I wanted to. You know, I'd be so small and able to go so fast nothing could stop me . . . yes indeed . . . I would love to be a hummingbird. So please remember to tell God to make it happen when I die. Okay, Dawn?"

If Dawn could have granted this wish, it would have been the most important thing she could ever to do for her mom.

A week or so after her mother passed, Dawn was out on her patio in the morning just having her usual cup of coffee with a little Smart Balance margarine and jam on toasted whole wheat bread—her standard kick-off for the day. This was a typical summer morning in New England—fresh crisp air and a deep blue sky. A slight breeze and an early sun were just breaking through the trees engulfing her home. A bombardment of mystical warmth and light seemed to be falling only on the patio, nowhere else, and Dawn was directly in the middle of it all. She was savoring the moment and, as usual during such times, just reflecting on her mother's wonderful life. She was recalling one her final conversations. She also remember how tired and sick she seemed but also how "ready and prepared" her mother was to leave this world and rush to the arms of her late husband—Bud. Lillian was far more at peace with her own death than Dawn was in letting her go. Then a gentle avalanche of thoughts and memories began filling Dawn's senses. She became cool and warm at the same time, as if that was even possible. Her backyard became so still and quiet at that moment she could actually hear a squirrel munching on an acorn across the lawn. The hanging menagerie of flowers along the patio railing also seemed to be providing an invisible barrier of some sort that was shielding her from all the noise and hustle of the outside world. It was a unique and peaceful moment, one she had never experienced before. As she sat there, deep in thought about her Mom, something very special happened. Directly in front of her, actually less than three inches away from her nose, appeared a beautiful hummingbird. It was just hovering there, seemingly floating on air. Dawn thought she was daydreaming, but she wasn't. She was wide-awake, staring into the face of a ruby-throated hummer, as her Mom called this special species. And more startling, the hummer was staring back at her.

"Inter-species eye-to-beak contact"—the orgasmic moment of any true bird watcher was at hand.

Because a hummer's wings flip eighty times faster than human eyes blink, it appeared motionless, suspended in time. The low-humming sound of such wings hard at work could be fully appreciated only by the most sophisticated birder ear. And, it was laser-focused directly at Dawn's nose at this moment. Fortunately, she had two well-trained ears both perfectly positioned allowing her to savor every sensual vibration. The bird then moved slightly back and forth then across the width of her face several times as if it were inspecting a new nest site for the first time. Dawn was reciprocating. She was now studying the hummer's long slender bill, white breast and red throat, as well as its strong emerald green back and white-tipped tail. She had never seen a hummingbird up so close.

That's when it hit her. This hummingbird had to be her Mom, just had to be. She then wanted to wrap her arms around the hummer and hold on tight forever. She began envisioning herself being embraced within its wings and then being gently picked up and safely carried far, far away to a place where all loving mothers and daughters embrace forever. Dawn couldn't believe her luck—her fate. Her Mom had indeed, come back to her just as she wished well before her death. And, Dawn now wished this moment would never end.

However, that's when her Mom spun around and zoomed into the trees as quickly as she arrived. A second later, she was gone forever.

Of course, Dawn was stunned at what just occurred. She was also very relieved, and so happy. No hummingbird ever came so close to her, never stayed so long, nor created such a calm sensation of warmth and peace in her heart as in that moment. That's when she knew deep inside that her Mom was happy and would be happy forever.

Both Bud and Lillian would be forever together, side by side in the Hillside Cemetery in Wrentham, Massachusetts. Even in death, Dawn continued the care of her parents by continually maintaining their grave site monuments—every birthday, every holiday, and every season change and even on both of their death days. Additionally, Dawn always sprinkled updates on how the Patriots, Bruins and Red Sox were doing. Any opportunity to visit her parents at Hillside, she gladly took.

Meanwhile back in Ken's MGB in Merrimack . . .

Ken was not only touched by her testimony, but he was also envious. He always wanted to experience such love for his parents. But it was just not in his heart as it was for her; he didn't share that with her. As the snow continue softly falling on the MGB with Dawn and Ken still warmly tucked into the front seats just talking, his mind seemed to wander deep into his own soul for a moment or two. He was searching for similar words, feelings, and sentiments that he could use to describe them about his own upbringing. But he could not find them at that moment. He didn't know if he should be feeling guilt or shame by not being able to do so. He and Dawn certainly had a lot in common. And, Ken wanted to learn even more about her, but now he was afraid she would one day learn about him.

Suddenly, the snow fall stopped, and so did their conversation.

She thanked Ken for a fine dinner, for the opportunity to get to know him better, and for a great drive in a MGB. He told her how much he too enjoyed the dinner and appreciated her taking the time after a long day of training to spend some time with him. He especially made it a point to say how much he admired her effort in caring for such wonderful parents, and how lucky they were to have such a fine daughter. "I am the lucky one, Ken . . . without them I wouldn't even be here."

Ken knew in his heart she was right. Dawn had asked about Ken's family early on during their dinner, but he just gave minimum information (two brothers, mother multiple marriages, moved around quite a bit—safe stuff). When she started inquiring further, he skillfully redirected the topic back to her and her family without being impolite. The difference between Ken's and Dawn's upbringing was as different as dogs and cats. However, he felt their commonalities were equally strong, and that's what he would always remember about her.

Ken slowly pulled away from the main entrance and headed over to her parked car. They said good-bye and shook hands. Dawn then drove out of the parking lot just as the snow started to once again lazily fall on Southern New Hampshire.

They would run into each other occasionally during many team meetings over the next five years or so, but they never had another dinner (a non-date) together. Dawn did come to West Boylston and attend one of Ken's classes the following year though. And, it was good to catch up with her again. Between 1980 and 1985, Ken would meet another woman and get married. Her name was Laura, a DEC software engineer. They met in one of Ken's training courses, dated, fell in love, married, fell out of love, and divorced around 1982. In total, they were married only about a year. Around that time, Ken also left the training organization of DEC and moved to New Jersey. There, he assumed an executive trainer position within DEC's Bell AT&T account management team. He held that position for several years.

"I Love You, But I Don't Like It!"

Then in the summer of 1985, five years after the dinner at Hannah Jack's on that beautiful snowy evening in Merrimack, Ken received a call from Dawn. Even though they had occasionally run into each other during training meetings, this was the first time she actually called him directly. Coincidently, Ken just so happened to be in Merrimack when she called. He was attending a Bell AT&T management meeting that just happened to be held in a local hotel not far from Hanna Jack's (the exact restaurant where Dawn and Ken had their "non-date" nearly five years before on a snowy night).

Dawn told him on this phone call that she was in the process of applying for an account executive position with the Bell AT&T management team—Ken's New Jersey-based team. She heard Ken was a part of that organization and called him to ask for some insight preparing for her upcoming interviews. Of course, Ken was delighted to hear from her, even more delighted to help her. He was even more excited thinking she may one day become a member of the Bell AT&T team. So he provided her with some information about the many people who were leading the team and other helpful information that may come in handy during her interview. Later that week, she interviewed with the group's leaders, and she was made an offer to join the team. She accepted and started the following month.

Ken and Dawn were going to be working very closely together from then on. He just didn't know how close.

After a few months, they started dating. She was making weekly trips to New Jersey as a part of the team and had a remote office located next to Ken's office. He had a condominium in Kingsberry Acres right on the Princeton, Pennington line—five miles from the DEC office. They dated mostly on weekends, but then they found themselves spending much more time together, including a weekend on the Jersey Shore as well as on long, country drives, including a week's long driving vacation together from New Jersey to Yellowstone National Park in Wyoming. It was in Yellowstone when they fell in love. A few weeks later, Ken proposed and Dawn accepted.

He was so very happy, but also silently concerned, not about Dawn, but about himself. He had tried marriage twice and neither worked out. While both were amicable divorces, he knew deep in his heart it was primarily his fault—managing close personal relationships as well as insecurities were the real problems. Both of his first wives were good, caring people and very good wives. Ken felt both of these good people just made a bad decision in selecting him as a husband.

He didn't want to hurt anyone ever again in such a way, especially Dawn who was now innocently entering a world totally different than the world in which she grew up. And, Ken knew this. So one night before they eloped, he tried his best to tell her what he felt, but it didn't come out the way he intended: "I love you . . . but I just don't like it."

Dawn was speechless.

She was happy and surprised. She was confused and bewildered at the same time. "OK . . . I love you too, but . . . please help me understand what you just said . . . especially the last part . . . what does . . . 'I don't like it' mean?" Dawn asked, truly perplexed. Ken was confused too, but he wanted to be open with her. He really did love her, but there was something else going on deep inside of him. It wasn't that he really didn't "like" it; he was "afraid" of it—of loving her and allowing her to love him.

His words just didn't come out the way he felt.

So they talked long into the night about things. He was as open as he could be about his feelings, about his background, about his fears and concerns, and about his relationship with his own family. While they discussed things of this nature before, it was never to this depth. She loved him and wanted to marry even more after his lengthy, genuine disclosure. Her heart was also broken for him when she learned the truth about his background and upbringing. And she now had a better understanding of his fears. He had been honest with her, and that was more important to her than anything. She, too, had been married and was just as insecure about some things as he. They held on to each other and talked until sunrise. Their love for each other had been significantly strengthened as a result.

A few weeks later, they eloped.

Since neither one wanted to go through a wedding again, eloping seemed the best plan. So they arranged a quick wedding ceremony to make things legal and official. And then, on February 14, 1986 (Valentine's Day), Ken and Dawn were married by a justice of the peace (JOP) in Hudson, New Hampshire. No one was present except the JOP, Ken and Dawn. The ceremony lasted about ten minutes. They were officially married at 7:00 a.m. then they boarded a plane in Boston at 10:30 a.m. At 1:00 p.m. they were on the pink sand beaches of Bermuda. Two and half decades later, on February 14, 2012, they would celebrate their twenty-sixth wedding anniversary together.

They would never have children of their own but had been international exchange parents to a young girl from the Philippines in the 1990s. Her name was Grendel and she came to the United States on an academic scholarship. While she lived most of the time on the campus of Sacred Heart College in Nashua, New Hampshire, she spent a lot of her nonacademic time with Angel Dawn and Ken. For the first and only time in their marriage, they felt somewhat like parents. They came to love Grendel as their own, and she in turn came to love them as well. Grendel and Angel Dawn became inseparable during this time. Actually, Grendel finished her undergraduate degree and went on to complete her masters in human resource management at Sacred Heart. And during this same period, Angel Dawn decided to return to school and obtain her own master's degree in clinical psychotherapy. She and Grendel studied together and they both graduated together in 1999 from Sacred Heart College—each with different degrees but both shared the graduation stage on exact same day. Grendel returned to the Philippines, and she continued her education there, eventually obtaining her PhD in human resource management and business. Returning to the Philippines brought her mixed emotions. She really wanted to stay with Ken and Angel Dawn and loved the United States, but she also had family and community responsibilities back in her home town of Davao, located in the southern part of the Philippines.

Ken and Angel Dawn became so proud of her for what she was able to accomplish in such a short period of time. They were also honored to have had the opportunity to "come close" to, while not actually touching, what it was like to be parents. Even though Grendel was thousands of miles away, they would still remain close for the rest of their lives.

CHAPTER 6

PTSD—
"Reluctant Husband, Reluctant Soldier"
(Massachusetts, 2009)

IT WAS ONE OF THOSE fluke New England days in February that comes only once or twice a century—back-to-back eighty degree sunny days. Somehow the position of the sun, tilt of the earth, and strong southern winds were perfectly aligned to transform the Dr. Zhivago-like, bitter cold Massachusetts landscape into a virtual Polynesian oasis. New Englanders were not only surprised but also very delighted. Even hibernating wildlife were fooled into temporarily believing mating time was upon them. Actually, history would show the six-month period between January and June 2009 was the warmest period ever recorded in New England history. And Ken loved it—simply because it meant he didn't have to put on three layers of protective running clothes before heading out for his routine, four-mile jog through winter's slush and snow. He felt the time it took just to dress for jogging (as well as removing the sweat-soaked garbs afterwards), took more effort than the run itself. Fortunately, he didn't have to go through such a routine this day. He just put on a synthetic shirt, nylon running shorts, cross-country running shoes, and his fireman's security belt holding his cell phone and knife. That was it.

He was out the door in a minute.

It was around noon and the sun was high in winter's sky without a cloud in sight; even people indoors had to wear sunglasses just to look out their windows as the snow on the ground intensified the sun's natural light. Ken was working in his home office and couldn't wait until his two-hour business conference-call on reverse mortgage mercifully ended.

He kept sneaking peeks out his window as everyone on the conference call discussed challenges facing this unique niche in the current mortgage industry. Even though his ears were listening to his colleagues, his eyes were jealously watching his neighbors who had already broken out of their igloo-like homes to seize the beauty of the day. His neighbors were dressed in short sleeves, cutoffs, and flip-flops as they pulled wagons full of screaming kids with one hand and managed leashed dogs with the other. Ken sensed the kids couldn't understand how they could be playing outside without boots, gloves, hats and coats. However, the dogs did care—they were happily prancing and sniffing around trying to keep their masters moving. Ken thought if the dogs had pulled their masters any harder, they would lift themselves high in the air like a kite, just as the baby elephant in Walt Disney's 1941 animated movie *Dumbo* hovered high above the circus while being chained to the ground. The dogs were energetic and alive, sniffing the sniffs of winter that hadn't been sniffed for a long time. It was as if someone had suddenly removed folds of packed Kleenex from their dog snouts and then injected them with high-powered nostril steroids and set them free. They were going dog nuts.

Families were also roaming through the perfectly plowed, perfectly paved streets of the "cliffs" section in North Attleboro, Massachusetts. Ken's second-story front window had a great view of everything going on. The two-foot-high snow piles scattered through the neighborhood were neatly stacked and well sculpted; the town's crew had once again done another fine job clearing snow and ice after the most recent storm.

Ken and his wife Angel Dawn lived at 220 Oldwood Road in the heart of North Attleboro's cliffs section.

Five minutes after the conference call ended, Ken was out the door—another "clean getaway" was at hand at least for the next ninety minutes or so. His routine four-mile jogs always started at the cliffs. He then quickly shuffled down Oldwood Road, and then turned right onto Raymond Hall taking his short cut through the narrow trail leading to the town's former airport area. Ken always avoided auto traffic by running on the dirt-packed alley behind Fitzie's Pub on his way to Watery Hill. There he entered the World War I (WWI) Memorial Park. He knew this was the ass kicker part of the run (all uphill), but at least it marked the halfway point on his jog. The WWI Memorial Park was Ken's favorite part of the run because of all the animals and their sounds. The area was more like a petting park than a zoo, and even in the winter months the animals were still caged outside most of the day. There were no real exotic animals just deer, goats, pigs, ponies, peacocks, chickens, ostriches, and a few wild turkeys. However, there was an emu sitting patiently waiting for any kid to come by to feed it. To Ken, it was the constant animal sounds that made him feel like he was running across Africa's Serengeti minus any big time fangs and claws.

Ken then headed down the back side of the park that emptied into the Westwood Estates, the premiere neighborhood in North Attleboro. Most front yards had electric fences enabling dogs to go through their pretend protective dance every time Ken jogged by. This routine had evolved into a ritual between Ken and the dogs even though each dog knew Ken's scent after hundreds of encounters over the years. They saw each other virtually every day in sun, rain, or snow. Yet, they still went through their *"don't you dare come near my turf"* dance even though Ken was no longer intimidating. Ken then hit Landry Avenue and headed down the hill taking a left at Animal Crackers Day Care. From there, he went straight up Oldwood Road to the monstrous blue water tower near his house, where he slowed to a walk and made it the rest of the way home at a more humane pace.

Ken was not a fast jogger, just a consistent one trying to sustain good health. And on this beautifully deceptive day in New England, he savored every blissful moment. He entered his home, quickly shed his wet clothes, showered, and logged his mileage into his physical exercise journal—a routine he started since he was diagnosed with adult-onset diabetes in 2008. Jogging represented about 50 percent of his daily exercise routine which also included ten minutes of tai chi stretching and bending, one hundred repetitions of twenty-pound free weights for strengthening, and three hundred sit-ups with his exercise ball.

At sixty, Ken was five feet eleven inches tall and weighed 188 pounds. He felt this was a well-balanced approach to maintaining good blood circulation, strong cardio performance, and healthy bones. His primary care physician, Dr. Sidney Bronson, concurred. The only daily medications Ken was taking at this age were one baby aspirin and twenty milligrams of Lipitor. Dr. Bronson viewed Ken as being "in great shape" for his age. Dr. Hawk, a cardiologist, had just administered a routine stress test as a part of Ken's annual physical and concurred that his overall condition was equivalent to a thirty-five-year-old man. By all standards, Ken was very healthy.

During his years in Okinawa in the mid-1970s (when he was in his mid-twenties and still in the military), Ken began jogging routinely. Just like eating, working, and sleeping, "sweating" became a natural part of his daily life. He never became obsessed with it; he just did it. And sometimes he'd even go several days without exercising at all without getting down on himself. He just did the best he could. And in the last several years, he had even cut down on the frequency and distance of his jogging merely to reduce the amount of stress on his joints. Despite the benefits to his respiratory and cardio performance, the constant pounding on his knees and hips had started taking its toll. So he now was averaging only three to four miles (versus five), and that was okay. He also began reducing the frequency of jogs to five times per week (versus seven). This too, was appropriate and welcomed by his body.

It was time he started to cut back anyway. From 1974 to 2009, he estimated that he had run a total distance that greatly exceeded the circumference of the earth—well over thirty-five thousand miles. In short, he had jogged around the world without once having his passport stamped.

Ken took a hot bath then went back into his home office to continue where he left off. He checked his e-mails then hopped on another conference call with John Titan, the president of Winter Winds Consulting, Inc.—the premiere consulting firm in the reverse mortgage industry. Ken had recently joined the South Carolina-based firm after completing nine years with Business of America, Inc. where he was a national learning and development manager within its reverse mortgage division. During that time, his office was located in Sagamore Beach, Massachusetts at the entrance to Cape Cod. In 2009, Business of America, Inc (BOA) exited the reverse mortgage business, not because of financial reasons, but because of the extensive government-driven, regulatory scrutiny that was being put in place to regulate the entire industry. As a matter of fact, all the biggest mortgage players also made the similar move. This business decision directly impacted Ken. He and over five hundred employees and managers in BOA's reverse mortgage division were laid off as a result. So Ken took a severance package and joined Winter Winds in the role of learning and development director. John Titan was one of the reverse mortgage industry's founding fathers who also helped lead BOA's reverse business. When he left BOA in 2008, he started the consulting firm.

While Ken was jogging that day, a BOA memory flashed through his mind. It involved a student who was participating in one of Ken's reverse mortgage training sessions being held in Minneapolis a few months earlier. The student was a veteran mortgage loan officer who was transitioning into reverse mortgages, and was required to attend Ken's training as a part of BOA's recruiting process. Anyone representing reverse mortgages for the company had to graduate from this training.

The man was not only a mortgage veteran but also a Vietnam veteran. It was through this man that Ken first learned about the Agent Orange / Adult-Onset Diabetes connection. After the training class ended that evening, he and Ken went out to dinner.

That's when it was discovered they both had been recently diagnosed with Adult-Onset diabetes. The veteran described to Ken how the federal government was specifically encouraging Vietnam vets who had such a condition to learn more about the Veteran Administration's (VA) new program—which permitted veterans who had been exposed to Agent Orange (a highly toxic defoliant) to participate. It enabled these veterans to receive benefits for their injury because a direct correlation was proven to exist between Agent Orange exposure and adult onset diabetes. Until that time, Ken had only taken advantage of one VA benefit that was available to him—the GI Bill, which helped him to complete his college education while he was still on active duty in the 1970s. He had not been familiar with other veteran benefits available to him, so he thanked the vet for sharing his insights about this program and promised he would definitely look into it.

And, he did.

Several weeks passed before he began exploring it further. He had started by researching it on the Internet and discovered helpful information there. He then printed out some literature and documents and shared it with Angel Dawn. After discussing it, they decided to learn more from those who really knew all the facts—the office of the Veterans of Foreign War (VFW) in Massachusetts.

VFW & VA

In the late summer of 2009, Ken set up a meeting with a representative of the Veterans of Foreign War (VFW), a man named Martin Finley.

The meeting was held in Martin's office in Boston. Ken had just assumed the VFW and the VA were one in the same, but quickly discovered they were not. Both organizations worked closely together yet they were officially separate entities. Actually, Ken learned the VFW was the largest organization of combat veterans in the United States. It received no taxpayer funds—supported only by charitable donations. All VFW representatives, like Martin, worked on behalf of veterans by lobbying Congress for better benefits as well as directly helping guide individual veterans through the vast puzzle of government procedures and policies. Martin's VFW office was located in downtown Boston within the State Street Bank building, a high rise structure overlooking the entire Boston Harbor, the historic Faneuil Hall areas and the Boston Common.

Angel Dawn was working at Massachusetts Medical Center (MMC) in the renowned Patient Advocacy Center at the time. On this day, Ken met her at the MCC and from there they took a brisk ten minute walk to Martin's office. It was located on the twenty-third floor. The extensive security screening process put in place after 9/11 took longer to clear than the time it took to walk from MMC. But they still arrived at Martin's on time. As they entered his office, they were immediately greeted by a petite, attractive woman. Her name was Ms. Harriett Bonin. She was a VFW's administrative assistant and made Ken and Angel Dawn feel very welcome and comfortable. "So very glad to meet you, please have a seat. Martin will be with you shortly. Oh, by the way, would either of you like a cup of coffee?" They thanked her but respectfully declined.

It was a typical small government office filled with lots of paperwork and sounds of people hard at work. Martin's individual office was equally cluttered but also seemed filled with a history of veterans' needs, ambitions and dreams. Martin was a young man about thirty-five. While he was dressed in civilian clothes, Ken sensed he had a natural military presence about him. He was equally cordial and friendly as Harriett, but then got right down to business. "Mr. Callahan, your DD-214 and your medical doctor's certification of adult-onset diabetes in 2008 checks-out. Thanks for sending these documents to me in advance. So, it looks like you are qualified to place a claim against the government for compensation. And I'd be glad to help you do so."

Martin continued to cite several military and federal regulations that Ken did not fully understand. He then started to explain a few more details of program and that's when Ken abruptly interrupted him, "Sorry Martin, but I didn't know this was about me suing the federal government or anything like that. Is this what you're saying the program is about?"

Ken was quite surprised; shocked was a better word. He didn't know he had to bring a lawsuit against the government. Martin responded quickly with genuine empathy, "Well Mr. Callahan, that's not totally accurate; it's really just a claim against the government—not necessarily a lawsuit or anything like that. And, in your specific case, this is more of an administrative action. You see, the status of the Agent Orange/ Adult Onset Diabetes program is what we call 'assumptive approval status' which means it becomes automatically available to you and other qualified Vietnam vets. That is, it requires very little proof and reviews, and certainly no lawsuits. But I understand how you could view it as a legal action especially hearing a word like 'claim' used in this context."

He then felt a little better after Martin's explanation. Ken didn't want to sue or take any adverse legal action against the government. Then Martin went on to explain in a little more detail the process of bringing such a claim "to" (versus "against") the government. "In your case, it's approved automatically. You see, several years ago, the federal government applied an 'assumptive' status on the Agent Orange/Adult-Onset Diabetes connection which requires only minimal qualifying proof. Your medical diagnosis in 2008 coupled with your DD-214 records proving you were on the ground in Vietnam is all that's really required. It will take only a couple of months, but afterwards you'll start receiving a monthly compensation for your service and suffering. This will be in effect the rest of your life."

Martin continued as Ken and Angel Dawn listened carefully, "In short, you deserve this, as all soldiers who served in combat in Vietnam on the ground do. Agent Orange was nasty stuff, real bad as you know, even though you may not have known it at the time. The government put you in that environment not knowing the full implications and the long-term side effects. They know now. And today, you and all soldiers exposed deserve compensation. It's that simple, really. They made a mistake and are attempting to rectify it."

Over the next hour or so, Martin asked Ken more questions and began reviewing more of his paperwork. Afterwards, he then suggested Ken and Angel Dawn think about it for a while before moving ahead. "Why don't you and Mrs. Callahan grab some lunch, discuss it, and come back and let me know if you would like to proceed. I want to go through the rest of your military records anyway. If you decide to proceed, I'd be glad to help you do so. If you don't that's fine, too. It's really your decision."

Ken and Angel Dawn thanked him and took his advice. They walked over to the Union Oyster House, the oldest restaurant in the America, located by the State Street building near Faneuil Hall, only a block away. There, they had some of the restaurant's famous clam chowder and they discussed things further. When they returned to Martin's office, Ken stated he would like to move ahead with his "claim to" versus "claim against" the government. He still wasn't comfortable with the use of the word "claim" but he would move ahead anyway. "I understand, Ken. Other vets I've helped also shared similar concerns . . . you're not alone. And I now believe I have everything that's needed to submit this on your behalf."

He shuffled through some more papers as Ken and Angel Dawn walked over to his window to admire the view. Then Ken spotted the renewed Millennium Hotel located adjacent to Faneuil Hall's Quincy Marketplace where he had conducted many training sessions for BOA over the years—each class being conducted right in Millennium's historic Williams

Dawes Conference Room, the perfect setting for learning anything in historic Boston. They then rejoined Martin at his desk. That's when Ken was asked a question he never had been asked before, "Oh, by the way, Mr. Callahan, when I was reviewing your DD-214, I noticed you also are a Bronze Star recipient. Congratulations. Would you mind telling me a little about it?" Ken paused, being surprised by the question, and then said "Sure." So he explained how it was bestowed on him in Lai Khe, Vietnam when he was with the First Infantry Division flying missions during his first tour of duty. As Ken was describing things to Martin, he noticed himself becoming somewhat uncomfortable simply talking about it, after all it was the first time anyone had ever asked him about his Bronze Star—in forty years.

When Ken finished his brief explanation, he then asked Martin a question of his own, "Help me understand why receiving the Bronze Star has anything to do with this, Martin."

"You're right, it really has nothing to do with you being exposed to Agent Orange or this claim. But since you were obviously in combat, as indicative of the Bronze Star, the stress and hardship you experienced could represent another type of benefit you may rightfully deserve and be fully eligible to receive."

Ken was more confused now. "Sorry, Martin, I'm still not following you on this." So Martin continued, "If you are currently suffering, or have suffered in the past from any psychological or emotional side effects as the result of your service, you may be entitled to other benefits."

Ken was beginning to understand what Martin was saying and what he was implying. That's when his facial expressions started to convey his feelings. He didn't answer Martin at first; rather, he just stared at him somewhat embarrassed at the insinuation.

Martin sensed Ken's discomfort so he continued providing more information, "Mr. Callahan, have you heard of posttraumatic stress disorder—or PTSD? That's what we're talking about here. If you are suffering psychologically today from any service-connected trauma incurred or aggravated by service in Vietnam, then you may be eligible to make an additional claim. It is not associated with the Agent Orange claim. It's totally separate, just another benefit you may have access to. That's all." Again, Ken was surprised and embarrassed at such a suggestion. He immediately shot it down as not being appropriate, not applicable to him. He was not suffering psychologically from his experiences in Vietnam—he was a "normal" veteran. Just the thought of it was ridiculous, even laughable. For forty years, he had been a very successful international trainer constantly working and excelling in business around the world. He knew anyone with PTSD could not perform at such a level of proficiency over the long term. As he thought more about the implications, he began feeling even more insulted.

Ken's emotional reply to Martin reflected this feeling loud and clear. "Look Martin, you seem like a good guy, and I really appreciate what you're trying to do for us, but you need to know this—I'm not mentally sick! I'm as healthy as an ox, physically and emotionally; probably healthier today than twenty years ago. My combat experiences were and will always be very personal, something I'll never forget, but compared to so many other veterans, my problems and reactions are trivial. I came back after two years in Vietnam without a single scratch—not one. There were many men who suffered greater hardships. That's where you should be focusing such help; they deserve and need it, not me." As Ken was talking, his emotions were steadily rising and Martin noticed it. He tried to explain things a little better to help Ken settle down. "Okay Mr. Callahan, I get it, I really do. Please understand, I'm not implying you suffer from PTSD. But I'd be remiss if I didn't at least share some details about this possible benefit. You see, there are lots of soldiers that don't know they've been suffering psychologically even though they may have been for decades since that war ended. Look at it this way, sometimes a soldier is the worst judge of his own needs. He's just too close to it. And, as time passes beyond his combat trauma, the more likely his hidden symptoms become a natural part of his life."

Martin then went on, "And another key thing to understand is that sometimes Vietnam vets are uncomfortable even talking about such things—no less considering that PTSD may be impacting them personally. Nevertheless, many vets are suffering without consciously knowing it."

That's when Ken became even more adamant, "I understand what you're saying, Martin, thanks for the education really, but this doesn't apply to me; it doesn't apply TO US . . . right, Dawn?"

Ken then looked directly at his wife. He was seeking her support and wanted confirmation of his view of things. But, it didn't come. Instead, she broke eye contact with him, looked down at her purse, and remained quiet. For a few moments afterwards, there was an uncomfortable silence in the room. Martin had experienced this exact type of moment many times between other veterans and their spouses. He knew to allow the silence to continue. This was very revealing, not so much for Martin, but for Ken and his wife.

Then Angel Dawn replied directly to Ken as Martin looked on, "I hear you, honey. I know what you're saying, really. But let's think this through a little bit more before we decide whether to move ahead with it or not."

Ken was stunned at her reaction. She then looked at Martin and asked, "I think I understand what you're saying but can you tell us a little more about PTSD. What are its exact symptoms and how are veterans usually diagnosed?"

Angel Dawn was using her most professional, clinical query voice in soliciting information now. Ken knew she was moving into her area of expertise—counseling. Martin then responded to her direct question, "Mrs. Callahan, I can't provide an in-depth medical explanation; I'm just not qualified to do so. But I can describe it in general terms and provide some literature on this subject if you like. And, I can also help you both understand PTSD a little better just by asking a few simple questions. You don't have to answer them aloud of course, just think about them now. This may prove to be helpful. Okay?"

"Sure, go right ahead!" Ken said immediately but in sort of defiant manner, as if he really wanted to say to Martin, ". . . BRING IT ON, MAN . . . GIVE ME YOUR BEST SHOT, MAN", but he didn't.

He was taking the suggestion more as a personal challenge while Angel Dawn was viewing it as an education. They didn't know it at the time but they would be changed forever just by listening and silently answering these few questions. With that, Martin slowly asked the following questions directly to Ken in more of a rhetorical way requiring no direct response; each was more thought-provoking in nature, designed to stimulate further insight and even more questions that could be discussed later in the privacy of their home.

"Again, you don't have to answer these questions now, just think about them." With that, Martin started his questions,

"Ken . . .

1. Do you have problems sleeping—reoccurring images or nightmares?
2. Do you experience any flashbacks to Vietnam?
3. Have you had problems with alcohol or drugs since the service?
4. How are you with maintaining relationships?
5. Do you have problems holding down jobs?
6. Do you avoid talking about Vietnam?
7. How do you view your personal role in Vietnam?
8. Do you associate with any other Vietnam vets?
9. Do you avoid identifying yourself as a Vietnam Vet?
10. Do you avoid participating in military programs or activities?
11. Are you easily startled?
12. Do you lose your temper over seemingly simple matters?"

Martin stopped there. He sensed Ken and Angel Dawn had heard enough and would likely need some time to think about it all, "What I've learned over the years is that it often comes down to avoidance of feelings or memories and/or guilt and shame associated with events that occurred in combat or other traumatic situations. These kinds of questions are examples of what medical doctors and clinicians commonly rely on when first attempting to help soldiers discover whether they may or may not have acquired PTSD. Answers to such questions represent potential indicators only, not definitive conclusions. Either way, just by thinking about these types of things may be helpful."

Angel Dawn nodded her understanding as Martin continued explaining:, "Technically, PTSD is an anxiety disorder that arises after a soldier has been involved, exposed to, or witnessed a life-threatening event. By doing so, it can often lead to an inability to cope in normal situations. It's complex, very complex."

Angel Dawn then looked over at Ken who now seemed miles away, still thinking about some of his unarticulated answers. He seemed somewhat uncomfortable by each question, even a little agitated. And she knew why but didn't push the dialogue further—it wasn't the right time or place. So she just placed her hand on his without Martin noticing.

Then she gave him a little squeeze and replied for them both, "These are very interesting questions, Martin, and it certainly gives us a lot to think about. Right, honey?" Ken merely nodded to himself without looking at her or Martin. She then said, "We'll have to get back to you on this." Martin understood and responded immediately, "Sure, I understand; it's a lot to absorb at once. I just want you to know this is only an option for you. As a combat vet, you deserve to know all your options; whether you act upon them or not is totally your call. However, if you decide to proceed, I'll be here to help guide you. Either way, I'll still move ahead processing your Agent Orange claim."

Ken and Angel Dawn then thanked Martin Finley for his help and left. They walked together in silence back to MMC, but it was a good silence. Their minds were going faster than a mouse on a treadmill, especially about the PTSD option. When they made it to MCC, they kissed and said good-bye. Ken went on to the next block and boarded a train for home, the same train she would take at the end of day.

They both had a lot to think about. Each of Martin's questions, combined with the way he so confidently presented everything about PTSD, had touched a long held uneasiness Angel Dawn felt about her husband. After twenty-three years of marriage, she knew Ken as well as he knew himself. It had been a very good marriage, ups and downs like everyone, but they truly loved and trusted each other more than ever before. Because of this, she also felt this thing called PTSD deserved to be explored a little further.

Later that week, Ken and Angel Dawn finally found time to discuss it in more depth while they were having lunch on their patio. She sensed he would be a little reluctant, especially considering so many years had passed since Vietnam. Never the less, by witnessing his emotional response and obvious resistance to Martin's questions in Boston, she realized Ken may be struggling with something. Helping Ken accept just the possibility that PTSD may have been playing some part in his life over the years was her only short term goal. She also sensed that Ken's only short term goal would be to avoid it—no matter what.

So, on that autumn afternoon, they both grabbed a sandwich and a cup of coffee and then headed out to their patio. Even though the leaves were just beginning to fall from their surrounding maples, it was a warm and beautiful day in North Attleboro. Their home was situated atop one of the highest points on Old Wood Road, giving them a good view of the forest and the nearby World War I Memorial Park. Angel Dawn always had a green thumb. She inherited it directly from her mom and dad who included her in every possible plant, vegetable, and flower adventure in their backyard as she grew up in nearby Wrentham. Even though she also had a "white thumb" when it came to cooking—everything else about her was green. "Look, we have to add some color to our deck and what better way to do it than with flowers. Besides, the birds love them, too."

On the other hand, vegetation (anything green) and Ken Callahan never got along, especially when it came to doing yard work. He simply hated doing anything in the yard, referring to it as—"domestic terrorism." "Listen, I had my full share of playing in dirt, mud, foliage and green everything while in Vietnam—just not interested in doing it here if I don't have to. Give me the good old asphalt and I'll be happy. Besides, I'd rather just pay someone else to come in and 'play' in the dirt. They'll end up doing a better job than me and get it done faster, too."

Such was Ken's philosophy toward yard work, and he stuck to it even when Angel Dawn occasionally coerced him into it. As a matter of fact, earlier that summer he had cut three different industrial power cords in-half "consecutively" within an hour by getting each cord mixed up with the electric trimmer as he was trimming their hedges.

Needless to say, their hedges were never clipped that summer.

Devil's Paintbrush

Her patio plants and flowers were still rich with color on this specific afternoon. Each was hanging from an extended metal bar placed strategically along the patio's wooden railing that ran along the back of their house. She had geraniums, roses, snap dragons, zinnias, chrysanthemums, and hydrangea; all proudly displayed and always well hydrated. Beyond the end of the patio near the woods, was a special place she reserved for her favorite plant—the devil's paintbrush. This beautiful and rare plant, a wild flower, is seldom recognized by most people; the plant is known as orange hawkweed. During her most recent surprise birthday party, held in Hudson, Massachusetts (a month before her official birth date), she was presented with "two" devil's paintbrushes. Ken had secretly tasked all her friends to comb the fields, mountains, and valleys of New England in hopes of finding just one for her as a part of her surprise.

Fortunately, Mickey London, a longtime friend took the challenge personally and eagerly. He was on it faster than a bird dog on a fallen goose. Yet even this seasoned hunter was coming up short. For weeks, he searched every inch of his vast backyard—the surrounding countryside and waterways of nearby Wachusett Valley, in the Leominster, Massachusetts area. He still came up short. He was about to give up entirely a few days before Angel Dawn's surprise party when he went on a fishing trip with his father in Rangeley, Maine about two hundred miles north of Leominster.

The luck of the wilderness was on Mickey's side that day.

He and his Dad were in a jeep driving along an old logging trail heading to a remote fishing spot in Maine. That's when Mother Nature called to Mickey's bladder. So he stopped the jeep, got out, and took a few steps off the trail to contribute a little human moisture to the surrounding vegetation. He was just about to take aim when he suddenly jumped back and nearly fell down. As any real man knows painfully well, trying to stop a dam from bursting after the first crack appears, takes Herculean effort. But Mickey, being a superman in the wilderness, was up to the challenge. He stopped immediately because smiling up at him in his direct line of fire were "two" beautiful devil's paintbrushes. Both were in full bloom, seemingly just waiting for him to finally arrive and free them from the forest floor. After his initial surprise waned and his bladder returned to normal, he yelled to his Dad who was still in the jeep.

"Hey, Dad, come here and take a look at this." Mickey could barely hold his excitement; he was now jumping around like a puppy just released from the house on the first day of spring. With the wisdom of any well-seasoned parent, Mickey's Dad, Archie, replied to his excited puppy-son without even glancing his way, "No thanks, boy . . . I've changed your diaper too many times as a child . . . just not interested at looking down there ever again. Do your thing and let's get going; we're running late."

Mickey was a little confused at first and didn't' get his father's sophisticated humor. Then he got it and yelled over to him once more, "No, no, not that. Just come over here and look at what's growing here. Remember, I've been looking for a devil's paintbrush for weeks. Well, guess what—there's *two of them* right here. No kidding."

Archie then exited the jeep, verified his son's claim, and then shared his excitement. Both devil's paintbrushes were true beauties. Then he gently dug up each flower, wrapped them in moist packed soil, and carefully placed them in a cardboard container in the back of the jeep. Next stop for the plants was Angel Dawn's surprise party.

Dawn was so surprised and delighted when she saw them at her party. It was her favorite flower, hands down. When in bloom, this small flower's bright yellow center surrounded by orange petals felt so soft and velvety. A devil's paintbrush is hard to locate even though it could grow almost anywhere in North America and Europe. It is also viewed as a noxious and invasive plant in several countries. Yet, technically speaking it is as much a weed as a wild flower, which made it even more resilient and capable of withstanding extreme weather conditions. And it is virtually impossible to remove once it gets a grip on the surrounding soil.

It was because of these characteristics that she felt the devil's paintbrush had a lot in common with her husband, Ken. She had always viewed him as such a plant, believing if he died and came back in another life form, it would be as a devil's paintbrush. Her logic was solid in her mind and went something like this . . .

Just like a devil's paintbrush, Ken was quite unique, extremely resilient, very strong, and attractive (even in his sixties). He most likely would be found alone rather than in groups; deep inside he was a solo guy even though he appeared to others as a gregarious sort. Additionally, she knew Ken always stood tall and proud on his own just like a devil's paintbrush would do in any open field or on the side of any mountain. Yet she also knew him to stand even taller when in the company of colleagues and friends. And like the devil's paintbrush, he could easily fit in wherever he was, even though he also could be quite noxious at times.

And, just as the devil's paintbrush could grow anywhere, anytime, he too was literally unstoppable when it came to achieving his goals. But the most salient characteristics he shared with a devil's paintbrush were his tenacity, resilience, resourcefulness, and adaptability. Ken had faced many challenges in his life, surviving on the edges of many extremes ranging from abandonment to abuse, from the Projects to Vietnam, from domestic chaos to military structure, from constant hunger to regimented diets, from systematic suffocation routines to burial in a bunker, from Darvon to Amyl Nitrate, from beer to marijuana, from small arm fire to incoming rockets, from cancer to vertebral dissection, from severe dog attacks to tarantula brawls, from layoffs to divestitures, and from divorce to sustained relationships.

Ken was still standing, even thriving. She admired his capacity to bounce back over and over and loved his relentless desire to keep moving ahead. Ken truly was a devil's paintbrush in her mind—just as beautiful and equally resilient. When Angel Dawn shared these similarities with him, he didn't know whether to take it as a compliment or an insult. So he decided to have a few laughs with her about it all. So Ken asked, "Let me see if I got this right . . . you're saying I'm a very rare and beautiful flower but also a dangerous weed that can't be killed; is that right?"

"Yep, good summary—you're my beautiful, strong weed man."

With that she leaned over and gave him a quick kiss. That's when he decided to really stretch her thinking a bit. So he told her he liked the comparison but believed he held a closer resemblance to another unique plant—one far more interesting. It was called a triffid. He thought it would make a better comparison from his view because it was more closely aligned to his true character. "Triffid, what the hell is . . . a triffid? Never heard of it?" she asked.

Ken was stunned—and also quite delighted. "Well, my dear, I can't believe I've finally discovered a plant that 'Ms. Green-everything' knows nothing about. Yahoo!"

So he started his "green presentation," savoring every part of his presentation. "A triffid is THE most deadly, most toxic, most dangerous plant on planet earth. That's all." Ken stated it as an assumed fact, one that every college student learned in a freshmen botany class. And he conveyed it proudly and boldly; it wasn't often he got the chance to educate Angel Dawn about plants and flowers, so he was savoring the moment and stretching it out as long as possible. He knew such opportunities rarely came along in the past.

Dawn responded quickly, "Never heard of it . . . describe more to me if you can."

Ken was now feeling his oats, "If I can . . . are you kidding me? Okay, try to keep up with me on this if you can. I'll go slowly. A triffid is a carnivorous plant that dwarfs even the deadly Venus flytrap. That's all. It even looks a little like a devil's paintbrush—big petals at the base, long thin needlelike stem, a colorful round crop on the top; it's just not as pretty. Actually it's a real ugly plant—more like a rag vine that had recently been tackled by a group of drunken chimpanzees. Oh yeah, almost forget to tell you, it also grows to be about five or six feet in height."

Angel Dawn was now going nuts at what was coming out of her husband's mouth about this mystery plant. She could normally tell instantly when Ken was playing with her, but this time he seemed too serious, too arrogant in his knowledge for her liking. She sensed he was feigning his knowledge and that's when she finally went at him. "What in the hell are you talking about? There's no such thing as a triffid . . . a five-foot-tall . . . carnivorous plant. At least I know it's not on this planet."

Then Angel Dawn tilted her head to the side and said, "Dog look?"

"Dog look" was a fun, personal code they used when questioning each other without wanting to come across too seriously. Dogs always seem to tilt their head to one side when hearing a strange new sound for the first time or when they see their master do something really stupid or out of the ordinary. A dog's pea-brain must process and make sense of new things before moving on. A dog head tilt was really a question—"What the shit is happening here?"

Then Ken continued his presentation: "Okay . . . let me help you out with this one. Triffids do exist, they're real. They are extremely venomous, and they are also highly mobile. Yea, I said 'mobile'—they can actually uproot themselves and run down slow-moving animals and even small children and old people. They also can shoot a paralyzing substance up to ten feet away, which disorients and blinds their victim momentarily. This gives triffids enough time to catch, overwhelm, kill, swallow, and digest their victims entirely. Come on, you may never have seen one up-close, but you must have heard of triffids. You must have."

Angel Dawn was becoming unglued by now at what her soon-to-be ex-husband was saying. She was getting close to committing this crazy man to MMC's psych ward, and she could do it very quickly and efficiently if needed. But she tried again to make sense out of what he was telling her, "Okay now, just knock it off. This is crazy. There's no such thing. I would have known about such a plant. More important, the world would have known about such creatures and destroyed them long ago. You're next stop will be the twilight zone if you don't knock it off."

That's when he busted out laughing and said, "Boy, you are so easy sometimes, Dawn; don't you remember the movie entitled *Day of the Triffids*. It was one of the best sci-fi flicks to come out of the 1960s . . . scary as hell . . . all about big carnivorous plants taking over the world, eating blind people who couldn't see them coming. Remember now? That's what I'm talking about here; it looks just like the devil's paintbrush, really. And, I wouldn't be surprised if that's what the movie folks modeled the plant creatures after—they're that similar in look and behavior."

She had to admit, he got her that time. And after more discussion, she finally recalled seeing that old movie. She just never knew it was based on a real plant. Still, she liked him much better as a devil's paintbrush; she would stick with it. Besides, she couldn't picture him going around eating blind people.

Ken was a devil's paintbrush—her devil's paintbrush.

Reluctant Husband, Reluctant Soldier

Meanwhile, back on the patio . . .

Angel Dawn had prepared a series of questions that may be helpful to Ken in getting a better understanding of things at least from her point of view. She felt her husband had been suffering for quite some time and may still be silently suffering today. She didn't know what it was, but sensed it had been present well before their marriage, and even before Vietnam. Even though she tried on many occasions to get him to open-up, he never did. She didn't really care if this was caused by PTSD or not; she just knew he had a problem and she wanted to help.

Martin Finley's overview of PTSD was making lot more sense to her every day. She felt this moment in time was a good opportunity to revisit and explore it further, now that she sensed the VFW and VA were there for them. As a result, Angel Dawn's confidence and her hope were building. The following dialogue took place on the patio that day; it went a long way in jump-starting Ken's ultimate decision to proactively learn more about PTSD. Angel Dawn started by asking Ken, "Listen sweetheart, what about your inability to sleep through a whole night. I've never seen you do so since we were married, not once. Why do you think that is?"

Ken couldn't' deny it, but he had his rationale well entrenched in his mind as he responded: "Sleep apnea. Remember when I was formally diagnosed with it a few years ago because of my breathing difficulty . . . that's all about physiology, not psychology. I think that's the driving force behind waking up all the time and not sleeping through the night."

Ken was comfortable with his response, but she was not.

Dawn continued, "Umm, that may be a factor, but what about having that 'K bartender's' knife, or whatever you call it, under our bed all the time; that's been going on for years, too. I've never known you to sleep without having it nearby . . . you even take some kind of weapon with you on business trips when staying over nights at hotels. Don't you think there may be something behind that, too?"

He answered this as swiftly as the first: "Honey, that's one of the most practical things I can do these days. It's a last line of defense in our protection at night, really. And it's not excessive nor an overreaction, not at all. You know as well as I do, we're a target, a big target for burglars. You even said you were concerned about the increase in the number of home invasions and break-ins lately. It's for that reason and nothing more, really."

Ken was now becoming a little defensive and it would continue to increase as her laser-focused questioning progressed. "And by the way . . ." Ken said, "It is called a 'Ka-Bar' not a K-bartender's knife; named after one the world's oldest knife manufacturers. It's the best knife ever made . . . geez."

Angel Dawn discounted that comment and continued questioning her husband. The education of her husband—the opening of his mind had just begun. "You know . . . more and more often I've been noticing how short-tempered you are with me, too. You've always been defensive when it comes to receiving personal feedback and criticism, and it hasn't been getting any better. You know, when I'm with you at work or in public, you seem to handle such things much better, but not interpersonally with me. I just assumed it would have gotten better as we aged, but I've not seen much change. Even some of our friends have pointed out to me just how sensitive and short-fused you've become even with simple things."

Ken didn't like the direction this discussion was heading and wanted to nip it in the bud: "Look, I just don't see it that way. After all these years, I just assumed you and friends would have come to know me by now; you know, would have come to understand my likes and dislikes and my priorities, just as I do yours and theirs. I make a lot of effort not to offend anyone, really, but I don't see it being reciprocated. It's as if I'm the one who always has to be the sensitive one. I think it's YOUR time to step up now, and make more effort along those lines. Remember, I'm the one who teaches interpersonal communication skills, so I know what it takes, and I apply such competencies well—I practice what I preach, not you."

Ken's direct and countering responses were clearly illustrating her point. He was getting more and more frustrated with her questions, but he just couldn't see it for himself.

So she continued, "Okay, I get it . . . and I promise to work on that for sure, but what about your nightmares? Those encounters with 'Mr. Dark', as you call him, have reoccurred many times throughout our marriage. The sweating, the yelling, and the kicking have only gotten worse over time, not better. There's something troubling you, Ken—there's something going on and it's real. Even if it exists only in your mind, that makes it real and very important for me to want to help you. Can't you see that?" Ken was beginning to hear her more clearly now. He hadn't known how much she felt about these things before, but it was now sinking in. "Well, I guess you're right there. But I'm handling it far better now than ever before. After all, it's been quite some time since I actually jumped out of bed in the middle of night and flew down the stairs head-first like a dog after a rabbit. Sure, I nearly broke my neck, but that was a long time ago, a real long time ago. Nothing that extreme has happened for years, has it?"

"That's correct." She had to admit it had been some time since anything that significant happened. But his steady resistance to discussing it further was confirming her observations of his continual nightmares. Certainly, the frequency had diminished, but not its presence.

She decided to go a little deeper this time, "And I know your drinking has decreased quite a bit since you were diagnosed with diabetes a couple of years ago, but you still drink routinely . . . just not as often."

Ken was really ready for this one; he was just kind of surprised it didn't arise earlier: "Yeah, that's true. But it's more to help me relax, not to hide or bury any deep problems. And, yes it is true I didn't start drinking or using drugs until Vietnam, but that doesn't mean anything—could have had my first drink anywhere—certainly can't blame the war for that. And besides, I don't 'need' a drink like some people do; I 'want' to have a drink occasionally. It is fun and relaxing, and I 'choose' to do so. If it changed me or caused me to do bad things like gamble, spend money needlessly, have affairs, or do other counterproductive behaviors, I'd agree with you. But it hasn't. And I can only think of one or two times in the last two *decades* when I even got drunk. I can't blame that on Vietnam. And you can't either. Look, you drink too, right? Every time we go out to dinner you have your standard gin and tonic, right? And you do something I don't do . . . you make a gin and tonic here at home now and then. I can't remember the last time I even had a beer at home without having guests over. I don't even drink when I'm alone watching the Patriots games. Never. So who's the one with a problem, really . . . you or me?"

Angel Dawn noticed the pitch and volume of Ken's voice rising, and he was starting to turn everything around by verbally attacking her; pointing to her own behaviors as an excuse, as a reasonable factor in his actions. But she discounted that for the moment and continued her questions, "Ken, you've got to admit that you have avoided direct contact with your own family for years . . . and you have always seemed to keep our friends and my family at a distance, too. And I hate to mention this, but you never have shared with me any relationship you made in Vietnam . . . not one. Why, I don't recall you mentioning a single person's name from that time and place. Something must still be bothering you about those days, at least to some degree. Isn't it at least a possibility?"

Ken became silent. He didn't respond to her for a few minutes. And, when he did, his response was direct and lengthy, "Wrong on both counts! My mother, her husbands, my father, my whole brothers and half-brothers, and little sister never wanted anything to do with 'me', not the other way around. That's 'their' problem, not mine. Have you ever seen them reaching out to me since we've been married? No you haven't . . . unless it's about money, of course? Well, have you?"

Angel Dawn did not respond; so Ken continued, ". . . and as far as Vietnam is concerned, I never spent much time in one place to get to know anyone too well. In two years, I was in eight different locations with many different teams. That's lots of people and not a lot of time to . . . 'kumbayah.' And besides, just like my own family members, I don't see anyone from Vietnam calling me, sending me e-mails, trying to locate me today either. Do you? They never had and never will. And you're saying that's my fault? That it's my problem I have to fix? Don't think so. There's no stress in this mind on that subject; no 'psychological discomfort' to use your terms. Look honey, it's just what most men do when they come back from war; it's just what they do; it's just what they do. I'm no different; I'm just as normal as the rest of them—a normal guy."

She didn't respond again. She just watched and waited patiently. Angel Dawn knew his heart had been broken by his family despite his words. Yet she still didn't understand why Ken couldn't cite at least one person he had served with in Vietnam, not one.

Her next question really caught him by surprise—it also was going to be her last, "Ken, please help me understand why you spend most of your off-time by yourself instead of socializing or seeking out others to relax with. You're always doing 'solo' stuff like . . . going on long runs, hours at a time. And, the time you spend on video games with your Xbox are always solo, too. I know you don't play war games nor kill other humans while playing, but you never do so 'with others.' And, going to movies alone every Saturday afternoon after I 'abandon you' (your word, not mine), at the Diamond Hill Reservoir in Rhode Island, is just more alone time as I see it. Ken, that's seven miles, an hour and half for you. Then you sit in the movies, again by yourself. And, each morning when you're not traveling on business, you hop in the car at sunrise and drive out to the reservoir, alone . . . alone.

Dawn was just getting going as she continued with Ken listening, "And, why are you so uncomfortable, so reluctant, when we get together with my family on special occasions like birthdays or holiday gatherings? I know you love my family, all of them, and they love you, especially the boys. They idolize you and really like the time they spend with you. I sense you are always participating reluctantly—it's never anything you initiate yourself or seek out on your own. Never. You got to admit you also get so sensitive about anything they say to you. I'm not really sure if you are avoiding something or just hiding from something beyond relationships. I just don't know, do you? Can you help me understand any of these things?"

Dawn stopped with that. She was now exhausted (so was he).

And Ken was surprised at this set of questions and observations. And more important, he was starting to notice just how hard it was for her to even ask such things. These questions must have been on her mind for a long time, but she never brought them up in all their years of marriage. She obviously observed his patterns, his ongoing unconscious habits, that until this moment had somehow eluded his own awareness. He tried to respond to the family questions and his "alone time" questions but couldn't right away. He never thought she noticed such things, yet he couldn't deny them either. Ken had to admit to himself that each of her questions as well as the clarity of her examples had been true for years, for decades. But, he didn't know just how much of all of this had been seen and valued by Angel Dawn. He did now.

So Ken thought more about everything in silence and then tried to answer the best he could. Only now, his earlier eagerness to rebuff everything had been slowly morphing into thoughtful awareness and self-discovery. He was beginning to see himself, and his wife, a little differently now. Then he responded. "Honey, I didn't know how much alone time I really had, that I really needed but it's true I guess. And, and I didn't know it was so obvious either. You know, I thought such habits were driven by a need for 'down time,' you know, after conducting training sessions with so many people all week. The degree of attending to students' demands as well as managing all the details necessary including the unexpected surprises that arise, can be draining on me. Getting away from it all seems just to be logical and natural to unwind, but now, I'm not so sure unwinding is the only reason."

Ken was examining his own words and thoughts as he spoke aloud to his wife—the one person he truly trusted in life. Her questions were causing him to look much closer at himself with a new set of lenses. He felt he addressed each of Angel Dawn's concerns but still wasn't sure.

She knew it too and replied, "Ken I love you, you know that. But your answers to these questions seem . . . well practiced. Seems to me you have a hundred excuses but real no reasons. I've heard you say those things before and I sense you believe them now and even though some parts may be true, discovering what's driving all of them may be helpful."

She went on, "And interestingly enough, most of these concerns were the same things Martin Finley shared with us when explaining PTSD in Boston. This is more than a coincidence. So let's consider at least learning more about PTSD. Let's just scratch the surface and see if anything is there, anything that may be even slightly relevant or useful to us. We have nothing to lose except a little time perhaps, but who knows, even if we learn just one thing, even one, then it may be worth the effort. We won't know unless we try, will we? What about it?"

Ken knew she was right. Angel Dawn always seemed to be right when it came to such things. Her logical, practical side had always seemed to bring balance to Ken's more expressive, impulsive nature throughout their years of marriage. But he couldn't verbalize it to her at that moment. Instead, he merely leaned over and gave her a long kiss and a hug. He was exhausted now. His shirt was full of perspiration; however, his face was now returning to its natural color. Being directly exposed to the sunshine of truth profoundly impacted him. As usual, she had used the word *we* throughout her questioning. She wanted him to know it was about both of them, and she also wanted him to know he was not doing any of this by himself if he chose to proceed—he wasn't going it alone.

The next day Ken promised her that he would eventually follow-up with Martin Finley. And after a few weeks of deep soul-searching, he did just that. Ken then called Martin saying he would like to learn more about PTSD and he could use his help and guidance in doing so. "Sure Mr. Callahan, glad to help. I'd recommend you set up an appointment in the VA's West Roxbury facility. I'll give you the number. Just call and tell them you're interested in talking to someone about PTSD. Here's their number. Oh yeah, take your DD-214 with you just in case you need it. This is where they will do an initial intake, kind of a quick clinical assessment and help you decide how to proceed. That should get the ball rolling. It's that simple, really. Good luck. Call me if I can help you in any other way. I'm here for you."

Ken appreciated Martin's help and especially his responsiveness. A few days later, Ken actually drove to the West Roxbury VA Administration Center. He did not call; rather he wanted to take this first step on a face-to-face basis, just to get a better feel for the people and the place. In other words, Ken wanted to "smell" the culture and environment of the VA. Specifically, he had heard a few things about how the VA treated Vietnam veterans after returning from the war. And what he heard hadn't been good. Admittedly, most of those stories came from the news as well as from articles and movies depicting veterans being poorly treated in such facilities. And since Ken never talked with other Vietnam vets, he wanted to get a feel for things, firsthand. He was basing his current feelings on such movies as *Coming Home* (with Jon Voight and Jane Fonda, 1978), *The Deer Hunter* (with Robert DeNiro, 1978) and *Born on the Fourth of July* (Tom Cruise, 1989). Movies had always served as a major source of information, entertainment, and escape for him growing up, and that continued into his adulthood. Even though Oliver Stone's *Platoon* (1987, Academy Award winner) was not about the VA at all, Ken found it to be the most relevant to him because of how intense and real the interpersonal conflict among soldiers themselves (versus the enemy) was captured and illustrated for the world to see.

Yet, something else seemed to be haunting Ken from the moment he saw and entered the West Roxbury VA, but he couldn't quite put his finger on it. Then it came to him. He had, indeed, been inside this exact facility a long time ago, in the late 1970s to be exact. It was the same place where he had his Vasectomy performed while still on active duty at Fort Devens—his memories were not good. He just hoped the VA had changed over the years because he was about to be thrust back into that environment for the second time in his life.

His hope was about to be realized.

Rather than a nightmarish ordeal, Ken found the people, the environment and processes of the VA, to be exemplary. His short meeting in West Roxbury VA was pleasant, personal and competently managed. Their professional staff met with him, openly discussed things with him (versus talking-down to him), and treated him respectfully and cordially. He left with a very clear set of instructions as well as another appointment. He couldn't have asked for a better first (second) impression of the VA and as a result, many of his reservations were beginning to fade quickly. Ken's next stop was the VA Campus in Plainville, Massachusetts, less than ten miles from his home in North Attleboro.

And, he was looking forward to it.

CHAPTER 7

PTSD—
"But, I'm Normal, Right?"
(Massachusetts, 2010)

ANGEL DAWN WAS GLAD HER husband was proactively moving ahead to learn more about PTSD. Whether it turned out to be PTSD or not, just watching him focusing on how to help himself was a good thing. She felt many things Martin Finley touched on had merit and her first-hand knowledge about just how troubled Ken's sleep had been over the years seemed to clearly connect to PTSD. Specifically, his reoccurring nightmare of being visited by "Mr. Dark" (the name he gave to an unknown, faceless shadow of a creature) came to mind. His habit of sleeping with a knife or short handle hatchet under their bed was always in her thoughts as well as his fear of being suffocated during sleep and even during waking hours told her something deeper was going on with her husband—more than he would ever admit. She also knew Ken had an unusual comfort, a need really, to keep family relationships, social relationships, and military relationships at a far distance. This was a stark contrast to her own style and desire to keep her family ties tightly wrapped, close by at all times.

On the surface, she knew Ken was viewed as a personable, social, and outgoing guy by others. But she also knew he could comfortably adapt to anything or anyone on a "short-term" basis, but not for long. With the exception of the professional organizations and institutions he belonged to, everything else was really transient. He didn't allow people to come too close for too long.

Ken always took his professional life seriously and did a good job in each company and organization he was a part of. His civilian training career progressed rapidly and consistently over the decades. But she always sensed there was something troubling Ken on a personal level. She knew of the turmoil and instability of his youth, and since Ken seldom discussed Vietnam with her or with anyone, she didn't know the extent of exposure he had to violence, trauma, and hardships while there. She had no doubt that Ken was a "company man"—ever faithful to his organization and always giving 100 percent of time—days, nights, weekends, and holidays. Even vacations were never "real" vacations because he'd always found some way to comfortably bring work into the picture. Angel Dawn accepted it but always attempted to help him achieve more balance in his life. At times she succeeded but most of the time it was a futile effort. She also thought he used "work" to hide or avoid other things. And, the only reason he once opened up about his childhood was because of his concern about how she would react to meeting his mother and family, as well as seeing where and how he was actually raised. That's when her mind flashed back to the first time she met Hilda Callahan face to face. It occurred several weeks before she and Ken were married.

"Hilda Time"

"She can't be that bad; after all she brought you in this world. Is it really that you don't want me to know the 'real' Hilda or could it be you don't want me to know the real 'you?' If it's the latter, honey, I understand." That was a good question—one that Ken had pondered for decades. Angel Dawn inquired about it many times with him in the past, but mostly before they were married. Specifically, she recalled discussing Hilda in detail during a drive from New Hampshire (where they both were living at the time) to Baltimore for her to meet Hilda for the first time. It occurred just before they eloped in the winter of 1986. He felt Angel Dawn's upbringing was so very different from his and exposing that difference to her could represent a big wild card in her decision. He knew they both also shared many common interests as well as many differences and it all rushed through Ken's mind on this drive.

He had moved twenty-one times before he graduated from high school; she never moved once in the same period. He had five "fathers" (five mother's husbands to be exact), she had one. She ate regular meals with her family; Ken couldn't remember a single time when his family sat a table to dine together. She had strong family ties, he had none. She went to elementary school, middle school, and high school with the same kids; Ken never shared a school with anyone consistently. She was never physically abused, but with him it was commonplace. She had been a hippie, and he had been a soldier.

But they also had many commonalities. They both liked sports cars, the movies, long car rides throughout the country on back roads, the Moody Blues, and the Alan Parsons Project, and they both had strong ties to their occupations; they both had a well-developed work ethic. And before getting married in their late thirties, they also realized having kids of their own was not likely.

As their drive continued, they openly discussed his family more than ever before. "Yes, my mother did give birth to me. That's true. But understand, you and I are about to spend twenty-four hours with her very soon. I know that seems like a short time at first glance, but believe me, it's a month in 'Hilda time.' You'll know what I mean and will better understand what I've been saying all along once you meet her; you can judge for yourself."

Ken was just trying to set proper expectations with Angel Dawn. Considering her background, he didn't feel she was prepared for what she was about to experience meeting Hilda. But he also knew she deserved to experience it firsthand before taking the plunge with him for life. There was also a side of him that was hoping everything he knew about his childhood had been just his imagination. Maybe Angel Dawn could help clarify some things just through her questions, observations and insight. He only told her about the physical abuse that went on within his family, about never living in the same place for long, and about always being hungry. There were also many other things he never told Angel Dawn about—many things. So Ken was interested to see how this meeting would go and what would come of it all. And, he knew there was at least one thing Angel Dawn was most interested in discovering for herself, "Ken, I do want to find out directly from your mother that story you told me about when you were a kid coming back from summer camp. No mother in her right mind could have done such a thing—I've got to find what really happened then."

Ken understood her concern and remembered how incredulous Angel Dawn found the story to be when he shared it with her. Ken forgot that he ever told her about the summer camp incident. But knowing the stable and loving home she had grown up in, he could understand how such a thing may be upsetting to her. "Okay . . . I get it. Just know there's one thing about my mother that's very predictable—she will tell you what's on her mind, straight up, so be prepared—good or bad. You know, I hope you remember to ask her about summer camp because I'd really like to know the truth myself. After all these years maybe I just made it up, got it all mixed up somehow, or perhaps I was just plain wrong."

Ken and Angel Dawn arrived in Baltimore and visited with his mother, Hilda Smith, and her last husband, Joseph. The entire visit was all about "Hilda"—she made it so. She never asked about them, their relationship, how they met, about their future plans together or anything. She also never asked about Angel Dawn's family or her background. Equally revealing to Angel Dawn, Hilda never shared any stories about Ken as a boy growing up, what kind of kid he was, any interesting or funny stories, no cute little habits, and absolutely nothing about her other children. Rather, Hilda talked incessantly about herself—nothing more, nothing less. It was all about Hilda all the time. There was another topic she seemed quite interested in addressing a lot of the time—just how stupid, weak, slow, and moronic her husband, Joseph, was. And her comments about him were always made in a very demeaning way while also in his presence. She disparaged the apartment house she lived in, their neighbors (because many of them were black, Hispanic, or Asian). She criticized the city of Baltimore, the state of Maryland, and the federal government's social security system. Nothing escaped her bitter judgment. Her incessant self-talk and disparagement of others quickly took a toll on Angel Dawn.

Ken was right about . . . "Hilda time."

Angel Dawn later admitted it was one of the longest trips of her life even though it only lasted last than twenty-four hours. On the second day, all four of them were walking down the stairs from Hilda's second-floor apartment together. They were on their way to lunch before Ken and Angel Dawn returned to New Hampshire. Joseph and Ken were slowly walking down the staircase with Angel Dawn and Hilda following. Angel Dawn was bringing up the rear and Hilda was directly in front of her. Hilda's nasty comments about everyone and everything continued even while walking down the stairs.

On the drive back home to New Hampshire, Angel Dawn confessed to Ken that there was one moment (just a second in time) when she felt like giving Hilda a little shove, a quick little push on her back as they were making their way down that staircase. She never did of course, but the fury and anger that had built up in her generated such thoughts to enter her head. They left as fast as they came. And as Angel Dawn was admitting to Ken how she had felt at that moment, tears started to billow in her eyes, and she actually started to tremble while just recalling it. She had never known such feelings before—had never experienced such rage about anyone, for any reason. And this all happened only after being exposed to Hilda for less than twenty-four hours. She then tried to imagine what it must have been like for Ken, her fiancé, to have spent years growing up with her.

Then she cried.

Once they had descended the stairs, Ken and Angel Dawn took Hilda and Joseph out to lunch. That's when Angel Dawn finally got the courage to ask Hilda about Ken and the summer camp incident. She just had to know before they left. So she interrupted Hilda in the midst of a long story at their lunch table. Hilda was talking about her love of dog racing. That's when Angel Dawn politely interrupted her, "Excuse me, Hilda, that's real a very interesting story about you at the dog tracks and all; sounds like a lot of fun. But I wanted to ask you one question before we headed out. Can you help me understand a story that happened years ago that I've heard about."

Hilda responded right away, "Sure darlin', what is it?"

At the point, Ken knew what was coming, so he did the only thing any real cowardly man would do—he excused himself by pretending he had to go to the restroom. He left them together at the table with Joseph.

Then Angel Dawn continued, "Ken told me it happened when he was eleven or so during the summer when he went to Summer Breakaway Camp. You remember that time?" Hilda thought for a while then replied, "Yeah . . . I do 'member. He got ta' go d'ere for two whole weeks . . . right in da' middle of school vacation. To tell ya' da' truth [she looked around quickly and started whispering to Angel Dawn] . . . I got's ta' admit, it was gud' ta' get rid of em' for a while . . . know what I mean?" With that, she looked directly at Angel Dawn and gave her an all-knowing motherly smile—from one girl to another, that is. Angel Dawn was glad that part of Ken's story was at least confirmed. So it did happen. She then continued by asking Hilda about the more important part of the story; the part about not coming for him after camp finished. "Hilda, tell me . . . when summer camp came to an end, he said no one came to pick him up in the city . . . and then he couldn't find you after he got back to the Projects because you had moved out . . . went to live somewhere else . . . without letting him know where you had gone. Did that happen, Hilda?"

Angel Dawn waited for her reply. So did Joseph because he had never known about it either. After a few seconds of thought, her response was simple and direct, said even with a bit of motherly pride: "Yeah . . . I do t'ink it happen da't way, as I 'member. Ya' see darlin' . . . I was pretty hard ta' keep up wit' in d'ose day, I guess. T'ings moved real quick for me back d'en. But it didn't matter really, I knew he'd catch up wit' me sometime . . . he always did. Little Ken was always able to find his way to his mudder'. No matter where I'd go, he'd somehow find me sooner or later."

After that conversation, Angel Dawn never questioned anything Ken said about his mother.

In recalling Ken's previous relationship with his mother, who had been dead now for over a decade, Angel Dawn became more compelled to find out as much as she could about PTSD—not just about the possible connection between Ken and Vietnam, but also with his childhood in the Projects of Brooklyn. She believed it was quite possible that Ken's emotions and self-image somehow had been severely impacted by exposure to "Hilda time" in his youth. Angel Dawn had been directly exposed to her for only a day or so during that trip to Baltimore—and had been changed forever by it. She then tried to imagine what prolonged exposure (eighteen years) to Hilda could have had on a young boy—but she couldn't.

It was after meeting with Martin Finley, the VFW's Legislative Representative in Boston, that Angel Dawn started wondering . . . *could an eighteen year old soldier go to Vietnam (or any war) having already been suffering from PTSD without even knowing it or without the army detecting it during the recruiting and enlistment screening process.* She didn't know, but if it was possible, she was beginning to sense Ken could possibly have been such a boy.

Whether Ken's emotional troubles, avoidance behaviors, and haunting memories were Vietnam-driven or Brooklyn-based, she just didn't know. She only knew he had been struggling with some heavy-duty things for a long, long time. Finding the source of it was important, for without such discovery, treatment would be ineffective, or worst, counter-productive. As a trained clinical psychotherapist, she knew the risk of exploring such things was low but the potential benefits of doing so could be high. Because of this, she was glad Ken was now beginning to proactively stretch himself in learning as much as he could.

Angel Dawn was going to support him all the way.

The Renowned VA PTSD Clinic of Plainville, Massachusetts

In 2010, Ken met with people at the VA's West Roxbury facility. They were competent, open and very responsive people who had helped him make direct contact with the PTSD Clinic located on the VA Campus in Plainville, Massachusetts. It took Ken only ten minutes on back country roads to drive through North Attleboro to the farthest part of Plainville. He merely followed Route 152, headed west on Route 106, and then headed north on 2A for about six miles and he was there. Even before he got close to the main entrance, he saw the facility's large purple and blue digitized sign broadcasting repetitive messages to the surrounding public. Each message lasted about ten seconds before moving to the next, and then repeated over and over—a series of free public service announcements, including:

1. Welcome to Plainville VA
2. Facebook address
3. The Day's temperature
4. The Day's date
5. The Day's time.

As Ken pulled in, a huge Garrison American flag was flying high above the digitized sign. The main building was a five-story structure that looked like a replica of the *Daily Planet* building where Clark Kent worked during the 1950s TV series, *Superman*. On top of this huge building was a vast array of various telecommunication satellites and electronic equipment. Twenty other single-story, red brick buildings were also neatly spread across and throughout the 1.3 mile circular drive shaped like an Olympic track that encompassed the entire VA installation. Each building stood alone or was connected by long enclosed walkways. They were also separated by several wide-open fields of well-kept grass with clumps of large maple trees strategically placed throughout. Every blade of grass was well-manicured just like the Boston Red Sox outfield at Fenway Park. It was as if the campus maintenance team trimmed and polished every single blade of grass by hand. There wasn't a piece of paper or trash anywhere. The walking pathways between the buildings and all around the campus were also immaculate. And even though it was late November, there was no snow anywhere. Year 2010 had been a mild winter so far.

That's when Ken's feelings of narcissism ("self-focus") and skepticism ("just can't be the right place") kicked in big time. He thought to himself, *"This has got to be a setup . . . just too pretty to be true . . . can't be the government . . . this can't be the VA . . . they must have phoned ahead and told everyone I was coming . . . better get the placed cleaned up quick . . .*

Ken's coming . . . got to make a good first impression on this guy or we'll lose him . . . he won't come back." Such thoughts entered and departed his mind quickly.

Ken arrived early and drove around the large circular road that surrounded the entire campus to get a feel for the place. It was a peaceful, slow drive. Actually, the environment felt more like a college campus than a government installation. Perhaps, that's why it was called a "campus"—the VA Plainville Campus. That's when he finally made the connection between college campus and government installation. As he slowly came around one curve, his eyes immediately were drawn to a shape in the center of a large field between two buildings. From a distance, the shape first appeared to be a big dog or fox. He just couldn't tell. The animal was standing perfectly still. It seemed poised in a ready-to-pounce position, staring intensely just at one spot on the ground. Its front paws were close together, and its hind legs were bent, ready to spring into action. And its head was cocked to one side, as if it was listening carefully to the ground.

Ken had to check this out.

So he stopped on the road to take a closer look. That's when he noticed other people were casually walking along the sidewalk, but no one was stopping to share his discovery of this big animal. He knew they could see it, but they were not concerned or interested in Ken's big discovery. *"Am I the only person with eyesight good enough to see this animal at this distance?"* Ken thought to himself. It was Ken's arrogance that was creeping into his assessment of the situation.

He now had three emotions (three insecurities, that is) going on at once—narcissism, skepticism and arrogance. And he knew it. Yet, Ken had to get a closer look at this phantom canine. So he reached under the front passenger's seat of his VW and pulled out his binoculars. He kept a set near him ever since Angel Dawn converted him a decade earlier from a "reluctant bird watcher" to a "passionate bird lover." When he focused the binoculars, he discovered what he was actually seeing wasn't a dog or a fox. It was merely a replica with the best features of both; a very good, life like replica at that. Later Ken discovered there were several similar dog/fox replicas placed strategically throughout the entire campus. It was an effort to keep geese and other foul from choosing to land, to rest, to eat, to poop on the grounds. The realism of the dog/fox replicas was very effective. If the realism fooled Ken, then a flock of geese flying at forty miles per hour at two hundred feet could also be easily tricked into thinking it was a hostile landing zone—a place where they could easily become fast-food.

Ken looked around and didn't notice a foul in sight on any of the campus' fields—hence, it worked and worked very well. Each of the many brown brick buildings across the campus was very well marked, clearly identified by names and numbers. Some the building names included: Spinal Cord Rehab, Arm and Leg Rehab, Chapel, Administration, Athletic Center and Gardening Center. There was even a Totem Pole Pond Recreation Area for veterans to kick-back and do a little fishing and relaxing during the day. And, all Ken had to do was stay on the single circular road, and it would take him wherever he wanted to go. He was searching for building 12—the renowned PTSD Clinic of the Plainville Veterans Healthcare System.

He found it easily.

When he pulled into the parking area closest to building 12, he started noticing for the first time the wide variety of military slogans and bumper stickers attached to cars. He hadn't seen so many military decals in his life in one single place. Stickers on parked cars and trucks included the following: Vietnam Veteran, POW/MIA, Wounded Warrior, America Love It or Leave it, Airborne, CIB, First Cavalry; Never Forget. He also saw a few official Massachusetts state license plates with a Purple Heart decal or the word, "Veteran", officially engraved right on the license plate number itself. Such license plates were familiar to him because he had one on his car, too. Ken had never been in a location where so many other soldiers were together at the same time, not since he served in the military. And it felt kind of good. It was there he realized just how "out of touch," how "detached," and how "alone" he really had been. All these cars belonged to brothers in arms. They were all probably here for help or for rendering help to other vets. In either case, they all were here searching for something. And, they were here because they had served their country, and because they loved their country (not necessarily their government).

Ken pulled into a vacant parking spot, grabbed his paperwork, and started to walk to the main entrance of building 12. He turned around to remotely lock his car. As he did, he noticed the license plate on the car right next to his own had a Bronze Star officially embedded in it. He had to do a double-take because it looked exactly like Ken's—an exact replica of his own Massachusetts plate only the numbers that followed the Bronze Star insignia were different. He had never seen two Bronze Stars parked next to each other. Little did he know at the time, but the owner of that car would turn out to be someone who he would, not only come to know well and meet with on a weekly basis for years to come, but also someone who would become a trusted friend. He then locked this car remotely and headed to building 12.

On his brief walk to the building, the image of double Bronze Star license plates sitting close together triggered a flashback to a special Christmas morning.

The year was 2001.

"Son"

Angel Dawn and Ken were on their living room floor opening Christmas gifts, having a cup of coffee, and listening to holiday music. Their two cockatiels, Stanley and Spike, were also watching everything from atop their respective cages in the kitchen area. Both birds were excited because of the brightly colored paper and all the new noises bombarding their little ears as Ken and Angel Dawn opened their presents. Both birds were now perched, staring down on them, like a pair of hungry hawks waiting to pounce on an unsuspecting rabbit. But they didn't.

"Okay . . . it's your turn. Open this one," Angel Dawn said excitedly to Ken, who was still half asleep. He took another sip of coffee and tried to open it. Usually he could tell just by the feel of a present and knowing who it came from exactly what kind of gift it was going to be. But, not this time. This present looked and felt different, very different. It was a small rectangular shape about six by twelve inches, like a large mailing envelope. He shook it, turned it upside down, and then felt all around it, but still had no clue. He even smelled it and still came up short. It didn't have a Christmas card on it either so he couldn't tell from whom or where it came. Angel Dawn was watching intently nearby, for this was a special gift. And she knew he would never guess its contents, not in a million years. This gift was from her late father, Bradley A. Brady ("Bud," for short). Actually, it was a late Christmas gift from a man who loved Ken like a son. Bud had passed away in April 2001 at the age of eighty-two, a few months earlier. He and Ken had become quite close in the first fifteen years of Ken's and Angel Dawn's marriage.

Bud also had been a soldier in the Army Air Corp during World War II, and that bonded them even closer. He was a bona fide member of Tom Brokaw's *Greatest Generation* for sure, having served honorably in WWII in several different theaters of conflict—India, Burma, Italy, and North Africa. When Bud came back from the war, he and his wife, Lillian, (of 'hummingbird' fame), started their family near the center of Wrentham, Massachusetts. There, they raised their two kids and became a solid member of that conservative New England community. Bud was also a master mason—a member of the oldest fraternal organization in the history of mankind—masonry. Each mason was special because of the generous services they provided to members of their communities in need. But Bud was a special master mason—a "Most Wondrous" master mason, which meant he was also the leader of many other masons. Bradley A. Brady was also the recipient the highest honor Masonry could bestow—The Joseph Warren Award. It was presented to him shortly before he passed away in 2001. Only a master mason who had served fifty consecutive years or more, constantly contributing in extraordinary ways to his local community, could qualify for such an honor.

He was such a special man.

When Bud was asked during his Joseph Warren Award ceremony, what had been his greatest memory he had as a mason, he paused for only a brief moment and then said to the packed auditorium of community leaders, other master masons and their family members (including Lillian, Angel Dawn and Ken), "It was when I had the privilege and honor of bringing my son-in-law, Ken, into the fraternity of master masons . . . when he chose to follow in my footsteps." Ken, of course, was stunned when heard those words. Bud, a man of very few words, seldom conveyed his true personal feelings in public, nor in private. But, he did that night. And, Ken was humbled.

Ken had become a master mason in 1991, five years after marrying Angel Dawn, and ten years before Bud's death. Masonry seemed so mysterious, caring and inviting to Ken that after a while he asked questions of Bud about it, "Bud, can you tell me a little more about masonry, seems like a good organization from what I have seen from a far. I just don't know much about it except what I've gleamed from watching you. Actually, I did learn two things—masons know how to help anyone in need and they like clam bakes." A big smile came over Bud's face when Ken finally asked that simple question. "Son, I've been waiting five years for you to ask me that." He went on to explain that masons cannot directly recruit anyone to join the fraternity. Individuals must come forth and directly ask about it—as Ken had just done. Then they can be invited to join masonry. It all made sense to Ken then. He had seen Masonic literature around, and often he noticed a single phrase that stuck in his mind but never understood it—*to be one, ask one*. He never knew what it meant until that moment. While the rules governing the recruitment of new masons had lightened up in recent decades, this phrase, *to be one ask one,* was still the dominate mind-set shared by most of the older, more veteran masons—to wait until being asked. Marketing and selling of masonry is a no-no, and it will always be that way. Yet Ken was even more surprised, very surprised in fact, by one single word Bud used when he was describing masonry to him. The word Bud used in referring to Ken, one that no man had never used to address him was . . . *son*.

Ken didn't even realize it at the moment because it flew by him so fast. It was also because that word was so foreign to his ears when referred to him. Throughout his life, he had been addressed by many informal and formal titles such as brother, nephew, cousin, colleague, neighbor, soldier, private, sergeant, lieutenant, manager, director, and friend, but never "son." He thought the odds were far greater that someone someday would call him—"Your Highness," "President," or "General" before hearing himself referred to as "son" . . . not until that moment. It took forty-two years for him to hear it, and it felt good, real good.

He came to love Bud even more.

Bradley A. "Bud" Brady died of a cancer on April 4, 2001 while sitting in his living room lounge chair watching TV. Lillian had been sitting close by at the exact moment he died. Ken and Angel Dawn arrived less than 15 minutes after his death. By the time Ken and Angel Dawn arrived, the ambulance was there. There was also a police car parked on their front yard with emergency lights flashing. Angel Dawn immediately ran to her mom's arms and comforted her. She couldn't bear to look down at her father who was lying on the floor. Bud had just been officially pronounced dead by the emergency medical team on the scene. But that didn't keep Ken from falling to his knees and holding Bud's head in his lap. Bud's eyes were still open. And, with one slow and gentle wave of his hand, Ken closed Bud's eyes forever.

Fortunately for Ken, being called "son" had come from a great man who he admired, respected, and truly loved. Bud Brady was the only real father he would ever have and the only father he would ever need. After fifty-two years, Ken then knew in his heart it was well worth the wait to become a "son" especially to such a fine, good man as Bud Brady.

Meanwhile back at the Christmas tree . . .

Ken kept touching and shaking the unidentifiable, alien present. He still had no clue what it was. "Okay, I give up, what is it?" That's when Angel Dawn said *"Open it."* He did so eagerly, ripping through the beautifully wrapped paper like a five-year old trying to free his first train set from its wrappings on Christmas morning. When Ken finally opened it, he just stared. He was speechless.

A new set of Massachusetts license plates was staring up at him. There was one thing significantly different from his other license plates—The Bronze Star symbol was beautifully embossed in front of the series of numbers. A thousand questions and another thousand feelings rushed through him all at once. Immediately, Ken thought Angel Dawn had done it, but she had not. "It's from Dad," she said softly, almost in a whisper. And then she continued, "Dad wanted to give this to you himself but he wasn't able to do so. He and I had been in the midst of finalizing all the lengthy paperwork needed by the government when he passed away last year. Ken, he was so proud of you, of your service, and also about how you always treated him and mom . . . he could not have been prouder. And he wanted the world to know what kind of man you turned out to be. That's why he did it."

Ken was nearly in tears listening to her story. Not because of the plates, which he actually had mixed feelings about, but rather because of Bud. He kept staring at the license plates as she came and sat next to him on the floor. She gave him a long hug from her and then another longer hug from her father. She then continued, "He knew you never would do such a thing for yourself, not you. So he went ahead and made it happen. These plates are meant to be forever. It was his personal, eternal gift to you; his second son."

Ken was genuinely touched at such a kind, thoughtful gesture coming from such a kind and thoughtful man. He just continued holding and staring at both license plates for quite some time. It was a very special moment in his life. Even though he was honored by what Bud had done, he had mixed feelings about the plates—about actually placing them on his car, that is. It would have been great just to frame them and hang them on his office wall, really. It was then 2001, and Ken still did not possess a good view himself or his Vietnam service, even thirty years since he served there. Being a Vietnam vet was not a good thing in many other people's minds either and he had always avoided drawing attention to this aspect of his life unless it was required. So to place a Bronze Star on the front and back of his car for the world to see would have to take some serious thinking time. Actually, it took several weeks before he placed the plates on his car. Ken was honoring memory and wishes of Bud, as well as what he had meant to him.

Nothing more.

The first time he drove his car with the Bronze Star plates attached, he felt like everyone was staring at him; he thought everyone now "knew" who he really was even though he didn't really know what that meant about himself. Ken really hoped others didn't think he was showing off or bragging which was another reason he hesitated in doing so. But because it came from Bud, he wanted to respect his memory and his love.

Later in his life he would be glad he did just that.

Meanwhile, back at the Plainville VA campus . . .

Just before entering building 12, years after placing the plates on his car, he recalled all those wonderful feelings all over again. His self-consciousness about the plates really hadn't changed much; he still felt somewhat embarrassed by having them on his car, but he felt more proud the plates had come from Bud. Perhaps by stepping through the doors of building 12, he would be able to obtain a better understanding, not about the plates, but about himself, and why he had so many mixed feelings about even being here. He was hesitant, yet kind of excited at the same time. So he walked up the cemented walkway to the front stairs of building 12 and stepped through its double glass doors.

It was November, 2010.

Kyle Armstrong

Building 12's lobby was surrounded by windows allowing the sun's light to enter at different angles throughout the day. It was divided into two sections—a sitting and waiting area with many chairs and a couple of sofas spread around, giving everyone lots of personal space. On each wall were VA posters describing various programs and there were lots of official looking pamphlets and brochures neatly placed at different locations in the lobby as well.

There was no elevator music playing—Ken was relieved.

A few men were seated together talking. They were wearing jeans, baseball hats, and sneakers. The only ties Ken saw were worn by staff members.

But he did not see any full suits. The place had a comfortable, casual feel to it. In back of the lobby was a chest-high reception desk and check-in area. Three young women sat behind it each with computers, telephones, and very big smiles. That's where all visitors and patients had to check in. They were cordial and pleasant women who were chatting with patients, setting up or confirming appointments, answering questions. A single line with a few men in it had formed in front of one young woman; the other women were on the phone and shuffling through some papers. The buzz of conversation was open and continual making for a very comfortable and pleasant environment. To Ken, it felt like a company-level orderly room within an army barracks where all a unit's administrative chores took place. There was also a big sign on the wall across from the desk: *"Please remember to check in here. We can help."*

So Ken walked over and stood at the end of a short line. He did this seemingly by nature, as if his military discipline automatically awoke after decades of hibernation. Then one of the young women gestured to him to come directly to her. He did so. "Hi . . . you must be new here, never seen you before. May I help you?" she said in a friendly way.

"Yes, this is my first time here. My name is Ken Callahan. I've got an appointment at one o'clock with a . . . Mr. Kyle Armstrong, I believe," he said this more in a questioning manner rather than as fact. "Kyle . . . sure . . . glad to help."

With that, she started clicking on her computer. She asked some basic contact information about Ken, and then directed him to Kyle's office. Building 12 was a T-shaped structure with offices and conference rooms aligned on both sides beyond the reception area. He made a left and proceeded down the hallway, passing several private offices and conference rooms. He then took a seat in a small waiting area at the end of the hall. At precisely 1:00 p.m., a man came around the corner and approached Ken. He was about forty years old, wearing gray slacks and white shirt, sleeves turned up between his elbow and wrist. He wore no tie (Ken was glad about that) but did have a badge dangling from a cord around his neck. Overall, the man appeared casual, yet he had an official look about him which Ken also liked. He was a handsome man with dark hair and a warm smile. He was wearing a pair of thin silver-rimmed glasses that covered only a portion of his eyes. He was not wearing a wedding band, so Ken wasn't sure if he was married or not. "Hello, you must be Ken Callahan. I'm Kyle, welcome. And thanks for being on time, really appreciate it." Ken was somewhat surprised because he had just assumed Kyle was going to be like other stereotypic government officials he met in the past—bureaucratic and pompous individuals with a holier-than-thou attitude especially those within public service organizations such as the department of motor vehicles, state unemployment offices, and town halls. Specifically, Ken was expecting the following attitude from the personnel at Plainville, VA PTSD Clinic:

"Look . . . we're doing you a favor just by seeing you. Our time is more precious than yours, we trust you agree with that; and we're more important than you. We also have something you need and we're not going to give it up easily. We trust you know that, too. You have got to adapt to us, to our schedule, to our rules or we won't help you. We have the power . . . you don't . . . so just bite me and get over it. It's our way or the highway; we don't care which way you choose. Now how can I help you so that you will go away."

Such people drove Ken crazy; they seemed to forget they worked for the citizens of their communities, towns, and nation, and therefore they are "employees." These people always reminded him of the 1960s *Laugh In* routine where Lilly Tomlin, playing an arrogant telephone operator, always treated customers with distain because she worked for the big and powerful telephone company (and the callers didn't).

Ken was delighted to discover that Kyle and the others he met in the VA thus far didn't possess such an attitude—just the opposite. Everyone was kind, courteous, accommodating, and competent. As a result, he started to become more comfortable and much more relaxed. Kyle did the three minimum things Ken expected during an initial contact—introduced himself, made direct eye contact and rendered a firm yet personal handshake. Ken also noticed Kyle conveyed a quick statement of gratitude, a simple "*thank you for your promptness*" even though it was not needed. "Yes, I am Ken Callahan; you're very welcome," Ken said.

"Would you please follow me."

Ken then accompanied Kyle to his office around the corner. The first thing he noticed upon entering his office was a long bank of windows overlooking one section of the VA's grassy field. The second thing he noticed out the window was a not-so-real dog/fox poised in the middle of that field. It was the same replica he saw earlier and it hadn't moved since he last viewed it with his binoculars. He was so glad about that—it made him feel "normal."

"Please take a seat, Ken and make yourself comfortable."

With that, Kyle closed the door and went to his desk. It was a small office, but the light coming in from the window made it feel much larger. Ken was relieved. He didn't like tight or closed spaces, even in 2010, at the age of sixty-one. He was even more relieved when he noticed there was no couch (the infamous "psychiatrist couch," that is). Ken could never picture himself carrying on a conversation with someone while in the prone position. To him, there were only two natural times in life when words should be spoken between two people who were prone—in a bed while exchanging personal intimacies and talking with a doctor or nurse before going into an operating room. Any other time just seemed a little weird.

He also feared he would fall asleep, snore or fart while on the psychiatrist's couch—or all three. Having never been on a psychiatrist's couch, he really didn't know how he would react, but he didn't want to find out. After taking one of the soft chairs across from Kyle's desk, he looked around the room surveying the environment, a routine he naturally did out of habit since he was kid entering a new place. It was a nice office with bookshelves filled with texts, journals, and several personal photos. One picture was a black-and-white shot of a man in fatigues standing in the bush. Ken sensed it was in Vietnam simply by the uniform, terrain, and by being a black-and-white photo. There were two lamps in his office, but only one was lit. It was throwing off a soft light that balanced the sharp daylight rushing through the window. On Kyle's desk were a large computer screen and several other pieces of technology Ken didn't recognize. His desk was facing the side wall, and Kyle's swivel chair was facing Ken. Kyle started out with casual conversation about Ken's trip to Plainville, the weather, etc. Ken had some questions for him about the campus, its history, as well as the rules surrounding PTSD discussions. He learned quickly that confidentiality was critical. Management of time (starting and finishing sessions promptly) and keeping appointments were also very important.

Those were the three big rules that stuck in Ken's mind. Then Kyle asked, "Ken, I did receive some information about you already, but not a lot. Before I explain the PTSD program and answer any questions you may have about me or the process . . . could you tell me a little more about yourself?"

"Sure. What would you like to know?" Ken replied.

"Anything about your military background, Vietnam service, where you grew up, type of work you do, any basics would be helpful. And take as much time as you like; our first meeting is just to get to know each other a little. And I'll also answer any questions you may have." With that, Ken explained a lot about himself. Kyle was a good listener and a good questioner. He never interrupted Ken except when he needed to clarify something, and when he did interrupt it was done politely. He also paraphrased now and then to ensure his own understanding as well as conveyed genuine empathy especially when Ken had shared some sensitive parts about his personal life. Kyle did all this naturally and sincerely, which made Ken feel even more comfortable with him.

In that first session, Kyle discovered that Ken's upbringing had been in the Projects of Brooklyn, Maryland had been somewhat tough and harsh. His childhood had been filled with constant abuse, insecurity, poverty, and violence. By the time he entered the army in 1967, he already had moved over twenty times and had no real personal stability until entering the army. Until then, most of his trust in people and institutions had been low. He had been married three times with no children. He also learned Ken's Vietnam experiences had been broad, varied, and very challenging, including two tours of duty—one year in a combat unit (First Infantry Division) and one year in the 525 Military Intelligence Command. He was a communication specialist. In such roles, he did many different jobs from ditch digging to shit burning to flying aerial combat missions as well as living with the Vietnamese on civilian status without a uniform or a gun. He left Vietnam as a buck sergeant with a Bronze Star after his first tour. Ken went on to serve over ten years of total active duty (including another two-year overseas assignment in Japan). And before he left the army in 1980, he had acquired a bachelor's degree from the University of the State of New York, as well as the professional credentials and certifications needed to conduct any phase of training within any type of organization or business. This had enabled him to have a viable civilian career in the training profession over a thirty-year period. He also left the military with direct commission to the rank of first lieutenant. Equally important, he had been honorably discharged.

Kyle also learned that Ken's overall view of the military (not the government) was a good one, a positive one. All in all, the military helped Ken learn to survive, not only physically and militarily, but also socially, professionally, and personally. He had come a long way since the Projects in Brooklyn, Maryland. However, he also discovered Ken was facing several personal, emotional, and psychological challenges associated with his service in Vietnam and from his childhood. Much of it was still unresolved, left dormant for decades, surfacing only as momentary flashbacks late at night as well as during challenging moments in the light of day. In short, Ken came to Kyle not really knowing what his problems were but hoped to find out. In 2010, at the age of sixty-one, he had deeply hidden feelings and false beliefs that were playing a large part in how he not only viewed himself, but also how he viewed many events, environment, and people around him.

Kyle's task was to help him see and understand himself better as well as help him resolve and manage his life with far more confidence and competence. He only took a few notes at first without distracting Ken. He was much more casual and unobtrusive about doing so—felt like he was capturing thoughts rather than collecting data. He would find over time that Kyle was focused more on the conversation, dialogue and direct interaction rather than documentation or note taking. Ken also assumed he summarized things after each session. And the only times he noticed Kyle actually writing anything down routinely during subsequent sessions was to ensure any commitment he or Ken made was clear. He would come to like that about Kyle. The vast majority of their time together would be in direct conversation, with direct eye contact and without major distractions.

"Thanks for that introduction of yourself, Ken. You've had a very interesting military and civilian life. It appears you've learned how to adapt and adjust to adversity very well." Kyle stated genuinely.

"It has been challenging for sure, but rewarding as well. Thank you. So would you tell me a little about yourself, Kyle—seems like I've been doing most of the talking." Ken asked, genuinely curious to learn more about the man who had just learned so much about him.

He discovered Kyle was a licensed clinical social worker with the outpatient mental health services posttraumatic stress disorder (PTSD) clinic within the Boston Healthcare System. He had been doing this kind of work for quite some time. Even though Kyle was in civilian clothes, Ken sensed he may have had military experience of some kind simply by observing his posture and personal demeanor, so he asked: "Kyle, are you a military guy . . . ever serve?"

Kyle was concise describing himself, but he was also very open and direct. Ken learned that Kyle, indeed, did have prior military experience himself—three years of active duty in the army. And coincidently, just like Ken, he had spent time at Fort Devens, Massachusetts, being trained as a US Military Intelligence Specialist. That's where Kyle received his advance military specialization as an electronic warfare Morse Code intercept specialist—that was exactly the same MOS (military occupational specialty) as one of Ken's. He had also been assigned to a California-based army facility during the early 1990s. That's when Ken quickly calculated that if Kyle were fifteen years older, he would have likely been one of his own students at the intelligence school in Fort Devens. But, one key fact that Ken would learn later about him, wouldn't come directly from Kyle. Rather, it would come from "Angel Dawn."

She discovered just how reputable Kyle was in the eyes of other PTSD clinicians around the nation. A few weeks after this first meeting, Ken was on-line when he received an email from Angel Dawn while she was at work in Boston: "Hey, check out what I stumbled across on "Med Web." "Med Web" was the world's top internet site providing forums for patient/doctor chats to occur on various health and medical issues. It also regularly announced breakthroughs in medical research and maintained a who's who of professionals across the world of medicine, sociology and psychology. Angel Dawn often used the site while doing research at the Massachusetts Medical Center. Her email went like this:

> Honey . . . are you sitting down? Kyle Armstrong is famous, named the recipient of the VA's Top PTSD Clinician Award for 2009—something called *"PTSD Clinicians Honors."* It's a very special recognition given out only once every three years and Kyle was the only recipient this time. Boy, I feel you're in real good hands. You're one lucky guy. Love ya . . . me. PS: Don't' forget to pick me up at the train tonight; should get in at 6:43."

That was comforting to Ken and equally comforting was discovering during a subsequent session that Kyle's father was a Vietnam veteran, too. That black-and-white photo sitting deep within his bookshelf, the one Ken noticed earlier, was indeed a picture of his father. In Ken's eyes, Kyle not only was more than qualified to help him with psychosocial implications of PTSD, but he also had been a soldier. That's when he sensed he had stumbled into the best of both worlds—a competent and caring PTSD clinician as well as a former soldier who possessed military experience and a great deal of empathy for veterans.

This was too good to be true for Ken.

The first session with Kyle flew by and then they set a schedule for their next few sessions—same place, same time, different days over the next two months. Ken couldn't wait to get back and report it all to Angel Dawn who would be expecting a thorough update for sure. And Ken really liked the Plainville VA Campus, even though he still felt compelled to take a closer look at that dog/fox thing.

During subsequent sessions, Ken came to appreciate and respect many other things about Kyle beyond his competence and experience. This helped Ken feel more comfortable in such a foreign setting—a clinical social worker's therapeutic office. Kyle never volunteered personal information on his own. That is, he'd never talk about himself unless asked. Ken assumed by doing so, he was maintaining that needed professional distance as well as keeping the dialogue focused on Ken. And even though he was very well educated, Kyle never came across professorial or erudite, the way Ken stereotyped all psychiatrists and psychologists. And, he never was condescending. Ken also came to appreciate how he answered every question asked, even if it was of a personal nature. He was open, honest, and immediate. He kept things moving along.

Equally important to Ken, he noticed Kyle never was afraid to admit he didn't know an answer to question posed by Ken; he never hesitated to say, "I don't know," "That's a good question," or "I'll have to get back to you that, OK?" This added even greater personal comfort and increased his confidence in Kyle. It was the relationship part of his PTSD treatment Ken also came to admire the most about Kyle. He was competent and caring, managing each session without strict control—he was flexible. He often allowed and encouraged Ken to set the agenda—topics that needed to be addressed. Unless it was a follow-up topic or an issue carried over from a previous session, Ken also seemed to determine the direction of discussion. Kyle seemed to know well in advance when to relinquish control in order to maintain control and Ken recognized this right away, feeling more secure with him because of it.

Ken came to appreciate his approach and style even more as time went by. Being a "process" kind of guy, Ken greatly appreciated a person's methods as much as their results. In business, he was always the go-to "process guy" in the organization. Whenever executives or team leaders were stuck simplifying the complexities of business messages, procedures, or tough concepts, they called on him. He could not only integrate lots of moving parts of problems into simple simplified process, but he also could help them explain and communicate it in simple terms, as well as convert it into a viable learning interventions. So, for Ken to witness and experience Kyle's techniques and methods specifically centered on helping him grow personally, it was a silent joy that he looked forward to each session. He discovered Kyle would systematically, casually and non-intrusively conduct his sessions in the following way:

Step 1: Always establish a little rapport—weather, family, sports.
Step 2: Elicit Ken's input on his mood or any outstanding problems.
Step 3: Bridge and process the previous session's commitments.
Step 4: Address issues of greatest need, first.
Step 6: Summarize and solicit Ken's feedback or for ideas on next steps.
Step 7: Give Ken assignments; set time and date of next meeting.

Ken just assumed this was one of the standard professional methodologies and protocols used by most clinical social workers in veteran treatment environments. But he wasn't sure. He also didn't really care. Kyle was a process-predicable guy, and that was very good for Ken. If any surprises arose, Ken would likely be the source of them, not the professional. And, he thought that was the way it should be.

"But, I'm Normal, Right?"

Early on in their relationship, Kyle concluded that Ken had been suffering for some time from prolonged PTSD (posttraumatic stress disorder). But he did not come right out and formally convey it to him, not at first. In retrospect, Ken sensed Kyle had been waiting for him to ask that specific question, but it never arose.

He ultimately concluded Ken had been experiencing the following symptoms over the long term—decades:

1. Fitful sleep (ongoing reoccurring nightmares, sleepless nights)
2. Short-temperament (quick to irritate)
3. Intense claustrophobia (unwarranted fear of close, confined spaces)
4. Hyper-vigilance (constant state of unwarranted suspicion or threat)
5. Emotional numbing (avoidance of past memories and relationships)
6. Avoidance of conflict—physically, socially and emotionally

Such symptoms were not exclusive to Ken. Rather, they were commonly experienced by many combat veterans. During the Vietnam War era, such symptoms were frequently discounted by professionals and institutions, commonly referred to using fashionable descriptors as "shell shock" or "combat fatigue"—temporary conditions that would pass with time. The thinking at that time was if a soldier was moved into an environment free of "shells" and "combat" then their symptoms would ultimately fade then cease altogether. As a result, direct psychological interventions, such as PTSD treatment, were not systemically made available to Vietnam veterans. No longer.

Since that time and especially during recent wars, including Iraq and Afghanistan, formal medical processes and resources were established and proactively administered to address the "hidden injuries" of vets coming home from war. This was "not" the case with Ken and his generation. Forty years is a very long time that enabled this condition to find deep hiding places within a veteran's mind and his soul. Kyle explained this history to Ken in an early session. "Thanks for the explanation, Kyle . . . that's real helpful and interesting. I'm glad to hear about the progress made, especially regarding the younger soldiers now returning from the Middle East." Ken found his overview quite helpful. "Yes, the government has made major strides in this area. They've also learned a lot from you and your generation, my friend," Kyle said genuinely. But Ken wanted to be sure he understood this.

"Just to get it straight, Kyle, you're saying this bullet I may have been hit by is a wound, not of the body but of the mind—a 'PTSD bullet' of sorts; a wound that does not come with any purple heart, right? Is that a simple way for me to view this?" Kyle found Ken's metaphor to be quite accurate and told him so. The only question Kyle had on his mind was whether the VA examiners would ultimately classify Ken's individual condition as either "aggravated" or "incurred" by his direct service in Vietnam. Given Ken's prolonged exposure to violence as a young boy, well before he stepped foot in Vietnam, was the real question. But he decided to cross that bridge when they came to it.

Kyle also noticed Ken's subtle use of the words *may have been* when he was referring to being hit by a "PTSD bullet" in Vietnam. That could be an unconscious yet important self-disclosure that Kyle noticed. So he thought it may be time to get things clearly on the table and move Ken closer to the reality of it all. So he asked, "Ken, I noticed you said 'may have been' hit by a PTSD bullet and not 'have been' hit. What do you mean by that?" He was taken aback by his question; he didn't even notice the words he used. "Oh, did I say that?"

"Yes."

Ken thought for some time and replied, "Well, maybe it's because I'm still a little unsure I even have PTSD at all. I mean, all this information is helpful and interesting, really, and you've been great in helping me learn about it, Kyle . . . but I guess I'm still not convinced I do have it. There's a big part of me that's rejecting this." Kyle responded empathetically, "I understand how this can cause some internal conflict, that's only natural, Ken. Let's explore this a little further. So, tell me more about how you're viewing yourself in relationship to PTSD thus far in our time together."

Ken just didn't know if all this was helping or hurting. Ken was "waffling" about PTSD in his mind. He and Kyle certainly talked about it, around it, over it, and under it in the past couple of sessions together, but he never really came right out and stated whether or not Ken had PTSD. He knew the first few sessions were designed to help Kyle gather enough information to make that professional determination. But, Ken just was not sure himself. And there was a side of him that was even hoping (wishing) he didn't have PTSD after all. So that's when Ken finally came out and asked him directly about it: "Well, I guess I'm still not convinced that I even have PTSD. So you tell me, do I or don't I have PTSD, Kyle? You should know by now."

Kyle didn't hesitate at all . . . he seized the moment: "Yes . . . yes, you do, Ken. I'm certain of it."

He then gave Ken a moment to think about what he just heard. Most of his patients were taken aback when they actually heard it confirmed for the first time. Some were surprised by it, some are relieved by it, and others were frightened by it. He wasn't sure how Ken would react. But he would soon find out.

Then Kyle continued his explanation, "Yes, I would also say that you are not only suffering from PTSD today, but have been for quite some time, without even knowing it. I say this primarily because of your specific symptoms which we'll also explore further together over the longer term, including: avoidance, denial, re-experiencing and hyper arousal. There's no question you've been exposed to a great deal of personal trauma both in Vietnam as well as in your youth. Whether it was incurred or aggravated by your experiences in Vietnam is not important at this time. But accurately identifying the sources of your PTSD, 'stressors,' will help us understanding it better, and then we can take steps to improve things. That's how I see things. And, you need to determine if that's the direction in which you would like to go."

Ken was listening closely now. His mind understood what Kyle was saying, but his emotions were someplace else when he eventually responded, "Well, I guess it makes sense, just seems like a lot to digest, you know what I mean? And what if I can't go through with it . . . what if I don't want to or can't continue? What then?" Kyle knew what was coming; Ken was entering "denial" and "avoidance"—the top two symptoms of PTSD. This hidden behavior was something Kyle sensed had been an unintended, but natural, part of Ken's life for a long time. Then he responded, "Ken, I understand your apprehension, really I do. I just want you to know that you're not alone in this. I'll be there to help, I promise. And I know your wife will be also be there for you, and our own Dr. Miller will be there, too."

Kyle was trying to reassure Ken. It wasn't working.

What had been driving Ken's concerns would eventually be uncovered but one thing standing in his way was how he viewed himself in all this. Kyle wasn't sure but he sensed that openly acknowledging and accepting his problems, the diagnosis of PTSD, was going to be big steps for Ken, perhaps the biggest challenges of all. Ken was resisting the fact that he may be suffering from PTSD after all. That's when the reality of the moment started to finally sink in. This became obvious because he then kept asking the same questions of Kyle expecting to get a different answer. The answer Ken wanted was "no" (you don't have PTSD), but it was constantly coming back "yes."

Then, Ken unintentionally and subconsciously repeated the same question to Kyle, "So you're saying I do have PTSD . . . right?"

"That's correct." Kyle paused and observed Ken's facial expressions and posture change drastically. Then he asked, "Ken . . . What are you feeling now that you've heard this again?" A few seconds passed before Ken repeated the exact question once again, "So you're saying I do have PTSD . . . right?"

"Yes," Kyle repeated his answer for a third time.

Something still didn't compute for Ken, and now his emotions were starting to get the best of him. "I get what you're saying, really, and I respect it, but I'm just struggling with one little thing right now."

Then Ken's voice exploded, "HOW IN THE HELL CAN I HAVE PTSD—I'M A NORMAL GUY!"

His mind was now moving faster than a speeding train. His emotions were also flying in every direction like a million birds scared out of a tree at once. That's when he let his true feelings and doubts out—those building for several weeks.

He dumped it all on Kyle's lap, "Look man . . . I've gone to work for forty-plus years since Vietnam; I'm as physically fit and healthy as any man twenty years younger, even my doctor says my metabolism is that of the thirty-five-year old; I run four miles a day; I do three hundred sit-ups and curl one hundred reps of 20-lb free weights each day; I'm highly successful—professionally and financially; I'm a published author and an international trainer, tops in my industry; I haven't missed a day of work unless I had been laid off or on my deathbed; I don't abuse drugs and only socially drink; I don't beat my wife; I don't gamble; I don't abuse kids; I never harm anyone; I don't think about blowing up any buildings or taking down any governments; I've been married for twenty-five years; I pay my taxes and vote regularly; I'm not depressed; I like myself—most of the time; I haven't thought about assassinating anyone or harming myself in weeks—only kidding, Kyle; I'm not mad at anyone; I don't blame the military for anything . . . and I'm a good citizen . . . so what the FUCK gives? . . . HOW IN THE HELL DOES THAT QUALIFY ME AS SUFFERING FROM . . . 'P' FUCKING . . . 'T' FUCKING . . . 'S' FUCKING . . . 'D' FUCKING, PTSD. HOW? HOW? HOW? TELL ME!'"

Kyle didn't respond right away, letting Ken have a little time to catch his breath. Ken was coming to grips with viewing himself in a new way, and he didn't like what he saw.

Kyle knew it would take some time to help him get through this. "I hear you, Ken. And, I understand how hard this can be, believe me. Listen, many vets, who are quietly suffering from PTSD, have been able to build good careers and raise great families along the way. They also have learned to manage, hide, discount, or avoid the severe pain that is not conscious to them. You're not the only one. It's true you've been a very successful man, and even that can be used to help hide other things. Your honest and open disclosures about yourself have been so very helpful to me throughout this process, and now that we're discussing things you've been silently avoiding and even unconsciously feeling may help start making your life even more satisfying and rewarding. I think that's where you are . . . right now."

Kyle continued as Ken was listening to him without making direct eye contact. "Ken, you've stated that you often relive stressful times in Vietnam . . . and your upbringing was equally disturbing and violent; your sleep has been poor with reoccurring nightmares; your fear about entering confined or crowded spaces is ever present; and being suspicious of people also seems to be continual. Such things are very real for you, even though you may not talk about or recognize them readily. And, you've still been able to lead a very successful professional life while also experiencing all this. You know, that's really amazing to me. Just imagine what may have been able to accomplish in the past, and much more important, what you could possibly accomplish in the future without carrying additional pressures in your life. Now that's something real amazing to think about, wouldn't you say?"

Kyle was trying to help Ken see the bigger picture of his life, but he still wasn't buying it. There was a part of Ken that was relieved to know there was something concretely wrong, but the other side of him kept viewing it all as some kind of flaw in his own character, something he had caused himself, something that was his fault. He could not articulate this to Kyle at the time because he did not know how. And he certainly couldn't do so without first admitting it to himself.

But he tried. "Kyle, I do appreciate all your effort in this, but I still don't believe I'm suffering from PTSD. Wouldn't I have known about it long before. I'm an intelligent guy—there's just no way I missed such a major 'character flaw' for so long; just no way."

Kyle replied: "I see. But sometimes we're the worst judges of our own behavior and needs. We're just too close. It's hard to be objective with something so subjective and personal as one's self. Besides, this is the first time you actually heard me or anyone specifically say . . . *you're suffering from PTSD'* . . . so like any surprise news (good or bad), it will likely take a little time to understand, even longer to accept. It's hard to wrap one's mind around such a thing at first. But, if you feel there isn't a reason to continue or if you still want to reject this view altogether, that's your call, too."

Ken still wasn't buying it.

"Blah, blah, blah . . . I DON'T HAVE PTSD! I DON'T HAVE PTSD! I'm not a basket case. I'm not nuts. I don't have reoccurring flashbacks of my combat days, well not often, certainly not regularly. And I don't harbor any bad thoughts about the Viet Cong—that's done, it's over. I hated the VC, then I feared them, and now I've come to respect them. The VC didn't kick our asses; we kick our own asses but they stuck in there and out-lasted us—that's for sure. Any Vietnam vet could easily agree with such a view. And, yes, I admit to still harboring bad feelings towards the US government about what happened in Vietnam, who doesn't among those of us who served there? So does this make me nuts? I DON'T FUCKING THINK SO!"

He was getting more and more agitated with each explanation that Kyle tried to provide and now Ken's eyes kept flashing toward the door. He was getting out of there in his mind, a "clean get-a-way" mindset was coming to a head just as Ken's hidden feelings were starting to resurface. Then Kyle responded, "Ken, we've been together for a while and I see you as an intelligent, competent, astute, and good man. But that doesn't negate the possibility you may also be suffering from something else, too. It doesn't lessen all your attributes or your successes, not in the least. If anything, it tells me how resilient you've must have been over the years and decades to have been able to balance it all—to succeed while also suffering."

Ken was quick with his response. "You see, there you go again. What suffering? What suffering? I'm not in pain. I'm not disguising or hiding anything, and I'm not running away from anything. Look, everyone in my life would have told me that something was wrong well before now if it were. I'm really an Okay guy, Kyle—as normal as can be. Really."

He knew Ken was getting very uncomfortable with this discussion, which compelled Kyle to continue along those lines. This opportunity may never present itself again, and this dialogue could help Ken recognize something very important. So Kyle continued, "I am certain that's how many others view you, Ken. You couldn't have excelled so well without the ability to relate well and manage your life as you have. However, most of those people see you in one or two roles or scenarios—business or social gatherings—not all the time and certainly not intimately, right? Only you see yourself all the time. Tell me, how many of those people you have worked with over the years have you actually discussed this level of personal information with? Not many, if any. Right? How many of your friends and associates, for example, actually know you sleep with a knife? Who really knows you were nearly killed in Vietnam when a mortar slammed into that bunker? Does anyone really notice (or care) that you take the stairs versus the elevators when given the choice to do so? Tell me, how your closest friends responded when you disclosed to them the sexual abuse you experienced as a child—not many of them even know about it I would guess. It's simple really; it's because you didn't, wouldn't or couldn't talk about such things with them, no matter how close they may seem to be, they're not THAT close, are they? What it comes down to is pretty simple too. Perhaps they just haven't earned the right to know your most highly personal, most well protected secrets. Ken, does this at least make a little bit of sense?"

Ken went silent. And, Kyle just allowed his words to marinate in the soup of Ken's mind. He was about to place all this in an even a bigger context for Ken and thought he needed a few moments to let it sink-in. He knew Ken was a "big picture" guy and this next appeal may help him see, understand and accept things better. So after a minute or so, Kyle tried again. "This PTSD environment and process and resources have been put into place for you, a combat veteran, to explore and discover things about yourself that may have been a silent burden to you for some time—something adversely impacting your ability to function and live as you should. We know how combat and prolonged exposure to violence can impact a person. We also know more about it today than we did yesterday, that's for sure. And to help soldiers who have gone through combat, who also return not knowing the full impact of it all . . . this was something we didn't do very well especially for Vietnam vets. But, no longer. You and other vets deserve this."

He then began to really hear Kyle—not just his words, but their meaning. Ken knew he was right, especially when placed in that context. Actually, he was blown away by it. If Ken had such help upon his return from Vietnam, it may have made big a difference. And Ken had to admit Kyle was right about how others in his life really didn't know him well—he hadn't given them a chance to. And besides, they wouldn't want to discuss such things either—who would? And, it just wasn't their business anyway. The only person who truly knew about such things anyway was Angel Dawn, and she learned about it the hard way—by living with Ken. "Ken, only you know how you really feel about what's going on inside you, and even so, much of that is likely very well hidden from you. Like you said in one of our earlier sessions, you probably could never accept that you have PTSD anyway because you see it as a 'character flaw.' Remember when you shared that with me? Well, PTSD has nothing to do with your ethics, morals, or values—your character, that is. It's more about your emotions, thoughts, and behaviors . . . not your character, not at all."

That's when something clicked for Ken.

He was beginning to better see and understand where Kyle was coming from. But *one* big problem he still had to deal with was also something he couldn't easily share. It was his overall perception of PTSD—the secret 'mother of all stereotypes' that Ken sensed would not be discussed openly; PTSD was not an "honorable" thing, not at all.

Character Flaw

In a follow up sessions with Kyle, Ken stated this secret view toward PTSD—it was *not* an "honorable wound;" not something a soldier should be proud of. Actually, he felt it was more about personal weakness, a mental and ethical deficiency, and to a degree, along with a slight touch of cowardice. Such implications represented something he could never accept about himself; he was not weak, wasn't deficient, and anything but a coward. Being afraid in combat was natural and expected; everyone in Vietnam was scared at one time or another (even if they never openly admitted it). Ken never viewed anyone he knew as a coward in Vietnam; most soldiers he dealt with had character. And it was on this subject that Ken started to do a "deep dive" regarding Kyle's next question. He would do so without answering him aloud. That is, he began "self-talking"—a silent, internal dialogue he did at times with only himself. He did so whenever he needed to analyze a problem that required total concentration, no interruptions, and without anyone's responses. That is, his own mind was the only audience during his "self-talks."

Kyle's question was, "Ken, my view of you is not as important as how you see yourself regarding PTSD. I've heard and do understand your perspective, but now let me ask you specifically, do you really believe that the symptoms you've been experiencing for so long are not related to PTSD at all?" Kyle then sat back and began observing him in silence now. He wanted to give Ken as much time as he needed to think things through. Knowing him as he did, Kyle sensed it wouldn't take long but he also knew Ken always wanted to think answers through before responding.

Ken's "self-talking" words, thoughts, emotions, and logic flowed through his mind in the following manner, but only in his mind—Kyle never heard any of following at the moment, only pieces of it during follow-up sessions together:

> "I view PTSD as a real "character flaw," something I am not willing or able to accept about myself . . . and certainly nothing I want to openly share with anyone especially those closest to me. To do that, I must first admit I have such a "self-inflicted" deficiency . . . one caused by me because of being so weak minded . . . and that is DIS-honorable.
>
> It's like being a wife beater or child abuser or even an alcoholic. I could never do or accept such things about myself nor allow them

to become known by others. PTSD and these traits are in the same category of such bad traits, and I'm not in that ballpark of people.

After all, PTSD is officially classified as a "mental disorder." That's what the government and the medical profession call it—PTSD (for disorder), right? Yeah. It's a mental disorder. Something is out of whack. And technically speaking, it is not even an official wound, not a real wound.

Right? Yes, again.

If so, the government would have classified it as such, you know . . . PTSI . . . for "injury" or PTSW . . . for "wound," . . . but they did not. Rather, they classified it as a . . . "D" (disorder) implying something is really screwed-up "inside" the soldier, something not "in order." It's so badly "out of order" and so deep inside a soldier even a surgeon's scalpel can't reach it.

Right? Yeah.

Any single bullet wound (even the smallest, most minor of physical wounds) is still far "more" honorable than even the most severe PTSD.

Right? Yeah.

I don't see the government giving a "purple heart" to anyone diagnosed with PTSD . . . no matter how severe or debilitating the problem nor acquired under the most severe of circumstances. Why? Because it's not a good enough wound? It's not a real wound. Right?

Yes, right once again.

And why is that? Whether a wound is caused by shrapnel or by horrific psychological pain, suffering is suffering! Don't all kinds of wounds (physical, mental, emotional) have lasting impact on soldiers? Don't all kinds of wounds change lives? Don't all kinds of wounds hurt people? Don't all kinds of wounds need to heal? Don't both kinds of wounds need treatment and care?

Right? Yeah.

Purple Hearts are not classified by severity either. It doesn't matter if a soldier loses both legs or loses an ear lobe. They both receive the same distinction, the same honor—a Purple Heart, and justifiably so. Both are honorable. But not PTSD . . . it's not "real" enough. It's not honorable "enough."

Right? Yeah.

To me, whether it's physical, mental, or emotional, a wound is a wound. Whether I get shot by a bullet, hit by a rocket, or step on Punji stick, my pain and suffering is real. Can't the horror of seeing your best friend blown apart by a land mine be equally painful, equally traumatic?

A wound is a wound is a wound is a wound.

I got out of Nam without a scratch. I was lucky. But if I had been physically wounded, I sense I could more easily accept such diagnosis and treatment and do so willingly and proudly. That's honorable and reasonable. But for me to admit to having a mental "disorder" is different, much different. A disorder is about a mental or emotional deficiency of some kind, and I view that as a . . . personal shortcoming of the mind or spirit, a weakness in one's character, as such it is and will always be a . . . Character Flaw.

And I can't admit nor accept that about myself. It's just not honorable. Not only that, I also have to hide it and disassociate myself from it . . . no one must know about me because it involves my "character," my sense of identity as a man, as a person . . . as a soldier. I can't live knowing that I have such a "character flaw." It's just not me. I'm not that kind of person and I won't allow myself to become one.

Right? Yeah.

Such was Ken's thinking. It was how he felt about PTSD overall and how it would impact him. Such thoughts were locked safely in his mind—a place he could revisit anytime, but no one else could. And, it would be a struggle to let any part of it out for the world to see. And that was one of the hidden biases and perceptions Kyle had to help him with, even though he didn't know it yet; it was one of Kyle's biggest challenges with Ken. He had to help him see that PTSD was not about his character at all; it was about his thoughts, his emotions, and his behavior. Such things were far more tangible as compared to one's character and far more treatable as well.

When Ken finished his "self-talk" a few minutes later, Kyle asked him about it. He tried to be open and explain how he felt but just kept coming up short. Yet, he still tried. When Ken completed his attempt to communicate this view of PTSD, Kyle understood Ken's resistance even more clearly and was glad he shared it with him. Kyle had seen it before in other veterans. And he acknowledged it, even confirmed Ken's view especially about honor, as well as the distinctions made among "wound," "injury," and "disorder." However, he also knew if he could help Ken see PTSD more objectively, more practically, it could also go a long way in helping him to help himself. Because that's what everything really came down to—helping Ken "help himself." Specifically, he had to assist Ken in realizing this psychological wound could also be "seen," "felt," and "touched" in many ways. Therefore, in that sense, it was real—as real as any bullet wound and as equally devastating. To do so, Kyle executed the following strategies to help Ken learn to . . . help himself:

1. Capture Ken's intellect—his willingness to accept will strengthen.
2. Stretch Ken's beliefs—his emotions will strengthen.
3. Broaden Ken's knowledge—and his self-image will improve.

Even though such strategies were never openly discussed, Ken's learning and eventual development was to be based on them as he moved forward in his treatment. "Okay Ken. I see where you're coming. You make several good points especially regarding 'wounds.' You know, it is a very valid view, one that's shared by others, including PTSD patients and professionals alike. As a matter of fact, currently there are official initiatives underway within the VA and other government agencies to change how PTSD is viewed and medically classified, that is. So, much of how you feel about things has some basis in reality."

Ken was so glad to learn about that. It helped validate a few of his basic views and helped him to back away a little from the cliff of craziness he was feeling. Kyle continued, "I sense you've been using a metaphoric mirror over the years in looking more closely at yourself. That's healthy—self-examination is a good thing. Keep it up. But moving ahead, let's consider using a different tool—instead of a mirror let's begin using a microscope, so to speak. This way you'll be able to take an even closer look at several other important things deep within yourself beyond character. How's that sound?"

"Okay . . . let's try it." Ken was still somewhat resistant but he was willing to move forward. Kyle knew Ken was an intelligent man and would be able to draw his own conclusions at what he found under the "microscope." He also knew Ken needed some time to chew on all this, so they agreed it would be the topic of their next session. And that's where they picked up the next time they were together. He quickly set expectations with Ken that he was going to help him see PTSD in a different light. "I'll be asking you some tough questions over time. These questions will be based on many things we discussed during our earlier sessions together. I do want you to know that you don't even have to response verbally to these questions, actually just by realizing how you're feeling about a question can prove as beneficial as the answer. I also want you to know if you still continue to feel PTSD is all about your character more than anything else, then we can reconsider other directions. Is that OK?"

Kyle was taking a huge risk because he knew Ken would hold him to it. He also knew Ken wouldn't intentionally deceive himself in the face of his own logic. If the math didn't added up, he'd know.

This approached seemed familiar to the way Martin Finely introduced Angel Dawn and him to PTSD when they first met him in the VFW legislative office in Boston several months before. Ken then responded, "Okay, I like this approach Kyle; questions that don't need a verbal response or immediate answer. Boy, I wish I had that kind of question in college on my final exams; it would have made things a lot more fun for me." They both laughed at Ken's attempted humor. Even so, Ken couldn't hide his obvious nervousness by using it. Kyle enjoyed Ken's wit, which was usually self-deprecating and always relevant to the discussion. Yet, he also knew Ken could use humor at times to change subjects, redirect the conversations, and minimize the impact of the tough moments. "Okay, let's do this. Fire away—no pun intended," Ken said.

With that, they had clear direction and were ready to embark on it. Ken would look back on these questions as if they all reigned down upon him at once. In reality, these queries were experienced over three sessions. Later on, Ken would look back at them as "death by a thousand cuts," in keeping with the ancient Chinese saying referring to the very slow, painful process of facilitating inevitable change. At least Kyle would render each "cut" with great skill and compassion. That was the one thing Ken trusted.

Each question was accurately targeted and purposefully delivered by Kyle. And each took Ken to a very sensitive, unspoken place in his mind that rightfully deserved greater understanding on the part of both Ken and Kyle. Kyle knew the answers to these questions could help identify some hidden origins of Ken's long-term, hidden pain and suffering. It took them a couple of sessions together, but each was addressed and openly discussed—some easily without emotion, others just the opposite. Kyle's questions then began: "Ken, can you describe what it was like when that bunker buried you alive in Vietnam—what were you thinking about, where did your mind go?" Then the following 21 questions were asked of Ken over time:

1. "How did you feel when you stepped off the plane back in the USA after returning from Vietnam?"
2. "Why is it so difficult, impossible, for you to name at least one person with whom you served during your two years in Vietnam?"
3. "You said that you not only feared your brother and mother but also hated both . . . please tell me more."
4. "What really happened that day in your mother's smoke-filled bedroom when you were a child?"
5. "How do you feel about your overall service in Vietnam?"

6. "Why do you always take the stairs instead of the elevators?"
7. "Why do you always take work along with you when on vacations?"
8. "How many people did you kill in Vietnam?"
9. "How many lives did you save in Vietnam?"
10. "When was the last time you actually got into a subway or train?"
11. "Describe that man, Mr. Dark, who comes to you in dreams?"
12. "Why did you start using drugs in Vietnam?"
13. "You lost your virginity in Vietnam . . . lots of young men did too, so why was that so hard for you to accept and get over?"
14. "Why haven't you ever associated with other Vietnam vets since the war?"
15. "Why do you need to sleep with a knife?"
16. "You stated the happiest day of your life was the day you left Vietnam. Yet you turned around and volunteered to go back less than a month after returning to the States. Can you please tell me more about that?"
17. "Why have you kept all your family members and personal relationships at a distance—a 'safe distance' as you call it? What's that mean?"
18. "Why did you decide never to have children, Ken?"
19. "Why do you think your first two marriages didn't work out?"
20. "Do you feel you deserved the Bronze Star?"
21. "How many American lives do you think were lost because of your actions or inactions in Vietnam?"

Exploring each of these questions helped jump-start and motivate Ken along his journey of self-discovery. As each question unfolded during subsequent sessions, Ken became more and more uncomfortable, not with Kyle, but with himself. It took a lot of time and personal effort for him to learn why. Some things he didn't have answers for, not at first. But as time went on, each exposed another part of Ken that deserved long-overdue attention.

It would prove to be well worth his effort.

CHAPTER 8

PTSD—"The Deep Dive" (Massachusetts, 2011)

KYLE AND KEN HAD BEEN meeting once or twice per month throughout 2010 and 2011. Ken's ultimate goal was to enter the final chapters of his life without suffering from needless emotional stress driven primarily by counter-productive beliefs about his past and self. Everything he now was doing focused at being able to better understand and manage his beliefs about his past which could directly enhance his day-to-day functioning and overall quality of life. Their face-to-face time together in building 12 was always cordial and professional, yet also quite intense at times while Ken was exposed to several well-proven PTSD therapies, techniques and interventions that could help him. These included the five following approaches:

1. Cognitive behavioral therapy (CBT)—one-on-one talk-therapy sessions with a professional PTSD clinician—with Kyle;
2. Group therapy (GT)—regularly scheduled sessions with other combat veterans—with a "vet-to-vet" peer-to-peer group;
3. Prolonged exposure (PE)—"going deep" during CBT with Kyle to re-experience specific traumas and significant past emotional events;
4. Writing therapy (WT)—describing specific events, thoughts, and feelings associated with specific trauma through written exercises and projects; and
5. Medication therapy (MT)—taking doctor-prescribed drugs to relieve PTSD-related symptoms, including antidepressants and anxiety reduction medications.

Kyle explained, "Ken, you may find each of these methods more effective than others. Each person is different. We've found this out over the years treating PTSD patients. There's no secret formula or right combination—some people respond better than others to different approaches. Much of it is really going to depend on you to determine which works best for you. But I'll be there for you and help in any way I can."

Ken would find the above therapies and techniques to be helpful in varying degrees. For example, he was prescribed an antidepressant over a several-month period but found it counterproductive physically and ineffective in stabilizing his emotional reactions to real or perceived stressors in his daily life. So he withdrew, with the PTSD doctor's guidance of course. He could have stayed "on that path," but he did not. So he engaged Dr. Miller, his PTSD medical physician, who was also located in building 12, and together they worked through the decision to stop. To him, this was an illustration of taking responsibility, active participation, and ownership for his own healing. Even though the medication was ineffective for Ken, he took away a positive lesson: "medications are not a viable tool to help right now, perhaps later, but not now." With that mind-set, he was able to focus elsewhere—on his writing, his journaling.

Writing Therapy (WT)

Ken found WT to be extremely helpful. It was also referred to as journaling. He had already possessed extensive writing experience before his PTSD diagnosis and was comfortable having written two books on credibility and professionalism. He also had several articles published in industry magazines and journals in the area of training and communication. But with even such writing competencies, he quickly discovered that writing about himself, his emotions, his experiences, his fears, his insecurities, etc., was far more challenging than writing about business stuff. For example, he found writing in the first-person form to be very different, even foreign to him.

Doing so required a totally different mind-set and perspective. Specifically, it was weird for him to write using phrases and concepts such as "I feel,"

"I am," and "We were" after decades of using "He is," "They did," and "You should." But once he mastered the first-person fundamentals, he found it helpful, even enjoyable at times.

Ken then became unstoppable, prolific in his writing.

It all began when he started writing a few words about a couple of events that happened to him in Vietnam, and before he knew it, it turned into dozens of detailed pages. It seemed that every time he'd describe the details of one situation or person, he would quickly find himself writing down related feelings (not just facts) . . . emotions he hadn't felt in decades and never articulated. This wasn't a conscious thing—more like afterthoughts. Never the less it was real. And later on he found that when he was writing about his feelings, all sort of additional long-forgotten facts and details would surface. Such things began endlessly popping out of his head and magically landing on his pages. In short, facts were driving feelings, and feelings were generating facts. It was weird, but he just went with it. It reminded him of the scene from National Lampoon's 1983 hit comedy *Vacation*, starring Chevy Chase. Chevy and his family finally made it across the country to The Wally World amusement park in California, only to find it closed. So they broke in and went on a wild ride anyway—on the largest mountain speedway ever built. They stayed on it seemingly forever at least until the police came and arrested them. The whole family had just gone wild on the ride and let it play out—whatever happened, happened. Wherever the ride took them, they went. That's how Ken felt while writing in this new way.

And, he liked it. Then something really strange happened.

He was attempting to capture an incident that happened to him when he was running toward a bunker during a VC mortar attack outside of Lai Khe, Vietnam, in 1969. His mind seemed to just magically switch from Vietnam in 1969 to Brooklyn in 1961—all by itself. It wasn't a conscious effort; it just happened. In no time, he then found himself writing about his childhood—ancient, personal memories that hadn't been dusted off for decades. His thoughts and feelings just seemed to endlessly flow like the waterfall at Yosemite National Park. He just dove in and went for the ride; he was unable to stop. Later, Ken discovered such a mental process was technically called a "flashback"—when a memory, thought or emotion links directly back in time to another moment, person or event, seemingly without an apparent or logical connection. However, subconsciously, lurking just below or deeply embedded within the mind, a more meaningful connection exists.

While writing, Ken found himself not only flashing-back, but also flashing-ahead, flashing-right, flashing-left, flashing-upside-down and every other way possible. He couldn't stop it. He didn't want to stop it. This was becoming intriguing, exciting and painful all at the same time. Regardless if he was writing about Phu Loi, Lai Khe, The Projects, Australia, Japan or Fort Devens, more and more flashes seemed to automatically and naturally surface in his mind; the more he wrote, the better he felt. And, the better he felt, the more he wrote. It became a wondrous cycle of emotions and memories—some good, some bad. Equally important, the more he wrote, the more he was able to share with Kyle when they got together. This turned out to be an excellent way for Ken to stay in control of his own treatment, while also learning how to help himself at the same time. WT was becoming more than a therapeutic exercise; it was also becoming a passion—a drug he didn't want to kick.

Ken also responded very well to CBT (one-on-ones) and PE ("deep dives" into specific incidents or feelings). And surprisingly, he found Group Therapy (GT) with other Vietnam Veterans to be most helpful. He was very reluctant at first to talk with other veterans but wasn't certain why he believed it would be uncomfortable or non-productive. Actually, he was quite adamant with Kyle about not being interested in doing so when he suggested it. But after the first few sessions, he quickly came to trust the veterans in his group. Each one of the four men had combat experience; had served in Vietnam; were about his age; lived in Massachusetts or Rhode Island. And, each had been suffering with PTSD for decades—doing so in their own, personal way. They came to trust and accept Ken as one of their own and he reciprocated. While discussions often took them all back to Vietnam from time to time, the vast majority of the time was spent sharing contemporary problems they were facing, including: family, finances, medical and healthcare issues, navigating the VA system, and day-to-day living challenges of all kinds. Mostly, they laughed and cried about things—all things, whatever topic came up. Equally interesting, it was just vet-to-vet, peer-to-peer sessions—no doctors, no clinicians and no professional facilitators involved. Every now and then, Kyle would drop in to say hello. He was always welcomed and trusted. That was a huge breakthrough for Ken. Until that time, he had never sat down with other vets and just talked about things. He always avoided doing so since leaving the army; but no longer.

Cognitive Behavior Therapy (CBT) and Big Time Avoidance

Ken recalled that Kyle was very clear from the beginning that he wanted him to take the leadership role in his own improvement. He must take responsibility and understand he could not just show up, sit back, listen, and then become "fixed." He needed to learn that Kyle was not the source of his healing. Kyle was Ken's facilitator, guide, confidant, and coach—his "clinician." He would guide Ken down the right path, but it was up to him to walk it. At the beginning, Ken often accidently stumbled into good and bad emotional terrain. In his view, the premise of CBT was to help people change bad or maladaptive thinking in ways that lead to positive and productive emotions and behaviors. Helping people like Ken think differently, not only about others but also about themselves is the goal of the clinician. By doing so, individuals develop, not only a more realistic view of who they are, but also experience decreases in emotional stress and self-defeating actions and behaviors. More importantly, they learn to use a personalized method to manage future maladaptive or counterproductive thinking. Talking about his feelings was far more challenging, even impossible at times. When painful feelings were being experienced, Ken always paused, sometimes for a very long time, seemingly to envision or relive the event. Kyle would always acquiesce and give him the time he needed during such moments. Ken would then try to articulate what he was thinking or feeling in response to a targeted question Kyle would ask, such as, "Ken, help me understand what you're saying or thinking; I sense it's something important to you. Can you describe what's going on or how you're feeling right now?"

Ken always tried but was not able to do so most of the time. Sometimes his own responses surprised even himself. In his effort to articulate things, he'd often stumble with words or become overwhelmed with emotion—tears, shortness of breath, reddening of his face. He would also break direct eye contact with Kyle, something Ken usually never did when talking with him. And more often than not, things would not be fully addressed in Kyle's office. When Ken departed, that's when his work really started. He'd rehash his conversation with Kyle over and over and do lots of soul-searching and "self-talk." He'd also jot down insights or questions to bring back to Kyle during the next session, and in this process, his written words and insights would prove to be far more helpful to him than actual dialogue. In short, Ken would take what he heard from Kyle (or what he thought he heard), apply it to an aspect of his life, capture it in writing and think it through even further, and then come back and share his thoughts and feelings with Kyle.

This process seemed to work for well for Ken; Kyle encouraged him to continue doing so. "That's great, Ken. You know, as an author yourself, you seem quite comfortable with writing. In the world of PTSD treatment, writing therapy has proven to be a very effective tool for individuals in enhancing their own understanding of themselves. You know these one-on-one sessions can be hard at times, especially when trying to respond instantly to questions and articulate new thoughts on the spot. Not everyone can do it. For some, they're just not comfortable or not skilled. But it seems to suit you."

Ken understood.

This combined process also allowed Kyle to work his magic in guiding Ken gently into or away from certain topics, depending on the situation. But there was always a deeper issue lurking just below the surface of Ken's mind. As motivated as Ken was becoming, there was also a side of him that was tugging to go in the opposite direction. Before he could "heal himself," he first had to understand and accept healing in a particular area was needed. Sure, in his mind it was still a "character flaw," but just accepting that was something he avoided, at least for moment.

Actually, he was still running from it.

Ken was "avoiding"—a major trait common to most veteran suffering from PTSD. Unfortunately, it was something he did well without realizing it. When it hit Ken that he and Kyle were about to enter a discussion that was uncomfortable for him, he would try to avoid it—not even showing up for a session or finding some excuse, any excuse, to get out of it. Kyle also recognized Ken's behavior as avoidance right away and called him on it. Ken "avoided" conflict, real or perceived, and it was one of the first things Kyle helped him see more clearly. Ken came to the PTSD clinic one day and then broke his appointment even after checking in. He didn't notify anyone he was leaving building 12; he just walked out. So this enabled Kyle to create a great learning opportunity at their next session. "Ken, from your background, avoidance seems to be a major coping behavior you've relied on for some time." But Ken was being "Ken" that day—somewhat resistant. "Not sure about that, Kyle, but tell me—how is 'avoidance' really defined? What is it precisely? I don't recall any avoidance patterns or habits of mine, none at all. Maybe at times, but no consistent patterns I'm aware."

Kyle then provided him with the following brief tutorial on the basics of "avoidance." "Okay, let me explain. We briefly touched on this a while ago, but now it seems to be a good time to go a little deeper. First of all, avoidance is a very common reaction to trauma—whether the trauma originated from a combat experience, a tragic car accident, or a sexual assault—trauma is trauma. Shock is shock—it's a mental, physical and emotional disturbance that disrupts everything. It can be short-term or long-term. It may vary in degree of intensity and is rarely responded to in exactly the same way by any two people. For example, two soldiers, who survive the same battle in the same place against the same enemy at the same time, could likely have different reactions. One guy may shake it off and move on to the next battle without any observable change, while the other guy may react highly emotionally by throwing down his weapon and choosing never fight again. In both cases, their behaviors (observable physical reactions) are quite different, but their inner feelings as well as their beliefs may be the same (disgust, anger, hatred, fear). No telling at that exact moment how they may react or remember things later on as time goes by."

Ken quickly interrupted, "Then wait a minute; maybe I've got it all wrong. I always thought avoidance was a good thing. In Vietnam, we avoided landing in certain areas because it was VC friendly. I take interstate 495 and avoid Interstate 95 in the mornings to avoid traffic jams. I steer away from and avoid certain people at work because they are natural-born assholes and I just don't trust them so I work around them. What's wrong with avoidance and what am I missing?"

Kyle responded quickly because he anticipated Ken's resistance. "Good illustrations and good questions. The difference is the degree of conscious thought that's involved. That is, regarding landing zones, traffic jams, and assholes at work, each comes as a conscious thought done with clear intent. On the other hand, 'emotional avoidance' is most often done subconsciously—not driven by reason, logic, or thoughtful intent. For example, avoidance driven by emotions such as irrational fears, like avoiding elevators, as you told me about yourself is a good illustration. That's a lot different than avoiding a nasty person at work. Avoidance behaviors allow and enable an individual to 'temporarily' escape thinking about or resolving uncomfortable situations associated with negative thoughts and feelings. The key concept is "temporary." Another example . . . you've stated you avoided making contact with other Vietnam veterans since the war? Why? Perhaps because of some negative experiences associated with Vietnam, but not because of an individual soldier . . . it's about something else that's causing negative behaviors. Until you realize what's driving such actions and feeling, your avoidance behavior will continue. You see, everyone brings a unique set of experiences, values, and fears with them to every situation, and when a trauma is added to the mix, anything can result."

This was making a little more sense to Ken, but he remained silent, just listening and thinking it through as Kyle continued, "It's also about the way the mind copes with bad feelings and memories, not just bad events—it avoids and it can interfere with the natural recovery and healing. Normally, once the traumatic event occurs, people come to understand it, and over time it fades in intensity—never totally forgotten; it's just no longer a persistent, debilitating problem. When people don't or can't make sense of it early on, that's when problems usually arise and re-arise, leading to chronic (long term) avoidance or denial. And, it can be buried deep in one's mind for days or decades afterward—usually the longer it's avoided or denied, the more difficult it is to fix."

Kyle went on; he sensed Ken was getting it now because he was listening carefully, obviously reflecting on what he was hearing. "And as we've discussed before—one's actions most often follows one's mind, Ken. It's not just how a person thinks that impacts him, but also what he actually does. The mind finds other things to focus on, more pleasant things, less threatening or less painful things instead of addressing the real issues. As such, avoidance can take the form of emotional avoidance, redirecting one's thoughts and feelings, or behavioral avoidance, physically maneuvering around situations or objects or people to avoid. Some examples—a victim of rape may avoid the act of sex again with anyone just to avoid painful memories that may reoccur associated with the rape; a person in a car accident may avoid driving ever again. Such actions and decisions may be helpful in the short-term, but over time they can become counterproductive, turning into more permanent, deeper problems. This is a lot to swallow I know, so let's bring things a little closer to home—much closer to you, today."

Before he continued, Ken interrupted, "But I've not been avoiding, Kyle, at least not to that extent. Well, I can't see it, that is. So it shouldn't really apply to me, right?"

Kyle responded:

"Not necessarily. Let's look at it from my view. Ken, you've been very open and honest with me, and I respect that about you. You've shared a lot and based on what I've learned about your background, both in the army and in Brooklyn, as well as in your life today, I sense you may have been avoiding lots of things—and have been doing so for some time. I just don't think you recognize it as such. This inability to see it, could be because you just have been too close, for too long or it's been too well hidden and integrated into your normal behaviors and thinking. That's all." Ken then quickly replied, "Umm . . . I just don't think anything impacts me that significantly. But if you think so, please give me an example how this applies to me. That would help me."

Kyle sensed Ken's resistance was steadily increasing. Then Kyle responded, "I could give you an example, but believe me it's much better if you discover it for yourself. I'll help you, though. We only have a few minutes left today, so here's what I'd like you to do at our next session. Try to identify one or two times when you felt like you had been avoiding something in your life (today or anytime in the past in military or civilian life—it doesn't matter which). Then we can use that as a starting point. That's your homework, Okay?"

Ken agreed. Kyle knew he liked "homework"—after session study work that he could do on his own, at his own pace, rather than responding right on the spot.

"This is sort of a search and destroy mission, huh?" Ken said.

"It's more like a search and 'discovery' mission. Hopefully, you will not destroy anything or anyone in the process." Ken laughed, he liked Kyle's humor and directness, but he also hoped Kyle was right about not destroying anything along the way. Usually Ken did a deep dive into any task or assignment Kyle gave him. But at their next session, Ken told Kyle he couldn't identify any avoidance-type behaviors. He just didn't find any.

Kyle didn't expect that from Ken. But knowing him, he also knew for Ken to admit to any shortcoming was consistent with his "character flaw" philosophy and mind-set. Nevertheless, he stayed on the task at hand. "Hmmm . . ." Kyle sensed he now may have to be a little more direct in leading Ken through this part of his work—his search-and-discovery mission on avoidance, that is. He may need more structure in an effort to help him. So Kyle embarked on a series of leading questions to stimulate Ken's thinking along these lines. Helping Ken see things more concretely while minimizing the effect of his disbelief and skepticism was a key first step, before any meaningful avoidance intervention could be applied. So he set off to help stretch Ken's view of himself, of his own world. He was going to reference a story Ken once told to him in a previous session; it may help restart his thinking. "Okay, let me see if I can help further. Think about this, Ken, and tell me what's it like when you are faced with the decision to enter or avoid elevators. Tell me your thought process and how you go about it, Okay? Specifically, what are you feeling, thinking and/or doing when you approach an elevator?"

Ken thought for a while then replied, "Boy, that's a lot to think about. But, okay, I'll try. Here's how I view elevators . . . first of all, I usually decide to take the stairs or wait until there are no other people getting on before entering the elevator. And, then I get in. You see, that's nothing really, no deep dark secret. I'm not hiding or avoiding. It's that straightforward. I just don't like having lots of people too close to me; some people just stink too much, or they push up against me, or they sneeze or fart. I'm uncomfortable with that stuff. That's not 'avoiding' anything; It's just me trying to be comfortable and safe, that's all."

Kyle knew Ken's rationalization was now kicking in. This was going to take some more time and work to help him see things beyond his self-imposed, blinders. Then he responded, "Yeah, I see what you mean, I don't like it either when someone's deodorant fails, especially when there is nowhere to run." They both laughed as Kyle continued. Ken needed more illustrations and Kyle quickly provided them. "Okay, but what about taxies, subways, and those small conference rooms you told me about in BOA. Or, how about crowded airplanes? Can you say the same thing about them? Any avoidance behavior or negative feelings there at all, or just more personal preference perhaps? What do you think?" Ken thought for a while. "Well, yeah. I did say that those were other environments I was uncomfortable in, not just like elevators, but they're different."

"How so?"

Ken thought hard but didn't respond. "Ken, perhaps on the surface they don't seem similar, but what does each one have in common?"

"Nothing . . . as I said . . . each is a totally different . . . a different thing."

"But I sense there may be at least one thing they all share, Ken. That's how you feel and react to them as 'threats,' at least to some degree. In that light could they all be the same?" Ken began thinking even harder as Kyle continued. He had to reverse this approach to help Ken get even closer to this distinction. "Then tell me, what does it feel like when you *don't* have any choice in these environments; you know, when its required to take that elevator, subway, or stay in a cramped airplane on the tarmac in the midst of a snowstorm as you told me happened recently to you? What then? How do you feel during such moments, even if it's not an elevator?" Ken was thinking harder now, but he still couldn't make the connection. He started to tell Kyle something but was having a little difficulty with word choices in his reply. It was apparent emotions were now getting into bed with his logic, and when that happened, articulating thoughts or feelings often blurred for Ken. And that's when Ken's direct eye contact, broke off. Then his emotions started kicking into overdrive without Ken even being aware.

Kyle just observed; he was now listening to Ken with his eyes, not his ears. Ken really wanted to tell Kyle something; he was making a strong effort to do so, but was stumbling. It was as if being trapped in an elevator, tarmacked on an airplane or packed in a stalled subway. Ken's words came out clumsily but his emotions were quite clear to Kyle: "Okay, in each situation, I feel like I'm going to . . . to . . . well . . . well . . . suffocate . . . suffocate to death. It's like the walls are all collapsing like a folding cardboard box around me . . . trapping me . . . taking away my ability to move and breathe . . . all at once . . . it's a super panic heat . . . a disorientation that won't stop moving . . . it's like being on an out-of-control roller coaster and I'm trying to hold on yet there's nothing to grab." Ken's mind was now spinning and Kyle could see he was thinking it through, genuinely trying to convey how he was feeling. But his words were coming more slowly and deliberately. Every consonant, every vowel, every phrase was like listening to Peter Boyle trying to utter his first words as the monster in Mel Brook's 1974 movie *Young Frankenstein*. And, he was finding it more difficult to breathe. Obviously, Ken was finding it harder to get his mind and emotions properly aligned with his lips and tongue. But he continued. Ken tried to describe the feeling of being in a confined space such as an elevator stuck between floors but his words were coming even slower now. Yet, his emotions were immediate and uncontrollable as he continued to envision himself locked inside the inescapable iron box hanging in mid-air by a single thread on the edge of the world. An innocent elevator had been suddenly transformed into an airtight, floating coffin with Ken's monogram stamped on it—that was all he could envision within his mind.

But he kept on trying, "It's . . . it's . . . it's as if every ounce of oxygen . . . every once moisture . . . is being squeezed slowly out of my lungs and body like a sponge forced in a glass of water . . . each exhale I attempt is making a beeline to my nostrils, by-passing my throat . . . it's so hard to inhale . . . to even take a single solid breath requires real conscious effort and every muscle in my body . . . everything else is secondary . . . everything and everyone around me no longer matter . . . they are expendable if I can't get air . . . then I feel compelled to strip every piece of clothing off my body . . . just to give me a little more breathing space—just a little more room would make a difference even if it's just a half inch—the width of clothing . . . and . . . and . . . because there is no escape, no way out . . . I begin scratching at the walls . . . banging on the elevator buttons with my fists not my fingers . . . then my screaming begins, first somewhere deep inside me . . . then I hear myself well before any sound even leaves my mouth . . . but no one else hears me . . . no one . . . it's just me and my screams present in the elevator just getting louder and louder . . . and . . . and . . ."

Ken then suddenly stopped.

There was a long silence. Kyle allowed Ken to stay where he was in his bed of feelings and images. The silence continued without interruption. Ken was still sitting in his chair, perspiring heavily, but Kyle knew Ken was still deep inside that elevator, even deeper in another very dark place of his mind. Then Ken slowly continued, his eyes were still open but focused on something in the distance well beyond Kyle. "And . . . and . . . I feel pity for anyone near me . . . I'm about to tear them apart with my hands . . . just to get them away from me . . . and get me out . . . or give me more space . . . they're in my way . . . they're taking up my precious air . . . my air . . . my air . . . and . . ." Ken was totally exhausted, totally drained. Pellets of sweat the size of quarters formed on his forehead and were now rolling down his face onto his already drenched shirt.

Then he stopped. More silence and more time passed. "Ken . . . Ken." Kyle handed him a tissue but Ken could not see it. More time passed. Ken slowly came back to the reality of Kyle's office. After a few more moments, Kyle softly asked him, "Ken—that must have been hard for you just now. Thank you for helping me to better understand what you feel like when in such places; Tell me if you can, do you know why you're perspiring and why you're out of breath at this moment, even though you were just picturing and thinking about being in such a place, yet not really there at all?"

Ken replied slowly, "I don't know."

"Ken . . . please understand me, if I felt as you do about elevators and those other tight places, I'd likely avoid elevators myself . . . all the time. Actually, I'd run from them faster than a deer from a wolf. I sense there's something that's causing you to feel this way, and it's not necessarily the elevator or plane or subway. Those are just objects that can't cause feelings by themselves. It's something else, something deep inside your mind that is bringing it all out. What do you think it could be?"

"I don't know." Ken responded quickly.

"Yeah . . . it must be difficult to put a finger on anything right now. But try. Could it be something you've experienced in your past? Think hard—go back in time to Vietnam or to your days growing up in the Projects." Kyle knew where he was taking Ken, but he wanted him to make the critical connection himself. Such a breakthrough, self-discovery, had to come from him, not from Kyle.

"I DON'T KNOW . . . I DON'T KNOW, I TELL YOU!" Ken yelled this time.

Despite Kyle's sensitive and supportive approach, Ken was still becoming more and more adamant, more uncomfortable, more frustrated, not with Kyle but with himself. This seemed to be a signal for Kyle to continue, only more slowly and with even more sensitivity than before. Ken wanted to articulate something but just couldn't do so on his own. He needed a little more help but couldn't ask for it, so Kyle gently continued, "Ken, please try again. Something may have happened to you in the past and it may have been something about the time that VC mortar exploded and buried you alive in the bunker in Vietnam? Remember? Didn't you say it took place around Lai Khe or Phu Loi? I'm just not sure."

Kyle thought by getting him closer to something more tangible, like the actual location of the bunker, could help him feel safer in describing what he was feeling about being inside the bunker.

A few more moments went by then Ken began responding a little more quickly than before—still without making direct eye contact with Kyle, "Right . . . right . . . yeah . . . the bunker was a few miles from Lai Khe . . . yeah, that's right . . . can't remember the exact fire support base . . . maybe FSB Marriott or FSB Hilton. No wait . . . Holiday Inn, yeah . . . FSB Holiday Inn. It was bigger than average FSBs . . . it was well-fortified . . . with a couple of well entrenched bunkers."

Kyle continued encouraging Ken, "Good, Ken, can you recall exactly where that bunker was—what it looked like?" He was inching Ken closer and closer to what could be a key memory for him that could help unleash more memories as well as ancient emotions. "Yeah . . . it was a big bunker . . . as wide as some of the bunkers we had on the perimeter of Lai Khe. These were just lower to the ground . . . it seemed out of place too . . . just didn't belong."

Kyle continued encouraging Ken and then sensed it was time to jump him into the event that nearly took his life, "That's good, Ken. Go on. Tell me, after the mortars started to hit, what do you remember? You told me something before about running to a bunker and then hearing a loud explosion . . . then seeing sandbags falling everywhere . . . right, Ken?" He didn't respond. There was longer silence. Ken's eyes were still focused at the floor; actually he was looking through the floor boards of the office, into the earth beneath Plainville's campus, and seeing all the way through the earth to Southeast Asia—to the other side of the world and to the other side of his mind.

Ken was back in Vietnam in a split second. He saw himself pinned solidly to the ground; he couldn't move. He couldn't see; he couldn't yell. He couldn't even breathe. Kyle didn't know where Ken really was, but he had a good guess. "Ken . . . Ken," Kyle asked, but again he didn't respond.

So he gave him even more time. After a few more moments of silence, Ken looked up and reconnected with Kyle, but then immediately his eyes went back to the floor—back to Vietnam. The front of his shirt was more soaked then before. His face was red, his forehead was drenched in perspiration, and his eyes were filled with a burning liquid. Kyle noticed this same physical reactions from Ken each time in the past when he flashbacked to Brooklyn—exactly the same physical reactions.

This was no different.

Kyle also knew Ken's feelings were no different whether he was in an elevator, in a bunker, or hiding behind the furnace in the kitchen in the Projects; it didn't matter—different circumstances, different places, different people, but the same caliber of fear and panic—exactly the same feelings, emotions and physical reactions. After a minute or so of more silence, Ken took out his own handkerchief this time and wiped his face and forehead. He looked around the office to refocus himself. Then he made brief eye contact with Kyle and slowly said, "Whew . . . I haven't been there in a long, long time, I guess, huh?" Ken said this somewhat embarrassed at having just gone around the world without even leaving his chair. He trusted Kyle but always felt a little embarrassed whenever he showed emotion of that kind. He still viewed emoting as a personal weakness versus a natural response—it was still a part of his "character flaw" mindset.

Then Kyle said, "Ken, I may be wrong, but I sense what you were feeling just now, when you were thinking about the bunker in Vietnam, was somehow quite similar to the way you feel in an elevator or other tight places today. Tell me if you can, are those feeling similar to you, too?"

If so, then such an awareness and understanding could represent a major breakthrough for Ken. There was a long pause, a very long pause, as Ken appeared to be doing so deep thinking. Then he looked directly in Kyle's eyes and very deliberately said, "Exactly . . . exactly the same . . . equally intense . . . equally real . . . not just similar . . . exactly the same."

Kyle was glad to hear Ken disclose this. It was key! "Ken, now listen to me very carefully. This is a good thing, really. Even though you may not see it now, it's a major breakthrough of sorts that could help you a lot. There may be an unconscious connection of some kind between elevators and bunkers, as well as with many other traumatic events that you've experienced over the years. Do you think that could be true?"

"Yeah . . . maybe . . . seems so doesn't it," Ken slowly replied.

Kyle then called it a day.

He promised Ken they would continue with this dialogue in their next session, which he moved up to the following week versus at the end of the month. Kyle didn't want too much time to pass without helping Ken work through this experience. Ken was exhausted when he left Kyle's office that day, and when he arrived back the following week, they picked up exactly where they had left off, just as Kyle promised.

"Ken, last week we were making the connection between your current feelings in the elevator and other confined places with your feelings the bunker from decades ago . . . remember? They seemed to be connected in some way, similar, right?"

"Yes . . . very much the same."

"Good, let's continue in that direction, Okay?" Ken then agreed.

"Do you also remember sharing a story with me about growing up in the Projects of Brooklyn, when your brother and mother tortured you in your home? I think it was a saying or rhyme of some kind that your brother said at such moments—'*suffocation no air can't breathe*' or something like that. That's what I'm talking about, remember?"

"Sure, I've never forgotten." Ken said solemnly.

"You described those times very clearly to me as I recall, every detail, what they did, what they said, the living room, the floor, the towels, their laughter and the cigarette smoke. But I don't recall you describing anything about how you felt when all that was happening to you. Can you now?" Kyle sensed he was treading on a very sensitive turf with Ken now, even more so than the elevator or the bunker, but he sensed this opportunity may not present itself again, so he went for it. If he could help Ken see the direct connection between childhood trauma, Vietnam trauma, and current behaviors and feelings, it could be a major step in beginning to help Ken to help himself over the long-term.

Ken didn't answer right away; his mind was back in the Projects. Then he slowly answered Kyle's question using almost the identical words he used when he was confirming the feelings with the elevator and the bunker, "It's exactly the same feelings, no different . . . exactly the same, Kyle."

Kyle noticed Ken was now making the connection on his own. He had seen it, articulated it, and was now feeling it. Long silence . . . then Kyle asked, "Ken, this is an important understanding you're forming right now. I know it must be difficult, and I want you to know I see you're working hard at it, too. You've also got to know that this is all good . . . natural and positive, especially at this time. Do you get this?"

He nodded without saying a word to Kyle. After a little time passed, they discussed his new awareness, how obvious it was becoming to him, but also how good it felt. "Like a bowling ball is being lifted off my chest," Ken said.

He didn't understand it fully yet, but he was becoming more comfortable with it and pleased that he had connected the dots in his mind. Kyle always kept a box of tissues on the table next to the chair along with a jar of wrapped mint chocolates. Ken never ate one before during any of the sessions with Kyle, but he did grab one at this moment. He opened it quickly, and then allowed the warm chocolate melt on his tongue and roll slowly down his throat. Then he took another chocolate and downed it faster than a Doberman on a hot dog. Being diabetic, Ken seldom, if ever, ate such things, but he did that day.

Kyle continued, "As I said, I see you working hard and making progress, Ken. There's just one more thing before we call it a day. This can help to tie together everything we've been discussing. This is also your homework OK, so we don't have to discuss this now . . . just think about what we've been discussing before we get back together again. I'd also like to encourage you to write about it if you get some time . . . just a few words to help capture your thoughts and feelings. Okay?"

Ken was again exhausted and just wanted to leave, but he would follow Kyle's directions and guidance. "OK . . . will do."

"Think about this—since you returned from Vietnam, during any time over the past several decades that is, have you ever had an elevator actually collapsed on you? Has any subway ever actually trapped you inside? Or, has any plane crashed pinning you solidly to the ground? Have any of these things ever actually happened to you, ever? If so, identify it and write about it. If not, write down your thoughts about that too. This is what I would like you to think about over the next few weeks."

Ken was momentarily puzzled by his question, and then he got the implication without needing further explanation from Kyle. Over the next several weeks, Ken found it to be an interesting homework assignment. It didn't take him much time to do, and things became clearer to him as a result. When they got back together several weeks later, he told Kyle what he discovered. It was direct. It was concise. "No . . . such events never happened to me . . . not once!"

Why hadn't he made this connection before?, Ken thought. This was an important moment even though he didn't fully understand all the implications. Now he was beginning to draw his own conclusions about things, and two key understandings stuck out to him like black seeds in a slice of water melon:

1. There was a solid connection between how he felt and reacted to perceived threats in his current life to events from his past even though they were completely different and unrelated.
2. Perceived threats in his life may be exactly that—"perceived" (not real)—happening only in his own mind, not in reality. They hadn't occurred in elevators, in the streets, in buildings, in subways or in airplanes. But they did occur in his mind.

This was a breakthrough for Ken. He had been avoiding such things out of fear even though the fear had only existed in his mind. Understanding this was one thing, but accepting it was another. Equally important, he had to determine what to do about it moving ahead. In subsequent sessions, Ken would come to understand that his tendency to "avoid" had very deep roots. It was more than just a tendency; it had evolved into a persistent habit that rendered only temporary and false comfort. The origins of his PTSD had roots in Vietnam for sure but also in the Projects of Brooklyn. They were well entrenched in his thoughts, feelings, and behaviors and undoubtedly counterproductive to his well-being. Specifically, his feelings of claustrophobia (the irrational feeling of being suffocated) were exactly that—"irrational."

Kyle knew that helping Ken understand these things was one thing. Fixing them was a different story. But, he also knew Ken was beginning to understand this difference. He was starting to "want" to understand more and more. If he could find a way, Ken could help himself cope with these situations. His ability to function and live a more ordinary life, one without needless or excessive worry, would be a good thing for him . . . a great thing. And acquiring a disciplined approach to all this was just around the corner.

Kyle would point the way.

The ABC Model

Ken was now learning how to view and understand things about himself in a different way—a more objective and realistic way. After decades of recalling and reliving events primarily through a set of "emotional" lenses, he had to change. That is, yesterday's emotions (how he felt) and his beliefs (how he thought) significantly influenced how he reacted (avoidance, denial, suspicion). Determining whether past events were accurate or not, or whether they even occurred was not the big challenge. Ken had to dive into a sea of conflicting emotions and beliefs that had been well embedded and reinforced for decades. Identifying, understanding and managing such things were the key competencies he had to develop and ultimately master. If so, many "truths and beliefs" that drove his emotions and behaviors in the past could turn out to be "untrue." He had to start there.

For example, Ken's emotional response to receiving a Dear John from Martha Elaine after only a few months in Vietnam did *not* really occur. That is, she never sent such a letter; it came from his best friend "about her," not "from her." He wouldn't learn the truth about everything that occurred at that time until he returned from Vietnam nine months later. But his emotions (hurt, betrayal, sadness, anger) became so intense that the "lasting revenge" campaign he enacted was focused only on hurting her and her family rather than focused on the truth. His understanding of things (beliefs) and his behaviors (reactions) were impacted and influenced by his feelings (emotions) . . . not by truth.

Ken's perception of the event as well as his beliefs and emotions were totally interrelated, but not based in fact or reality.

Another example: Since returning from Vietnam, Ken believed he was a baby killer, a war monger, a real bad man. That's how he secretly viewed himself because of all the perceptions he felt others had towards him and his brother soldiers. His emotions (shame, guilt) ran deep and had been well hidden since then. When he arrived back in the USA, the public's negative view, attitude, and actions taken toward him and other Vietnam vets only reinforced and strengthened his feelings of self-loathing and shame. Subconsciously, these emotions and beliefs intensified over time, driving his avoidance and disassociation with Vietnam in general and other Vietnam vets as well. Yet the truth, the actual reality of it all, was just the opposite. Ken never killed anyone with his hands or with a gun in Vietnam—not a single VC or an NVA and certainly not any children. As a matter of fact, he couldn't even recall firing his M-16 or 45, not once. Even though his helicopter team's actions, maneuvers, and commands may have directly contributed to the death of many enemy combatants, he had never killed anyone personally. Yet he still believed that he did—he was a killer in his own mind.

Also upon returning to the States, his homecoming in Brooklyn was that of hero, not a villain. He was a Bronze Star recipient who was welcomed home with a celebration, flying banners, and even local press coverage. Yet in his mind, he still viewed himself as a villain hated by some, despised by others. Despite such reality, over the years he still loathed himself for what he thought he had had done, not what he actually did.

To complicate things even more in his mind, Ken simultaneously felt he should have done more, much more in Vietnam. He believed he hadn't done his fair share as his fellow soldiers who found themselves killing every day. Such beliefs generated even more confusing feelings, thus causing him to avoid having anything to do with "them"—he was unworthy in the eyes of his brother soldiers. Again, this was an untruth.

Ken's perception of the event as well as his beliefs and emotions were totally interrelated, but not based in fact or reality.

Another example; Ken's claustrophobic behavior (avoiding elevators, car trunks, closets, subways, taxis) while likely incurred during real-life traumas growing up as a kid in his home (torture, beatings, sexual abuse) and directly aggravated as a young soldier (mortar attacks, aerial missions, buried alive under a bunker), were also based on inaccurate beliefs and perceptions ("all confined spaces will kill and suffocate.")

Such beliefs were then reinforced over decades by his deeply hidden emotions (fear, dread, shame, guilt, and self-loathing). All this directly influenced his ongoing avoidance behaviors of events and people.

His perception of things as well as his beliefs and emotions were interrelated, but not based in fact or reality.

Because of such "thinking," it was imperative for Ken to understand the dynamics among a triad of interrelated, integrated factors—his thoughts and beliefs, his emotions and feelings, his behaviors and actions. Without doing so, Kyle knew it would be difficult for Ken to move ahead in his life effectively, and his future would likely continue to reflect much of his past—filled with fractured and false memories as well as conflicting personal feelings—most of which were not warranted or deserved.

Equally important, he had to learn how to consciously cope and manage in the future. If not, his emotions were destined to continue driving his behavior and negative self-view.

Kyle was committed to helping him reach a state of positive and productive functioning in his daily life. This was his job, his challenge, and his greatest reward. Helping veterans like Ken move ahead in their lives in a better place mentally and emotionally was his calling, and he did it well.

During a late 2011 session, Kyle introduced Ken to a method of approaching and managing his emotions, beliefs, and behaviors. This was designed to help him, not only make better sense of his past, but also to be far better prepared to function on his own in the future. In simple terms, this methodology was called the ABC Model.

This simple three-step approach helped people suffering from PTSD (which was technically an anxiety disorder) and from other illnesses, including depression, bipolar disorder and substance abuse, just to mention a few. The model's primary purpose is designed to help individuals with their ability to change their own thinking, behaviors, and emotions specifically in responses to severe trauma and related experiences. It just so happened to be PTSD in Ken's case. "Ken, professionally speaking, this model is called the rational emotive behavioral technique—REBT. It's focused at addressing psychological disturbance and change."

Kyle noticed Ken's eyes rolling back in his head but he continued, "Don't worry, you're not going to be tested on this, I promise."

"Thank God" Ken said with great relief. They both laughed.

"Simply put, this is merely a simple framework designed to help people view traumatic experiences by first developing a more realistic and accurate understanding of the trauma. It helps strengthen understanding about how one's beliefs influence their feelings and behaviors. The ABC Model provides a step-by-step approach to doing this. And with your passion for writing, transforming your thoughts and feelings into written form, I believe this model is going to be right down your alley—very appropriate for you to use today and well into the future."

"Okay, tell me about it. How does it work?"

Kyle then explained the ABC Model for Ken and provided a clear and simple example: "Look at it in the most simple way—something traumatic happens to a person, we'll call it an *a*ctivating event and label it 'A.' Then, based on that *a*ctivating event, the person forms *b*eliefs in order to make sense of it—we'll label that 'B.' And, based on those *b*eliefs, the person reacts emotionally or behaviorally. We'll label that 'C.' Hence, 'ABC.' In short, a traumatic *a*ctivating event (A) triggers *b*eliefs that are formed in the mind (B), and that leads to emotional or behavioral *c*onsequences (C) that become a part of the person."

Ken was getting it, but needed more clarity, so he asked, "You're saying when something happens (good or bad) to me (A), my mind tries to understand and make sense of it (B)' as a result (consequence) I react in a certain way (C). Is that correct?"

"Yes, perfect, you got it, Ken. All the rest are details, really. Let me give you an example that may help. A woman is walking home alone late at night when she sees a man cross the street and he is quickly approaching her—that's the *a*ctivating event, the 'trigger.' Her mind interprets it as a dangerous threat—*b*elief, so she panics and screams for help, which is the *c*onsequence—emotion and behavior. Hence, you got the 'ABC Model.' Now, let me raise the bar a little on this. However, if the same woman sees the same man approaching (the *a*ctivating event) and when he gets closer she recognizes him as an old friend and therefore is not viewed as a threat (*b*elief). Instead of panicking and screaming (*c*onsequence), she is happy and joyful, could even end up hugging the guy. Again, 'ABC.' You see, Ken, one's belief, attitude, or perspective on things makes a big difference in what people do and how they feel, not only about the event itself, but also about themselves. Does this make sense, Ken?"

Ken was silent, obviously thinking it through even further. Then he asked Kyle, "OK, I think I get it. Since you know a lot about me and my background, can you give me a real-world example that is applicable to me; one that I can relate to, personally. You know, an example that brings this a little closer to my world. That could really help me."

Kyle replied to Ken right away. Actually, he would have been surprised if Ken didn't ask for such an example. "Sure. There are several examples that come to mind, but I'm not going to, not now. But what I am going to do is to help you do it yourself. It will be far more impactful and meaningful if you do it. So I want you to do some homework, some more serious thinking and some of your best writing as well. For example, I want you to view your elevator event as the activating event to start with. Try that and see what happens. Then add as many other activating events as you like; I'd like to see you come back with the ABC Model exercise applied to at least three; entering elevators being one of them, Okay?" With that, Kyle handed Ken a single sheet of paper. It was a template, a fill-in-the-blanks tool.

The "ABC Model" template consisted of three major components (boxes to be filled in with words/thoughts/feelings). The first box was marked "A"—used to describe what actually happened (the triggering activating event). The second box was marked "B"—used to describe what beliefs were held about "A." And, the third box was marked "C"—used for describing the consequences (what was felt about "B"). Also included at the bottom of the template were two key questions designed to help stimulate even further self exploration. "Is it reasonable to tell yourself "B" (in short, are such held beliefs logical), and "What can you tell yourself in the future if or when such things reoccur?"

This was a very simple process for Ken, easy to understand and easy to use, even though it involved many highly complex ideas and concepts at the same time.

Then Kyle continued, "The reason I'm introducing you to this model is to help you develop 'your own approach' to thinking about all this. Look, it comes down to this—*what you believe directly influences your emotions and behaviors.* That is, how you actually respond and react to things is driven by your understanding of things. By being able to objectively assess things and manage your beliefs (your thoughts), you can directly change your reaction—for the better. You see, the more explicit and accurate you are in describing your traumatic events in life and the more open and flexible you are in analyzing your beliefs (how you see and think about things)—the more constructive your emotional responses and behaviors will be. Look at it this way—all three parts represent a piece of the puzzle.

If one piece is missing or not accurate, your reactions may become counter-productive and self-defeating."

Kyle went on, "Over the next few weeks, I want you to consider selecting different events from your entire life—past, present, or future. Fill in the blank areas of the ABCs, and answer the questions below. We can talk about each when we get back together. I suggest starting with some routine things, you know every day kind of concerns or activities in your life, and then expand to more serious concerns. In other words, don't try to tackle the big things first—just try to master the process and the three key components will likely just come to you, naturally."

Ken was clearly following Kyle's explanation and guidance. The ABC Model seemed simple at first glance, but he needed a little more information to absorb it all. "Yeah . . . I think I got it . . . but tell me a little more about how I should start using it . . ." So Kyle continued, "Try this—identify a simple concern you've had for some time—something not as serious as claustrophobia. That will come later. For example, you've shared with me your fear of losing your job and/or being laid off recently. Start with something like that. Apply the ABC Model to that and then move on from there. That way you can get comfortable with the process and concepts before applying it to more complex and important issues."

Ken got it, now. "Well, this may help me get going, Kyle. Let me talk through one example with you. I'll use 'losing my job'; that's a good one since it's still fresh in my mind having just been laid off from BOA and all." Then Ken started slowly walking through the ABC's steps in his mind applying it to "being laid off." He was holding the paper model in front of him, using it as a guide and focusing on each step in the diagram while also talking and thinking aloud to Kyle.

"The A—*a*ctivating activity—describes what's happening/happened . . . OK . . . being laid off from my job. That's the activity, my issue, my stressor. Right?"

"Correct," Kyle replied.

"OK then . . . the B—_b_elief—describes what I think about it, what are my thoughts and perspective of it—my point of view about being laid off, right?"

"Yes, exactly." Kyle sensed he was working hard at getting the concept first. Ken continued, "Alright . . . I view being laid off as . . . a . . . a . . . a . . ." Ken was struggling here. It suddenly was getting more difficult for him to describe what he really thought about it. He hadn't articulated it ever before, but tried to do so on the spot with Kyle: "I feel being laid-off is a . . . an inadequacy, a personal failing on my part . . . a shortcoming of my own making . . . something I caused or should have at least seen coming and thus avoided . . . to me, it's a punishment based on a flaw in my own competence . . . my character."

Kyle gave immediate feedback and insight, "Ken, I sense this is kind of hard for you, and that's very good to recognize, really. Remember, in describing your _b_eliefs—how you view things, it doesn't mean right or wrong or accurate or inaccurate. It's more about being honest with yourself and being as open and objective as you can. That's good enough. Just describe the event without adjectives, feelings, etc. Okay? Try that."

Ken was still struggling a little. Kyle then said, "Let's move on to the 'consequences' for the moment. That is, how you feel about being laid-off. Take a moment and then try to describe your reactions." Ken thought for a while as Kyle watched him trying to connect the dots; he was working through it. Then Ken responded after a few more moments of thinking, "Okay . . . C—_c_onsequences—describe how I feel or what I do based on my _b_eliefs and thoughts about being 'laid-off.' Okay, let's see . . . I feel . . . a . . . a . . . I feel afraid. I also feel guilty for not working harder. I also feel I'm not liked or trusted, and as a result, I feel bitter toward everyone involved in laying me off. I feel betrayed and used. And, now I feel a desperate sense of panic coming over me because I will no longer have money or income for my family. I'm also afraid I won't be able to find another job at my age. And, there's even a side of me that really wants to get even—to punish them. I blame my boss and even go so far as disparaging the company whenever and wherever I can. I'm pissed, really pissed, but mostly I'm afraid . . . mostly."

Kyle allowed Ken a little more time after that lengthy and powerful self-disclosure. He sensed Ken had indeed touched some feelings that he hadn't articulated ever before. He was correct. Ken had never talked about it like that before. "Listen, Ken that was a fine first effort, really. I think you got a good handle on this ABC Model. Remember, we discussed how one's *b*eliefs—how things are understood (the truths, the facts, the logic) directly impact one's feeling and behaviors. So now I want you to try to change how you look at (not feel) being 'laid off.'"

Then Kyle asked a series of questions surrounding his "beliefs" that kept Ken thinking for days. "Tell me, do you think it is reasonable to believe the people you worked with all those years, those you contributed so much to, let you go because they no longer trusted you, or suddenly found out you're really incompetent after all, or that they suddenly just stopped liking you? Is that even reasonable? Or could it have been something else? What's more reasonable or more logical in this case?"

Ken chewed on those questions for a while then shared his thoughts with Kyle: "Well, I think I really was a good employee . . . a good team member . . . always completed my work on time and always helped others . . . never hurt anyone over the years . . . so maybe it really could be something else at play here . . . maybe something else is driving my feelings or how I'm viewing things."

"Like what?"

Ken thought some more. "Maybe . . . it actually was the reason they gave me in the first place. Maybe it was what they said—a major change in the organization was needed and my department, not just me, was no longer needed. The reverse mortgage business environment had changed which meant that BOA also had to change."

Kyle was quick to respond, "So you're saying it could have been a business decision, after all, not a personal decision or an attack on you, right?"

"I guess so . . . yeah, right," Ken replied after more thought. "Good, now try to convey that possibility to me, as a new and different '*b*elief.'"

Ken formulated what he was going to say several times before replying, "OK . . . here goes—I was 'laid off' because of a business decision taken by the company, nothing more, nothing less. It was all about business. I did not cause such a decision . . . I was just in the way . . . my layoff was a 'result' of that decision, not the 'reason' for it."

"That's great, Ken, perfect really. So with that viewpoint—*belief*—do you think it could impact or change your emotional reactions or consequence, in any way, to some degree?"

Ken paused. He really wanted to think this part through. Then it came to him. "Well, I probably would not feel bitter about anyone . . . and certainly not feel I had been personally attacked, that's for sure. And you know, I don't think I would feel so guilty either knowing that it wasn't anything I did to cause it or even anything I could have done to have prevented it for that matter . . . it was something bigger than me and not about me. Yeah . . ."

Kyle didn't respond right away. He was allowing Ken time to realize what he had just said, what he had just done "for himself."

Kyle then responded, "Ken, I think you got the basic process and concepts down pat now. Great effort! Let me suggest you take these additional blank copies of the ABC Model and fill in the blanks applying it to other aspects of your life, too, beyond being laid-off. For example: your childhood, Vietnam, military life, civilian life, work, family, even PTSD. It's really your call where you go with it. But, remember to do "elevators" as a minimum. Okay?"

"Sure . . . will do." The session ended there, and Ken departed Kyle's office and set off to do his "homework" over the next several weeks before their next session.

Ken's ABCs—his "eternal" home work

He was really curious and somewhat excited about trying it out but was a little reluctant. He had come to trust Kyle's guidance and partnership with such things by now and would move ahead. He had originally planned to do only a few examples to just master the process and the ABCs. However, a funny thing happened in the midst of his homework. When he finished his first several examples, one automatically led to another, then another, then another. He found the ABC Model was not only easy to understand and master, but also very practical and even fun in helping him see things more objectively, more accurately, more reasonably. As a matter of fact, Ken did about twenty-five examples for his homework and shared them all with Kyle during their next session.

Ken wrote an illustration of this tool in detail following the model's template. He selected MRI (magnetic resonance imaging), something Ken definitely held a strong opinion about—mostly because of his fear and his claustrophobia. Ken felt there were not enough drugs in the world that could adequately sedate him to enter a MRI tube. This was a very good application for the Model.

A-B-C Model Worksheet	Date: _____ Patient: _____	
"A" Activating Event	**"B"** Belief	**"C"** Consequence
"Something Traumatic Happens" (Triggering)	Thoughts that arise when Activating Event Happens"	Feeling and/or behaviors generated based on Beliefs
"What's going on / what just happened to triggered my thoughts or feelings ..." *"My doctor wants me to get an get an MRI as a result my recent head injury."*	"I think about what just happened or what will happen in the following way ..." *"MRI s are too constricting, not reliable ... it's a coffin ... I'll be stuck inside ... won't be able to breathe or move .. no escape."*	"Because of what I believe and think about what happened, I feel or act like ..." *"I'll suffocate to death ... I'll feel helpless and alone ... vulnerable ... I wont be able to manage my fear*

Is it reasonable to tell myself "B"? Yes ____ No X Why: *MRI's come in many sizes and styles and now medications are available to help to relax and comfort patients.*

What can I tell myself when, if, this happens in the future? *MRI's don't break-down; MRI's have several safety mechanism; MRI are design to heal, not kill; Music and voices humanize the technology and make it a more comfortable experience.*

Over time and with more practice, Ken found this simple ABC Model to be helpful in taking a more disciplined approach. It could not only help in viewing and better understanding past events and beliefs, but also in assessing (and even anticipating) situations and feelings during his current daily life. As a result, his list of "*a*ctivating events," "*b*eliefs," and "*c*onsequences" grew and grew.

When Ken and Kyle reconnected in their next session, he shared about twenty-five illustrations of how he applied the model in his life—past events as well as current activities. Kyle had told him to start with a few simple events and concerns and work from there. So that's what he did. As a matter of fact, he applied the model to so many aspects of his life it evolved into a natural way of thinking for him. Ken had now become very comfortable at consciously thinking, writing, and sharing his problems in this way. Doing so enabled him to think things through more thoroughly, go deeper or wider on issues, uncover hidden and long-forgotten facts, as well as even dissect some feelings that have been a part of him for some time.

Topics ranged from fear of spiders to Dear John letters, fatherhood, elevators, aging, alcohol consumption, lay-offs, and even the US Congress entered his thinking. He felt there wasn't anything he couldn't apply this disciplined approach to and couldn't stop applying it once he got going—sort of a natural assembly line of new thoughts and insights. This reminded him of one of his favorite scenes from the 1950s *I Love Lucy* TV series. It was the scene when Lucy and Ethel were trying to package hundreds of chocolate candies on an automated conveyor belt, one after another, until they became so overwhelmed when they had to keep up with the ever-increasing speed. Like Lucy's chocolate assembly line, uses for the ABC Model just kept coming and coming to Ken.

The following list of just a few "*a*ctivating activities" from many aspects of his life, military, business, and even his childhood, were identified and addressed using the VA's effective "ABC Model."

Ken's ABCs ... (2010 to 2012)

Activating Events ("Triggers")	Beliefs (Thoughts/Attitudes)	Consequences (Feelings/Reactions)
....	....	....
Diabetes	Yesterday ... Result of Careless Habits	Pity & Apathy
	Today .... Manageable Disease	Self-Respect
Alcohol	Yesterday ... Regular Necessity	Sought After Fun
	Today .... Social Use Only	Still Fun but Not Needed
Nightmares	Yesterday ... Ever Present Realties	Fear/Sleeplessness
	Today .... Indifference	More Restful Sleep
Abandoned Relationships	Yesterday ... Not interested in Me	Avoidance
	Today .... Interesting & Positive	Actively Sought
Vietnam	Yesterday ... Worst Life Experiences	Avoidance & Guilt
	Today .... Positive Life Experiences	Pride & Honor
Vietnam Homecoming	Yesterday ... Neg. Public Treatment	Shame & Guilt
	Today .... Positive Public Reception	Pride
Vietnam Vets	Yesterday ... Victims of War	Avoidance & Pity
	Today .... Brothers	Admiration & Sought
Bunker Incident	Yesterday ... Near Death Experience	Fear/Nightmares
	Today .... Test of Personal Resilience	Pride
Dear John's	Yesterday ... A Cowardly, Vengeful Act	Anger
	Today .... A Disparate, Ignorant Act	Sadness
Viet Cong	Yesterday ... Evil and Ruthless	Hatred & Anger
	Today .... Committed Fighters	Respect
US Congress	Yesterday ... Competent, Daring Leaders	Prideful
	Today .... Woefully Inept People	Vote Differently
The VA	Yesterday ... Incompetent & Uncaring	Avoidance
	Today .... Competent & Caring	Proactively Support

Hyper-vigilance

Kyle also helped Ken see how the concept and components of the ABC Model could be a tool in better understanding and addressing hyper-vigilance. There was no doubt that Ken's hyper-vigilance began in Brooklyn, and then greatly aggravated in Vietnam. Never the less, Ken seemed to always be on emotional "high alert." That is, he always found himself looking over his shoulder or behind him, anticipating threats or over-reacting to loud noise or surprise encounters (even in nonthreatening situations). While direct, personal threats to Ken seldom, if ever, materialized in reality once he left Vietnam, his feelings and thoughts about threats were ever present. From the time he arrived in Phu Loi, Vietnam, in March 1968, mortar and rocket attacks were commonplace. And when the First Infantry Division's artillery relocated from Phu Loi to Lai Khe, incoming mortar and rocket attacks increased even more. He learned to always be ready for anything day and night. Lai Khe was considered a "forward base camp," which meant it was in harm's way especially considering there really were no real "front lines" in Vietnam at all—no completely safe areas existed. Ken actually felt safer at times flying missions than when he was sitting on the ground in base camps. He sensed a moving target in the air was much harder to hit than a stationary target on the ground. And besides, while flying he could actually fire back—be on the offense, that is, versus never being able to respond to incoming rounds at base camp. Still he was ever vigilant in both scenarios—in the air and on the ground.

While landing in direct fire zones, his fear of snipers and small arm fire was also ever present. Day-in and day-out thoughts of being attacked became second nature to him; he wasn't alone. All soldiers in combat felt this vulnerability. He was no different. How soldiers reacted to such constant threats was also different for each soldier. However, when they left Vietnam, many soldiers couldn't turn their "radar" off, even though the actual daily threats disappeared. Ken was one of those soldiers. While actual threats seldom, if ever, manifested back in the States, his feelings and thoughts of impending doom and ever-present harm were always present. "I thought it all could have really started in the Projects, in 4139 Martin Court . . . you know . . . in my childhood, not Vietnam . . . I sensed that during my first few days in Vietnam because I already was on 'high alert' in a way, certainly as compared to the other newbies who landed with me. Being on high alert—already "hyper vigilant" . . . was kind of normal me, you know." Ken explained to Kyle.

"Your symptoms of hyper-vigilance likely did start at home in the Projects when you were young boy, well before Vietnam. That's reasonable considering the continual violence you were exposed to there at a young age. You had to be ever ready for anything, anytime even at night, right?"

"Yeah . . . guess so."

"No guessing here, Ken. You were definitely predisposed to hyper-vigilance well before Vietnam. Remember that mental step-by-step process you told me about, you know that process you used whenever you entered a bedroom, an alley, a classroom, even the movie theater . . . you called it your 'survivor scans' or something like that, right?"

Ken was very forthcoming in his response, "Yeah, that's right . . . was my way to get ready for worst-case scenarios. Just seemed to help me better prepare for tough situations, you know, just in case. It was always the surprises that threw me off."

Kyle continued, "Well, that was your way of adapting to threats—real or perceived as a young boy—it was mentally and emotionally draining, and likely counterproductive to you as a kid. The good news was when you went to Vietnam, you already had a built-in defensive and offensive mind-set which meant you likely learned to adapt to combat stress early on while others had to develop it in real time on patrols, on the perimeter duty, in the air, or during incoming rocket attacks."

"Are you saying it was a good thing I was predisposed and hyper vigilant before going to Vietnam?"

"No, I'm not. It's just another reality, however; being accustomed to danger came natural to you as compared to many others young boys arriving in Vietnam."

Kyle went on to explain hyper-vigilance to Ken in more contemporary terms. "Ken, being on constant "high alert" as you described it, is called hyper-vigilance. It's just like being in a constant state of mental tenseness, you know, like landing in a fire zone all the time, a never-ending scanning of the environment for the enemy. It's natural to have a sense of danger to some degree, but when a person becomes preoccupied with doing so, even in non-threatening times or places, it can lead to problems—additional, needless and undue stress."

Kyle continued, "In your case, it was like the way you described feeling during every landing and taking off in the Huey around Lai Khe, remember? That's when you stated always feeling most vulnerable, when your mind and emotions were on high alert, right?"

"Yeah . . . that's when I felt most vulnerable."

Ken discovered one of Kyle's major strengths was being able to simplify highly complex subjects and make it relevant to him and more easily understood. Kyle then went on. "Hyper-vigilance occurs when one the hyper arousal symptoms directly associated with PTSD keeps soldiers seemingly on high emotional and mental alertness concerning their surroundings. It's constant, even when a threat is not even present—that's the real danger, Ken."

"Sounds like I'm kind of . . . paranoid, right?"

Kyle responded quickly to this question, "I can see how you could conclude that but—no. You're NOT paranoid, not at all. Listen, paranoia, while appearing to be similar to hyper-vigilance is different. Paranoia is a mental disorder that can come about because of chemical changes in the brain—it's more of an internal thing. Hyper-vigilance is driven primary as a result of some kind of external trauma such as rape, sexual abuse, car accidents, and combat, of course—all externally driven things. You do not have a mental disorder, Ken, but you have been responding and trying to cope with external traumatic experiences; you've been hyper-vigilant. Get it?"

"Yeah . . . that's a helpful distinction to know; just thought perhaps I was nuts or something for feeling this way."

As Kyle continued explaining hyper-vigilance, Ken couldn't help but recall one of his favorite movies about things such as hyper-arousal, hyper-vigilance, and paranoia. The movie was called *Marathon Man* (1976) starring Dustin Hoffman and Laurence Olivier. It was about an ex-Nazi dentist (Laurence Olivier) on the run from authorities after WWII. He mistakenly engages Dustin Hoffman (an innocent marathoner), captures and tortures him, trying to determine the safety of a location where he can sell some stolen diamonds. "Is it safe?" becomes the key phrase that brands this movie forever. It is the question asked of prisoner Hoffman over and over each time the ex-Nazi's steel dental probe is sunk into a live nerve in Hoffman's teeth. With Ken's newfound knowledge, he could see the ex-Nazi could have been "paranoid" all along while Dustin Hoffman merely had been hyper-vigilant—justifiably so.

Kyle continued his overview of hyper-vigilance, "It really comes down to how you view such external threats—what you think or believe about them. It's about your thoughts, Ken. So perhaps by using the ABC Model, it can help you think about events differently. Remember, we discussed how thoughts drive feelings. And feelings definitely impact behaviors—what you do, that is. So let's use the ABC Model and apply it to hyper-vigilance. Okay?"

"Sure . . . let's do it."

"But let's take a more direct, practical way this time. Instead of you going off and writing the ABCs regarding hyper-vigilance situations, let's take it head-on by just talking—like you did when you first were mastering the model, Okay?"

"Sure."

"Great. I'm going to ask you a series of questions that may help jump-start your thinking about certain hyper-vigilant situations that you're very familiar with. At the end, I think you'll be able to see how your new thinking has impacted your feelings as well as your future behaviors in such situations. So let's begin. This is going to be quick, direct, and impactful, I promise."

With that, Kyle proceeded. "Ken, for decades you've viewed many things as threats, and even today, you still do. So let me ask you some questions that are very close to home for you. Some answers may be more difficult than others, so feel free to take your time; we have plenty. Just answer yes or no to each one for now. Let your feelings lead you. You don't really have to think through every question. Ready?"

"Ready."

Ken then sat back in his chair prepared to go on another journey of self-discovery with Kyle. He wouldn't be disappointed. "Ken, tell me simply 'yes' or 'no' to the following questions. No explanation or reasons are needed at all—just 'yes' or 'no.' Got it?"

"Got it."

"Okay, let's begin." Kyle then embarked on his questioning of Ken. It lasted only a few minutes in reality, but to Ken, it felt like days and weeks.

Q1: "Was 'Mr. Dark', that faceless figure who has been showing-up at night in your dreams for decades now, *ever* actually in your bedroom or hotel room when you abruptly awoke from a nightmare?"

Ken thought about it for some time, and then replied,

A1: "No . . . he was never there. One time when I was really convinced he was in the room, I got on all fours like a Doberman and chased him down two flights of stairs. I really wish he were there that night . . . I would have had a much softer landing at the bottom of stairs with him beneath me to break my fall. But he wasn't."

Kyle responded,

"Okay, I get the picture, but remember—no explanations and no reasons are needed—'yes' or 'no' will suffice."

He then continued with his questions:

Q2: "Has any elevator _ever_ trapped you inside and suffocated you?"

Ken thought about it for some time, and then replied,

A2: "No, not once."

Q3: "Were you _ever_ taken prisoner by the Viet Cong and tortured?"

Ken replied immediately,

A3: "No."

Q4: "Has anyone _ever_ shot at you while in the USA?"

A4: "Nope."

Q5: "Have you _ever_ needed to use your knife in the middle of night?"

Ken thought about it for some time, and then replied,

A5: "No, not once."

Ken was getting the picture and the pattern already. His thoughts were starting to change already. But Kyle continued; he was relentless.

Q6: "Have you _ever_ been mugged walking down the street?"

A6: "No."

Q7: "Have you _ever_ been fired from a job?"

A7: "No."

Q8: "Have you *ever* been trapped below ground in a subway?"

Ken didn't have to think about that at all.

A8: "Nope"

Q9: "Did you *ever* kill another US soldier while you were in Vietnam?"

Ken had to think long and hard about that one . . . then replied,

A9: "No . . . not that I know about . . . hopefully not."

Q10:"Have you *ever* been in an airplane that crashed and burned?"

A10: "No."

Q11:"Has an MRI *ever* blown up, collapsed, or pinned you inside it?"

A11: "Never."

Q12:"Outside of Brooklyn and Vietnam, have you *ever* been attacked?"

Ken thought about it for some time, and then replied,

A12: "No."

Q13:"Have you *ever* been sexually abused?"

A13: This was the only question Ken could not answer 'yes' or 'no.'

After his final question, Kyle remained silent for a while, allowing Ken to think through what had just happened. Then he questioned him a little more. "Okay, good job, Ken. So what can you conclude from this exercise? What did you get out of it? Any surprises?" In the midst of these questions, the pattern became even quite clear to Ken.

Much of his long-term fear, nightmares, claustrophobia, and even his self-image had been based on flawed or inaccurate thoughts (beliefs).

While most of his original triggers (the activating events) were accurate, his own beliefs and emotions formed about them over the years had been based on false assumptions, vague memories, or narrow viewpoints—not facts, evidence, or truth; certainly not total reality.

In short, they never actually occurred in real life as much as in his mind.

Ken then recalled a communication seminar he attended in Massachusetts during the early 1980s. It was held by a communication specialist named Ryan Tostanti. He used a phrase called "stinkin' thinkin" to describe the long-term counterproductive nature that negative thoughts could have on a person's ability to excel—even with intelligent and competent people. Ken had been "stinkin' thinkin" about himself for so long it had become a natural, a normal part of his thought process, without even knowing it.

The bottom-line to Ken was his hyper-vigilance was much more about his thoughts and how he actually viewed threats, than anything else. His hyper-vigilance was being driven by past thoughts and memories that generated endless feelings of suspicion and vulnerability as well as the defensive behaviors of avoidance. Being able to better understand this, he would be able to develop a more disciplined, more "thought-FULL" approach when needed. Doing so wouldn't remove all his fear and defensiveness totally, but it was enough to reduce his suspicions significantly. Therefore, his *beliefs* would also be changing which implied his feelings and behaviors would become much more appropriate to the situation, too.

It was all good.

Kyle also helped guide Ken to more sources of self-study in this area and helped him customize and personalize a simple 5 step process of his own—one he could use when coping with future when hyper-vigilance symptoms and scenarios:

> Step 1: Acknowledge to yourself that a perceived threat may indeed be just that—"perceived" by your mind, "nonexistent." Just entertain the possibility of it not being real.

Step 2: Be mindful of your surroundings . . . stay in the here and now; determine if it's reasonable that such a threat is even possible.

Step 3: Try to relax the body by taking deeper breaths and more oxygen and sitting down and resting, if at all possible.

Step 4: Share your perceptions with others who you trust—a "sanity check" on things—most people respond well to such requests.

Step 5: Take away a lesson. If it was a "perceived" threat, not real, try to learn from it so it's not repeated.

Ken even added this list regarding hyper-vigilance to his list of ABC Model examples.

After one of Ken's peer-to-peer group sessions with other Vietnam vets, he was just leaving building 12. Instead of taking the stairs down to the ground floor, he chose to take the elevator. As he was waiting for it to arrive, a fellow veteran from his group came up and stood next to him also waiting for the elevator. They had been just discussing perceived threats versus real threats and fear in the group that very day. That's when Ken first openly shared his claustrophobic reactions based on being buried alive in a bunker near Lai Khe. This other veteran had shared similar feelings with the group too. However, this marine had been a "tunnel rat," which meant he entered and cleared out VC tunnels and underground passageways during the war—just as Ken had developed claustrophobic and hyper vigilant feelings whenever he found himself in tight spaces. They quickly talked about it while waiting for the elevator and even shared a little nervous laugh as they both then entered the elevator together. During their brief ride down to ground level, they talked about how difficult and ever present claustrophobia had been for them over the years. But they both were determined to beat it. That's why they took the elevator rather than taking the stairs on this day. They had shared and faced their fears together—something neither would have ever considered doing only a few months earlier. Their thinking was changing; therefore, they were feeling more confident and less threatened which in turn changed their behavior. From then on, they both took the elevator together after every peer-to-peer group session.

The Bunker Revisited

Another in-depth application of the ABC Model involved a long-held, deeply hidden feeling about a combat incident in Vietnam. He couldn't recall ever talking about it with anyone in his past, yet it seemed to be ever present in his mind for decades, just lurking somewhere between his hippocampus and neocortex, but never quite nearing his lips. This memory seldom stuck its ugly head out. In 1969, not far from Lai Khe, Ken had been buried alive beneath a collapsed bunker as a result of a VC mortar attack. Even before this incident, he always viewed bunkers as "necessary evils;" he didn't like or trust them very much. He viewed them as strong defensive objects for sure, but he also saw them as dens of scorpions and spiders as well as puddles of ever-harassing, malaria-carrying mosquitoes. As such, bunkers represented a good illustration of an "*activating* activity."

His *b*elief (thoughts, attitudes, and viewpoints) toward bunkers was a *break glass only in time of emergency* kind of thing. Otherwise he had nothing to do with them. Bunkers also made him feel like he was entering a huge sandbag or suffocating coffin (*b*eliefs) and thus had to be avoided (*c*onsequence) at all costs. Just like visits to dentists, bunkers were to be avoided. Yet, he did survive this bunker incident in 1969. Whenever his deeply buried emotions or fear arose regarding bunkers, he'd immediately close it off—he'd avoid it. However, once he started applying and understanding the ABC Model way of thinking, his emotional response and behaviors changed. Specifically, while the detailed description of the "*a*ctivating activity" (being buried in a bunker) remained the same, his *b*elief and his *c*onsequence changed, as follows:

Ken's thoughts, attitude, and viewpoint toward bunkers changed from that of a suffocating, poisonous insect-ridden, bad thing (*b*elief) to a necessary, protective and good thing. He realized that if that bunker wall hadn't collapsed on him when it did, it was highly likely Ken would have been hit directly by flying shrapnel off the exploding mortar. He would have been killed. He never viewed it that way before. His emotions were always leading the way, not his thoughts. In cold reality, the bunker likely had saved his life—not tried to take his life.

With such new thoughts and a refreshed point of view, Ken's feelings of fear and avoidance began dissipating—decreasing substantially to the degree of a benign presence rather than overwhelming terror. And that was good enough for him. In short, whenever his mind revisited that event by seeing bunkers in a movie, whenever bunkers were referenced or discussed by other vets during group sessions or whenever he came into contact with similar "tight spots," Ken was no longer emotionally paralyzed or intimidated as in the past. Far more important to him, his use of the ABC Model was applied to all things potentially suffocating in nature within his daily life (e.g., elevators, closets, car trunks, subways). The model had become a viable tool, a self-imposed, disciplined process he could use anytime. Whenever confronted with such potentially threatening activities, he could now allow his thoughts and logic ("Is it reasonable for me to think this way . . .") help lead his emotions and behaviors.

Transference of such a mental discipline (ABCs) regarding past experiences and counterproductive feelings of today had now become a current practice positively influencing his daily functioning. This was one of the ideal outcomes of PTSD treatment as Ken understood it. And he used it. There didn't seem to be any area in Ken's current life or his past where the use of his ABC Model couldn't be applied. Each time he used it, his understanding of the process was reinforced. He'd even used it to help think things through while working out and jogging, preferring it over listening to music on his MP3 player as he sweated. He was hooked.

Ancient Writings / Modern Perspectives

As time went on with Kyle, he moved from just casually jotting things down using the ABC Model to writing complete sentences, paragraphs, pages, and chapters "about himself." The more he wrote and shared with Kyle, the better he was able to convey feelings and facts more clearly. It was through this new passion for thinking, writing, discussion, and study that his confidence in applying lessons from PTSD strengthened. As more ABC discussions unfolded, the more confident he became. As a result, instead of just waiting and responding to Kyle's questions in sessions, Ken began to proactively introduce the issues and topics from his past experiences. In short, he was taking more and more control of his own healing and learning—his understanding of himself was blossoming from within, not from external sources. This was good. Then one day, he casually shared with Kyle something he had written nearly twenty-five years earlier, around 1990—truly ancient writing in Ken's mind. He had forgotten all about it until recently. The story was about a boy and his experiences growing up in a hostile domestic environment of poverty and violence. As he could recall, Ken had written it in third-person format. Yet he didn't remember exactly why he felt compelled to start writing about such a thing at the age of forty, but he had. Once he started thinking about it more and more, Ken sensed it had a very familiar feel to the work he and Kyle were doing.

Then it clicked.

Perhaps the story wasn't about a fictitious boy at all; maybe it was about himself—his own childhood. Perhaps because he wrote it in a third-person format, versus first-person memoire style, he never made the connection that it could actually have been a personal, true story about himself. "Kyle . . . I'm not sure if I can even find it now; been so long ago. And besides I think it was even written on an old DEC-Mate II system, one of Digital's first PCs back in the 1980s; used it more as a word processor than a computer, but it worked well for me."

Kyle sensed Ken was coming up with every reason "not" to locate it (to once again, "avoid"). Even so, he was truly intrigued and suggested Ken try hard to locate it and recover its contents. "Ken, seems like your excuses for *not* finding it outweigh your reasons for finding it. Well, perhaps there's a little déjà-avoidance going on here. What do you think?"

They both grinned. Ken was somewhat embarrassed but he was also enlightened by Kyle's insight. "Yeah, good observation. I guess I'm still learning how to recognize it when I'm doing that. It's something I've got to do a better job at. Thanks for the reminder." Ken replied.

"Seriously, your past writing may be worth checking out, Ken. Sounds like it could be very relevant to our discussions, especially surrounding your early years." So Ken took Kyle's advice and over the next several days he scavenged through tons of boxes and filing cabinets at his house. On his hunt, he was amazed at how many old discarded computers he still had lying around, including Digital, Hewlett-Packard, Micron, IBM, and a Dell. He tore his attic and basement apart determined to find those specific files. Angel Dawn always became panicky when Ken went on a search-and-destroy mission to find anything in the home. This particular quest was no exception. She was just hoping nothing important would be broken or damaged on his quest.

It took Ken a couple of days to locate it, but he did. It also took about a dozen Advil to keep Angel Dawn as pain free as possible along the way while Hurricane Ken came rushing through and eventually came to a peaceful end. She and the house survived another Ken quest. Of course, the wake he left behind was another story. He eventually found what he had been seeking—two five-and-a-quarter inch floppy disks (the kind he sometimes used as Frisbees in the 1980s). They were "huge" disks—the size of archery targets in his mind as compared to the tiny thumb-size storage devices of today. Both floppies had been well buried under inches of dust, three-ring binders, boxes, and piles of paper within his seldom-touched roll-top desk located in the far corner of their basement. As usual, the disks were buried in the very last place he had looked. Since he couldn't extract the information from such an outdated technology, he hired a company in Hudson, Massachusetts called Advanced Recovery Technologies, Inc. They were very familiar with old Digital systems and technologies and were not only able to recover the data, but they also converted it to Microsoft Word format. It only took them a day or two, but they did it. Advanced charged him about $150. And when Ken finally reviewed his twenty-five-year-old writing, he felt they could have charged $500 and he would still have felt it was worth every penny.

As Ken began reading it, he immediately became overwhelmed. Stunned would be more accurate. It pulled together so many pieces he had been struggling with throughout so many PTSD sessions with Kyle and his peer-to-peer group of Vietnam vets. So many activities, events, ancient feelings, disturbing personalities about his upbringing in the Projects came screaming off the pages. The fictitious story about a boy growing up in a rough way was not so much of a fiction after all. Specifically, one part of the story was about this boy coming home from school on a cold afternoon in February and was sexually abused by his mother and her boyfriend. Ken read it and reread it. Then he brought it to Kyle, who also read it over time. Together, they used his "ancient writings" to identify and discuss many current, relevant issues. Angel Dawn also became involved in helping pull things together. Ken even shared parts of it with his PTSD group of vets, who were always responsive and supportive.

Kyle now guided Ken, "I think it would make sense for you to use the ABC Model to develop a more accurate understanding of this whole thing, Ken. It may not be applicable to everything you wrote, but it may be useful when focusing on some key events; then we can discuss it in that context, Okay?"

And, Ken did just that.

CHAPTER 9

PTSD — Order out of Disorder
(Massachusetts, 2012)

FROM 2010 THROUGH 2012, KEN participated in nearly one hundred formal PTSD treatment sessions conducted primarily by the VA's PTSD clinic professionals in Plainville, Massachusetts. At first, he participated reluctantly, but as Ken learned how to assume more and more personal responsibility in helping himself, he began participating eagerly and proactively. Each session was highly personalized and dynamic—ranging from one to three hours in length and involved PTSD clinicians, PTSD medical doctors, PTSD case examiners, and VFW representatives, as well as other Vietnam veterans within peer-to-peer group settings. With access to all these fine support resources, Ken felt his greatest progress occurred "after" and "beyond" these official PTSD activities. Early on, Kyle had told him this may be the case, "Ken, you should expect that most of your real progress, your major breakthroughs, that is, will likely occur after you leave your sessions. Actually, your mind will be actively engaged during the sessions but when you leave your intellect and emotions will kick-in; you'll be working things out continually no matter where you are."

As usual, Kyle was correct.

Ken's "post" session efforts (efforts made outside the safety of the clinic) included the following activities—self-reflection, journaling and writing exercises, self-study and research of professional web sites, book and article reviews (even film reviews), participation in public PTSD charitable events, direct interaction with other veterans (from all wars, not just Vietnam), and direct disclosure and queries with friends and relatives. The ultimate outcome for Ken was to enter the next chapters of his life without suffering from needless emotional stress caused primarily by counterproductive beliefs, emotions and behaviors from his past. He had successfully avoided addressing this over the years by allowing his work to occupy the vast amount of his attention, and since he was very successful, professionally and financially, he was able to continually avoid helping himself grow emotionally and socially.

Ken's professional success was also his greatest personal liability.

It would take his current level effort to achieve such a worthy goal; everything he was now doing in the PTSD program was focused at obtaining the following result:

> "*Managing his emotions, beliefs, and behaviors in a more disciplined way that enhances day-to-day functioning and overall quality of his life - to live without unwarranted fear and anxiety. In short, to allow himself to be happy.*"

The Breakthrough—a long, long night

In 2012, the key activating activity involved a boy, his mother, an older brother, a strange man and sexual abuse that took place on a cold afternoon in February 1961. The boy was in the seventh grade; he was about the age of twelve. The more Ken reread and discussed this "fictional" story of that boy he had written about nearly twenty years earlier, the more things became clear. And, using the ABC Model's framework everything was becoming clearer at lightning speed.

However, the clearer things became, the more things also changed. The most important change being the boy in question on this cold afternoon in February 1961, just happened to be . . . Ken Callahan. The fictional life he originally had written about was quickly morphing into a stark "non-fiction"—the secret life that Ken had been living with for decades without knowing.

Ken and the boy were the same person.

Many aspects of this story were absolutely true; others were totally inaccurate. Ken's emotions had held a strong grasp on his Brooklyn memories for quite some time, yet the more he re-read and re-discussed it with Kyle and Angel Dawn, the more quickly he was able to separate emotion from the fact. He was then able to re-write it, not just on paper, but also in his soul. And, he couldn't stop.

Doing so became a double-edged sword for Ken. On one hand, he was beginning to see things much more clearly. On the other hand, each time he had a breakthrough (a new understanding), he also became more emotional and uncomfortable with himself (consequence). During a couple sessions with Kyle, Ken's feelings became so intense discussing this specific late afternoon activity in his mother's bedroom, he lost control of his breathing, began crying uncontrollably, and even became temporarily disoriented. Fortunately, Kyle was with him all the way, which was comforting and reassuring. But then Ken avoided bringing it up with Kyle for some time and for some reason (consequence). Kyle wouldn't push it either, knowing Ken would revisit the subject when he was ready. Even so, he continued his re-writing efforts whenever or where ever he could—at home, on airplanes, at his office, during business meetings, on conference calls, in the evenings, over weekends, and even while in his car with the aid of his Sprint voice recorder capturing flashes of insight at the moment later to be transformed into text.

Yet, something critical was still very uncomfortable and unresolved in his mind. He couldn't identify it specifically, but he could feel it tugging on his mind. So many feelings and memories now seemed to be constantly resurfacing after decades of occupying the darkest places of his memory. The fog of the past was starting to fade each time he'd write or discuss things. Simultaneously, many of his long held beliefs, seemingly held together only by fractured emotions, were now shattering faster than window glass in a high-speed car crash.

His use of the ABC Model, that Kyle had so carefully ingrained in him over months, was now a fun and natural way of thinking. Ken's understandings (beliefs) were changing, which would inevitably impact his feelings and behaviors (*c*onsequences). The ABC Model had not only become a sound working framework, but also served as a common language between Kyle and him. Ken was getting close to something, a breakthrough of mega-proportion regarding that late afternoon in the Projects; but something kept eluding him, and it was driving him crazy—like the proverbial itch that always finds that one spot on a person's back where it can't be scratched.

Then, one night well after Ken and Angel Dawn had gone to bed, he awoke startled; he sat up in the darkness of their bedroom and yelled out a single word that never wanted to end. Actually, it sounded closer to a deep breathless howl—a non-human noise, rather than a recognizable word,

"Aaaahhhhhhhhiiiioouuugggg!"

It was a loud, very startling resonance that took all the air out of his lungs in a second. He swung his body to the right side of the bed and just sat there, his feet touching the carpeted floor. He was staring straight at the bedroom wall, seeing nothing except everything that was rushing through his mind. His hands were held up near his head, seemingly suspended in midair by some unseen tether hanging from the ceiling; he was like a puppet being controlled by a hidden marionette.

Angel Dawn awoke immediately. She was around the bed and upon him in seconds. "What is it, what's happening . . . you OK? Wake up, wake up!" Angel Dawn said as softly as possible but assertively. She could hear and feel him breathing heavily, more rapidly than she had ever seen him do even when he was exercising. She did not touch him, afraid to startle him even more. Rather, she just sat next to him.

After a few moments, she hugged him tightly with just one arm. They both were now facing the side wall of their bedroom. After a little more time passed, she then asked, "Honey . . . did you just have a Ned Racine moment or what? You scared me to death. What's up . . . talk to me." But Ken still didn't reply. His body was right next to her, but his mind was somewhere on a distant planet, in another time.

A Ned Racine moment was an epiphany—an out-of-the-blue surprise, an "aha" of mega importance. It was like finding the final key piece of a jigsaw puzzle needed to complete a whole picture. Just between Ken and Angel Dawn and their close friend Jonathon O' Donald, the phrase, a Ned Racine moment, had become a personal reference to a specific scene from one of their favorite movies—*Body Heat*, the 1981 sultry drama starring William Hurt and Kathleen Turner. In the final scene of this great movie, an imprisoned Ned Racine (William Hurt) is suddenly wakened by a startling awareness that dragged him to the realization of an elusive truth. His lover, Kathleen Turner, was not dead after all. He had been duped, big time, and she was on a Pacific island beach sipping Rum Punch for the rest of her life in luxury, while he remained imprisoned for a murder she orchestrated. But on this night, Ken didn't have an ordinary "Ned Racine" moment, no "aha." Rather, it was six epiphanies of awareness exploding in his mind at once. He responded to Angel Dawn after a few more minutes had passed, "Yea, you can say that . . . a Ned Racine moment for sure, more like several at once."

"What was it, what was it?" she asked, trying to get him more awake so the moment wouldn't be lost forever as dreams and other fleeting thoughts often do in the middle of the night. But he went silent again; then after a while, he said very slowly and deliberately, "It was Butch . . . it was Butch . . . the Butcher-Bird . . . it was Butch." That's all he kept repeating over and over again.

Angel Dawn didn't get it; she didn't understand. She knew of Butch, his brother, even met him once, but she was unclear about the context. "Butch . . . okay . . . it was Butch . . . what about him?" After more silence, Ken then replied more slowly and more deliberately—each word now coming out of Ken's mouth and mind were separate and distinct like a young boy reading a book for the first time, "I . . . I wasn't in the bedroom . . . I wasn't under the pillowcase . . . It wasn't me being raped by her and that man. It wasn't me . . . It wasn't me . . . IT WAS BUTCH."

Then a much longer silence followed as Angel Dawn remained motionless and stunned. She didn't know what to say. So she said nothing.

"Aha" Moment #1 (the first of the six "aha's," "oh boy's," "oh no's," or "oh shit's"). Ken now knew everything that had happened that late afternoon in 1961 was real; it did happen; it wasn't just a dream, nightmare, or his imagination. Everything took place, really took place. He just had some facts mixed-up all this time. The key mix-up was—it was Butch who was on the bed with his head deeply buried inside a pillowcase, not Little Ken. Butch had been the object of their mother's "abusive affection" all along, not him.

And, he told this to Angel Dawn. It was just the first of long series of Ned Racine's to follow on this long, long night. "What?" Angel Dawn was shocked. After all this time, how did this awareness come about? Why now? What caused this new insight? She was struggling at what she just heard her husband say because she thought she knew this story well. "Honey . . . what makes you think this? Tell me more?"

It took some time to pull all the pieces together, but Ken was finally able to convey his new awareness, the "reality of it all" versus his ancient beliefs and fractured emotions. He had been using Kyle's ABC Model to revisit this specific childhood experience many times over the past several weeks, and he was also bouncing it off her at times, too. Angel Dawn, being a clinical psychotherapist herself, easily followed his explanation as he consistently referenced the three components of the model while doing so. "Dawn . . . the *activating* activity—the bedroom event on that day . . . was real. It did occur just as I had known all these years. Sexual abuse did in fact happen on that afternoon at 4139 Martin Court and likely other times as well. I've seen it in my mind for decades . . . every detail, every smell, every sound, every action, and every word . . . I remember Mr. Penn's Buddy Holly glasses and how he always rubbed his eyes without taking off the glasses . . . I remember the lazy pattern of drifting cigarette smoke throughout the bedroom . . . I remember my mother stepping over Mr. Penn's collapsed body on the floor as well as her facial expressions throughout it all . . . I remember the picture of Elvis Presley on the wall and the country music playing in the background . . . I remember the smell of stale whiskey . . . I remember the fish-ashtray brimming over with butts, and so many things. But mostly I remember . . . the pillowcase . . . that pillowcase, and . . . and . . . and . . . her lingering stare at the crack between the bedroom door as she was straddling the body within the pillowcase on the bed. I know it all happened. I was there. I saw it all. Those were not dreams, not nightmares—it all was real."

Angel Dawn was trying to follow him, but it was getting harder now. "Okay, all those explicit memories are real events, but what was it about Butch? Where does he come into this . . . help me. That's the part I'm missing. Go on, honey."

Ken thought some more and then slowly continued, "The pillowcase . . . it was the pillowcase . . . that was the key to everything. That's what clicked, that was the single piece of the puzzle in my mind for so long I couldn't figure out . . . you know, that itch I had in my mind for weeks now but couldn't scratch . . . . it was all about the pillowcase . . . it was the pillowcase."

Angel Dawn quickly responded, "Honey . . . Okay . . . the pillowcase . . . I got it . . . what about it?"

Longer silence, then Ken continued. He was now lying down on the bed once again. Angel Dawn had moved back to her side and was lying close to him. They both were wide awake just listening, questioning and talking. The lights in the bedroom were still off; they were staring into the dark looking up toward the ceiling with their eyes wide open.

"The pillowcase . . . that was the key to everything." Ken said once again.

"What do you mean, key to what? You always told me your mother placed a pillowcase over your head and pulled back the top edge so you could breathe during those times, right? I remember that."

Longer pause, then Ken said, "That's what I always thought . . . but . . . but . . . but . . . . it wasn't me in the pillowcase . . . because I was not in the bed nor was I in the bedroom at all. It was Butch! It was Butch! And, I never had sex with my mother that day."

Ken slowly continued, "I had watched her having sex many times in different parts of the house in many of our apartments over the years, including the pillowcase time in the Projects. Each time it happened,

I was also always hiding, watching from afar, but I never actually participated."

"What? What?" Angel Dawn was very surprised to hear this, even confused. She had read his writings many times and heard this exact story on occasions the past several months, but this was a major change from his long held version. "Ken, tell me more . . . keep describing things. Why do you feel this? What triggered this new thinking? Go on. Don't stop."

Long silence again.

Then Ken was finally able to convey more clearly what he had come to realize—what it was that shocked him out of sleep that night. It was lengthy, detail description that unfolded as Angel Dawn listened in amazement. "Dawn, it was the pillowcase . . . the pillowcase that held the key to everything. After revisiting this event and discussing it with Kyle and you as well as using the ABC Model so many times analyzing it, things finally came together in my sleep tonight. You see, it would have been <u>impossible</u> for me (or anyone, really) to have seen all those little details, all those specific actions, all those quick gestures and movements, all those looks and glances, including: Mr. Penn's sweating and how he always was rubbing his eyes underneath his glasses . . . the late afternoon gray stream of light in the room . . . the lingering path of cigarette smoke . . . everything. It would be impossible for me to see all this "*if*" <u>my head was inside that pillowcase.</u> How? How could I see such details if my eyes were constantly covered?"

Ken paused, then continued, "Dawn, it was the pillowcase that kept haunting me all these years; The pillowcase was not a frightening reminder or ceaseless haunting memory from which I couldn't escape no matter how far from Brooklyn I ran; rather, it was a "clue"—the missing piece of the puzzle that my mind kept secretly seeking in order to discover the truth about what happened so long ago. Don't you see . . . the pillowcase was a "key," not a crucible; it was a good thing, not a bad thing. It's the pillowcase that was trying to set my soul free all along, not drag it to hell."

There was a longer silence now. Even Angel Dawn's questions stopped. She too, had to admit to herself this change had to be thought through. It was more than a curious notion; it was a practical possibility worthy of further consideration, reason and logic. She then encouraged her husband to continue.

"Dawn, all this time I believed it was me inside that room, buried deep within that pillowcase; but I wasn't. All this time, I thought I was there 'doing my part,' 'obeying my mother,' 'being the good son,' . . . you know—my *be*liefs; but it wasn't me. She responded quickly as she saw a flaw in this thinking, "Okay Ken, let's say you were not INSIDE the pillowcase, nor even inside the room, then how did you see all these little details and actions going on there?"

Ken responded right away: "Because . . . I was there alright . . . only on the sidelines all along, not in the bed. I was watching . . . watching it all from the crack between the door and the wall that she always left ajar—on purpose. That's how."

"Aha" Moment #2: Ken had been witnessing everything from a safe distance of sorts just outside the bedroom, not inside it. He did not actually participate.

"Go on." Angel Dawn said.

"Honey, I was there alright . . . but in the hallway on my knees like a mouse hiding in a corner, watching as it all took place. I was staring through the crack between the door and the wall. She always left the bedroom door opened just a little, remember? I just never knew why until now. But now I do—*it was for me* . . . to watch her and see everything. She must have known I was there watching, even though I thought she couldn't see me. I sense this was her way of showing affection for me. She made eye contact with me all the way across that room, every time she had sex, not just this time when Butch was being pillowcased, but every time that I snuck up to watch her with other men. It was many times. She knew; she had always known even though I believed she didn't know I was watching."

Angel Dawn was very silent now as Ken continued slowly talking in the dark with her by his side. They were still facing the ceiling together as many strange images, wild thoughts, and crazy feelings kept bouncing around her mind.

"Aha" Moment #3: Ken's mother had known he was watching her every time she had sex; she enabled it; she made it happened; she enjoyed it.

Ken's words were coming slower but more deliberately now as he continued. Before the night was over, he'd have a few more "Ned Racine moments" to share with Angel Dawn.

He continued, "And I don't know how to say this, but . . . there was side of me that . . . that . . . enjoyed it. I mean . . . I liked it . . . I liked watching her . . . it was fun for me . . . not scary at all. The weirdest thing was my fear of the pillowcase (dread of being smothered) was not as overwhelming as my fear of getting caught by her. Yet, overall I wasn't afraid."

It was getting more difficult for him to talk about this specific "aha." Feelings of shame, guilt, and personal embarrassment were steadily mounting and that's when his words became entwined with tears. But he tried to continue anyway; he had to continue it with as much clarity that he could. Ken sensed this moment may never present itself again. He wanted, needed, Angel Dawn to hear it all. "I wished it was me . . . me . . . in the pillowcase . . . instead of Butch. I would have hated putting my head inside it, but I would have been closer to her. It *should* have been me . . . I was the good son . . . not him." Now, it wasn't hate, fear, or anger that Ken was feeling. He came right out and said what he was really feeling, for the first time, ever. "Oh God . . . I was jealous . . . I was envious . . . I was not mad or angry or even frightened of Butch, not really. I was *jealous*. Butch had been getting all her attention . . . he was being touched by her . . . her affection was being given to him, not me . . . and all the time she knew I was watching. I had wanted to be with my mother too, even though I didn't even know what that really meant at that age, but she never wanted me. This was a special kind of torture that she was doing to me, to my young body and to an even younger mind . . . these were new and exciting feelings, I sensed it was wrong, but I still liked and wanted it . . . all along my mother was allowing it . . . even enabling and empowering me to watch it. That's why she always left the door cracked open—that's when she had both her sons, and/or her boyfriends under her spell . . . *at the same time.*"

"Aha" Moment #4: Ken hadn't hated his brother after all those years of torture and torment; rather, he had been envious of him all along. While he feared Butcher-Bird's tortuous ways that were lavished on him outside of her bedroom, Ken's jealousy of his brother out weighted his hatred.

Hearing all this, Angel Dawn was now deep in thought trying to truly understand what her husband discovered about himself. She understood the Oedipus complex very well, having studied it as a part of her masters' work in clinical psychotherapy. She also knew it to be a natural stage in the psychosexual development of most boys—the desire to sexually possess one's own mother. Yet, to hear it conveyed in this context by her own husband was somewhat shocking, just not at all surprising, especially knowing what kind of woman Hilda was. And being so close to Ken, she also knew how difficult this was for him to accept, no less to openly convey to it anyone, even to her.

So she tried to help him through these tough moments; she held him even tighter and talked to him. "Honey, I understand, really. It's a hard thing to envision, even harder thing to accept. But in many ways having such sexual feelings about one's mother is natural especially during your youth. It's especially challenging for you considering the abusive home environment and life style you were forced to endure as a kid as well as considering your mother was really a very, very sick woman. It really wasn't your fault, Ken. You must accept that fact. You were a young boy; you weren't responsible for your emotions or your behaviors."

"Aha" Moment #5: Ken liked it; he never really feared the pillowcase or her bedroom after all. Actually, he secretly desired it; he never ran from it; he actively sought it out. And, he had coveted his mother's attention; he hadn't feared that either.

Even when she beat him with her extension cord throughout the years, at least that was some kind of attention—physical contact. And there was also a side of him that sensed he misbehaved at times just to get her attention, even if it meant more beatings. In reality, "Little Ken" had never participated in "high times" with his mother; he had only watched and witnessed things. He had desired his mother; he wanted to possess her, and he wanted her to possess him. And all along, she had been preparing him, likely in the same manner she had done with Butch as well as his oldest brother, Walter, before he ran away from home.

Ken continued, "She'd been grooming me. I believe my time was coming soon, just as I was old enough, I guess . . . just like Butch when he too reached the right age."

Angel Dawn had never considered that dynamic. Ken continued, "I guess that's why Butcher-Bird bolted when he did, just like Walter—he just had enough. I don't really know why Walter left because I was just too young to know what was going, but he bolted around the same age as Butcher-Bird did when he turned seventeen. I knew she physically beat and abused Walter with our frying pan—the same one I used to make 'naked-pancakes' with. I just don't recall ever seeing him and her in a pillowcase situation or in 'high times.' And even if I did, I likely wouldn't have understood it back then."

Ken was tiring now, but tried to go on, "Dawn, I sense my turn was coming . . . I was next! And on that cold afternoon in February when I got home from school, when she was upstairs with Mr. Penn and didn't let me in for a long time and I nearly froze to death . . . that day, I think was to be *my* first 'high times' day."

"Aha" Moment #6: Ken felt he was being prepped—emotionally groomed all along. He sensed it was a part of his mother's ongoing secret plot to control and manipulate; the two things she seemed to need the most.

Ken continued talking with Angel Dawn as the darkness in their bedroom began slowly transforming into early morning light. They now had been awake together for hours. She eventually concluded the older Ken got and the farther he was distanced from his mother and memories from the Projects, many of his unresolved conflicting emotions transformed into permanent feelings of guilt and low self-esteem. While Ken had briefly discussed these times with her, he had never really conveyed his feelings. She knew what he was now doing with Kyle and the PTSD team in Plainville was a healthy thing for him, even decades after all the traumas took place. Her personal and professional understanding of her husband was also strengthening. She now had a better grasp on why Ken had such conflicting views of women at times, why his previous marriages (and almost their own) didn't work out, why his sleep had always been troubled, why he kept his family and personal relations at a distance and why he never sought to have kids of his own.

While lying in bed with Ken that night, Angel Dawn was engulfed in a sea of mixed emotions about his mother, Hilda, even more so now than when she first met her in the late 1980s. Her feelings ranged from anger, disgust and pity to sadness. She was now seeing Hilda M. Callahan much more clearly than ever before. What she had done to Ken, Butch, Walter, and her daughter, Sandy, over the years was now coming to light in a much bigger, horrid picture. It was an image of needless and endless torment, ever-present suspicion, ongoing personal insecurity, betrayal, and manipulation "for everyone." Hilda's behaviors and values had not just adversely impacted the "Callahan kids," but it also affected everyone each of her kids touched throughout their lives—wives, husbands, children, friends, relatives, and even colleagues. This stark realization struck her mind like a sledgehammer smashing on an anvil. It was so foreign and bizarre compared to her own upbringing. She had a difficult time even visualizing it all, let alone understanding and accepting it. Even her professional training was limited when it came to applying it to someone so personally close.

She and Ken were now silent, lying in sweat-soaked sheets. After twenty-five years of marriage, she believed she had come to know her husband very well. But she really hadn't, not until this night. She loved him now more than ever before. They just held each other close, then eventually fell asleep, totally exhausted.

The next day crawled by.

As Ken and Angel Dawn were having a late lunch together on their patio, she asked him to once again describe that cold afternoon in Brooklyn, but to now include the new revelations from the other night. She wasn't being cruel by asking him to revisit it; she just knew he had only conveyed bits and pieces (important ones for sure, but still just parts of the whole story) about that afternoon. It was now vital for him to pull it altogether into a single understanding of the whole experience. By doing so, it could help him solidify his understanding and refine his emotions. This was an important step for him. Without doing so, such an understanding could remain fragmented and never come together in a meaningful, lasting way for him. Even though he would be discussing this with Kyle in their next session, she wasn't certain Ken would be able to recall all the important things he had discovered, and he may not be willing to go through the whole thing again.

So now was the best time for him to solidify it in his mind, once and for all. Ken hesitated at first, and then acquiesced. Not only that, he followed-up the whole thing with Kyle in his office. Additionally, Ken wrote it and rewrote it. His passion for writing was now being applied to a very critical part of his healing. His efforts were not academic any longer, it was therapeutic and life altering. She had to keep encouraging him to write about it.

And, so he did. The following is best truth about what actually happened at 4139 Martin Court on that cold afternoon in 1961. It was the best understanding Ken now possessed, and thankfully, this is the way he would come understand and view it as he moved ahead in life.

Here is what really happened on that cold afternoon . . .

A Mother's Wicked Sinful Ride . . . "Revisited" (1961)

Little Ken made it to the doorsteps of 4139 Martin Court from school on that cold, overcast afternoon in February, 1961. His mother took some time but finally opened the door and let him in, after a half hour of routine pleading. She then turned him around and sent him back outside to the store to get a pack of smokes for her and her boyfriend.

"Listen, I want ya' ta' go to Giles Food Market and get me some cigarettes . . . and get back with 'em right away. D'ers someone upstairs I want ya' ta' meet." she directed (it was not a request).

"Ah, Mom . . . I still haven't even warmed up yet. I promise to get your cigarettes later after I have a chance to do the . . ." But before he could finish his sentence, he saw the back of her hand coming up from below her waist directly toward his face. He swayed at the last moment, avoiding the full impact of her blow. "Don't give me any crap, ya' hear. I'm going out later ta' night, and I don't need any of ya' bullshit . . . understand? Just do it." With that, she threw a quarter on the table and departed the kitchen as quickly as she appeared. Hilda did not wait for Little Ken to say "Okay."

It was not an option. Hilda knew he understood.

So he put his shoes and jacket back on once again and headed out the back door. He also remembered to unlock the door as well as unlatch the kitchen window to ensure he had at least one way to get back in without another afterschool, beg-to-get-in routine. Little Ken got to the store in no time and bought the smokes. It took him twenty minutes or so. He yelled upstairs that he was home. Little Ken threw his jacket on the sofa and began re-embracing the furnace. Once he was close to feeling somewhat normal again, he headed to the refrigerator to see if there was anything to eat. Only the usual suspects were there—a container of canned milk, several bottles of beer, half a bowl of leftover pancake batter, a jar of mayonnaise, and an untouched bag of M&Ms.

So he took out the canned milk and pancake batter, got the frying pan from the cabinet, and started making his dinner—an exact replication of last night's dinner and the night's before. There was never any syrup or jelly for the pancakes, but even "naked pancakes" (as he called them) were filling and hot. That's all he had—all he needed.

Suddenly, he heard the back door to the kitchen slam shut. He turned around and saw his brother standing there—it was Butch (the Butcher-Bird). They didn't say a word to each other; they didn't have to. Butch walked into the living room, took off his brand-new, fully insulated winter coat, wool sweater, thick warm gloves, knitted red hat, and rubber-soled winter boots, and then returned to the kitchen. "Hey, little shit, what do you think you're doing with *my* pancakes?" Little Ken was always nervous and tense when Butcher-Bird was in the house, and with his mother present too, he had to stay on hyper-alert, ready for anything. He had every right to be nervous—Butch was older, bigger, faster, and much stronger even though he was only about two years older. "Come on, there's not much left. I got here first, so they're mine." Little Ken stated without any real hope of satisfying the Butcher-Bird. "I'm just kidding . . . don't' worry you little shit . . . it's your lucky day. Mr. Carbina took me for some dinner after school, and I'm full . . . full to the brink right now . . . so go ahead and eat your precious pancakes. I don't care," he said with the pompous pride of a spoiled kid with power.

Mr. Carbina was Butcher-Bird's homeroom teacher at PS 239. It was the same Mr. Carbina who also bought Butcher-Bird all his warm clothes. He was always helping Butcher-Bird in some way—buying him stuff and taking him on long drives through the country, going to the movies, and going out to dinner. Butcher-Bird liked the attention. And for some reason, Mr. Carbina liked Butcher-Bird, but Little Ken didn't know why. At this moment, Little Ken was just relieved Butcher-Bird wasn't hungry. On the other hand, Little Ken was really hungry now and would have eaten Butcher-Bird's fine knitted hat if he was allowed to touch it. But he had rules about all his "stuff"—no touching, no using, and no looking, no anything. If he caught Little Ken anywhere near his stuff, there would be hell to pay. And the Butcher-Bird loved bringing hell to his little brother, but not this afternoon.

Meanwhile, Little Ken was still trying to get his pancakes going with Butcher-Bird hovering nearby. Then they both heard their mother calling to them from upstairs. However, her tone was different from when Little Ken went to the store to get her smokes. She was now using her most contrived, most loving feminine voice, which was usually reserved for special occasions. "Listen . . . won't ya' please come up here for a moment, darlin'? I want ya' to meet someone. And please bring up da' cigarettes too. Okay, sweetie?" She heard Butcher-Bird and Little Ken talking after he came back from the smoke run. And whenever they heard that specific tone of voice coming from upstairs, filled with words such as *darlin'* or *sweetie,* they both knew the nature of the next routine.

It was time for "high times."

Little Ken removed his hand from the frying pan, turned, and looked at Butcher-Bird in a questioning way. Butcher-Bird also had a puzzled looked on his face. "Is she talking to you or me?" Butcher-Bird asked. Their eye contact was direct and questioning. "I don't know, but I hope it's you. I'm really hungry . . . haven't had anything to eat since this morning." Ken's response was more of a plea than an answer. Butch understood what his little brother was really asking, what he was requesting, and it had nothing to do with food. "Who's up there with her this time, you know?" Butcher-Bird asked. "I'd don't know, haven't been up there since I got back."

Then they heard their mother call once again. Neither brother replied. Instead, Little Ken crossed the living room and threw the newly purchased pack of smokes up the stairs, then ran back to the kitchen; the pack landed on the second floor in the hall. There was no reply from her. After a minute or so, they heard the weight of her footsteps making their way deliberately across the bedroom floor, along the short narrow hallway between the two bedrooms and bathroom, then down the stairs. Each step became louder and louder in their minds while they simultaneously exchanged glances of fear. Subconsciously, Little Ken's grip on the frying pan handle also tightened with each of her steps. Butcher-Bird backed away and stood right next to the furnace at the far side of the kitchen, knowing she'd arrive shortly. By the time she entered the kitchen, their senses were on heightened alert. They both knew they had to be ready for, not only the impact of her words, but also the impact of her fists. They sensed her two greatest assets (fists and words) would be felt shortly, simply because they did not answer her immediately when she had called.

But she did not arrive bearing fists or vile vocabulary, not this time. Rather, she approached Little Ken directly and, in her most sweet, motherly voice, said to him, "Ken, please turn off da' burner now and come upstairs w'it me, darlin'. I'll give ya' some money later on so ya' can go and get somethin' ta' eat down at Central's Restaurant . . . I promise."

Hilda Callahan didn't wait for a reply from her son. She reached over and turned off the burner herself and took him by the hand and headed to the stairs; to what both brothers knew would to be more "high times" (the name she gave to such special physical moments with men). But this would be the very first time Little Ken would have done so—he really didn't know whether to be scared or excited. He also didn't really know what to expect even though he had secretly witnessed it many times between her and many of her boyfriends.

As Little Ken was being lead out of the kitchen by her, he glanced at Butcher-Bird without a word needed to be spoken. They held each other's eye contact for a second or two, for they both knew what was about to unfold, and there was nothing that could be done. It was to be Little Ken's first time in "high times," just as Butcher-Bird experienced some time before. Ken couldn't remember for sure if Walter had been exposed to the same abuse; he was just too young to remember. He wasn't really afraid, thinking it was just a rite of passage of sorts—his time to step up to the plate, he guessed. Somehow, Butcher-bird also knew it was to be Little Ken's maiden voyage through the waters of "high times."

Just as Little Ken and their mother were crossing the living room to go up the stairs, Butcher-Bird intercepted them by putting his hand on his mother's arm and saying, "Mom . . . let's let the little shit get back to his pancakes and eat. I'll go this time." With that, Hilda Callahan paused and looked at Butcher-Bird curiously, as if seeing him for the first time. She quickly questioned Butch Bird's motive for replacing his brother. After all, she thought he disliked his little brother. And, it had been some time since Butcher-Bird's last flight into the land of "high times," and she had noticed he was being more and more reluctant each time. So she was somewhat suspicious at this gesture being extended to Little Ken. She turned and looked directly at him and asked, "Okay . . . what da' hell gives . . . what's really goin' on here?"

This had never happened before.

Knowing his mother very well, Butcher-Bird sensed he better have a good response, one that made sense to her, or it would not be worth trying. So he replied in a way that didn't show any outward compassion for his brother—that would be a clear giveaway. He also knew he had to come up with a more practical, even slightly reasonable explanation for doing so, and it had to be specific. "I'm not hungry at all . . . Mr. Carbina took me out to Gunning's Crab House after I helped him clean up the classroom after school today. I'm full, real full now. Oh, by the way, Mom, Mr. Cabrina says to say hello to you, too. Who is this guy upstairs? He been here before? Do I know him?"

Butch was trying to momentarily distract her by asking her a series of quick questions along with providing a simple answer to why he wanted to do this for his brother. It worked. She bought it. "He's Mr. Penn . . . owns da' Downton's bar on Patapsco. He's a new friend of mine . . . so be on y'ur best behavior, just do what I say," she said as a matter of fact, still a little curious about what just happened between Butch and his brother. With that, she released Little Ken's arm and then she and Butcher-Bird started up the stairs to "high times." On the first step up the stairs, Butcher-Bird quickly glanced back at his little brother and said, "Hey, little shit . . . don't let those pancakes burn." Little Ken nodded.

They then made their way upstairs, leaving Little Ken downstairs in the kitchen where he was finally able get his pancakes going—after three unsuccessful attempts since coming home from school. Ken, too, was a little confused and very surprised about what his brother had just done. He had mixed feelings. On one hand, he didn't want to go upstairs; he was still real hungry. On the other hand, he wanted to go having never actually participated in "high times" himself and was kind of excited about doing so. So, after he quickly downed his pancakes, he turned off the stove and quietly made his way up the stairs. He then slowly and quietly crawled down the hall to the entrance of his mother's bedroom. As usual, the door had been left slightly open—about the width of an eyeball, just wide enough for a young pubescent boy to see everything going on, seemingly without being seen himself by someone else. That is, unless that someone actually wanted him to watch.

And Hilda did.

Little Ken watched until she and the man finished their business with Butch. They both then collapsed from exhaustion on the floor. Then there was nothing.

At that moment, everything in the room became hauntingly still, silent and sullen. Even though the radio could still be faintly heard in the background, not another sound was present. And the only motion that Little Ken could see through the crack in the door was a thin path of cigarette smoke drifting from a lit cigarette on the vanity. This slow steady stream of gray smoke was hauntingly hypnotic, forming an endless trail of shadows circling the bedroom, crawling up the mirror, rolling along the wall, and casually coming to rest on the floor before lazily making its way to the ceiling above. The three human bodies in the bedroom were motionless, cadaver-like, really, like a scene from a B-rated horror film depicting the aftermath of a psychotic butchery of a family of three. The only difference was there was no blood. That's when Ken slowly backed away from the doorway and quietly went back downstairs. It was to have been his turn to be in "high times;" his turn inside the pillowcase; his turn to be nearer to her than he had ever been before, but Butcher-Bird had gone instead . . . on this day.

Whether Butcher-Bird did it out of empathy and kindness for his little brother, or out of personal greed and cruelty to deprive him of being close to his mother in "that" way, Little Ken would never know. But, he did know this—after that cold afternoon in February 1961, Hilda began to date a man she had known earlier. He was the only man who would come to the house on a regular basis and Little Ken remembered him because he always brought boxes of stale cookies, cakes and a carton or two of Tang orange drink with him. From the time she began dating him again, she didn't have any other men in house and "high times" just seemed to fade into the dark history of 4139 Martin Court. And, so did any opportunity for Little Ken to enter the pillowcase world of "high times."

And, he owed it all to his brother, Butch, the Butcher-bird.

Ken finished reconstructing the entire story for Angel Dawn just as she suggested. And afterwards, he was very glad she encouraged him to do so. Everything, all the pieces of this puzzle in his mind, made better sense to him now that he talk through it again, captured it in writing, applied the ABC Model to it once more, and discussed it later with Kyle in his office. Kyle and Angel Dawn met during one of Ken's initial PTSD sessions in his office; that's when she knew he was going to be able to help her husband.

"Thanks Ken for sharing this with me. It appears it was an emotional time you and Dawn experienced that night. Yet, you still seem somewhat concerned about something. What's on your mind?" Kyle asked, sensing Ken's uncertainty about something. There was something Ken still needed to make better sense of, and he knew Kyle could likely help. "Kyle, there are two things really. It's about my own feelings toward my mother growing up and Butch's relationship with her, too. You know, Butch never talked to me about any of this, never confirmed or denied it, never said a word about it, not once over all these years, even when we were alone together in Vietnam. So I never really knew how he felt about things. Maybe that's why we always kept a distance from each other; same with my other brother Walter. Maybe none of us really wanted to be placed in the position to have to talk about such things—just too embarrassing, too personal, you know?" Kyle then replied, "Considering your own prolonged avoidance behavior and the obvious avoidance habits of your brothers over such a long time, I feel it clearly indicates some kind of trauma or bad experiences were shared among all three of you."

"Yeah . . . such are the consequences of being driven by tainted beliefs, huh." "That's exactly right." Kyle noticed Ken's understanding of the ABC Model was becoming well refined.

Then Ken continued, "Anyway, the other thing I've been struggling with was, without confirmation or acknowledgment that all this really took place, I still think perhaps I had just been imagining it all along . . . you know . . . just the fantasies of a pubescent boy or something, I guess. I just don't know."

Kyle did understand what he was saying and replied, "First of all, you will likely never have firm confirmation, real proof, that is. Too much time has passed and the people involved have mostly passed-on. And, the feelings you had about your mother around that age were natural. Most boys are somewhat younger when they look at their mother in more than a 'motherly way.' So, just let that go for now or put it in a good place in your mind. Such thoughts were normal and considering the amount of emphasis and exposure you had as a routine part of your home during those years, I can see how it could easily impact your thinking and your emotions as you matured. You know, what's far more important here is how you feel about it today and will feel about tomorrow. And, what you're doing today in trying to make some sense of it all is a good, real good."

Long period of silence, then Ken continued, "Well, I now realize I was not responsible being just a kid, didn't know much, and there was no one there to guide me or my brothers, really. I was feeling ashamed of myself and actually blaming my brother when he was equally as much of a victim as I was. I also believe if Walter wasn't forced to flee our home, he would have protected me and Butch from her, but without a father, a man, or anyone to around to help, we were really at my mother's mercy. I guess I'm just now forgiving myself for carrying it so long."

"Good. That's where you need to be, Ken. Now, let's talk about your brother Butch. Why didn't you ever ask him about his relationship with her or was it just too uncomfortable for you as you referred to earlier?" Ken had to think this through. "Don't know why we didn't discuss it, but we didn't. We had a few opportunities to talk about it, like when we were both in Lai Khe, Vietnam, together or when Walter, Butch, and I drove from California to Texas together over a three day period. But again, we never did. It was a secret taboo of some kind that I sensed we all knew about but would never dare to talk about."

Ken continued, "However, there was one time when this topic was addressed by Butch; it came about after my mother's death around 1998. Butch sent me a letter, a highly encrypted one. It was the only letter I ever got from him since Vietnam."

"What did he say in it?"

"I still have it, over ten years now, and we can review it together; it's very brief but loaded with emotions. Dawn and I read it many times without really getting the essence of it. But I did take two messages from it—he admitted having sex with our mother, and I should never contact him again. He also said lots more, perhaps you can help, Kyle. I'll bring it in, and we can review together, Okay?"

"Sure, glad to."

Before Ken brought Butch's letter in for Kyle to review, he rewrote it word for word, comma by comma, because Butch's handwriting was so difficult to read. After years of hatred, anger, and fear of his brother, he was beginning to understand that Butch had been more of a victim than he was. Butch lived it, lived through it all. Ken had only experienced the physical and emotional abuse parts, but he had been exposed to physical, emotional and sexual abuses. And, Butch never had an opportunity like Ken had today to receive help and support from the VA's PTSD program in order for him to help himself. It wasn't until Ken shared the actual letter with Kyle that things finally came together for him. Butch had really benefited just by writing and sending that single letter to him. Ken never looked at as a sort of a cathartic healing effort for his brother, but it was. He introduced Butcher-Bird's letter to Kyle in the spring of 2012.

Butcher-Bird's Letter—"Revisited"

It had been the first chance Ken had to inform Butch about their mother's death in 1998. He had tried to find Butch when she passed away but just couldn't. Then out of the blue, Butch called him. Coincidently, it came only a few weeks after her death. The purpose of his call was to ask Ken to co-sign a loan for some furniture he wanted to buy. While it was good to learn Butch was still alive after ten years of silence, their conversation didn't last more than a few minutes. That's when he was finally able to tell Butch about their mother's death. Butch's reaction was minimal, impersonal, and dismissive, saying something along the line of . . . "Ding Dong the witch is dead . . . bout' time." He had been living in the northwest and that's all Ken learned about him on that phone call, except how he felt about his mother's passing.

However, a few days later, Ken received a written letter from Butch—the only written letter he had received from him since Vietnam. It had the look of a real letter, but felt more like the kind of message a person would find inside a bottle that had been washed ashore. It was a series of fragmented thoughts and jumbled images linked together by a few commas, periods, and six highly emotional exclamation marks that screamed out at Ken. His "almost letter" was hand scribbled using a dull pencil. It looked like a ransom letter—the kind bad guys constructed using cutouts from different newspapers and magazines so police officials couldn't identify them. Most of words were printed, some written. There were misspellings; some i's were dotted, some not. Periods were missing; sentences were not complete. It seemed more like a series of splinter statements fused together which could have been written in a minute's time or over several hours or days.

The letter also had been written on four very, very small sheets of spiral notebook paper that had been ripped out of its binding—the kind of little notebook that engineers and computer nerds seemed to always carry in shirt pockets. The envelope and the letter were both very well encrypted with Butcher-Bird's secret messages and meanings. It had been years since Ken had heard from Butch, and after decrypting this "almost letter," he sensed the Butcher-Bird hadn't been flying well psychologically for some time—certainly not since his frontal lobe brain injury caused by his motorcycle accident years before.

It was really Butcher-Bird's direct, but belated response to the news of his mother's death. It was his response; he just couldn't or wouldn't verbalize it to Ken over the phone when they spoke. The envelope was postmarked March 17, 1998, Seattle, Washington.

The envelope's "addressee" was:

> 'Yen Yen' Callahan
> 332 Sleep Hollow Rd
> Nashua, New Hampshire, 03062.

"*Yen Yen*" was the name given to Ken by his little sister, Sandy, when she was about the age of two. Sandy was still too young to pronounce

K sounds, so she merely said "Yen" (for Ken). And for some reason, she always used his name twice whenever calling him or referring to him, for example, "Mommy, where's Yen Yen?" or "Yen Yen, tuck me in bed." or "Yen Yen, I hungreeee (hungry)." Before opening the letter, Ken knew it just had to be from Butch. Besides his mother, only Butch had such knowledge of his sister's ways. And since their mother was dead, Ken knew it had to be from him.

The "return" addressee was:

J. Doe
69 Lone
Anywhere USA

Ken sensed this was Butch's way of letting him know that he didn't want to be found or contacted later on. The contents of the letter also conveyed his very desire to remain undisturbed. As a matter of fact, it was the only message explicitly conveyed in the entire letter. He was hesitant in opening it. If he even saw a pinch of white power, he'd freak out. (That's where his mind was with the letter still in his hands.) So he was very relieved to find only paper inside. As usual, Angel Dawn had a way of cutting through the crap and going right to the core of problems, especially when it pertained to relationships, medical issues, or financial problems.

They both sat down and read the letter as best they could—Butch's poor spelling, grammar, and penmanship caused problems right away, but his encryptions and scrambled emotions were what required extra thoughts. They then tried to decipher the following:

98

Hey, Little Shit,

The wicked witch Bitch is DEAD (AKA)
taking a dirt nap forever & a day

The Devil said your mother was to ugly to go to hell!

Yes, I was a mother fucker, when I was 12, 13 on Herdon ct

It fell naked as a Bluebird on it's back shitfaced!

You'll love this one, everyone here thinks Im an only child
with no family.

I like that way. Old family problems suck.

My new life & what I call a family was as nice surprize for
me forever

I'm back on the Coast that's the <u>most!</u>

The lesser coast to the East sucks the most, I know it!

Loose my # or you'll have a ear drum <u>Busted!</u>

P.S.

con—sucks

Lib is freedom

Butch, your has been BRO!

Butch's handwriting seemed more like the psychotic chicken scratch of a prisoner on death row rather than man writing to his brother. It took Ken and Angel Dawn hours trying to decipher the meaning of it all. Not a word was spoken as both of their minds went racing.

This was Kyle's first time reviewing the letter; Ken's twentieth. Kyle took some time to thoroughly read it, then looked over at Ken and asked, "This is certainly a revealing and emotional letter to you from your brother, very impactful. Since you had this for some time and have certainly worked hard to make sense of it much longer than I, tell me, what do you think Butch was really trying to convey to you? What do you think this is all about?"

Kyle asked this with genuine curiosity as well as to help Ken draw specific conclusions of his own. Even though one very clear message jumped out at Kyle immediately, Ken would have to think harder about the question before Kyle would share his own perspective with him. By doing so, Kyle was hoping Ken would develop a better understanding of it in the process. This would be a far greater benefit than merely analyzing his dead brother's motives.

Ken struggled at first. He was trying hard to look at it beyond the written words, just as he had tried many times before. "I guess Butch was yelling at me or at my mother or at himself . . . Butch was getting it all off his chest finally . . . something that he had been carrying for a long time, something he never could talk about before because he never had the opportunity to do so. I sense he was kind of taking a last shot at revenge of some sort, getting even by finally being able to point the finger at where it belonged as well as say what hadn't been said before."

Kyle thought about Ken's answers and replied, "Yea, I think that's part of it; he's certainly getting something off his chest as you said. So let me take you a little farther in that direction, Okay?"

Ken replied quickly with a touch of frustration, "Kyle, if you know something just tell it to me please. Why do I have to do the work all the time—just give it to me. Okay?"

After several years with Kyle, Ken understood the process and the reason for it, but he was just hoping Kyle would relent just this one time. But, he didn't. "I know this is a tough one for you Ken, but now you know it's more helpful if you let me guide you to your own conclusions rather than tell you what your conclusions should be, right?"

"Yes."

"Good, so let me guide you there. Here goes—Why, do think he was driven to write to you about this. What was compelling him, really?"

Ken thought harder then he replied, "Butch was mad and wanted to scream this message out. He needed to blame, to get back at her, and

I was the only way to get this off his chest. Now she was dead, he must have felt much more freedom somehow . . . . to let it out. I guess it was something he couldn't do face-to-face or over the phone with me or anyone while our mother was still alive."

Kyle continued, "Yes, his words are filled with sarcasm and bitterness. But why? And at whom is it really directed?"

"I don't know . . . at me? . . . at my mom?" Ken calmly stated.

"Perhaps, but who else could it be directed at?"

"Not sure there is anyone else; perhaps at Walter, our older brother who ran away from home and abandoned him?"

"Could be, but think harder . . . you can do it."

"Okay. Maybe it's directed at our father, her husbands, for leaving us with that crazy lady; you know, for running off."

Ken was becoming louder now and obviously becoming more frustrated at not getting it.

"Good, keep in that direction." Kyle stated.

"CHRIST . . . I DON'T KNOW . . . I DON'T KNOW," Ken yelled out. But Kyle kept guiding him.

"Yes, you do know. Try again."

"There's no one left in his life, no one else. If he's not directing his anger at her, me, Walter, our father, or her husbands, who is left?"

"Ken, why do you think he's venting 'anger'? No one said his letter was based on anger. I know I didn't say that and never even considered anger was there. But, could it possibly be about blame, you think?"

Ken's mind was now grinding on all cylinders, and his oil light was flashing at him. Then he got it. "At himself . . . Butch was blaming . . . himself! Butch was blaming himself for what happened. Yea, that's it!" Ken felt relieved and also sorry at the same time. Butch had been blaming himself for everything all through his life.

Kyle was glad Ken had reached that level of understanding for himself and let him know, "Yes, Ken! You got it . . . I know it must have been tough, but you got it."

Kyle went on very slowly, "Now let me ask this. Think back to one of our earlier sessions together when we first met? What is it called when someone 'blames' themselves for something that was not really their fault?"

Ken got it correct, right away. "Guilt . . . guilt . . . Butch felt guilty. And it was directed at himself, not anyone else! That's what his letter was really about—guilt. Even though he wasn't responsible, not accountable, and not at fault . . . he still felt guilty all those years."

Kyle was quick to reply, "Yes! Yes! Now hold that thought. We're going to come back to it shortly. Trust me on this one; it will be well worth the deviation from this specific topic."

Kyle knew Ken had to make this breakthrough on his own; he was certainly getting closer to understanding his brother Butch, but more important, he was about to learn much more about himself. He just wasn't quite there yet, though. So Kyle continued, "You're doing fine, Ken, and I see you're working hard, and I understand how difficult this can be, so hang in there. It's going to be well worth your effort, I promise . . . just stick with me."

Kyle then shifted gears and took a different approach, "Let's go a little further but now in a slightly different direction. Tell me, what was the biggest reason for you coming here, to the PTSD clinic, in the first place—two years ago? That is, what was really driving you to help yourself after so many decades of avoiding discussions or having anything to with Vietnam or other veterans?"

Ken had to take time to readjust his thinking. Kyle continued, "What was eating away at you for decades that you didn't even know about until you discovered it for yourself here in this office and within your Vietnam veteran peer group sessions?"

Kyle was guiding him more gently now when Ken responded, "I was having a hard time sleeping, having nightmares, drinking a lot, avoiding personal relationships; I felt shameful and embarrassed about my service in Vietnam, too." Ken was trying to capture it all but couldn't.

"Yes, good. And what did you eventually discover that had really been at the root of some of your pain? What were you feeling but just couldn't articulate? It wasn't fear or anger?"

Kyle was being strong and forceful now, yet his tone of questioning was, as always, kind and caring. It made Ken think even harder. There was a lot of silence that followed as Kyle allowed him to think things through.

Then Ken got it, "Umm . . . guilt. I, too, had been feeling guilty all along; guilty for coming home after two tours in Vietnam without a scratch: guilty for not getting wounded or killed; Guilty for not doing more; Guilty for surviving. You called it 'survivor's guilt,' right, Kyle?"

"Yes, exactly. And after so many of our discussions, after using the ABC Model so often, after so much direct dialogue with other Vietnam Vets . . . you now realize what, Ken? What?"

More silence. The Ken slowly restated his first major lesson taken from his PTSD treatment. "Well . . . my first big lesson was learning the difference between shame and guilt—that was a key for me . . . shame being painful feelings about myself as a person and . . . guilt being painful feelings toward something I did, my past actions. Shame implies there is something wrong with me—that I'm no good; but guilt is about something I did, a mistake of some kind; an action or inaction of my own that lead to a bad thing. I eventually realized I was not responsible for the wounds of my fellow soldiers; I wasn't the cause of the war; I had done my best at the time, the best I could at eighteen, and yet my brothers in combat were still lost; I also learned I should not blame myself nor feel guilty for that which was not my fault, nor my responsibility; I shouldn't blame myself. I had been getting my feelings of genuine sadness and sorrow for the loss of my brother soldiers mixed up with my manufactured feelings of shame and guilt."

More silence. Then Kyle responded by pulling together all the previous pieces of dialogue he had with Ken during this sessions, "Yes. And you know something, your brother, Butch, and you shared the same feelings of 'guilt' over all these years and decades. You both felt and carried 'guilt' even though it was triggered by different events in different times and in different places and involving different people. It doesn't matter if guilt is incurred in the Projects of Brooklyn or in the jungles of Vietnam. Feelings are feelings. Guilt is guilt. The only practical difference is you were able to come to that realization with the help of others. And now you feel much better about yourself because your understanding and your beliefs changed . . . do you get that, Ken?"

"Yes, yes I do," Ken said slowly and gratefully. Then Kyle continued, "Unfortunately, your brother, Butch, never had an opportunity to go through such a formal process of healing, not like the one you are going through here in Plainville. He couldn't or didn't seek the support he needed that may have helped stop his suffering. Ken, that's what I sense was really driving Butch to write that letter, even in such a raw form. And considering his head injury, it was probably the best way, the only way he could do to express himself. Perhaps that's why he couldn't do so over the phone when you both talked just before receiving his letter."

Kyle continued as Ken was thinking harder about what he was learning, "Ken, to me, Butch's letter was all about guilt, lots of guilt—decades of carrying the guilt around about his sexual relations with his own mother. And like your own feelings of guilt about Vietnam, it wasn't his fault. He was just a young boy, not responsible for his actions and therefore should not have had to feel guilty about anything. He just didn't have anyone or anyway to help him see it."

Silence continued. Ken was connecting the dots, and Kyle allowed him the time to do so. After a few more minutes Kyle broke the silence, "Ken, its highly likely Butch never before conveyed the emotions he was able to capture in his letter to you. By you just being there for him after your mother's passing, may have provided him with a final opportunity, for him to let go of a lot of built-up negative, counterproductive feelings the only way he knew how—by writing it down and sending a letter to *you* . . . *t*o you, Ken . . . to his little brother. You! It was you who helped him relieve some of his suffering merely by being there for him."

Ken's emotions were all over the place now. Something was getting to him, slowly at first, but it all was becoming clearer as Kyle continued encouraging him to think it through aloud. Then Ken tried to respond further. He had to be certain about what conclusions he was drawing from all this. "So Kyle . . . writing this letter was Butch's way, his only way, to express his feelings—primarily his guilt. It was his guilt that likely drove him to write it . . . just as my own guilt, in part, drove me to come here to you . . . to the VA?"

"Yes, yes."

"Yet, Butch died with so much guilt on his mind and in his heart . . . how horrible . . . how terrible." Ken's genuine empathy for his brother was building and about to overwhelm him. That's when Kyle helped get Ken to a much better place. "Perhaps . . . but not necessarily, Ken. You may not see it quite yet, but let me say it again . . . Butch got an opportunity, a final opportunity in his case, to express his feelings of guilt—to vent, express, release his long-held feelings, not only of guilt but also some shame, too. And, by doing so, a lot of suffering and pain was released that had likely been building for decades. And it was done in one simple, hand-scribbled letter to his little brother. And equally important, he was able to do so with someone he valued, someone he knew would understand what he was trying to convey . . . probably the only person in the world who would truly 'get it.' That was critically important to him. Again, that someone was—*you*."

Ken's eyes then quickly filled with tears. Then he got it; he truly got it. He was not feeling pity or remorse or anger or sorrow for his brother, Butch, Butcher-Bird, Butch E. Callahan—it was empathy and love.

Ken cried in Kyle's' office until the session ended.

The letter had confirmed that Butch, indeed, did have sexual relations with their mother in some way; it wasn't just in Ken's mind after all. And Butch carried that needless guilt for such a long, long time. Equally important, the letter also confirmed Butch never wanted to talk about it again. That's why there was no understandable return address and why it was reinforced by giving Ken a clear warning never to contact him again. Now, Ken could even understand that.

In 2009 (ten years after the letter), Ken received another letter. But this one came from the state of California. It was about Butch's death. He had been incarcerated in a secured mental health facility for the last three years of his life; he died there of multisystem failure—advanced dementia/ vascular. They tried to locate any friends or relatives upon his death but were unsuccessful. Eventually they located Ken. Butch had been cremated by the state of California a month earlier, and they sent his remains to Ken. A month later, Ken buried Butch in the Massachusetts National Military Cemetery. He was given a proper military burial and will spend eternity in the beautiful and peaceful surroundings of Cape Cod.

Change—for the good

The ideal outcome of Ken's treatment was to help him manage his emotions, beliefs and behaviors in ways that enhanced his day to day functioning and overall quality of life. Throughout it all, he found the VA experience to be extremely positive, supportive, and highly effective. It wasn't what he expected—it was much better than expected. Most important, Ken found himself in a far better place psychologically, emotionally, and socially as a result of actively participating in the VA's PTSD program.

He was also able to document his key lessons, observations and actual changes throughout his two years and then share with his family and with Kyle. In late 2012, he placed a written summary of all his experiences into a six part summary. Of course, the VA kept their own clinical and medical records of Ken's official journey through PTSD, but he felt his own summary was far more practical and useful to him.

The six part summary follows:

Part 1: What was wrong with Ken before coming to VA PTSD Clinic?
Part 2: What happened to Ken in Vietnam?
Part 3: What happened to Ken during his childhood in Brooklyn?
Part 4: What changed for better since involvement with the PTSD Clinic?
Part 5: How were achievements reached via PTSD treatment?
Part 6: What's next for Ken?

Part 1: What was wrong with Ken before coming to VA PTSD Clinic?

    A. Afraid of closed spaces, confinement—claustrophobia
    B. Distrust of long-term personal and social relationships
    C. Inability to recall anyone's name he served with in Vietnam
    D. Fear, anger, and hatred of brother and mother
    E. Guilt ridden about service in the Vietnam War
    F. Major measure of success was only professional & financial
    G. Experienced continual disruptive sleep & nightmares,
    H. Slept with a knife nearby at all times
    I. Excessive alcohol consumption
    J. Troubled perspective towards women

Part 2: What happened to Ken in Vietnam?

    A. Continual fear of death from mortar and rocket attacks
    B. Constant fear of being taken prisoner by the Viet Cong
    C. Direct exposure to Agent Orange
    D. Used drugs (Darvon, marijuana, alcohol, "liquid speed")
    E. Abandonment by fiancé
    F. Contracted Hepatitis B
    G. Lost virginity
    H. Experienced significant hearing loss
    I. Buried alive during direct enemy engagement
    J. Flew 250 combat missions in a Huey
    K. Recipient of five Army Air Medals
    L. Recipient of the Bronze Star

Part 3: What happened to Ken during childhood in Brooklyn?

    A. Exposed to continual poverty, hunger, violence, and abuse
    B. Exposed to extensive instability (21 addresses in 17 years)
    C. Mother married five times but no father in his life
    D. Sister adopted at age of three
    E. Exposed to constant alcohol and drug abuse
    F. Lived with untreated amblyopia
    G. Graduated from high school

Part 4: What changed for the better since Ken became involved with the PTSD Clinic?

    A. No longer sleeps with a knife or other defensive weapons
    B. Decreased frequency of reoccurring nightmares
    C. Improved sleeping and eating habits
    D. Re-established abandoned relationships
    E. More open to personal feedback and criticism
    F. Stronger, more positive identity with Vietnam War service
    G. Proactive participation in military charitable initiatives
    H. Direct interaction with Vietnam veterans
    I. Utilizes a systematic, disciplined approach to managing emotional stress, hyper-vigilance and claustrophobia
    J. Able to identify 3 people with whom he served in Vietnam
    K. No longer fears or hates family members
    L. Personal identity expanded beyond professional and financial
    M. Significantly reduced use of alcohol
    N. Learned how to forgive others and to forgive self
    O. No longer possesses feelings of guilt about Vietnam
    P. No longer possess feeling of shame about childhood
    Q. Possesses more realistic, positive view of self
    R. Learned to share problems and to ask for help from others

Part 5: How were achievements reached via PTSD treatment?

    A. One-on-one CBT sessions with a PTSD clinician
    B. One-on-one medical counseling sessions with a PTSD doctor
    C. Ongoing peer-to-peer group sessions with Vietnam vets

D. Extensive writing therapy and practical application
E. Extensive application of ABC Model framework and process
F. Assumption of personal responsibility for self-healing
G. Integration of friends and family into self-healing process

Part 6: What's next for Ken?

A. Continued involvement in VA Plainville PTSD program
B. Continue involvement with Vietnam veterans peer network
C. Continue refinement of coping disciplines (e.g.: "The ABC Model")
D. Proactive forgiveness ("reburial") of brother and mother
E. Proactive forgiveness ("reburial") of the Vietnam War

A few years after his extensive experiences at Building 12 in Plainville, Massachusetts, Ken would then voluntarily participate in the VA's advanced, six week PTSD program held at the highly reputable PTSD Clinic in Western Massachusetts. There, he would join twenty other combat veterans who had served not only in the Vietnam War, but also in Korea, Iraq and the Afghanistan Wars as well. Participating along-side younger veterans and several Vietnam Veterans would significantly help reinforce his empathy towards fellow veterans struggling with PTSD, acquire new coping skills and techniques, and reinvigorate his personal motivation for staying focused on proactively helping himself learn and grow over the long term.

One of the Ken's biggest lessons that came from his journey within the VA's PTSD program was learning how closely interrelated his childhood traumas and his combat experiences in Vietnam really were. "One person's fear is another's joy; that's why feelings are so hard, if not impossible, to objectively assess no less measure consistently." Kyle said this to Ken during one of their most recent sessions together in 2012.

Ken responded, "I guess I can appreciate that better now than two years ago. At that time, I wouldn't even have known what you were talking about. So I guess that's also true when it comes to how the VA Services Center's examiners view my PTSD as well . . . right?"

"Yes."

The Projects of Brooklyn—Worse than Vietnam?

When Ken entered the VA PTSD program in 2010, it was in parallel with requesting compensation for several other service-connected disabilities, including,

1. Loss of hearing due to auditory impairment caused by extensive artillery and aerial noise during Vietnam,
2. Adult-onset diabetes caused by direct exposure to Agent Orange defoliants in Vietnam,
3. PTSD as result of exposure to sustained combat stress in Vietnam.
4. Hepatitis B caused by direct exposure to indigenous populations
5. Skin cancer caused by chronic, prolonged exposure to the sun

After a lengthy, but relatively simple process, two of Ken's five compensation requests ("claims") were approved—hearing loss and Agent Orange exposure. Both of these areas were quantitatively and medically measurable with direct supportive evidence at hand. That's why he felt they were approved so readily by the VA. However, Hepatitis B and Skin Cancer were denied due to lack of direct evidence connecting them to service in Vietnam.

Also, Ken's PTSD request was also denied, even after several appeals. As Kyle stated—"feelings and emotions are not as easily measured or quantified." Specifically, the VA examiners denial for PTSD compensation was primarily based on the following: "(his) PTSD was more likely caused by childhood trauma than trauma caused by combat service in Vietnam." Ken was supported and even encouraged to appeal the decision of the VA examiners regarding his PTSD on such grounds. This encouragement came from members of the Plainville PTSD professional staff, Veteran of Foreign War (VFW) legislative representatives, members of his peer-to-peer vet-to-vet PTSD group, and his wife, Angel Dawn. Each adamantly disagreed with the decision of the VA Services Center's final assessments.

Kyle's position was also clear, "It may have been *incurred* during your childhood, but it was definitely *aggravated* by your service in Vietnam, and according to 83 CFR sections 3.1, 3.304, and 4.125, I believe your case certainly meets such a standard, a threshold of reasonableness."

His Vietnam vet-to-vet group members stated, "You got to appeal it for the younger vets who are now coming back from Afghanistan and Iraq who will be facing this same process, this same standard."

Martin Finley, the VFW representative, stated, "You got to fight this . . . you're a Bronze Star recipient . . . you served two tours in Vietnam . . . you flew over 250 missions in combat . . . you must appeal."

And Angel Dawn's position on this was a little different but equally compelling to Ken, "Listen to me. If anyone knows what your PTSD really looks like, it's me. I see you every day and sleep with you every night. Your nightmares haven't gone away totally, not really. I know. Just look at our bed each morning—my half is as flat and as undisturbed as the white sands of Bermuda's Grotto Bay lagoon, while your side looks more like the aftermath of a terrorist's detonated IED. While your sleep has been getting better lately, twenty-five years of consistent bad sleep doesn't change things. Vietnam impacted you in many ways, well beyond the childhood traumas that you took to Vietnam with you . . . so you must appeal it!'"

Ken was still reluctant to appeal, but he did just that. He wasn't convinced it was the right thing to do, but one thing he had learned over the past two years of PTSD treatment was how to listen carefully to the advice of others, especially those he loved and trusted. So he did appeal.

Ken was then required to undergo a personal examination by another Veteran Service Center examiner. And this time he also had additional written evidence from Dr. Miller, Plainville's PTSD medical doctor, and additional written evidence from Mr. Robert S. Kenaly, a seasoned VFW Legislative Representative. Both new sources of evidence were placed within the appeal. And several months later, it still came back denied once again.

He then discussed it with Kyle during a subsequent session. "Maybe they're right, Kyle. My childhood, as you know, was tough, really tough. And, it was cited among the major reasons for denial, I guess."

As Ken was talking, Kyle was reviewing the actual VA Service Center's written denial then responded, "Well . . . at least they do acknowledge the fact that you, indeed, have PTSD as determined by their own VA examiner, not just me. That's good. However, they also go on to say 'all' of your PTSD symptoms are driven by your abusive childhood environment . . . 'all.' They're saying *none* of your symptoms have even been 'aggravated' by your service in combat in Vietnam."

Kyle continued to carefully read the denial documentation even more closely now, then he said, "Ummm . . . I'm curious how they can conclude that with your history of substance abuse since Vietnam, your persistent hyper arousal symptoms directly connected to mortars, rockets, small arm fire—all those things didn't affect your symptoms to any degree. I bet no such 'stressors' were involved in your early childhood within Brooklyn. Also, your self-injurious behavior as well as your persistent avoidance symptoms had been suppressed for decades . . . they're saying none of these have any connection to Vietnam? . . . None? I just don't understand this."

Ken replied, "Kyle, I don't know either. What also gets me is how they can think _you_ are not competent to make a determination one way or another about PTSD service-connected disability. That's what really got to me. What's up with that?" Kyle was stunned at hearing that, "Hmmm, I didn't see that part . . . where does it reference that?" Ken then showed Kyle the exact excerpt; it read as follows:

> *"Your mental health counselor (Kyle) is not considered competent to either render a diagnosis or link that diagnosis to your military service."*

It was the first time Kyle had ever seen the VA Service Center actually put something of that nature in writing, especially directly within correspondence sent to a patient. It may have been technicality accurate given Kyle's master's degree was not aligned with the official credentials required to render formal diagnosis, but the work of the Plainville VA PTSD clinic was specifically set up to do so, in addition to treat PTSD soldiers; he just couldn't determine compensation. Besides, Kyle worked under the direct supervision, in concert with, a PTSD Psychiatrist (a Medical Doctor). Regardless, such reasoning and detailed justification should never have been placed in writing within a denial justification provided to a patient. It seemed to Ken that he was now caught in the middle of dueling conflict between government organizations over turf, charter, policy, and even accountability issues—his care as a veteran now seemed secondary in the bigger scheme of things. "You know, I don't really care what they think, Kyle. You and everyone here in Plainville have been so helpful, so competent, I can't be more pleased and proud to have been served and supported by you."

Kyle was sincerely flatter. "Thanks, Ken, but this is bigger than the both of us. May I make a copy of this document? I need to let our director see this and makes some sense out of it."

"Sure."

"Here's how I see things, Kyle. It really doesn't matter if I am compensated financially for my Vietnam service-connected PTSD, really; Oooops, sorry—I meant to say my . . . 'Brooklyn-connected' PTSD."

They both had to laugh at that one.

Then Ken continued, "Wow . . . you know I just had another 'Ned Racine' moment (Ken had to explain the movie *Body Heat* and what a Racine moment was). What's so funny is the VA, an arm of the federal government, is concluding that 'all' my PTSD symptoms are *absolutely* associated with my childhood; 'none' are Vietnam related not even 'aggravated' one bit by my combat service. Well, this helps me clearly see for the first time in my life, just how bad it was growing up in the Projects with my mother and brother."

Ken paused for a moment. He was about to put a few missing pieces of the puzzle together in his mind. Kyle listened as Ken went on, "Let me see if I got all this right, Kyle. I want to be sure this is clear in my mind. My mother, my brother, and the environment of Brooklyn's Projects in the 1950s and 1960s had a much more detrimental impact on me than the Viet Cong, NVA, mortars, rockets, small arms fire, being buried alive, combat aerial missions, black scorpions, prostitutes, drugs, and even bird-eating tarantulas—all combined? Is this what they're saying here, or is my conclusion way off base, Kyle?"

Kyle knew exactly where Ken was coming from. Either the VA Service's Center professional staff was smoking something interesting or Ken's childhood growing up in the Projects deserved to be placed in the same lore of Charles Dickens's *Great Expectations*. Perhaps more practical and more relevant, the Projects of Brooklyn itself should be placed on the government's "most dangerous travel destinations." Either way, something still just didn't feel right.

Then Ken stopped suddenly; he just had another "Ned Racine" moment. "And here's the real kicker for me personally. Knowing my mother, Hilda M. Harrington, Lang, Archer, Callahan, Mytus, Smtih—I believe her response to the VA Service Center's conclusion would have gone something like the following if she were still alive today: 'Well, ya' see boy . . . I dun' told ya' all along d'at I was hard ta' keep up wit' in d'ose days, real hard, right? If ya' could *survive* me and the Projects all d'ose years as a kid, d'en what could a place like Vietnam really do to ya' in a year or two . . . nutt'en . . . nutt'en at all. Don't ya see, boy . . . I was preparin' ya' for Vietnam all along . . . why, even the VA comes right out says so, right here in writing. Vietnam was nutten' compared to me and da' Projects. Guess I wasn't such a bad mom after all, huh? I rest ma' case."

There was either a lot of truth about how his mother would have seen things, or Kyle really did hit it right on the head when he said earlier in the day: "One person's fear is another's joy; that's why feelings are so hard, if not impossible, to objectively assess, no less to consistently measure."

So Ken resubmitted another appeal (a PTSD "claim") in October, 2012 through to the VA Service Center's official appeal process. And, since there was no limit on the amount of appeals an individual could make, he still believed this claim would likely be his last. He was going to follow the recommendations of those personally and professionally closest to him this time, including Kyle, Dr. Miller, his PTSD group members, the VFW, and of course, Angel Dawn. Ken believed he already had been more than adequately "compensated" just by learning how to "help himself." There was no monetary equivalent to such learning and personal growth. None.

Much more importantly, he was now re-appealing to assist younger veterans facing similar situations down the road, especially those sharing comparable childhood and economic backgrounds as he had growing up. Young soldiers who had been predisposed to PTSD prior to experiencing direct military combat should not be penalized or denied benefits simply because of growing up in severe domestic or community environments. Ken also believed that when it came to such individuals, their PTSD could reasonably be classified as not being "totally incurred" by prolonged exposure to combat. However, under no circumstances can it be concluded that their prolonged exposure to direct combat wasn't at least "aggravated" to some degree by it. After all, being "aggravated" is adequate to meet the minimum threshold of fairness, and within the VA's own official standards.

Ken summarized his position in writing for Kyle (and other PTSD professionals in the VA) with hope that it may be helpful in treating other vets in the future.

"To me, it really doesn't make a difference if my PTSD is classified as 'incurred,' 'aggravated' or even 'nonexistent' for that matter. All I know is this, I am today far better off (mentally and emotionally healthy) than I ever have been. As such, I am already ahead of the game then when I started this journey. Everything that follows from this point is just a bonus in my life."

Before Ken departed this session with Kyle on this early Autumn day in 2012, he had one more question for him: "Kyle, we've been together for a couple of years now, and I never asked this question of you. But, can you tell me now . . . am I Okay. I mean at sixty-three, am I sane, you know, am I normal? Based on everything you've come to know and understand about me that is, I guess I'm asking if I mentally and emotionally healthy. Well, am I Okay?"

Kyle paused for a moment to think his answer through. And, Ken would have been disappointed if he hadn't done so. Then he replied, "I get what you're asking me. And you know, I'm a little surprised it took you so long to ask. Usually, people ask that much earlier, but it is an expected and reasonable question. So just let me say this; it always comes down to a single word from my point of view—*functionality*. Are you functioning well—mentally, emotionally, physically, and socially better today than yesterday? That is, is your day-to-day life better than before? Are your relationships better? Do you view yourself more positively and honestly? How are others open to you and engaging you? Are you more confident than before? Are you liked and do you like yourself? In short, are you happy? Ken, only you can answer such questions, my friend. And knowing you, I bet you'll strive to answer all of them for a long time to come."

As usual, Kyle didn't directly provide the answer to such a personal question. He just asked more profound questions for Ken to figure it out on his own. And he was right to do so.

But then Kyle continued. He left Ken with a final perspective before this day's session came to an end. "Ken, I've been doing this a long time, and I've got to say that I've seldom seen a man work so hard at learning how to help himself than you. You may recall, I've often used the word *resilient* to describe you, and I meant it each time—even more so now. Considering all the things you've been through and how you always found a way to bounce back from adversity is admirable, remarkable, really. And I'm sure your personal *resilience* will also keep playing a key part in sustaining your motivation to answer such enduring questions you just asked—'*Am I Okay?* I think your *resilience* will continue to guide you; it's served you well throughout your life thus far and it's now just a natural part of who you are."

With that, Ken thanked Kyle once again. Together, they scheduled their next session for late October 2012 and then Ken left building 12—the "renowned" VA PTSD clinic in Plainville, Massachusetts. As he was slowly driving off campus on this early autumn afternoon, he was savoring the many open fields of grass, the full clumps of well-manicured trees in the midst of the slow changing seasonable colors, as well as the bright blue sky above it all. He had come to like this place a lot. He was also thinking about Kyle's view of his "*resilience."*

That's when another flashback quickly came to mind. It was a moment during Angel Dawn's sixtieth surprise birthday party being held in Hudson, Massachusetts, a couple of years before. The gift-giving part of her party was about to end when she was handed one final, delicately wrapped package. The gift had come from Mickey London. It contained two devil's paintbrushes—her most adored flower. When she opened it and discovered the contents, she was so surprised and delighted that she nearly cried.

Looking down upon both plants, the only word that came from her lips was . . . *"resilient."*

EPILOGUE

(Massachusetts, late in 2012)

A FEW WEEKS AFTER HIS MAJOR breakthrough occurred with Kyle and Angel Dawn, Ken decided to capture some of his learnings on paper, starting with the moment he reluctantly began his PTSD journey. He felt compelled to put everything in writing and share it with those who may benefit the most:

- Vietnam Veterans
- Younger Veterans (returning from Iraqi and Afghanistan)
- Family and friends of Veterans, and
- Civilians suffering from the aftermath of violence and trauma.

He sensed civilians who had experienced significant emotional trauma associated with automobile accidents, tornados, rape, domestic violence, or cancer treatment, could find some comfort and practical ideas helpful in their own recovery efforts. To capture his insights, Ken once again went to his patio and began writing. Six days later, he finished. Many of his key lessons, insights, and take-away messages regarding his PTSD experience were captured in the following pages.

First, he provided a quick summary. From 2010 through 2012, Kenneth A. Callahan had participated in one hundred sessions regarding psychological, social, and medical aspects of PTSD as a patient within the Veterans Administration's Healthcare System of Massachusetts. He entered the world of veteran care suspiciously, skeptically and reluctantly. Yet, his attitude changed rapidly as he experienced the genuine compassion and competence of the people at the VA. Today, he feels his life has changed for the better because of doing so. For decades, Ken had been suffering and struggling with deeply hidden feelings of shame and guilt as well as hyper-vigilance and chronic avoidance behaviors; yet he didn't know it; none of this was consciously disturbing to him. Forty years after Vietnam he felt such things were just a natural part of his character and personality that had evolved over time. Specifically, he had been experiencing fitful sleep, including reoccurring nightmares; he slept with a knife at home and while traveling for work; he avoided making genuine, long lasting relationships; he kept family members at a "safe" distance; he constantly over-compensated for his perceived personal weaknesses; he feared all kinds of confined spaces; he experienced prolonged feelings of guilt and shame associated with his service in Vietnam and with his turbulent childhood; he was easily startled and continually suspicious of others. Ken also possessed a very poor self-image even though he was able to effectively manage the perceptions of his colleagues and associates who viewed him as the opposite—a confident, out-going, open and competent professional.

"Decades" is a very long period of time for anyone to learn how to hide, avoid, and rationalize things. And Ken learned it very well. He did so by unknowingly allowing his professional and financial success to hide intense personal insecurities and fears. Unfortunately, this also allowed him to avoid fixing things and healing himself.

In short, Ken just couldn't see what he would not allow himself to see. Over time his ability to avoid and minimize the impact of deeply hidden memories and feelings (originally caused by prolong exposure to violence) just couldn't be sustained. Then a long series of PTSD interventions coupled with the proactive involvement of a strong, loving wife, helped changed his view, his understanding, and his life. He became empowered (emotionally) and enabled (cognitively) to learn how to "help himself" by breaking through a façade of personal success that had engulfed so much of his true identity.

Simply put, Ken's goal in PTSD treatment came down to one key goal—*learning how to help himself.* And, that is the key message he wanted to share with other veterans and civilians or anyone currently living with suppressed feelings of anger, fear, guilt or shame incurred or aggravated by prolonged exposure to combat violence, domestic abuse or other traumatic life experiences. From his view, "assuming personal responsibility" for one's own healing is the most critical step in PTSD treatment and recovery. Without it being addressed early-on, the road to personal recovery would be much more challenging for anyone.

Today, Ken can see a brighter future ahead, one in which he can now actively participate, not just observe from a far as he had been doing for so many decades. Also, he can now accept for the "first time" just how wonderful his life has been despite the emotional baggage long carried from his childhood experience in Brooklyn and combat experience in Vietnam. Making such a personal transition reminded him of the turning-point scene in the 1939 movie—*It's a Wonderful Life* starring James Stewart as George Bailey—a man who could not see all the good he had in his life despite being constantly surrounded by it every day. As Clarence the Angel said to George when he was finally rising out of his own self-inflected despair: "You see, George . . . you really did have a wonderful life after all." Implying of course, all that George had to do was to first give himself permission (assume personal responsibility) to see what had been in front of him all along.

Ken's severe up-bringing made him feel falsely unique as compared to other Vietnam veterans. He long believed that no one entered Vietnam in the 1960s with his load of emotional baggage. But, with further examination later on in life, he discovered his social and economic demographics were actually the norm as compared to the official demographics of all the boys who served there. Specifically, he entered Vietnam at eighteen when the average age of soldiers serving in Vietnam was nineteen. He came from a low-income home, while 76 percent of all soldiers serving in Vietnam also had come from low-income, working-class families. He was a high school graduate while 79 percent of all soldiers in Vietnam were also high school graduates.

With that understanding alone, he started to begin viewing himself more reasonably. Unfortunately, such realization didn't come until he was in his sixties. Ken's situation, his plight, and his history were like many other kids on the bus of life within his generation; he wasn't special after all; he was like most of his peers.

The Message

So, Ken was determined to send at least one tangible message to other Vietnam veterans and younger veterans returning from Iraq and Afghanistan. The message he hoped would be heard, understood and acted upon was a simple one: "One's past doesn't predetermine one's future." By understanding and accepting such an idea, a veteran would be assuming a great deal of personal responsibility for their own healing; Ken was living proof of it. Without having been exposed to the VA's PTSD program, he would have continued to allow his past to silently impact his life in negative ways—as illustrated throughout his story. While Ken's memories of everything will likely be with him forever, the way he now reacts to and manages them no longer is counter-productive. Because of this, he sensed many other veterans were still "crawling" (metaphorically) on their knees toward the future because their past was weighing them down when they should be "sprinting." To do so, he knew PTSD interventions could help such veterans learn how to let-go and to better manage counter-productive feelings from their past.

In short, PTSD interventions could help veterans "sprint."

"Sprinting versus crawling" was the best metaphor Ken could use to help convey this key outcome of PTSD treatment and recovery. To him, by not taking charge of one's life and/or by not asking for help from others, a veteran is destined to throw away their chance to be fully alive, to be happy, and to feel human once again. To do so, veterans first need to give themselves permission to "sprint" versus crawl. And, that's the hardest part for many. It starts there. Again, this is an example of assuming personal responsibility—the ability to lead one's self. That's where his successful recovery actually began.

If any veterans know they are experiencing any of the symptoms Ken experienced in his story, and does not assume personal responsibility for fixing things (i.e., merely asking for help to start with), they are more likely to end up crawling for the rest of their lives. The saddest part of in-action is veterans who do not assume such responsibility may unintentionally be taking family and friends down with them. That is, through their "in-action," they'd be making loved-ones "crawl," too.

The VA's PTSD process is not perfect, but it is quite excellent when fully executed. Even though it didn't exist as a viable option for returning Vietnam veterans during the 1960s and 1970s when they needed it the most, it's here today. It's available now. It's real. And, veterans have not only earned it, but they also deserve it. So, if any veterans are hesitating or reluctant to ask for help (as Ken was), he believes they must get over it. They should reach out and take it.

That's a key part of the message Ken wanted to share with veterans and anyone suffering from PTSD-based symptoms—*take personal responsibility and start by asking for help; your past doesn't have to control your future.*

He also wanted to provide veterans with a few illustrations of his own "sprinting" experience as a result of his experiences within the VA's PTSD program. Specifically, he used to hate and blame his mother and brother for much of his sorrow in life (as reflected in his story). He no longer does. Ken buried his mother in 1998 and his brother in 2009. But in 2012, he "reburied" both of them. Only this time, he buried them in his heart (not in the ground); it was something he wasn't able to do the first time around. Ken felt fortunate now; he had a second chance and PTSD treatment helped him understand this. That is, he actually went back to his brother's and mother's graves in Massachusetts and Maryland respectively, and reburied them in his heart. Angel Dawn, his wife, was at his side both times.

It went this way:

Jonathan O' Donald

Ken's longtime friend, Jonathan O' Donald, joined Ken and Angel Dawn at Butch's reburial in Massachusetts. Jonathan was a kind and good man who befriended Ken in 1980 at Digital just as he was transitioning into civilian life from the army. He and Ken were colleagues and became solid friends right away, sharing the same office space in Digital's West Boylston facility for years. Without his friendship and tutelage, Ken was not certain he would have been able to make a viable transition into the civilian world. Jonathan made a huge difference, not only as a professional trainer, but as a friend. He had served in the navy as a younger man. Specifically, Ensign O' Donald was part of naval history in a couple of interesting ways. First of all, he was the very first electronics officer to serve aboard the USS Stormes (a naval destroyer) on its maiden voyage. For several years afterward, during a challenging period in the Cold War, Jonathan sailed the north, central, and south Atlantic Ocean protecting the USA from harm. While doing so, he also somehow found time to visually document some key naval operations at sea by just using his personal, handheld 8 mm movie camera (state-of-the-art technology at that time). And today, his home-movie footage of these live naval events represent some of the only visual documentation ever captured of the USS Stormes and other naval ships at sea. Through his personal efforts, such precious and historic moments are now publicly archived and accessible for the entire world to see anytime.

Jonathan certainly had an honorable tour of service protecting our country, just as he so freely did protecting and helping Ken and Angel Dawn over the decades. As such, Ken felt it was more than appropriate to ask Jonathan to join them at the reburial of his brother Butch. He gladly accepted the invitation and provided personal support and love at the re-burial. It was so good to have Jonathan present sharing such a personal moment with Ken and Angel Dawn. Before PTSD treatment, Ken would never have chosen to include anyone in such a personal part of his life. This was another illustration of "sprinting" versus "crawling" in Ken's mind.

So here's what happened standing over the graves of Ken's brother, Butch E. Callahan (at the Massachusetts National Cemetery in Bourne, Massachusetts) and his mother, Hilda M. Smith (at the Memorial Park Cemetery in Hagerstown, Maryland). The following were the exact steps he took in reburying them in his heart—same steps, same process, different times, and different locations:

Step 1.   He described their life (as positively as he could)
Step 2.   He told them he forgave them (for the bad things) and then asked for their forgiveness of him

Step 3. He then told them he loved them (no longer held hate or anger in his heart)
Step 4. He thanked them for being in his life and then said good-bye (he let them go)
Step 5. He left a personal family photo on their graves (to remember).

Then he and Angel Dawn walked away.

The photo he left showed his mother, his brothers (Walter and Butch) and himself sitting atop the Empire State Building in 1954. It was the only photo of them taken together before they moved into the Projects. No other such photo exists of Hilda and her three boys. This positive, happy picture, a split second of time, is how Ken wanted to always remember them from then on, and he hoped that's how they would remember him.

It was in the midst of these symbolic reburials that Ken realized he wasn't only forgiving them, but he was also forgiving himself. Specifically, he was forgiving himself for carrying so much anger, fear, hate, and suspicion around with him for so long. And, he was also forgiving himself for having been so afraid for so long, for avoiding and hiding for so long, and for blaming everyone else for so long. By forgiving himself, he truly experienced a sense of personal relief. It was like lifting a fifty-pound emotional weight off his chest. By letting them both go in this way, he was also allowing himself to move ahead, to go on with his own life. He was emptying his life of so many negative emotions, thoughts, and memories that had been silently holding him down for decades.

Ken then conducted a similar reburial ritual at the Vietnam Memorial Wall in Washington, DC. The memorial was not very well lit on this wet, rainy night, and there were only a few people visiting the Wall. He wasn't there this time to rebury any individual soldier, but rather, to rebury all fifty-two thousand fallen service men and woman—at once.

First, he thanked them for their sacrifice and let them know how proud and honored he was to have served with them. Ken then let them know he no longer felt the guilt and shame that had been needlessly festering in his mind for decades—about coming home alive without a scratch, not dying alongside of them, for blaming himself and for hiding for so long. That was the hardest part, but he did it as Angel Dawn held him close.

Somehow he sensed that's what those fine, fallen soldiers wanted all along. And, he also felt they were encouraging him to begin moving ahead in life, at last. It had been too long and too wrong for Ken (or any veteran) to carry such unwarranted, self-inflicted baggage. After Ken and Angel Dawn reviewed the entire list of names the best they could in near darkness, they thought about three individuals who were from neighboring towns and childhood friends of Angel Dawn. They had been killed in Vietnam in the late 1960s. While Ken never met these fine men when they were alive, he still felt he had known them forever.

That evening at the Wall, Ken was also able to leave behind his feelings of continual self-blame, any thoughts of culpability, and every remnant of guilt and shame. However, the things he did not leave behind were his memories of those veterans and of Vietnam. They would stay with him forever.

Ken felt by conducting the reburials of his mother, brother and Vietnam, which was a process of forgiveness, his entire PTSD experience with the VA had become far more powerful and meaningful. Doing so seemed like he finally closed a circle without ever knowing where it really began or ended. As such, he helped himself not only to put many things to rest, but also allowed himself to move ahead with far more confidence in his life than ever before.

Whether the act of "forgiveness" involves family members and a war (as with Ken), or the Viet Cong, other soldiers, colleagues or bosses, ex-spouses, horrible deeds or horrific events, the results are the same, even though the process of doing so may be different for each. Forgiving others is not forgetting; it benefits the forgiver as well as those the forgiveness is directed to.

One's Past Doesn't Predetermine One's Future

Another example of assuming personal responsibility ("sprinting") in Ken's life happened in 2012 as well. He had an opportunity to raise funds for veterans in need—something he had never done before. Specifically, this fund raising event was for younger veterans returning from Iraq and Afghanistan who were suffering from PTSD and/or traumatic brain injuries. The program was called "Run to Home Base" sponsored by the Red Sox Foundation. Over 1,400 runners, walkers and joggers generated well over $2 million in donations by completing five miles. The run started at historic Fenway Park (home of the Boston Red Sox), went around much of the city of Boston, and ended back at the park by crossing home plate.

Ken ran the race on behalf of his PTSD vet-to-vet group in Plainville, Massachusetts. His team's slogan was "PTSD—Order Out of Disorder" and it was reflected on his running shirt. Until that day, Ken had never participated in any military charitable event. He found it to be fun, challenging and personally rewarding. He crossed the finish line with a much younger vet who was also undergoing PTSD treatment at the time. He had recently returned from Iraq and was accompanied on this run by his faithful PTSD dog, a beautiful female, chocolate Lab. Throughout the final mile of the run together, Ken and the young vet talked about a lot of things. That's when Ken learned how this young veteran's PTSD dog helped him through many tough moments, especially at home at night whenever nightmares overwhelmed him. When the dog noticed a change in her master's behavior in the midst of a nightmare, she would automatically hop off the bed and snap on the bedroom light switch, immediately waking him from his nightmare. He and his PTSD dog were inseparable.

Ken's experience participating with other veterans on that day resulted in greater understanding and even greater empathy for his brother and sister veterans. To proactively reach out to other veterans was another example of personal responsibility in his mind. Such an experience was immeasurable.

When Ken crossed the finish line at home base in Fenway Park, he had his photo taken just as all the runners had done before him earlier that day. There he noticed Senator Steven Blyhle (State Senator from Massachusetts) who was finishing an interview with local reporters. So he approached the Senator, introduced himself, and chatted one-on-one with him for a few minutes. Senator Blyhle had also completed the run earlier that day and was very cordial and open talking with Ken. Then he asked about Ken's slogan on his shirt ("PTSD—Order out of Disorder"). Ken proudly told him about it. The Senator paused for a moment and then a big smile came across his face, "That's a real interesting and appropriate slogan, Ken . . . I only wish I could bring a little order to the constant disorder that takes place in my own kitchen every morning when my family is trying to get out and get going." With that, they both laughed. Ken got his message. The Senator was referring to being the only male in a household of women—his wife and five daughters. It was local humor many Massachusetts folks shared about him and his wonderful family.

Before participating in the VA's PTSD program in Plainville, Ken never would have been involved in a veteran fund raising event or any such activity, and he certainly never would have approached a Senator on a veteran-to-veteran basis. He did now, and with pride and honor. His previous negative stigma of being a Vietnam Veteran was still present at times in his mind, but it no longer adversely impacted his emotions or his behavior. Assuming personal responsibility for his feelings, choices and actions had made a difference once again.

After his brief meeting with Senator Blyhle, Ken was so inspired by his sincerity, his commitment to our nation, and the genuine love he openly showed for his family, he felt compelled to read his recently published autobiography, entitled—*Steven Blyhle: "The Leader"* (2009, Eagle Publishing). And, guess what Ken quickly discovered—the Senator also grew up in a very troubled domestic environment. Specifically, he had lived in seventeen different houses before graduating from high school; he had always been in search of food as a boy; he had been physically abused; and he was forced to adapt and recover over and over at a time when stability and security were needed the most in a boy's life.

Sound familiar?

That's when Ken knew Senator Blyhle likely had a little bit (a lot, really) of the "devil's paintbrush" resilience quality deep inside of him, too. More meaningful, the key message in Senator Blyhle's book hit home to Ken right away: *"The past does not have to determine the future."*

Ken also came to realize "sprinting" ahead in his life also included the capacity to look back and recognize people who had helped him sprint. He didn't know if it was luck or fate, but each of the following people significantly impacted his life at a critical moment. Only the passing of time enables a person to have such hind-sight, never the less, he felt by acknowledging such awareness was just another way of assuming personal responsibility. It's a humbling and rewarding process for anyone to undertake at least once in their life time. Ken did exactly this after the "Run to Home Base" in Boston and discovered each of the following people directly influenced his life (by accident or by intent) at a very critical moment when he needed it the most as a young man—even though he couldn't recognize it as such at the time. Interestingly, he also noticed half of these fine people impacted his life before he was nineteen years old, and all but two were men:

- Mr. Williamson, a recreation director—taught Ken self-respect, charity, tolerance and non-violence.
- Daniel Harrington, an uncle—demonstrated what "relatives and family" should really be about.
- A High School Administrator—illustrated forgiveness and leniency.
- Mr. Francis Jackson, a music teacher—taught Ken social skills and the importance of formal education.
- A Young Army Enlistment Doctor—illustrated to Ken that sometimes it's best to take one for the "team" (even if it's the wrong thing to do).
- Captain Butta, an Army Chaplain—taught Ken to rely on insight as well as eye sight, to offer help even when it's not requested, and to believe in something bigger than himself.
- Annette, a high school sweetheart—helped him learn to distinguish between revenge and forgiveness.
- Mrs. Baumann, an adult neighbor—helped him experience the essence of "motherly love."
- Thomas Lancer, a friend—taught him that stretching beyond perceived limitations is often the only way dreams can be reached.

- Bud Brady, Father-in-Law—taught him how to lead by example and what it felt like to be a "father's son."
- Lillian Brady, mother-in-law—taught him how to be humble, patient, and compassionate.
- Manny Lawrence, a friend—illustrated what good parenting really looked and felt like.
- Mickey London, a friend—taught him tenacity and kindness.
- Kyle Armstrong, a PTSD Clinician—helped him understand the lasting value of resilience and how to stretch and grow his mind.
- Jonathan O'Donald, a friend—taught Ken about loyalty and autonomy.
- Angel Dawn, his wife—taught him that it's actually possible to love as well as like someone at the same time.

Ken never before thought about where many of his values came from. But after this exercise, he realized most things he had come to stand for took root by being touched by someone. He wondered if most people ever took the time to reflect on their life in such a way. This too, was a form of assuming personal responsibility ("sprinting"). Being able to help others was a noble and rewarding thing for Ken, yet he found being able to ask for help from others was challenging, even impossible at times. Not any longer.

In early October 2012, Ken and Angel Dawn felt the first breath of early autumn in New England as they sat on their patio having breakfast. Mother Nature's cool breezes were beginning to make their presence known and Ken knew that Angel Dawn soon would be asking him to move the patio furniture back to the basement for its long winter's nap. He also knew she soon would be asking him to water the flowers just one more time before the season ended. But, he didn't know she was about to ask him this, "So . . . have you confirmed your next session with Kyle, yet?"

Ken paused before replying. He just wasn't expecting that topic to come up. "Well . . . I'm not really sure. We left it kind of open for the time being . . . you know how those things go." Angel Dawn knew her husband all too well and she sensed he may be waffling about continuing with his PTSD sessions, especially after the reburial of his mother, brother and Vietnam. So she called him on it, "No, I don't know how those things go! You're *avoiding* again, aren't you? Ken, everything you've been going through has been so beneficial . . . so good for you, I'd hate to see you not keep it up."

Ken replied after a few seconds of thought, "I don't know . . . I'm feeling pretty good about myself and about things in general now, not really sure if I need to continue. You know what I mean?"

That's when she put down her coffee cup and looked him directly in eyes and said, "No . . . I don't' know what you mean." She said this strongly and then continued, "Okay . . . come with me. I want to show you something. Then you can decide whether to continue with Kyle or not." With that, she took his arm and walked him into the house and then together they went upstairs. There, they stood at their bedroom door entrance and just looked in. After a moment of silence she said, "Take a look at that bed . . . tell me what you see . . . I rest my case." Ken looked but didn't see anything special, nothing out of the ordinary. So he looked at her and simply said, "What?"

They were facing their unmade bed, untouched from earlier that morning. Her side of the bed was flat, neat, almost as if she hadn't even slept there at all—as usual. Her pillows were perfectly aligned with only the slightest indention where her little head always rested in the same spot throughout the night, every night. She never seemed to move in her slumber. That was her routine, her trademark. The position that Angel Dawn falls asleep in is always the same position she awakes from.

On the other hand, Ken's side of the bed looked as it usually did. That is, his "sleep signature" was the same as a thousand previous mornings. It appeared as if a terrorist had just pulled the pin on a hand grenade, placed it under the sheets and then quickly fled the scene before it exploded. Some of his blankets were on the bed and some were on the floor; there were pillows up and down the length of his side with none at the head of the bed where pillows belonged. His sheets were crumbled and intertwined with blankets appearing more like a psychotic spider's web rather than a restful place for a human to sleep.

Ken didn't need an answer—he got her message. Maybe the first couple of years with Kyle really just marked the beginning of his PTSD journey, he thought to himself. Ken had made a lot of progress, but as he surveyed his half of the bed once again, he sensed his journey was just beginning—he had a lot more to learn.

So he placed his arm around Angel Dawn, kissed her check and then said to his wife, his best friend . . . his love, "Okay, I'll call Kyle today and reconfirm our next session."

ABOUT THE AUTHOR

K.L. Arthur was raised in the Projects of Brooklyn, Maryland. He served two tours in Vietnam and was a recipient of the Bronze Star bestowed by the First Infantry Division in Lai Khe. He received a direct officer commission to the rank of First Lieutenant while serving on active duty at the US Army Intelligence Command and Training School at Fort Devens, Massachusetts.

Today, he is one of America's top corporate trainers and an author of numerous books and articles on the subjects of professional credibility, interpersonal communication skills and occupational professionalism. K.L. has been formally diagnosed with PTSD and actively participates in the VA's PTSD program within the Massachusetts Healthcare System. He and his wife, "Angel Dawn," live in Massachusetts with their pet cockatiel, Lucky.

INDEX

Printed in the United States
By Bookmasters